Habsburg Honor and Nazi Duty

Habsburg Honor and Nazi Duty

Tom Joyce

authorHOUSE®

AuthorHouse™ LLC
1663 Liberty Drive
Bloomington, IN 47403
www.authorhouse.com
Phone: 1-800-839-8640

Published by AuthorHouse 08/19/2014

ISBN: 978-1-4969-3507-6 (sc)
ISBN: 978-1-4969-3508-3 (hc)
ISBN: 978-1-4969-3506-9 (e)

Library of Congress Control Number: 2014914711

CONTENTS

CHAPTER ONE

On Monday, March 14, 1938, Adolf Hitler triumphantly entered Vienna standing upright in a roofless car. His right hand was stretched outward in salute while the vehicle was driven down the Ringstrasse, the great boulevard circling the inner city. Crowds on the sidewalks shouted with enthusiasm.

Heil Hitler!
Sieg Heil!
Out with Jews!
Heil Hitler!
Kill Jews!

When Hitler's car left the scene, Vienna police stood back while large numbers of people went running off to penetrate the areas of Vienna where Jews were most likely to be found. Viennese faces famous all over the world for geniality had become contorted masks of hate. The plundering continued all night.

A few weeks later, on Palm Sunday, April 10, 1938, a day beginning the Holy Week leading to Easter, an election was held. On that day, the vote was virtually unanimous. It was officially recorded that 99.73 percent of the voters approved the Anschluss, the incorporation of Austria into the Greater Reich. Nazi officials closely monitored activity at the voting booths, but foreign observers close to the scene concluded that even with a totally fair vote, Adolf Hitler and National Socialism would have overwhelmingly won the election.

On Thursday, April 14, 1938, late in the afternoon, Police Inspector Karl Marbach opened a door on the second floor of the Vienna police headquarters building. He nodded at the watch commander, a bulky man standing behind a high-paneled wooden desk. Positioned behind the desk like a bartender behind a bar, the watch commander was using thick, stubby fingers to get relief from the tight collar of his uniform.

Marbach glanced at the watch commander's collar. On that collar was a button with Sig-Runes, two silver runic characters, twin lightning flashes—the double S of the SS. Like the watch commander and others in Kriminalpolitzei (Kripo), Marbach had one of the SS buttons on the collar of his coat, and, like everyone in Kripo, around his waist was an SS belt buckle containing the words *My Honor is Loyalty*. He didn't like those words. He believed those words reduced loyalty to blind obedience. Although born into a family that sometimes knew grinding poverty, his father had taught him to identify with the values, discipline, and demands of the royal House of Habsburg. The Habsburg honor he had been taught by his father required that honor never be diminished to the level of blind obedience.

He was resolved to remain faithful to his Habsburg honor. He had managed to hold onto his Habsburg honor when the Habsburg Empire came to an end twenty years ago, and he hoped he would be able to continue holding onto his Habsburg honor while living and working in Adolf Hitler's Greater Reich. What would be accomplished if he gave up his job? What would he live on? How could he meet his responsibility to his wife and daughter? It had been terrible in recent weeks listening to all the Nazi talk. There was praise for Hitler and curses for Jews. For him, it had become necessary to avoid drawing unwanted attention. He found that because he was a police inspector, he could get away with a lot by just listening with a solemn look on his face. Sometimes he had to echo the praise and the curses, but not often.

He opened the time sheet with Kripo on the cover, turned the page over, and searched for the place to sign out. A new requirement introduced by National Socialism a couple of weeks earlier required police inspectors and police detectives, not just the lower ranks in Kripo, to record the hour and minute when each workday began and ended. This applied even to out-of-town workdays.

The watch commander addressed Marbach with conventional formality. "Herr Police Inspector, it is good to see you. I didn't expect you to be back until tomorrow from straightening out that administrative problem in Switzerland." The watch commander paused. "Ach, is it reasonable for me to have to keep my collar buttoned at all times?" The watch commander had one serious criticism of the current state of affairs. The new National Socialist requirement that Kripo headquarters staff had to keep their shirt collars buttoned was an onerous burden for a man with an oversized neck.

Marbach pulled the Kripo time sheet closer. He was ready to record his hours of work for today and for the two days he had spent taking care of Kripo bureaucratic business in Switzerland. All he needed was a pencil. There was supposed to be a pencil tied to a string attached to the time sheet, but for some reason the pencil was missing. He wondered if the explanation for the missing pencil was that the watch commander wanted him to go on a case. Watch commanders were responsible for sending police sergeants and Kripo personnel of lower rank on cases, but they had no authority over police detectives, let alone police inspectors. Watch commanders could, however, request police inspectors and police detectives to volunteer to go on cases. The watch commanders had a big incentive to occasionally make those requests. Unless most of the cases under each watch commander's jurisdiction were promptly closed, meaning there had been an arrest or a dismissal, the watch commander ended up with a poor evaluation record. For countless years, back to the previous century, the requests sometimes made by watch commanders had been called "ensnarement" by everyone in Kripo. Police inspectors and police detectives had long ago agreed among themselves that the best thing to do when a watch commander tried to "ensnare" one of them was to be on guard unless the case was of professional interest or, at the least, genuinely interesting, and, of course, providing that the pitch was being made on a day and at a time when it wouldn't be personally inconvenient to take on the case.

For Marbach, it would be personally inconvenient to go on an extra case today. He had important plans for tonight, and if he agreed to go on a case this late in the day, those plans might be seriously jeopardized.

The watch commander stared at Marbach for a few moments and then gazed off into the distance. "I believe that we of Kripo have deep bonds of comradeship."

Marbach believed the bonds of Kripo comradeship were deep, but he also believed that sometimes one was entitled to put his own needs first. He was convinced that people who never put their own needs first were not showing loyalty; they were just conveying that their own needs had little or no importance.

"I don't see a pencil," he said, allowing his voice to express a small note of irritation.

The watch commander leaned forward. "I know you must be worn out getting back from Switzerland early this morning and then doing your job here today, but a call just came in from Garlic Island."

Those words confirmed to Marbach that this was, indeed, an attempt at ensnarement, but he didn't immediately call a halt to things. He was curious about what might have happened in Leopoldstadt, the ghetto area of Vienna, the place called "Garlic

Island" by people like this watch commander who were conveying prejudice against Jews.

Marbach hoped that the worst was over for Jews. He found encouragement for that hope in Vienna Mayor Hermann Neubacher's recent public statement that anti-Jewish activity that had recently been highly active in Vienna was "only a temporary thing." The words affirming that the recent anti-Jewish activity was "only a temporary thing" were being widely repeated, even printed on posters pasted on lampposts, billboards, and walls. Marbach liked thinking that things were going to get better for Jews. He had found confirmation for that earlier today when he saw in a prominent drinking establishment some Vienna citizens, swastikas prominent on their lapels, sitting contentedly at a table with two people he knew to be Jews.

Anxious to get signed out on the time sheet, Marbach asked, "Where is the pencil?"

"The pencil?" The watch commander's heavy eyebrows arched upward.

"Yes. Please. The pencil."

"Oh? You want a pencil? … Here."

Marbach accepted a pencil brought out of a coat pocket by the watch commander and then, after taking a deep breath, applied himself to filling out the hours and minutes when his police work had begun and ended in recent days. The only thing he was required to do was account for the minimum required work time. There was no incentive for him to include the extra hours and minutes he had actually worked. There was no overtime pay for police inspectors or police detectives, like there was for those of lower rank in Kripo.

Finally, the frustrating chore with the time sheet finished, Marbach set down the pencil, stood up straight, and asked, "What is going on in Leopoldstadt?" He wanted very much to avoid getting ensnared on this day of all days, but he was curious about what might have happened in the Jewish ghetto.

The watch commander shook his jowly cheeks while handing Marbach a Kripo Flash Sheet, the official police description of a matter needing Kripo attention.

Marbach started reading the Flash Sheet containing a description of the incident in Leopoldstadt and immediately saw that this was, indeed, an interesting case. Ordinarily, he would be glad to get "ensnared" for such an interesting case, but not today. If things worked out as he hoped, he wouldn't be going home to see his wife and daughter, he would be spending tonight with Constanze Tandler … marvelous Constanze, the Italian actress who had come to Vienna to star in a play at the Vienna Volkstheater and had become his lover. During his married life, he'd had many lovers, but he had always felt that could be reconciled with his Habsburg honor. His Habsburg honor permitted unfaithfulness to his wife as long as proper protocol was observed. Proper protocol meant not doing anything that might publicly embarrass his wife. Habsburg honor could be demanding, but it wasn't unreasonable in its demands.

Marbach concentrated his attention on the Flash Sheet. The case was a 71, a murder case. The number 71 derived from the number of the streetcar that stopped at the main cemetery near the outskirts of Vienna: the 71 streetcar. The Flash Sheet provided fascinating details for this particular 71. For one thing, it recorded that a Jewish prostitute had been killed in the Hotel Capricorno, identified on the Flash Sheet as a Jewish brothel. Jewish brothels had been ordered closed after the Anschluss, but that order was imperfectly enforced. Marbach smiled, seeing the Hotel Capricorno identified as a Jewish brothel. He knew it wasn't a Jewish brothel, that it had never been a Jewish brothel. Doing routine police work, he had learned that the Hotel Capricorno was a brothel owned by Gentiles and that the prostitutes there were Gentiles hired to pretend to be Jews. The arrangement was not unique. Several other Vienna brothels operated the same way, even now after the Anschluss. The explanation given for the longtime commercial success of the Hotel Capricorno and other so-called Jewish brothels was that many Gentiles, for their own reasons, liked having sex with prostitutes they believed were Jewish. Some said this made Gentiles feel less guilty. Others said it made things more exciting for Gentiles. Marbach believed that a fully correct answer included both of those explanations.

He stared speculatively at the pencil in his hand. He knew he ought to agree to take on this case. If he worked on this case, that might keep some junior police officer in Kripo from getting into a mess. Any Kripo police officer that didn't know the situation at the Hotel Capricorno could make trouble for himself by accepting at face value the story of a Jewish prostitute involved with Gentile clients. A false arrest might be made, and that could mean a lot of trouble, perhaps disaster, for the police officer making the arrest.

Marbach examined the situation for a few moments. He knew what he felt obligated to do, but still …

The watch commander, not an unobservant man, took advantage of Marbach's hesitation. Continuing to use conventional formality, he said, "Herr Police Inspector, you read it for yourself. It is all contained on the Flash Sheet. A Yid whore was killed. A worthless creature. That is unimportant. Read more of what is on the Flash Sheet. Three young army officers are involved, and you know what happened to Police Sergeant Schramm when he mishandled a case involving a Yid and an army officer."

Marbach wasn't surprised the watch commander was ignorant about the way the brothel at the Hotel Capricorno operated. He knew a couple of Kripo police officers close to the scene who were just as ignorant as the watch commander.

The watch commander made a low groaning sound.

Marbach knew he was getting more and more entangled, but he continued to listen while the watch commander talked.

"For this case today, I had no choice except to send the only Kripo man available to me. This could be worse than what happened to Police Sergeant Schramm." The watch commander lifted his hands in helpless supplication. "Such a small error Police Sergeant Schramm made and look where he ended up."

"I know about Schramm. Who did you send on this case?"

The watch commander seemed not to hear. He began talking in detail about the error made by Police Sergeant Schramm three weeks ago. Marbach listened even though he already knew everything there was to know about the fate of Police Sergeant Schramm. A week after the Anschluss, Schramm had found an army major and the major's Jewish mistress sharing a flat together. Schramm made an arrest, but quickly all charges were dropped against the major, and the Jewish mistress was allowed to flee the country while Schramm, a fourteen-year police veteran, was being held on an unspecified charge in the local jail. The message was clear to everyone in Kripo: although the law titled Protection of German Blood and German Honor was going to be enforced, it was hazardous to proceed too aggressively when privileged people were involved, privileged people like the army major arrested by Schramm.

The watch commander made a shrugging motion. "Willie Holder was the only one I had available to send over to the Hotel Capricorno." The jowly face swung from side to side. "You know Willie. He is only a Kripo police assistant. Not regular police, just a police assistant. He won't be regular police for another two months. He's a fine young man. Everyone likes Willie. But … well, he's young and inexperienced."

Marbach heaved a sigh.

The watch commander pursed his lips. "I told Willie to be careful, but the lad is so inexperienced … and army officers are involved." The watch commander's porcine eyes entreated. "We wouldn't want to see Willie sharing a cell with Police Sergeant Schramm, would we?"

Marbach didn't find Willie Holder to be particularly likable, but that was unimportant. What was important was the obligation owed to anyone who was Vienna Kripo, even Police Assistant Willie Holder. Marbach sized things up. Very clearly the watch commander had been cunning with this ensnarement. Maybe the watch commander didn't know about Gentile prostitutes in so-called Jewish brothels, but he was clever with ensnarement. He had taken his time, gotten the whole thing out in the open: there was a dead prostitute, some army officers were involved in whatever had happened, and, regardless of his deficiencies, Police Assistant Willie Holder was Kripo. If there had been a blurting out of what was going on, followed by a plea to keep Willie Holder from getting into trouble, there would have been a quick refusal to get involved in anything that might interfere with what was planned for tonight with Constanze. But the watch commander had been clever. The ensnarement was total and complete.

There were things Marbach needed to think about. He and Constanze had agreed that during the few days he expected to be out of Vienna, she would be providing some of the extra room in her flat as an accommodation for an actress friend visiting from Italy. Constanze's flat was modest: a living room, a bedroom, a kitchen, and a bath. It wasn't a large flat.

Marbach silently cursed himself for not having contacted Constanze earlier in the day to announce his unexpected return, one day early, from Switzerland. If he had called her on the telephone, she'd have been able to make other arrangements for her Italian actress friend, but he hadn't telephoned. He had thought it would be better to play a surprise by suddenly encountering Constanze in one of the places he could usually expect to find her on an afternoon in the city. There were some personal problems between them, not serious but troublesome, and he had thought springing a little surprise might help mend things. But unexpected police business came up early in the afternoon, and it hadn't been possible to go out, find Constanze in one of the places she liked to frequent, and enthusiastically surprise her.

Marbach was convinced that the major reason he and Constanze had a personal problem was because Constanze, for all her intelligence, was too emotional, not rational like she ought to be. Case in point: she didn't merely deplore National Socialism like he did, in the manner of a rational person. Instead, she allowed herself to be carried away by deep, emotionally-based hatred for Adolf Hitler and National Socialism. And that was dangerous. It was putting her in jeopardy. A few days after the Anschluss, there had been a public incident in front of the Volkstheater that could have spelled disaster. She had expressed loud anger upon seeing a poster announcing that the Volkstheater was "Jew Free," that Jews would no longer be performing for the Vienna Volkstheater.

Fortunately, he had been with Constanze and had been able to spirit her away before too much attention was attracted. He had managed to get her back to her flat, but then, within the safety of the flat, when they started talking about the incident, she had lost control emotionally, threatened to leave, go outside, and make a very public scene against Hitler and National Socialism. It had been necessary to use physical strength to keep her in the flat. She did a lot of kicking, but he knew ways to restrain people without hurting them. She also did a lot of shouting. Some of her words were cruel. Again and again, she had called him *"Nazi policeman!"*

Again and again, those awful words: *"Nazi policeman!"*

She had struggled desperately. The conflict between them hadn't ended until she finally collapsed into exhausted sleep. Hours later, when she finally woke up, all of her fury was gone, but in its place was melancholy, a tenacious melancholy.

Even three weeks after the public incident in front of the Volkstheater, Constanze was still afflicted by melancholy. She was getting better, but a lot of the melancholy still remained. Hopefully, she would become more like her old self when she was told about the good deed accomplished because of the trip to Switzerland. Calling the trip "official police business" had just been an excuse. There had been some bureaucratic police business that called for Kripo presence in Switzerland, and he had volunteered to do the chore. The reason for him doing that was because he could use a police car to go to Switzerland. Using a police car made it possible to take one of Constanze's friends to safety, a man who, after the Anschluss, had become homeless and hunted in the city where his role as a political leader had once brought him respect even from those who professed dislike for Jews. As things had worked out, Constanze's Jewish friend was now safe in Switzerland.

Taking that fine man to safety in Switzerland was a good deed that could be shared with Constanze. He didn't like sharing with her most of the things he did as a police officer. Even before the Anschluss, he had avoided sharing with her the things he did as a police officer. He wasn't ashamed of what he did as a police officer— quite to the contrary. Police work for him, even now under the Anschluss, was something he took pride in doing. But he didn't like talking about police work with Constanze or with anyone who had no firsthand experience, no way of understanding what the work was all about. It was the same way with the things he had done as a young mountain soldier during the war of twenty years ago, the deeds that had won him fame and medals. For what he did at Monte Ortigara, he had received the Maria Theresa Medal, the highest honor the Austro-Hungarian Empire awarded to a soldier. But, like it was with his police work, he avoided talking about the Ortigara with Constanze. He could talk about the Ortigara freely and easily when he was with people who had backgrounds or experience that made it possible for them to understand, people who wouldn't say foolish things or ask nonsense questions. Whether with police work or mountain fighting, there are some things that can be shared with a stranger that can't be shared with a friend or a lover when the stranger has background and experience that the friend or lover doesn't have.

Marbach told himself that soon, hopefully tonight, there was going to be a sharing of the good deed accomplished by getting a very fine gentleman to safety in Switzerland. It was something she didn't need special background and experience to understand. He would enjoy her endless questions about the doing of the deed. He very much wanted the sharing of the deed to take place alone tonight with Constanze in her modest-sized flat. The two of them alone. No visiting Italian actress present. But at this time of the day, it was impossible to contact Constanze, even by telephone, to let her know he was back from Switzerland and suggest that she find another place for her friend to stay tonight. At this hour, late in the afternoon, she would be keeping herself isolated from everyone. This was her required time of emotional preparation before going on the stage tonight. If he didn't find some way to get word to her before she went on the stage, the actress from Italy was going to be sharing the flat tonight.

The watch commander made a quick movement with his bulky body, stared at the clock, and murmured, "The play begins at seven o'clock."

Marbach bristled. The watch commander was making an intrusive observation by deliberately talking about what time Constanze's play began. Things concerning Constanze were not for discussion with this watch commander … or any watch commander.

Oblivious to the distress caused by his intrusive observation, the watch commander began talking about the current sorry state of theater in Vienna.

Stifling irritation, Marbach listened. The watch commander was simply saying what everyone was saying: all the theaters in Vienna were providing poor plays this season. As he babbled on, the watch commander made his comments specific to the Volkstheater. "I must say *A Serious Guy* is a horrible title for a play. I took my wife to see it on Saturday. We are both big fans of Constanze Tandler. Everyone loves Constanze Tandler, of course. But even with her sparkling performance ... well, I have to say it: the play is an awful piece of fluff."

Marbach said nothing in reply. *A Serious Guy* was indeed a miserable play. Everyone knew the play was awful, and no one was quicker to affirm that than Constanze. She could be roused in an instant to a fury of expressive curses about the play, the ridiculous title, and the mediocre playwright whom she always referred to as "the alleged playwright Herr Dohm."

Marbach knew that Constanze regarded the theater as a sacred place, like a church. Many times since the play began three weeks ago, he had heard her strongly assert that no sacred place should have inflicted on it an awful play like the one by "the alleged playwright Herr Dohm." And Viennese theatergoers seemed to be of the same mind. They had quickly rendered their judgment about *A Serious Guy*. Attendance at the Volkstheater dwindled the day after the opening, even as the ticket prices dropped, first by one-quarter and then, at the beginning of the second week, by one half. It was a certainty that any day now *A Serious Guy* would close.

Yes, Marbach told himself, it was a poor play, but doing the play had helped with one thing. The sheer hard work and the need to master an incredible amount of memorization had seemed to help roll back a lot of Constanze's awful melancholy.

There was something else that Marbach figured had helped to relieve some of Constanze's melancholy: Romani jazz music. Bubili Mirga, Marbach's Romani friend from boyhood days, was now also Constanze's friend, and one of the things Bubili and Constanze shared was enjoyment of gramophone record platters containing Romani jazz music.

Like other Romani, Bubili hated the word *gypsy*, a word used by Gentiles. Bubili took pride in being Romani. He was highly intelligent, and although he didn't have much formal education, he could hold his own with most of the intellectuals who sometimes engaged him in conversation in cafés and coffeehouses.

Early in the afternoons, beginning a couple of weeks ago, Bubili had begun bringing Romani jazz gramophone records to Constanze's flat. And sometimes, when it was possible for Marbach to get away from police work, the three of them listened while the gramophone played Romani jazz. Marbach had trouble understanding the music, but he found it a joy to watch the two of them, Constanze and Bubili. He enjoyed the way Constanze moved her head and shoulders, and the way Bubili closed his eyes and tapped the floor with his feet.

An especially enjoyable thing for him was how any expression of perplexity on his part about any piece of Romani jazz being played ignited exasperated scorn from Bubili and Constanze, scorn directed at the one they called "the clown." He enjoyed playing the clown. He enjoyed seeing his lover and his friend rise to high spirits while shouting disparagement at him for being a clown. He fully accepted that some sort of deficiency on his part prevented him from fully appreciating the musical sounds that captivated them, but as hard as he tried, he couldn't identify what they called "the hypnotic rhythmic pulse." It wasn't at all like the music he loved, the music of Strauss, Mozart ... Beethoven.

Marbach knew his life was good, that no man could ask for more than to have a lover like Constanze and a friend like Bubili, but he decided that right now it was time for him to think about immediate things. The watch commander's prattle was becoming hard to ignore.

Marbach interrupted the prattle. "I'd like to use your telephone."

"Of course, Herr Police Inspector." The telephone was shoved across the top of the bench. The watch commander was going to hear what was said, but that couldn't be helped. There wasn't time to spare.

Marbach put through a call to the Alpen Café, got connected with someone whose voice he didn't recognize, and with no preliminaries, he asked to speak to Bubili Mirga. He waited until the familiar voice came on the line.

With no request to know who was calling, Bubili asked, "What do you want?" That was the only way Bubili ever answered a telephone call, regardless of who might be calling.

Like Bubili, Marbach spoke with no preliminaries. Most of his conversations with friends and colleagues made use of conventional Viennese preliminaries, but not when he talked with Bubili.

"Do you know if Constanze will be providing a place in her flat tonight for that Italian actress friend of hers?"

"Constanze is often unpredictable, but I predict it will be safe for the brave police inspector to pay her a call tonight after she finishes her performance."

"Have you talked with her since we got back?"

Bubili's voice dropped to a low pitch. "No. You very specifically asked me to avoid doing anything that might cause her to find out that you are back. You didn't want to spoil your chance to personally surprise her with the early return. But I happened to encounter the marvelous Anna taking a walk over by the Opera House. She promised to not tell Constanze that you and I have returned, but she did tell me that Constanze's Italian guest acquired a Viennese lover last night. Anna and I discussed the implications of this development, and she assured me that Constanze's flat will not be crowded tonight."

Marbach appreciated hearing that good news. "I have to go on a case, old friend. I don't know how long it will take, but I will probably be late, maybe very late. Please get a message passed to Constanze saying I'll be at her flat tonight whenever I can get free."

"That is easily done," Bubili said. For a moment there was silence. Then Bubili asked, "Anything else?"

"No."

Immediately, Bubili disconnected. As usual, Bubili provided no Viennese salutation.

Marbach hung up the telephone.

"Do you need an automobile?" the watch commander asked.

"No, I'll take the streetcar," Marbach said while placing his Tyrolean hat on his head. Of course he would take a streetcar. Within the city, he seldom used a police car, and he didn't own an automobile of his own. To get around on police business, and for his own purposes, he relied on streetcars and taxicabs.

"It is the Hotel Capricorno," the watch commander said, making an unnecessary observation.

"Yes, the Hotel Capricorno," Marbach said, nodding agreeably and delivering a polite farewell as he went on his way. He moved quickly. There was police work to be done in the ghetto.

CHAPTER TWO

Marbach caught a streetcar. After a short ride, he transferred to a second streetcar and remained on board until it came to a stop in Leopoldstadt, the Jewish ghetto. He got off the streetcar, reached behind, and secured his truncheon—a ten-inch wooden club—into a snug place at the back of his trousers. Carrying the truncheon was bothersome. Most Vienna police inspectors avoided lugging one around. They preferred to pull out a pistol when it was necessary to quiet things down. But Marbach had long ago learned that he could quiet things down by gesturing with the truncheon. Of course, sometimes he had to do some hitting, but any weapon—truncheon or pistol—that is pulled out will sometimes have to be used aggressively.

Marbach looked around. There was a policeman in a flapping green cape and shining helmet pacing outside a building identified by a tattered sign as the Hotel Capricorno.

The policeman saw Marbach, stepped forward, identified himself, and delivered a precise hand salute, not the Heil Hitler salute of recently required protocol. In reply, without hesitation, Marbach identified himself and returned the hand salute, using the tips of his fingers to touch the front brim of his green Tyrolean hat.

As if it wasn't significant that no Heil Hitler salute had been exchanged, the two men entered the Hotel Capricorno and walked up a wooden stairway. It was a narrow stairway, but they walked side by side, and, although they had never before exchanged more than perfunctory greetings, they talked in detail about the different mountain soldier units each had served in during the war of twenty years ago. In response to a question asked by the policeman, Marbach talked about the Ortigara. He talked in specific detail about the deed for which he had been awarded the Maria Theresa Medal. He provided the important particulars because he knew the policeman with a background in mountain fighting wouldn't say foolish things and wouldn't ask nonsense questions.

When they got to the fifth-floor landing, they walked a few steps toward a room with an open door. Voices were coming from inside the room.

Marbach halted, turned half-around, faced the policeman, and thrust forward his hand. "Thank you for this good talk we have had."

The policeman grasped the extended hand and said, "I have learned more than I have told." After that, the policeman turned around and headed back to duty on the street. His shoes lumbered heavily going down the wooden stairs.

Marbach stood still for a moment and then took several steps and walked through the open door. He came to a halt a few paces inside the room. Police Assistant Willie Holder, in civilian clothes, was talking to a uniformed Kripo police corporal. Willie had a puffy face, was softly muscled, of average height.

Ignoring Willie and the police corporal, Marbach performed what for him was a required ritual upon arrival at this type of crime scene. Waving a hand to assure he wouldn't be interrupted, he surveyed the entirety of the room, studied the walls, the ceiling, and the floor. He took mental note of what was present in the room and what was absent. There was a bed. No chairs, no dressing table, just a bed. And no other furniture in the room except a floor lamp. There were several pictures on the walls and a small window with a drawn curtain. On the bed was an army officer's tunic.

There was something else in the room. On the floor lay the body of a very young woman.

Marbach pulled a notebook from his suit pocket, marked the date, the exact time, and began sketching—first, an outline of the room, then, with rough proportionality, what was inside the room. The final thing he sketched was the position of the body. When finished, he returned the notebook to his pocket, stood rigidly still, and stared down at the body that was lying on the floor, face upward, eyes closed. Garish red lipstick dominated the pale face. The victim was wearing the signature garb—revealing and lewd—of a prostitute. Her body was sprawled on the floor with the ragdoll looseness of the dead.

Marbach once again waved his hand to assure he wouldn't be interrupted and started moving around while doing another survey of the room. Systematically, he sought out small details. He checked one thing, then another, but he was cautious where he stepped and what he touched. He halted beside the bed, carefully picked up the officer's tunic, emptied the pockets, and found papers bearing a name: Lieutenant Paul Neumayer. According to the papers, the lieutenant was assigned to the Forty-Fifth Aufklarung Abteilung of the Wehrmacht, a Third Reich unit recently posted to Vienna.

Where the lieutenant was posted wasn't important. The important thing was his name. Lieutenant Paul Neumayer wasn't just any young officer. He was the son of Colonel Count Neumayer. The colonel count was high-level SS in Vienna, among the half-dozen most powerful people in National Socialist Vienna.

Marbach quietly tossed Lieutenant Neumayer's tunic to Willie, stood very still, and, one final time, scrutinized the entirety of the room. When ready, he pulled out his notebook, made one final notation, returned the notebook to his pocket, glanced at Willie, and, with an upward movement of his arm, delivered the Heil Hitler salute, the signal for talk to begin.

"Heil Hitler!" Willie proclaimed, making a vigorous upward thrust of his arm. There was a proudly beaming smile on the face most people found likable. Willie's voice dropped to an artificially low octave. "The Yid whore was dead when I got here about an hour ago. There were some army officers here, three of them. The Yid whore was killed by the army officers. They had no sex with her. Before they left, they provided full information: how they can be contacted and so forth. The officers were, of course, justified in killing the whore when they found out she was a Yid."

Marbach wasn't surprised Willie hadn't tried to keep the officers from leaving. This was, after all, National Socialist Vienna. That meant a lot of conventional law had been repealed. Willie opened and closed his mouth but spoke no more words. Willie's eyes conveyed anxiety. This was a messy situation.

With a hand gesture, Marbach signaled for Willie to say more.

Willie's eyes opened wide. "No crime was committed here, just the death of a Yid whore."

Marbach wondered which word was more cruel—Yid or whore. He pondered that thought for a moment. Then he thought about the Flash Sheet back at police headquarters. On that Flash Sheet, there had been no names of the army officers. Would he have gotten ensnared, agreed to take this case, if he had known that the son of Colonel Count Neumayer was involved? The answer was no.

Marbach stepped away from Willie, went to where the victim was lying, and looked down at her. He fished in his pocket and brought out a packet of Reemtsma, an inferior brand of cigarettes. He had given up smoking years ago, but a foul-tasting cigarette would make it easier to get an unpleasant job done.

Marbach placed the Reemtsma cigarette in his mouth, fussed inside his pocket, and pulled out a small box of wooden matches. When his attempt to ignite a wooden match with his thumbnail yielded only a failed popping sound, he walked over and scraped the match on the wall. The match flared and fizzled before burning brightly. He lit the Reemtsma, inhaled, and proceeded with the unpleasant business.

Kneeling down, he touched the young face. The face felt warm. That was surprising. She looked like she had been dead long enough to have a face that would be cool to the touch. He put his hand on the neck. He frowned, then moved the head around. There were slight bluish marks around the left eye and the left side of the face. She had taken a beating, but the wounds didn't look bad enough to have caused death. Was it possible she had some sort of head injury?

But when he moved his fingers through her hair, he found nothing. He was still frowning as he slowly stood up. He pulled the Reemtsma from his mouth, tossed it onto the floor, stamped it out, and stared down at the victim. Shaking his head, he again knelt down and carefully examined the skin on the face, then the neck, and, finally, the bare arms. Taking out his handkerchief, he began gently wiping the cheap red lipstick from the closed mouth. When he finished, the lips looked almost fresh. He lifted one of her hands. The fingernails were free of polish. That was unusual for a prostitute. But there was something more important. The nails looked very fresh, yet she looked like she had been dead long enough for the nails to have begun to pale.

Uncomfortable in the kneeling position, afflicted by an ache in his knees, Marbach fussed with the box of wooden matches, withdrew one match, placed it between his teeth, and gently used the fingers of one hand to open the victim's eye. He saw that the eyeball had not yet begun to flatten. Ignoring the discomfort in his knees, he scratched the wooden match across a patch of floor. When he brought the flame close to the opened eye, the pupil fluttered. Quickly, he pulled the match away. "You're alive," he whispered.

He tossed the match away and gently placed the young head back onto the floor. He was checking for a pulse when he heard a gurgling sound, followed by the sudden presence of a foul smell. Urine and bowl discharge was taking place. The young woman had been alive when he held her head in his hands. It was only in the past few moments that she died. It didn't look like a beating had killed this young woman. If the beating didn't kill her, was this a poison case? Yes, it did look like a poison case.

Getting to his feet, he was determined to not to miss anything that might be important. Frowning, he stared at the young face. Even with all the heavy makeup and the bruises on her face, she looked more like a sleeping child than like a corpse. As he continued staring, he found himself thinking she looked familiar. Did he know her from somewhere? If so, where?

After a long moment, he knelt back down again and checked the pockets of the clothes. But there was nothing to be found. He used his handkerchief to wipe some of the makeup from the lifeless face. She may have never been a beauty, but beneath the outrageous makeup and the cheap lipstick was the attractiveness of someone very young.

He made his decision. Regardless of who the victim was, for himself, just for himself, he would ask for police laboratory tests. He was determined to find out what had happened here and why it had happened. If he learned anything that couldn't be disclosed, his sense of honor would permit him to live with that. He wasn't going to commit an act of futile martyrdom, but one way or another, he intended to find out what had happened. That was the only way there could be peace with his sense of Habsburg honor. He had to try to learn what had happened here even if he would have to keep secret everything he learned in a case that involved the son of Colonel Count Neumayer.

Marbach had one troubling thought. Before the Anschluss, he had regarded Willie as a hired dog. But right now, wasn't he also a hired dog? Beginning at this moment, wasn't he as much a hired dog as Willie? He wondered if it was going to be possible for a hired dog to hold onto Habsburg honor.

Deeply troubled, Marbach left the room. He went downstairs to the hotel manager's office. There was no one in the office. No one was in charge of the brothel. He wondered about that. Of course, whoever was in charge might have fled, but that didn't seem likely. Owners of brothels make it clear to the ones they put in charge that they must never do anything that might result in loss of a license, which would be the likely consequence if no one was around to answer questions when there was official police business on the premises.

But finding no one in charge of the brothel was something that could be dealt with later. Right now there was something much more important to do. Marbach picked up the telephone, connected with an operator, and asked to have a call placed to Commander Stephan Kaas, Chief of Vienna Kripo.

Commander Kaas, a Berliner, had arrived in Vienna on the first day of the Anschluss. Marbach's opinion was that the new Kripo chief was good at his job. In addition, he found Commander Kaas to be more civil and friendly than most of the other SS who had come to Vienna because of the Anschluss.

Marbach knew that some in Kripo made humor about how much alike he and Commander Kaas looked: same size, tall and husky, similar facial features, about the same age, early forties. He had dark brown hair, and the commander had slightly reddish hair, but they looked enough alike to pass for brothers. He wondered if Commander Kaas had heard any of the humor about how much alike they looked.

Holding the telephone earpiece close to his head, Marbach learned from a police secretary that Commander Kaas had left his office for the day. Speaking into the telephone mouthpiece, he informed the police secretary that the commander had to be contacted, that a matter of urgency had arisen requiring the commander's immediate attention.

Upon receiving assurance that the commander would be quickly contacted and given his telephone number, Marbach hung up the telephone and waited.

Approximately ten minutes later, the telephone rang. It was Commander Kaas.

After greeting protocols were completed, Marbach explained that he was in Leopoldstadt, in a hotel that had long functioned as a brothel. He told the commander that the place presented itself as a Jewish brothel, but the owner and the prostitutes were all Aryans. Then he went directly to the purpose of the call. "There is a dead woman here. It looks like she was a prostitute. I don't know if she is a Jew. I don't rule anything out. Three army officers are involved in whatever happened. I am not sure what did happen. The important thing is that one of the officers is the son of Colonel Count Neumayer."

There was silence. Then Commander Kaas said in a low voice, "What a mess."

"Yes," Marbach said in reply.

Commander Kaas delivered instructions quickly, crisply, with clarity: "I will be taking over. I will see the colonel count. Wait half an hour, then telephone the colonel count. That will give me a chance to talk with him on the phone. He and I will sort this out. When you talk with the colonel count, it will help if you put his mind at rest about any possible problems for his son. Tell him his son's name won't be on any police reports. I'll tell him that too, but it will help for him to also hear it from you. You can give me the evidence tomorrow, whatever you find. Put it in a bundle, and I will personally destroy it. Hell, what a mess."

There was nothing more to be said. Commander Kaas rang off.

Marbach waited exactly one half hour and then asked the telephone operator to connect him to the residence of Colonel Count Neumayer.

The connection went through quickly. The colonel count came on the line, but what happened next was totally unexpected. In a nervous voice, the colonel count implored him to come immediately to the Neumayer estate.

"What about Commander Kaas?" Marbach asked.

The nervous voice said, "I have talked with him. I don't need to see him. Just you. Come immediately. Right now. Come to my estate. Don't waste time. Bring whatever … bring whatever you have collected."

Marbach would have been relieved to turn this messy business over to Commander Kaas, but there was nothing for him to do except listen while the colonel count continued sputtering, mostly just repeating what he had already said.

Where do such men come from? Marbach wondered. *How do they rise so high?*

When the telephone call with the colonel count was finally completed, Marbach made a second telephone call, this time to the Alpen Café. He wanted to learn if Constanze would be expecting him in her flat tonight. He wanted to be sure they would be spending tonight together, hopefully without the presence of the actress friend from Italy. Franz Krofta, owner of the café, came on the line. Bubili wasn't there, but a handwritten message had been left. It contained a communication from Constanze.

Franz comically professed to not understand what the message could possibly mean as he slowly read it over the telephone, pausing after each word. The words were from the chocolate soldier operetta by Oscar Straus: "Come … hero … mine."

CHAPTER THREE

Holding the bundle containing evidence of a crime under his arm, Marbach left the hotel and caught a streetcar. The loudly clanging red-and-yellow streetcar, the number 71 prominent on its front and on both sides, slowly lumbered toward the Neumayer estate. It bothered him that he was on a 71, a case involving a murder, and traveling on the streetcar that stopped at the cemetery—the 71 streetcar. This wasn't the first time he had taken the 71 streetcar to go on a 71 case, but those other times he had been doing proper police work, not helping to cover up a crime. What about his Habsburg honor? That would have to be sorted out later.

As the streetcar moved forward, he looked at the bundle in his hands. The awful bundle troubled him more than the truncheon jammed against the small of his back. He edged around on the wooden seat. Soon he was in a state somewhere between sleep and wakefulness. This long day had begun in Switzerland many hours ago.

It was well into the evening when Marbach got off the streetcar. He was not far from a heavy wooden gate, the main entrance of the Neumayer estate. Carrying the awful bundle, he walked to the gate and stood still for a few moments. He rubbed his hand over the stubble on his face. When had he shaved last? If it wasn't for this befouling business, right now, at this very moment, he might be shaving and cleaning himself up in Constanze's flat, waiting for her to return from the evening performance at the Volkstheater.

He took a moment to anticipate what it was going to be like when he told Constanze about the Switzerland adventure: a good deed done. That was going to be grand, but first there was this garbage work to do.

While looking at the Neumayer shield on the wooden gate, Marbach jerked hard on an iron handle. There was a clanking sound as the heavy gate swung open. After the gate shut behind him, he walked up a long path toward the door of the main building. The evening darkness was thick and heavy. From deep inside that darkness he heard a rustling sound. Somewhere in the darkness was an animal. Judging from the noise being made, it was an animal larger than a dog, probably a deer. There were a lot of deer on these large estates.

He continued walking while wondering what was waiting for him inside the main residence of the Neumayer estate. On the telephone, the colonel count had been nervous, but by now he'd had time to pull himself together, and the colonel count had a reputation for being nasty to people of lower status than himself.

Being subservient never came easily to Marbach.

At the front door of the main building, a waiting servant took him inside and led the way down a hallway. When they got to the end of the hallway, Marbach paused when he spotted an impressive-looking gun rack. One of the weapons on the gun rack was a 12-gauge, double-barreled shotgun. He studied the shotgun with professional interest while, a few steps ahead of him, the servant pulled open a glass-handled door.

When the servant stepped back and made a gesture with his arm, Marbach moved forward and entered a cavernous room. In front of him stood Colonel Count Neumayer immaculately dressed in a black SS uniform. The colonel count was tall and fat, with a very round head covered by a smattering of wispy hair. There were three men standing with the colonel count. The tall, young man in an army uniform was the son, Lieutenant Paul Neumayer. The two others, both wearing black SS uniforms, were aides.

Marbach quickly saw that he didn't need to be worried about being treated arrogantly. The colonel count had a pleading look in his eyes as he made a gesturing movement and said, "I am honored, Police Inspector Marbach. I am truly honored. May I present my son, Lieutenant Paul Neumayer."

The son of the colonel count stepped forward. He was in his early twenties, as tall as his father, but thin, almost skinny. Despite his height, Lieutenant Neumayer looked more like a frightened schoolboy than a young army officer.

The two aides were not introduced.

Marbach held out the bundle.

The colonel count snapped his fingers, and one of the aides stepped forward, grasped the bundle, and quickly left the room.

While the colonel count dabbed himself with a handkerchief, Marbach nursed a vivid recollection of the last time he had seen the colonel count. That was two years ago in Munich at the Theater am Gärtnerplatz. He had been there for a night of enjoyment. After the performance began, from his seat down below, like the people around him, he had looked upward several times to the prominent balcony where the colonel count sat beside the Führer of the German people, Adolf Hitler. The colonel count kept wiping the opera glasses the two men shared while casting their eyes upon the scantily clad "Beauty Dancer" known as "Dorothy."

Dorothy's real name was Ilse, and Marbach was in the theater because Ilse had agreed to share a late-night meal with him. It was a meal a police inspector could afford. Goodhearted as always, Ilse hadn't complained about sharing a modest meal with a man who had to watch his pocketbook. Afterward, like many times in the past, she had been generous in bed.

A year later, Marbach's lover was Constanze. And, naturally enough—anyway it seemed natural to both of the women—Constanze made a fond friend of Ilse. Recently, Constanze had been putting a lot of effort into making arrangements for the Beauty Dancer known as Dorothy to perform in Vienna. It looked like that was going to happen in another month or two.

Constanze and her friendships, Marbach thought. Especially her friendships with those who were his former lovers. Among men—certainly for men like himself—it was unthinkable to actively seek out friendships with a lover's former bed partners. But for women, he had learned long ago, the rules could be different, totally different. And, truth be told, he did enjoy seeing the way Constanze fussed over, fondled, and laughed mischievously with Ilse and with others who had shared their favors with him.

But Marbach knew that now was not the time for idle thought. Not here in this cavernous room at the Neumayer estate. He paid close attention while the colonel count put away his handkerchief and began talking.

"I know you will agree that in these dangerous times all that counts is what is good for the Greater Reich."

"Of course," said Marbach. What else could he say?

Suddenly, a telephone rang.

The aide who hadn't left the room rushed to a small table, picked up a telephone receiver, stood rigidly at attention, and spoke solemnly into the mouthpiece: "The residence of Colonel Count Neumayer."

Pausing for a moment, holding his hand over the mouthpiece of the telephone, the aide said, "Herr Colonel Count, it is Herr Direktor Hugo Rainer."

"Excuse me," said the colonel count, making a flustering motion while he went to answer the telephone. "The call is of only modest importance, but it is best for me to take it now."

Marbach nodded agreeably. Then he walked over to where Lieutenant Neumayer was standing, took a moment, and matter-of-factly put forth a question. "What happened at the Hotel Capricorno?"

"I didn't mean to kill anyone." Lieutenant Neumayer nervously raised his right hand to his face.

"What do you remember?" Marbach asked while surreptitiously studying the fist on the right hand, a pale, fleshy hand. The knuckles were totally unmarked, not at all like knuckles that might have delivered the beating suffered by the young woman at the Hotel Capricorno. But had Lieutenant Neumayer's knuckles been protected by a glove?

Marbach recalled that there hadn't been a handshake at their introduction. A handshake might be a way to find out if a pale, fleshy fist had recently been used to cruelly beat on someone.

Lieutenant Neumayer hadn't replied to the question he had been asked, so it was repeated: "What do you remember?"

Lieutenant Neumayer looked confused.

"Who was killed?" Marbach asked, as though making an inquiry of no large importance.

"I didn't mean to kill her."

"Who was it you didn't mean to kill?"

"He says I beat Julie ... that I killed her."

"Who said that?" Now Marbach knew the victim's name, a first name anyway. But what was Julie's last name? And, very important, who told Lieutenant Neumayer that he had killed the young woman named Julie?

Lieutenant Neumayer opened his mouth, but no words came out.

With calculation, Marbach ended the awkward silence. "I seem to have lost my gloves. I am always losing gloves. Do you wear gloves?"

"Gloves? No. Not in this weather."

Marbach was debating whether to repeat his question about the name of the one who had made Lieutenant Neumayer think he did the killing when the colonel count, having completed his telephone call, walked over, and said, "You have performed a good service for my son and the other two officers this night, Police Inspector. I thank you. There is nothing more to keep you here. I will handle everything now. I ... I am in your debt."

Marbach stood stiffly and made a slight bowing motion.

Colonel Count Neumayer nodded his head. "A Yid whore was killed tonight by men who had no sex with her. There is no police case. Nothing important has happened."

Marbach reflected bitterly that he would only bring trouble on himself if he reacted in an honorable way to what had been said. He couldn't even say that the young woman probably wasn't Jewish. His thoughts were bitter, but he didn't permit anything negative to show on his face as he allowed himself to be led to the front door by the colonel count. The son trailed along behind them.

All three men came to a halt outside the building. The colonel count held out his hand. Marbach grasped the hand, gave it a shake, then turned and held out his hand to the son. With no reluctance, no show of discomfort, a firm handshake with Lieutenant Neumayer was completed.

Of course, there was still the left hand, but Marbach doubted that Lieutenant Neumayer had used either of his soft, fleshy hands to inflict the blows suffered by the one named Julie.

Who, indeed, was the one named Julie? And what was she? A prostitute? She was dressed like one, but even more important than whether she was a prostitute was learning what had caused her death.

Making a point of keeping an untroubled look on his face, after farewell words were spoken, Marbach took leave of the colonel count and his son. He walked alone down the path to the main gate.

Moving at a quick pace, he was a short distance from the front gate when he came across four groundkeepers with lanterns, standing over something. Pausing, Marbach saw what the groundkeepers were surrounding: an injured young deer lying on its side. The four groundkeepers weren't aware that a stranger was watching them.

The face of the young deer had a stricken, frightened look. The tormented creature was making an agonized, choking sound. One of the groundkeepers, a man with a thick moustache, took a deep breath before saying, "One of the heavy stags must have tried to mount her. Poor little thing. She was old enough to want the attention but too small to bear the weight."

The stricken young deer's choking sound became a helpless wail. The four groundkeepers shared a look of distress. The one with the thick moustache said, "Her hind legs are splintered. A shame. Nothing to be done. Poor little thing. Well, give me the hammer. If neither of you two is willing to do it, I'll take care of this nasty piece of business. I just hope I'm up to doing it right."

Standing off to the side, still unnoticed by the four groundkeepers, Marbach found himself thinking about a game sometimes played in Vienna, mostly by teenage boys, but sometimes by older men as well. In that game, the males called themselves "stags," and the willing—and unwilling—females were called "deer." Stagging was supposed to be only a teasing game, but sometimes teasing can become cruel. After the Anschluss, stagging sometimes involved Aryan girls and women pretending to be Jews.

The groundkeeper who had been talking reached out for the hammer, and with that movement, he became aware of the presence of a stranger. He stopped, turned fully around, and stared at Marbach. Quickly, the groundkeeper moved the fingers of his right hand up to touch the tip of his cap, the obligatory sign of deference, but Marbach shook his head vigorously, and the hand halted in midgesture.

"The poor thing is in misery," Marbach said. "Get on with it, man. You have a bad thing to do. Do it bravely."

The groundkeeper turned back to his responsibility while Marbach headed for the gate. He had only taken a few steps when he heard the blow struck: a leaden sound. There was one final tortured wail from the young deer—and then silence.

Marbach continued moving toward the front gate. When he got there, he placed his two hands forcefully on the solid wooden frame and shoved. Slowly, very slowly, the heavy gate swung open. He passed through and pushed the gate shut.

Far away in the distance was the familiar clanging bell of an oncoming streetcar. He walked fast, heading for the nearby streetcar stop.

When the streetcar arrived at the stop, Marbach was waiting. He stepped on board and found a seat. With an effort of will, he put his mind on where he was headed and banished all other thoughts. Soon he would be with Constanze. He reached into his pocket and brought out his handkerchief. He was ready to start wiping his face when he saw that the handkerchief had incriminating lipstick on it. It was the handkerchief he had used while examining the young woman murdered at the Hotel Capricorno. He tossed the handkerchief onto the floor at his feet. It was a good handkerchief, but he didn't want to take the chance of having to explain to Constanze about the lipstick.

A short time later, he made connection with a second streetcar, one that would take him to a stop near Constanze's flat.

CHAPTER FOUR

Karl Marbach stood in front of the door to Constanze Tandler's flat, trying to gain entrance with his private latch key. To his distress, the key worked awkwardly and noisily. He shoved it forward, made left and right turns several times, but there was no success. Finally, he jerked the key out but made a fumbling motion, and it fell with a metallic clink onto the wooden floor. While picking up the key, he heard the patter of feet from inside the flat, then the hard mechanical sound of the lock being turned.

The door came open, and a disheveled Constanze, passionate, sweetly fragrant, making soft exclamations of joy, flung herself into his arms. "Karl … Karl … oh, my love!"

Holding Constanze tight, he enjoyed the sweetness of her mouth. He was delighted when spontaneous trembling movements erupted from the tops of her shoulders to down below her waist.

Later, when they were together in her large bed, she made laughing sounds while he held her close and let his passion join with her laughter. He was grateful there was no trace of her melancholy.

After the lovemaking was completed, they lay together on the bed. He was almost asleep when he became aware that she was pressing one of her fingers onto his lips. He opened his eyes, and she withdrew her finger and rolled over to the other side of the large bed. He smiled as he gazed at her. Both pillows were under his head. He listened while she mirthfully lamented her sad fate: no pillow for her.

He stared appreciatively at her lying with her hands above her head on the side of the bed with no pillow.

"How did the play go tonight?" he asked.

"The play is dreck, and the audience knew it!" she declared.

He stared at her until she began to laugh. Gradually, it became musical laughter, E-flat laughter. It seemed to him that it had been ages since he had last heard her laugh in E-flat when they were in bed together.

He made his voice sound matter-of-fact. "I didn't think the play was so bad when I saw it. Playwright Dohm isn't a Schnitzler or a Hofmannsthal, but he does all right."

As he expected, she wouldn't tolerate that kind of talk.

"The alleged playwright, Herr Dohm." She offered that correction before lifting her tousled head upward for a moment or two, then dropping it back onto the bed. She had no bun in her hair. He had undone it as a prelude to their lovemaking. Her unbound hair framed her face. To him, she was a wonderment.

She made a low, growling sound as though angry and then playfully punched him. He grinned amicably and watched as she stretched lazily on her side of the bed. Her voice was raspy from the night's work on the stage. "Is it any wonder the public is staying away from the theaters when everything being performed is dreck?"

"Whatever you say, my love."

"It isn't just the Volkstheater. Things are bad for all the theaters in Vienna. Why should anyone go to the theater these days? There is nothing but dreck. It isn't difficult to understand why there is nothing but dreck. Did you read that awful boast Herr Blaschke put in all of the newspapers today?"

He expressed his reply with exaggerated innocence. Of course, he had read Herr Blaschke's boast, but in the spirit of spoof, he said, "I was pretty busy, getting back from Switzerland and everything. I haven't had much time for newspapers today. What did Vice Burgomaster Blaschke have to say?"

For the past couple of weeks, neither of them had made use of spoof talk. Before the melancholy became a problem, there had been lots of spoofing. She had taught him about spoofing a year ago when they first became lovers. There were spoofing rules, her spoofing rules. According to those rules, spoofing couldn't be cruel, not in the least way. Spoofing was different from teasing. She had instructed that the spoofing could be a series of playful interactions lasting for hours, or it could be just one isolated verbal exchange. Spoofing was part nonsense, part vivid truthfulness. Spoofing wasn't just a way to play. Sometimes it was a way to communicate about things that were difficult to talk about openly and directly.

He knew his spoof was a success when she jumped out of bed and shouted, "This isn't for spoofing, you rotter. You damned rotter."

She flipped on the light, grabbed a newspaper from a nearby table, scrambled to find her black-rimmed eyeglasses, and hopped with a deft movement back onto the bed. She pushed her fist against his shoulder, edged into a sitting position up against the head of the bed, and declared, "This statement was in every single Vienna newspaper today! I know *you*. I can tell right now just by looking at *you* that you read this newspaper today."

He began laughing. He was delighted his spoof had elicited such success.

"Oh, stop laughing!" she said, like one delivering an order. "All right, you fooled me with a spoof. Now listen to this. I will read the article to you, even though we both know you have already seen it. Pay attention! Listen!"

She drew the newspaper up close to her face. She looked like a precocious rabbit. He lay back and watched her.

She stared at the newspaper and recited in an affected stage voice:

> *The great cultural mission which Vienna will fulfill in the German hegemony requires the remodeling of the Viennese stage whose great past looms as a legacy and a duty in these modern times. To bridge over the difficult transition from the aborted stage to the stage of the people, I beg the people of Vienna to heed the call of the theater and to give us a shining example of active racial cooperation in this field as well.*

Abruptly, she halted and then repeated the words *active racial cooperation* in a voice filled with indignation.

He stared at her and marveled at his great good fortune. His life was good. His life was very good. And this woman was the best thing in his life. Even now, with her hair askew and the ridiculous spectacles perched on her tip-tilted nose, she was a feminine wonderment. She began reading out loud from another article in the newspaper. He didn't listen to her words. He allowed himself to become lost in his appreciation of how visually fascinating she was.

But the bliss didn't last. He was startled when she suddenly asked, "What do you think about that?" She was staring at him, awaiting his reaction to the other article she had been reading to him. He had gotten so lost being fascinated at how marvelous she looked that he had stopped listening to her recitation. There could be a price to pay for having no idea what she had just finished reading to him. But all was not lost. It might be possible to bluff his way out. He vigorously clapped his hands together and continued to clap for a few moments.

Her mouth collapsed into a smile. An actress to her core, she loved hand clapping, whether one person was watching her perform or countless people were watching her in a very large theater. But she wouldn't be played for a fool. Not now, not by him. Making a vigorous feminine sound, she leaned forward and slapped the open palms of both her hands onto his chest. After doing that, she jumped out of the bed and, without a backward glance, scampered out of the bedroom.

In the next moment, he heard her puttering around in the kitchen. She was making a snack for herself.

"Do you want anything?" she called out.

"No," he called back. Of course he didn't want anything to eat. She was the one who always wanted to eat after making love. Not him.

He secured a comfortable position on the bed and began thinking about that lucky day one year ago when this extraordinary woman first came into his life. He had been sitting in the Café Central when she entered the café attired in a way that concealed her identity and her femininity. She was wearing what he later learned was her "anonymity garb."

On that day, one year ago, he had watched with some puzzlement and only a small amount of professional policeman's interest as the dowdy-looking woman, lumpy figure, wearing grotesque eye glasses, poked her way from one table to the next.

He might not have paid her any serious attention, but the way she moved caught his attention, and he was quickly convinced that something was amiss. He wasn't long fooled by the heavy coat at least four sizes too large, or by the hair pushed up under a ridiculous wide-brimmed, floppy hat that was battered and bloated. Nor was he fooled by the grotesquely outsized, black-rimmed eyeglasses.

He had quickly concluded that this was someone who—for reasons legitimate or not—was concealing her identity.

As she moved from one table to the next, the combination of authority and grace in her physical movements brought him recollection of a certain dancer he used to know, and when she paused at a nearby table, and a glove was pulled off, he stared with curiosity at an exquisitely manicured hand with silvered fingernails.

A few moments later, she advanced on his table, stood up straight, and said she was seeking an elusive copy of an Italian newspaper—a Milan daily—that might have somehow ended up mixed in with the four or five newspapers on his table.

The odd eyeglasses disguised much of her face, but the instant he heard that voice asking him if he had the Milan newspaper, he knew with certainty who she was. The revelation that the dowdy-looking woman was Volkstheater actress Constanze Tandler had hit with stunning force. Among the things giving her away, causing him to pull together other critical clues he had been recording, was the distinctive voice, a Viennese voice but with a Mediterranean undertone. Almost ten years before the meeting at the Café Central, he had been in the audience at the Theater in the Josefstadt when, as the understudy, she had filled in for the more established actress, Paula Wessely, in the role of Margarethe in Max Reinhardt's production of *Faust*. Constanze played Margarethe for only a few days, but those few days put her on the road to becoming a recognized figure in Vienna theater.

Now, lying on the bed, he told himself that he had been incredibly fortunate to have been in the audience ten years ago when, in one of the first scenes as Margarethe, she had riveted herself to the stage, no movement at all, until she abruptly began a majestic march from stage left to stage center, drawing forth a spontaneous and unexpected gasp from the audience.

When Margarethe was played by other actresses, no similar physical action was ever performed. Some critics at the time had said that she must have taken her own liberty within the play, but shrewder ones speculated it was all Director Max Reinhardt's doing.

Settled comfortably on the bed, he indulged himself the pleasure of thinking about having seen Constanze play Margarethe ten years ago and then meeting her one year ago, him at his table, her in the anonymity garb looking for a newspaper. At the encounter one year ago, he had stood up and uttered the word "Margarethe." That was the first word he ever spoke to her. He had followed that word, which brought a smile to her face, with an invitation for her to join him at his table.

To his delight, she had agreeably accepted the invitation. She took off the ridiculous eyeglasses and began fussing with her coat. He stood up, moved around the table, helped her off with the heavy coat, and guided her into an available chair. When her coat came off, there had been the flowery scent of her perfume: violets mixed with a musky fragrance.

After he sat back down, the first thing he had asked Constanze was why she was dressed in disguise. With luminous amber eyes, remarkable shifting shades of brown mixed with a grain-like color, she had stared directly at him and answered. "The clothes I am wearing, along with the hat and the bulky coat, are good for my purposes. And the spectacles also help. Besides, I need eyeglasses to see with. The important thing is that I like being able to move around the city without being bothered too much by the theater public." And then, with calculation, she had added, "Or by married men on the prowl for a flirtation."

He'd had the wit to reply, "I am the worst sort of Schnitzler character, just hoping to lead astray some sweet, little lass."

Tightly shutting her eyes, she had repeated the words "sweet, little lass" and then began relating details about her many portrayals of the archetypal sweet, little lass, the unmarried innocent involved with married men in various Arthur Schnitzler plays. At the beginning of her career, the sweet little lass was the role she had most often played. She had played that part until Schnitzler was banned by the Austro-fascists in 1934.

As their first encounter continued, Constanze had described the transitions different types of sweet little lasses made in Schnitzler plays, making it clear she had little interest in the Schnitzler lasses who simply endured a sad fate. She claimed a strong identification with the sweet, little lasses who were equal to or even superior to their lovers. "I have Italian blood!" she had declared, as though that was the complete and total explanation.

At the beginning of their first meeting, they had both known she had him enthralled. Very early in his life, he had learned the importance of letting women know when they had him enthralled.

At that first meeting, when she had expressed doubt that he could remember very much about the performance as Margarethe she had given ten years earlier, he asked, "Would you expect a man to forget eternal womanhood as described in the final lines of *Faust*?" After pausing for dramatic effect, he added: "The feminine image that leads men on."

In response to her skeptical smile, he stared into the amber eyes, took an appreciative inventory of her treasure house of a face, and spoke immortal words:

> *Here the ineffable wins life through love;*
> *Eternal Womanhood leads us above.*

Of course, he had overplayed himself. And her reply came quick and tart. "Viennese men, more than any other men, are always using the closing lines of Goethe's *Faust* to try to convince women that it is the image of the eternal feminine that is drawing them forward, and not their eagerness for a temporary place in the woman's bed."

With calculation, he had placed a look of torment on his face. Later that same night, when she asked about the look of torment, he told her the truth—that calculation on his part led to the look of torment on his face. His Habsburg honor required that the truth be told in an initial encounter with a woman if he hoped to ever see the woman again.

Near the end of that first encounter, he brought up for discussion the majestic march she had made for her first scene as Margarethe, and she provided the explanation.

"I got that walk from Maestro Max Reinhardt. It was entirely his doing. He planned it for me. He said it would work for the play and that it would work for me. The Maestro is a genius. Simply a genius. I learned more from him in four months than I learned before that in all of my theater training—and I began training for theater when I was twelve years old."

After saying that, she had leaned across the table and said, like one revealing a great secret, "The Maestro is a tyrant but also a genius. Simply a genius! He instructed me that before doing the walk, the important thing was for me to stand on the stage with the weight of my entire body in my legs. Not with any weight in my bottom or in any other part of my body, but only in my legs. The Maestro said that when I did that little march in *Faust,* or when I did any similar movement on the stage for any serious play I might be doing, that I was to remember to keep my weight fixed in my legs and keep my feet directed toward the very center of the earth. He said I should imagine that the soles of my feet were drawing energy from the very center—the absolute center—of the earth."

After that powerful statement, Constanze had continued. "In addition to learning how to connect with energy from the center of the world, I learned my Goethe during that time with the Maestro. In German philosophy, there is hardly any sympathy for femaleness. Goethe is the exception! And he also teaches about the redeeming nature of action. It wasn't just the Maestro. My father often spoke precious words from *Faust* that are always in my heart: 'The glory's naught, the deed is all.'"

The words he had chosen for his reply to her were words that many people frequently used to identify her father. He had spoken the words solemnly: "Commander Friedrich Tandler, the man of the deed."

Constanze's eyes had filled with fierce pride at mention of her father, who'd had to flee to Vienna when Mussolini took power in Italy in 1922, her adored father who was killed in the 1934 worker uprising in Austria. Her voice had dropped to a low pitch as she talked bitterly about the crushing of the Austrian workers in 1934. She talked about her own role in the fighting, how she got wounded. After that, she had talked about her childhood. With breathless enthusiasm, she had said, "When I was a little girl, my heroes were the Alpini, the Italian mountain soldiers."

He had answered her with simple honesty. "I fought the Alpini."

There was a quick reply. "My uncle was an Alpini. He always said your mountain soldier army, like his own, was filled with brave and honorable men."

"I was at Monte Santo."

"At the surrender?"

"Yes."

"Did you see Maestro Toscanini?"

"Of course."

"Maestro Arturo Toscanini won the Italian Silver Medal at Monte Santo."

"And the respect of those of us who were made prisoners at Monte Santo."

"Tell me about it. I want to hear every detail. I know the story, but I never heard it from anyone who was actually there."

So he had told the story in detail. Staring at Constanze's fascinating face, he began by saying, "In the war, it was routine for bands from opposing armies to be at the front and play their music before and after battles, but what Maestro Toscanini did that day was extraordinary, very totally extraordinary."

He had continued. He described the scene at the Monte Santo surrender in detail, every word spoken with absolute honesty. He told how he and the soldiers of the defeated Austrian force had marched from the place of surrender while the Italian bandmaster Maestro Toscanini, out of a generosity of spirit, played the Austro-Hungarian marching tune. Such a march it was: victors and vanquished exchanging tribute to each other with music and song.

When he had finished telling the Monte Santo story, Constanze had asked him with blunt directness about his adjustment to civilian life after the war. Unsure how to answer the unexpected question, he had told her about an incident he had never before shared with any woman, and, in fact, with very few men. In frank detail, he told her about an experience in the cruel winter months of 1919, after the war was over, and the only thing that kept him from starving was hard manual labor. He had been able to get a job, but to keep the job he'd had to learn how to handle an awkward wheelbarrow, a wheelbarrow that was a devil to handle. Everything had been hopeless until he got help from a woman construction worker who had taught him how to handle the monster.

After telling her that story, Constanze had signaled it was time for the two of them to leave the Café Central. They went to a hotel, signed in, went to their room, and made love.

That was one year ago. At this moment, lying comfortably in bed, he was still recalling his first encounter with Constanze when she returned from the kitchen munching on a sausage. On the occasions when she didn't stay locked in his arms, at least until he fell asleep, she often got up and had a snack. It had been that way ever since their first lovemaking. Somehow, she never seemed to put on extra pounds.

"You are much too thin," he said, letting his eyes reveal how pleasured he was watching her stride back toward the bed. He marveled at her tall, commanding posture, her long and perfect dancer's legs. Mostly, he marveled at her face sculpted like a beautiful piece of Italian art, punctuated with expressive amber eyes that could shift from joy to sadness in the beat of a heart.

She slowed as she approached the bed, her long, brown hair flowing down onto her bare shoulders. The nightgown offered tempting glimpses of the trim but generously attractive figure. She stood at the side of the bed and declared, "I am not *mollert*. You like your women *mollert*."

"*Mollert*," he said, repeating the Viennese word derived from Italian, a word used to describe women with extremely full figures.

"Well, I eat lots of Lekvar," she chirped, before swallowing what remained of a piece of bread pasted thick with Lekvar, delicious prune butter.

"But you don't get *mollert*," he said in a contrived, complaining voice.

Constanze laughed as she slid into the bed.

He still had both pillows. Edging apart from her in the bed, he said, "You really ought to be ashamed of yourself—using your female wiles to take advantage of a tired civil servant just back from doing an important service for the Greater Reich."

She lay on her back, face up, on her side of the bed. When she spoke, her voice was crisp. She hadn't recognized that she was hearing more spoof talk. This time, not a short, quick spoof, but one that was going to be drawn out. She said, "I hate hearing about any of your service for the Nazis. All I want you to do is help keep Marianne safe. Is that too much to ask?"

He proceeded with the spoof. In a voice feigning irritation, he said of Marianne, a close friend of Constanze, "I like Marianne Frish … As far as I am concerned, she isn't a Jew."

There was an angry reaction. "Karl, why are you talking this way?"

It delighted him that she was taking so long to recognize he was indulging in a spoof. He deliberately added a little more provocation to the spoof by saying, "Just who is and who is not a Jew is something I decide for myself." Those were words spoken by Karl Lueger, the turn-of-the-century Vienna mayor who had maintained private friendships with individual Jews while building political power on the basis of explicit anti-Semitism.

Constanze lay rigidly on the bed. She didn't realize she was being spoofed. She attempted to change the subject. "Tell me how your trip went. What time did your train come in?"

"I didn't take the train," he replied. "I motored over to Switzerland on Saturday, and today I got back to Vienna."

"That must have been a lot of motoring," Constanze said crisply. "Why didn't you take the train like you usually do?"

"Oh, it was a pleasant motor trip this time of year. Bubili did the driving."

"I know Bubili went with you," she said testily.

He waited a moment, pleased at how well this spoof was proceeding, then said, "We used a new, black limousine with the SS markings. There was a very important traveling companion with us. A great patriot. An honored hero in the 1914 war. With your excellent university education in philosophy, you might have understood better than I could what he said about good and evil."

Constanze drew herself into a tight bundle for a moment and then, with a strangled cry, gave vent to her anger: "Why do you bring this garbage talk into my bed? I don't want to hear about philosophical discussions on the nature of evil between you and those who ride with you in SS limousines."

"Oh, I don't know," he replied, smiling slightly, intending for Constanze to see the smile. "I know I am only a poor police inspector. I don't have the fine university education you have, but I am capable of philosophical talk about evil."

Constanze bolted upright in bed and spoke angry words in unintelligible Italian. The flow of Italian continued as she propelled herself from the bed. On her feet, she shifted to Viennese German. Again, as at other times in recent weeks, she used the words that had created a barrier between them: "*You goddamned Nazi policeman. You goddamned …*"

But almost as soon as Constanze's bare feet hit the floor, she spun around as though a bomb had gone off in her brain. He was able to see the precise moment when recognition hit her.

"Rabbi Leichter!" she exclaimed, swaying awkwardly.

He took delight seeing Constanze not simply recognize he was spoofing, but figure it all out and make a connection to one particular individual. That was the most marvelous part of it.

"Rabbi Leichter," he said, confirming her friend was the one in the SS limousine. The Rabbi, a former political leader of some note, had dropped out of sight before the Anschluss. The National Socialists had put Rabbi Leichter, an honored hero from the war, at the top of their list of fugitive Jews. That must have been an important clue she had recognized: the Rabbi had been an honored German war hero. She had obviously put that together with Bubili driving the automobile. Bubili had been looking for Rabbi Leichter at her insistence.

Constanze almost choked with joy. "Rabbi Leichter. Rabbi Leichter. Oh, my God! I know you, Karl. I always knew you. You are a rotter. You made me a prisoner right here in my own flat when I expressed outrage at that poster declaring the Volkstheater was *Jew Free*. That almost destroyed me. But I know you. Oh, Karl, oh my lover, my hero, you saved Rabbi Leichter. I was tired and stopped paying attention, and you fooled me with spoof talk. Oh, it was spoof talk. Such spoof talk. I love you. You are my hero! I love you! I love you!"

Lying on the bed, he held out his arms and said, "Your friend was as talky as ever. There was a lot of philosophy talk that I didn't understand. Rabbi Leichter is a very intellectual man, and he and Bubili together, well, all I could do was sit quietly and listen."

Laughing uncontrollably, Constanze took a step back away from the bed.

He closed his eyes and said, "Of course, I didn't remain totally silent. I talked about Boethius."

Constanze attempted to temporarily stifle her laughter. "Oh, you would talk about Boethius. Of course, you would bring in the only philosopher you have ever seriously studied."

"You should have heard Bubili use his Romani philosophy to explain why it was unnecessary for Rabbi Leichter to thank us."

"I can imagine. I can hear Bubili now: You are what you do. Do your good or lose it."

"Do your good or lose it has always sounded fine to me."

"Bubili is a wonderful fool. Both of you are wonderful fools." Her face was wet with tears, her body was heaving in uncontrollable sobbing. She took a tentative step toward the bed.

He reached out, grasped one of Constanze's hands, and drew her into the bed beside him.

"Come on now, sweetheart, don't be a baby," he said while holding her tight. "It was a fine coup. Bubili was the one who found the rabbi. The rabbi is a brave man, but his health was too frail to risk getting him out on foot or using any of the other ways we might have used to try to get him out of the country. He greatly enjoyed the ride in the SS limousine. Bubili was an excellent driver. You should have seen your Romani friend driving that SS limousine with a cigar in his mouth and his Romani scarf wrapped around his neck."

"I can see it in my imagination," Constanze said, amidst choking laughter.

He held her in his arms and joined in her laughter. With playfulness and tenderness, he drew her close and began the preliminaries of again making love to her.

The lovemaking had no beginning or end. From interval to interval, Constanze demanded repetitious descriptions of every detail connected with the rescue of the rabbi and his ride to Switzerland in the SS limousine. And, again and again, she erupted with joyous E-flat laughter. Not until early in the morning did he finally fall asleep.

CHAPTER FIVE

Karl Marbach was sitting in a chair at the kitchen table. It was almost seven o'clock in the morning, and he was watching Constanze fix breakfast. Long ago he had accepted the fact that cooking was something she attacked with ferocious intensity and none of the competence she demanded of herself in the other areas of her life. Plainly and simply, she was a terrible cook. But from their first time together, she had made it a condition of peaceful relations that if he stayed the night and wanted to part without spoiling the joy they had shared, he was not permitted to say or do anything that suggested criticism of any breakfast she might prepare.

He attempted to make himself comfortable in his chair while watching Constanze. She was preparing eggs and little pink sausages. He tried to console himself with the thought that there was little harm that even Constanze could do to eggs and sausages.

While he watched, she leaned down and aggressively poked a lit match into the oven to heat some *mohnsemmel*—poppy seed rolls. The oven came on with a distressingly loud noise, and at that same moment, on top of the oven, the eggs on a low-lit burner began making an odd popping sound. She was doing something strange with eggs this morning.

He decided it was best for his peace of mind to go outside the kitchen until this meal was fully prepared. Quietly, he got out of his chair, left the kitchen, and retreated into the living room of the flat.

He stood still and stared at the living room walls. The pale yellow walls were covered with a pattern of bluish stains, some vivid, others light. The stains were from glasses of wine thrown against the walls, a few of them by Constanze, most of them by friends. Many of the glasses had been thrown in expressions of joy, but some of the glasses had been thrown in bursts of anger. He stared at the pattern of wine stains and smiled when he spotted the one stain for which he could claim credit. It was a modest stain, but he felt good as he recalled why he had thrown the glass.

Stepping back, he thought about what friends liked to half-humorously say: that the pattern of wine stains on Constanze's walls was artistic.

At that moment, an odd sound came from the kitchen. Something had dropped onto the floor. He wondered if Constanze would throw away whatever had fallen. Maybe she would, and possibly she wouldn't. He told himself it was a good thing he had temporarily retreated into the living room. If one had to eat Constanze's cooking, it was best to not be present at the preparation.

He returned to contemplation of the living room walls. The wine stains were a good topic for conversation when friends gathered. Which stain was created by whom? On what occasion? Was this one a stain of joy and celebration, or was it one of anger, perhaps even rage?

A loud noise erupted from within the kitchen, and he apprehensively rubbed his hand across the back of his neck. He remained silent. He knew that anger would be directed at him if he was foolish enough to call out any word of concern.

He decided to put out of his mind what was going on in the kitchen. He accomplished this by thinking about the actress in American films who physically resembled Constanze. The actress was often in adventure films with a swashbuckler. The audience line in front of the Kino Schloss—one of the best Vienna film theaters—was always long when American films were shown, especially the films with the handsome swashbuckler. *The Charge of the Light Brigade* was a recent film. The actress, her name was Olivia de Havilland, was in that film, and she did, most definitely, favor Constanze in the face.

Without much question, Constanze Tandler and Olivia de Havilland looked a lot alike. They had very similar faces: the same set of jaw, the same wistful eyes. On movie screens, the de Havilland eyes often looked dark, but in the movie magazines, when there were colored photographs, her eyes looked soft brown, maybe even almond-colored. Regardless of the exact color of Olivia de Havilland's eyes, Constanze and the American actress looked very much alike, but, of course, Constanze expressed distress whenever anyone called attention to that.

Feeling restless, he surveyed what was contained in the large living room of the flat. There was the piano. Lying on the piano seat was a newspaper with the entire front page filled with a celebration of National Socialism. He scowled at the newspaper. Beside the piano was Constanze's treasured gramophone. And next to the gramophone were four long shelves of carefully stacked gramophone records.

He approached the collection of records. There might be disorder in Constanze's kitchen, but never with her gramophone records. In an especially hallowed place on the top shelf were the records that contained Romani jazz music.

He pulled out one of the Romani record albums and read the English words: *Tiger Rag*. A strange title, incomprehensible to him, but he knew the album contained some of Constanze's favorite Django Reinhardt music.

With a soft laugh, Karl recalled Constanze's highly emotional reaction the first and only time he had provocatively inquired why she had no Richard Wagner records on any of her shelves. That was several months ago, before the Anschluss. At the end of a long litany of expressive Mediterranean curses, she had declared her enmity to Wagner, to his music, and to the effect that music was having on the German people.

The next morning, when he went into the bathroom to shave, he had found pasted on the mirror a newspaper article with a reference to one of Adolf Hitler's quotes:

> *"Whoever wants to understand National Socialist Germany must know Wagner."*

After that, from time to time, with wicked delight he brought Wagner gramophone records to her flat. They were surplus items liberated from the evidence room at Vienna police headquarters. He believed that because he was a rational person, it was possible for him to take Wagner or leave him alone, and because Constanze was emotionally driven, she made sure the Wagner records quickly disappeared, never to be seen again. He was rational, and she was emotional. That was all there was to say.

He was careful as he put the Romani album back where he had found it. A man could be careless with many things in Constanze's flat, but never with records by Django Reinhardt.

His thoughts were interrupted.

"Come and eat," came a call from the kitchen.

He walked back into the kitchen and sat down at the table. The eggs looked odd to him, but the most distressing thing was that the servings were extremely large.

He took a bite, chewed, and kept chewing until he was finally able to swallow. Whatever had been done to the eggs this morning gave them a fishy taste and made them incredibly chewy. How could anyone make such fishy, chewy eggs? He hazarded a glance at Constanze. She was chewing thoughtfully.

He pecked at his breakfast while Constanze ate what was in front of her. There was a contest going on here. Always there were contests between them. About the contests involving meals cooked by Constanze, the rules were never articulated but were clearly understood. He could win as long as he ate all that was on his plate as though it tasted all right, and Constanze could win if he gave up before finishing the meal while she kept on eating as though the food was all right. Usually, he managed to win.

He watched with fascination as Constanze chewed. When she became aware he was staring at her, she conveyed a cheerful smile.

He ate most of what was on his plate but finally gave up and watched helplessly as Constanze chewed the final morsels on her plate. This time he had played the game and lost, but he couldn't eat any more of the awful-tasting eggs, and, besides, it was time for him to leave for work. He rose from his chair, put his suit jacket on, and wandered around the kitchen, reluctant to be too far from Constanze before the final moment of leave taking. Finally, he placed his Tyrolean hat on his head, knowing she would recognize that as a signal he was ready to leave. He was pleased when she put down her fork and gave him a silent plea of longing.

Usually, whatever might happen when he took his morning leave of her did not take place in the kitchen, but she abruptly stood up, grabbed him tight, wrestled him back into his chair, and slipped onto his lap.

Constanze's words flowed rapidly. "My lover! That was dangerous—what you did for Rabbi Leichter. I don't care what you said last night about not taking any risk. Both you and Bubili took big risks. You are both wonderful, but you are like little boys. What would have happened if the limousine had broken down? Or got an unpumped tire? There are always unexpected things that can happen."

"Bubili and I know about unexpected things—even unpumped tires."

Constanze bristled.

He knew she was angry at herself for what she had just said. Whenever she used what she called "mouse talk," she got angry at herself. But the important thing for him at this moment was the feel of her in his lap. He loved her totally and completely. She had changed him. Of that he was certain. For him there would be no more sexual adventures with one woman after another. He was no longer a wandering man. He was in love with Constanze, and that love was so powerful he could never be unfaithful to her.

He began thinking about what they might do this coming weekend. He was still thinking about the weekend when Constanze interrupted his thoughts by placing her hand on his mouth and saying, "I can't declaim my indignation about how people these days stand aloof while awful things are going on and, at the same time, fret about what you and Bubili did for Rabbi Leichter."

He decided this called for some spoofing. A small spoof might keep Constanze from getting too angry at herself. "Declaim?" He put a thoughtful look on his face as though puzzled by that word. It pleased him to make a spoof using just one word.

"Yes, *declaim!* You know what I mean."

"Declaim?"

"Don't try to *spoof* me. It won't work. I am on guard."

"Such words you use, and to me who never went to the university."

Predictably, Constanze went on the attack. "Oh, let me hear now about the poor little boy who had to go into the army, who was never able to go to the university."

"I never went to the university," he said with contrived melancholy.

Secure in his lap, Constanze placed one hand for a moment on top of his Tyrolean hat, then wrapped both arms tight around his neck. "You rotter."

"I am just a humble Habsburger."

"You and your Archduke Otto. Where is your archduke these days?" Constanze edged back a little. Settling herself more securely in his lap, she stared at him appraisingly and then kissed him with feminine assertiveness. When she drew her face away, she spoke like someone delivering a lecture to a schoolboy. "Your emperor lives in a foreign land. He will never come back to Austria."

"I am a man with his hopes."

"I am a woman with her fears."

He used one hand to edge his hat back on his head and then used both hands to hold Constanze secure. "You are braver than anyone I have ever known."

Constanze pressed tight against him. "I am a coward."

"Don't talk like that."

"It is true."

"It is false."

Constanze kissed his face again and again. She murmured the word "chocolate" while kissing him. He wondered about that. Why that word? He knew that whatever she was up to—and it was a certainty she was up to some sort of mischief—it had something to do with chocolate.

When they finally finished kissing, Constanze remained in his lap. He stared at her face for one long moment before reluctantly saying, "I really do have to go to work."

Constanze's voice was lighthearted as she said, "The chocolate soldier has turned into the chocolate policeman." After saying that, she laughed in distinctive E-flat laughter and said, "You *are* the chocolate policeman."

He shook his head. "What do you mean? ... The chocolate policeman?"

"Yes, the chocolate policeman."

He knew what the operetta about the chocolate soldier meant to Constanze, the delight she had taken performing in the Oscar Straus operetta, *Der Tapfere Soldat*. Deep in the core of her being, Constanze was a singer and an actress. In the operetta, she had sung to the chocolate soldier, the soldier who spent more time in ladies' bedrooms than on battlefields, the soldier who kept his ammunition sack filled with pieces of chocolate rather than bullets.

He held Constanze tight. He was grateful for the feel of her body, grateful for this moment, but he couldn't help wondering how far she was going to go with the chocolate policeman foolishness. There was for him one consolation. Without question, "chocolate policeman" was better than "Nazi policeman."

He listened as Constanze hummed the notes of the "My Hero" song from *Der Tapfere Soldat*. When her humming began fading, he said, "I am no chocolate policeman, and I have no chocolate bonbons for Constanze."

"No bonbons for Constanze?" Sometimes, when alone with him, Constanze spoke of herself in the third person. He never did that, didn't think it would work for him.

He moved his hand from the small of Constanze's back up to her neck and said again, "I have no chocolate bonbons for Constanze."

A large pout captured the expressive face. "No bonbons for Constanze?"

He asked a wicked question. "In the operetta, wasn't the 'My Hero' song sung to the rival of the chocolate soldier?"

Constanze ignored the tease, became very loose in his arms, and moaned as though in distress: "You have no bonbons for Constanze?"

"I have no bonbons for Constanze."

Constanze deliberately put a crestfallen look on her face.

He was about to call attention to what time it was when Constanze turned in his lap and grabbed his head in her hands. He thought she was going to kiss him again, but instead she stiffly held his head in front of her, stared into his eyes, and declared, "You really are the chocolate policeman … and most certainly you are my hero."

He started to look around the kitchen, but the hands holding his face gripped him tightly. Constanze was determined that he would not look at anything but her face.

Staring at Constanze's wonderful face, he said, "A chocolate policeman, eh? Well, I am hiding from my duty. And I am almost in a lady's bedroom, even if I have no chocolates."

Constanze kissed him. Then they locked together in a long embrace. He was conscious of every slight movement she made as she edged around on his lap.

Finally, she leaned back slightly, stared at him sadly, placed one hand on his stomach, and began murmuring words to him in Italian that he wasn't able to understand.

Her hand moved round and round on his stomach, and he became as helpless as a puppy having its belly rubbed.

Constanze asked a question. "Do you know why I fell in love with you at our first meeting that time at the Café Central?"

"I remember everything about that first meeting," he said, hoping Constanze wouldn't stop rubbing his stomach. "I suppose you were impressed because I paid proper respect to the Alpini in the war."

Constanze's hand stopped the rubbing activity. "Your respect for the Alpini meant only that you might be a good and decent man, but that wasn't why I fell in love with you that very first time we met."

"Well, I did mention your early triumph in *Faust*."

"*Quatsch!*" Constanze declared, using the mild vulgarism to make it clear she regarded that comment as nonsense.

He was grateful when Constanze again began moving her hand on his stomach. When he shifted his weight in the chair, he became aware of some sort of bundle in the pocket of his suit jacket. He reached into the pocket to see what the bundle was and pulled out a full packet of French cigarettes—Laurens Green cigarettes.

Constanze often put small presents in his pockets or left them in places where he was certain to find them. He had stopped smoking cigarettes, but the packet of Laurens Green was a good present. He would be able to use those French cigarettes to pay for information and assistance in connection with his police inspector work.

Constanze laughed. Always, ever since they first became lovers, she had been expressive with delight whenever she successfully surprised him with a gift.

Constanze wrapped her arms securely around him and then edged back, smiled, and said, "I know you have to go to work, but first I want you to tell me a story."

"A story?"

"My favorite story. That story was what made me fall in love with you the first time we met. Oh, there were other things about you that impressed me mightily, but it was the story you told me that made me certain you were a man who might be worth knowing. You only told it to me once. Many times I have wanted you to tell it to me again."

"What story? … Why didn't you ever say anything?"

"I was waiting. I wanted it to be the right moment. This is the right moment. Right now, this moment, this exact moment is the perfect moment for you to tell me for the second time in our life together about the woman and the wheelbarrow. Please, my love, tell me that story again."

The woman and the wheelbarrow: he had thought about that last night. Before that, he hadn't thought about it for a long time.

"Let me tell it to you tonight," he said. "Tonight there will be more time. I don't understand why you kept quiet about this for so long."

"Tell it to me now," Constanze ordered.

He knew there was nothing to do but get the story told. Once Constanze got started on something she really wanted, it was almost always impossible to make her be reasonable.

So he began the story. "All right, well, like I told you the first time, it was the summer of 1919, and I was not long back from the war. Those were hard times. I had nothing but my uniform to wear. I was just looking for a way to survive. A lot of civilians reviled any soldier they saw in those days. We soldiers were the ones who had lost the war."

Constanze was staring at him with deep intensity. He steadied her on his lap, stared into her eyes, and said, "I fought most of the war in snow and ice. I was safe in the mountains. If I had known about the malaria, I might not have ever come down from the mountains. That malaria was the best weapon you Italians ever had."

"But you didn't stay forever in the mountains."

"No, I didn't. I came down from the mountains, and I got malaria. And then, sick as I was, I roamed and plundered with other soldiers. We did plundering. I make no excuses. It was wrong. As bad as anything I ever did in the war. As bad as anything I ever did in all my life. Anyway, I finally broke away from the plundering and struck out on my own.

"Poor chocolate policeman."

"I had to get a job to keep from starving."

"Poor, *poor* chocolate policeman."

He decided to show Constanze that he could counter her teasing talk. Constanze and her theater friends sometimes used the words "empty costume" to refer to actors who gave nothing to other actors on the stage. Actors who were said to be empty costumes were often popular with audiences, but on the stage, there was nothing for their fellow actors to play off of, nothing inside the clothes being worn. With that in mind, he said, "I was still wearing my army uniform. I wore it during the plundering, and then later. It was all I had. I was nothing but an empty uniform."

Shifting her weight in his lap, Constanze declared, "You were never an empty uniform. Never a day in your entire life."

"You must have been just a child at the time. You may not remember how hot the summer was in 1919."

"I remember the heat of that summer, and I know how desperate those times were. In 1919, my family was always hungry. I was a child, but I still remember the hunger. I remember never having a full stomach, always going to bed hungry and waking up hungry."

"You poor kid."

Constanze placed her arms around his neck and stared at him.

He knew it was time to get on with the part of the story Constanze wanted to hear, but he couldn't help wondering why, if the story was so important to her, she hadn't brought it up before. One thing was certain. He had to get finished with the telling of the story if he was going to get to work at any reasonable time.

He pursed his lips for a moment and said, "Times were bad. Terribly bad. One day I got a job helping to remove bricks being torn up from an old factory. I was wearing my officer uniform. There were more than a dozen of us working together, but I was the only former soldier. We had to push heavy wheelbarrows—big, wooden, three-wheel monsters loaded with bricks—along a path on the muddy ground from the pick-up area to the bin area. When we got to the bin area, we had to heave the wheelbarrows upright and dump the bricks. Then it was back to the pick-up area and start all over again. Each time we unloaded our wheelbarrows, we got some chits, depending on how heavy the load was. At the end of the day, we got paid on the basis of how many chits our wheelbarrows earned for us."

Constanze moved slightly. He held her tightly while he told more of the story. "I was weak from that damned malaria. And I was having a lot of trouble figuring the ways of wheelbarrows and muddy paths. I had one calamity after another. I was clumsy and weak, kept dropping my wheelbarrow, losing the load. Several of the workers cursed me and laughed at me. Finally, I ended up rolling on the ground, gasping for air, sweating like a pig, shaking uncontrollably. I was having a malaria fit. That damned malaria! I was helpless and exhausted. I felt like I had a body too broken up to work."

He paused a moment. He was providing a lot more detail than he had the first time he told Constanze this story.

"Go on," Constanze said almost in a whisper. "Tell me all of it."

Feeling uncomfortable, unsure whether it was smart to tell this story in so much detail, he nevertheless continued. "There were some women working with us. One woman, in particular. She didn't laugh at me."

"Tell me," Constanze whispered. "Tell me about that woman."

He nodded. The woman was, after all, the point of the story.

"The woman walked over to where I was collapsed on the ground. She was tall."

Constanze closed her eyes, cradled her head against him, and murmured, "Oh, my beloved, I don't want you to ever lose your memory of that woman." Constanze's voice was soft. "Keep that memory in your head forever. I'm more grateful than you can ever imagine that you have the memory of that good woman in your head."

He breathed his lover's musk fragrance and held her close in his arms. She lifted her head and kissed him. Her mouth was moist and sweet. He told himself that if only he didn't have that damned business from the Hotel Capricorno to clear up, he might make up an excuse and stay with her all day. But the Hotel Capricorno business was important. He had to go to work today, and already he was going to be later than was best for what he needed to do.

"Tell it all," Constanze pleaded, moving slightly on his lap. "Tell me all of it. You were lying on the ground, and the woman came to help you. Tell me what happened so I can see it in my head."

He continued. "The woman was tall. She was very tall. Much taller than you. And tremendously healthy looking. She was dressed in overalls, just like the working men. As for myself, I was wearing my officer's uniform. It was all I had to wear. I had no other clothes. The woman came out of nowhere, just suddenly appeared. I was lying on the ground, and she asked me to give her my wheelbarrow. She said she would show me how to control it. She was very sure of herself. She told me to watch her. It seemed ridiculous. I had half a mind to get up and try to shove her away, but I was so weak I couldn't do anything but let her do whatever she wanted."

He paused for a moment and then spoke in a reminiscing voice. "You should have seen what that woman could do with the wheelbarrow. There were tricks to controlling the monster, but nobody had taken the time to explain things to me. She picked up the first load and ran with it down the muddy path. Then she emptied it with strength and skill that was amazing to behold. She was better than any of the men. She could do incredible things with that treacherous wheelbarrow."

He related more of what he remembered. "After the first wheelbarrow run, she came back to me, and I started to get up, but she shoved me back down. She told me to pay close attention, and she explained the mysteries of handling a large, heavy wheelbarrow. After that, she said for me to watch her do a second load. Before she left to do the second load, she pointed at the insignia on the soldier's jacket I was wearing and said that her brothers had served in the First Imperial and Royal Division. I told her I had only been in the First Imperial and Royal for a short period of time right at the end of the war, but she didn't seem to care about that. She went back to work with my wheelbarrow. There were tricks to loading the wheelbarrow and separate tricks to navigating it successfully down that muddy path. It was amazing. She was better than any of the men workers. And … and they hated her for being so good."

He looked away from Constanze and stared around the room without focusing on anything in particular.

In a quick movement, Constanze lifted the Tyrolean hat from his head and tossed it onto the floor. Then she clutched him tightly and nested her head firmly against his chest. "Tell me the rest of the story. Tell me the total and complete story."

He knew he had to tell it all. He took a breath and said, "A while later, after doing several loads, I collapsed again. She did more loads with my wheelbarrow, and after each load, she came up to me and pushed the chits my wheelbarrow had earned into my hand. Even as skilled as she was, it was a lot of work to do for a stranger. But she was insistent that I keep the chits. All of them. After I managed to get started again, I got through the rest of the morning—then the afternoon, too. But there were several times when she found me worn out, and each time that happened, she took up my wheelbarrow again. For each of my wheelbarrow loads that she did, she gave me the chits. She gave me a lot of chits by the end of the day."

He stopped for a moment, deep in recollection of memories from long ago, and shook his head. "When the day's work was done and we were paid off based on our chits … I … well, I rather expected her to be waiting for me. After all, even as ragged and weak as I was, I wasn't really a bad-looking fellow, and I rather fancied that she must have had a … well, you know … some sort of interest in me. I mean there had to be some reason why she went to all that trouble to help me."

"You blind fool, Karl." Constanze's voice was a soft whisper.

He told more. "The last time I ever saw that woman, she was running across a field away from our work site. She was shouting to a man. I stood and watched them embrace. I heard him call her his wife and heard her call him her husband. He told her to hurry so they wouldn't be late for the service on that Friday night."

He knew what Constanze was thinking. He said, "Yes, it was a Jewish service. I never saw that woman again after that day. A friend got me a better job in Linz, and I had to catch a ride there that very night. I didn't get back to Vienna for six months. I never learned the woman's full name, but her husband called her Marsha."

"Marsha." Constanze spoke the name fervently.

He was silent. This was the first time he had spoken that woman's name to Constanze, or even, for that matter, to men friends when he had told them the story. He had kept that name private, just for himself … until now.

"Thank you, Marsha," Constanze said in a low, soft voice.

He held Constanze tight. She moved in his arms, lifted her head, and kissed him for a long time. Her kiss was soft and intimate. She continued kissing him softly while speaking lover's words. Her voice was a melody of sounds. Finally, she said, "When you tell that story to your mountain soldier friends, is there anything else you tell them?"

"What?"

"Tell me what you tell your men friends about how she looked."

"What I tell …?"

"Describe her to me."

He wasn't prepared for that, but he knew he had to answer and that he had to speak truthfully. "Her face was beautiful. Her hair was black. Her eyes were wonderfully dark brown." He stared at Constanze's reddish brown hair and amber eyes. "I tell those who are men friends and understand such things that the woman was beautiful. I tell them that when she ran across the field to her husband, she took off her worker's cap, pulled the rest of her head wrap off, and her coal-black hair fell down her back, far past the middle of her body. And I tell men friends that, as dirty and sweaty as she was, even wearing those ungainly worker's clothes, she was a precious feminine image."

He had spoken without reservation. But the need to tell the truth—full and complete—had been overwhelming. Constanze was kissing his face again. Her mouth traced a journey from one side of his face to the other before concentrating on his lips.

They kissed and fondled for a long time.

Finally, with reluctance, he said, "Damn it. If it wasn't for a case that has come up, an important case, I would stay with you all day today."

Tears were working their way down Constanze's cheeks, but her face was lit by an extraordinary happiness.

It took a long while before they finally got disentangled and Constanze was able to rise to her feet. He stood up, straightened his suit jacket, went to a nearby table, and picked up his truncheon.

Constanze retrieved the Tyrolean hat from the place on the floor where she'd thrown it, put it on his head, gave it a few taps until it was placed exactly the way she wanted, then helped him put on his light overcoat.

They walked toward the door of her flat.

"You look very proper," Constanze said, making a point of staring at the Tyrolean hat. She had one final thing to say. "Please do what you can do to keep Marianne safe."

"Of course." He paused. "Are you all right?"

"No. I am not all right. It is wrong to be all right when all this evil is going on."

He regarded Constanze's words as emotional nonsense, not at all rational, but he resisted the inclination to disagree. Instead, he moved up close and wrapped his arms around her.

Constanze buried her face up against his chest, took a deep breath, and said, "You are afraid of my moods." She took a deep breath. "I am not like you. You take pride in not letting your emotions influence your rationality. I have rationality, but I trust my emotions even when things happen like my tantrum at that awful Volkstheater poster against Jews. Oh, my love, my precious love, you shouldn't have made me a prisoner. That was wrong. It was wrong! I needed to do some shouting, but I am no idiot. I wouldn't have let it get out of control."

"You *were* out of control."

"Holding me against my will was wrong."

"I had to keep you safe."

"You didn't have the right to make me a prisoner."

"I had to keep you safe."

"*Safe? ... Safe?*"

"Yes."

"I had to protest. Don't you understand? It was wrong of you to make me a prisoner just to keep me safe. Awful things are happening. It is wrong to do nothing, to keep totally silent when such bad things are happening."

He came up with the best answer he could think of. "The great philosopher Plato tells us that when there is no hope in making a protest against overwhelming evil, sometimes all a person can do is refuse to join in the wickedness. When protest is futile—like it is in this awful time—sometimes a good person can only do what reasonable people do in a storm of dust and sleet. Plato says that when the storm is really bad, the best thing to do is find a wall and get behind it until the storm passes."

Constanze uttered a gasp. "Oh, you and your coffeehouse philosophy."

They embraced one final time before he opened the door leading out into the hallway. Constanze kissed him while slipping something bulky into his coat pocket.

After leaving the flat, he caught a streetcar going down the Wiedner Haupstrasse. At the Ringstrasse, he got off the streetcar and began the long walk to police headquarters. It wasn't until he got to police headquarters that he absentmindedly put his hand inside his coat pocket and brought out the extra surprise Constanze had put there: a handkerchief containing chocolate bonbons.

CHAPTER SIX

A familiar face was waiting for Karl Marbach when he entered his office.

"Herr Police Inspector?" Police Assistant Willie Holder's puffy face was troubled.

"Give me a moment, Willie." Marbach took off his truncheon and sat down. After he felt reasonably comfortable in his chair, he lifted his hand, the signal for Willie to speak.

"The victim at the Hotel Capricorno wasn't a Jewess," Willie said in an urgent voice.

Marbach would have been surprised to hear otherwise.

"She was Fräulein Julie Thimig," Willie said.

Julie Thimig! Marbach felt like he had been struck a physical blow. Julie was the teenaged daughter of Judge Thimig, a fine man, a close friend.

Marbach lowered his head. Now he knew why that battered young face at the Hotel Capricorno had looked familiar. When was the last time he'd seen Julie before yesterday? It must have been only a couple of weeks. But yesterday he hadn't recognized her. Not even twenty years of police work was preparation for this. What was there to say? Poor Julie ... God help the judge.

Marbach wished he could be alone, someplace where it might be possible to groan, show a more human reaction than was possible in the presence of Willie, who, having delivered news more hurtful than he knew, was continuing his report, communicating his opinion that Judge Thimig's son was the most important member of the Thimig family—not the judge. That made sense to Willie, who knew that the judge's son, Monsignor Eugen Thimig, was a protégé of Cardinal Innitzer. It was common knowledge that Monsignor Thimig was the one who drafted the cardinal's first pronouncement after the Anschluss, a letter signed by the cardinal that ended with the salutation "Heil Hitler!" And it was rumored that the monsignor had arranged the meeting at the Hotel Imperial between the cardinal, the primate of Austria, and Adolf Hitler, Führer of the Greater Reich. What was indisputable was that Monsignor Thimig was now playing a key role in assuring that the faithful, whenever they attended Mass, were informed about the virtues of National Socialism.

Such a son for a man like Judge Thimig to have, thought Marbach. He addressed Willie in a firm voice. "Be quiet."

Startled, Willie stopped talking.

Marbach stared at Willie and asked, "Has Judge Thimig been notified yet?"

Willie shook his head. "No."

Marbach clenched his fists. Without delay, the judge would have to be told about the terrible thing that had happened to Julie. But what exactly could the judge be told? What details could be told? What details would have to be withheld?

While Marbach brooded, Willie apparently believed it was all right for him to resume talking. He said, "Monsignor Thimig is the brother of that murdered person at the Hotel Capricorno."

The words "that murdered person" became a throbbing sound in Marbach's head. He told himself that the murdered young woman was "Julie Thimig." Her name was "Julie Thimig." She wasn't "that murdered person." She was "Julie Thimig."

Oblivious to the effect of his words, Willie continued talking.

Marbach interrupted. "Tell me about the brothel in the Hotel Capricorno."

"What do you want to know?"

Marbach was beginning to get angry. "In your police assistant training classes, they must have instructed you how to give reports."

Willie swallowed. "Well ... uh, the Hotel Capricorno is a brothel owed by Aryans. The prostitutes are Aryan women pretending to be Jewish prostitutes."

Marbach thought that maybe Willie wasn't the idiot he appeared to be. He had learned what was important to know about the Hotel Capricorno.

"What is the next thing for you to do?" asked Marbach.

Willie looked totally confused.

Marbach deliberately added to Willie's distress. "I trust you know enough about police work to know you are going to have to check things out. You will begin by getting some names."

"Names?"

"Yes, names. You are going to have to get the names and information about everyone who was in that brothel yesterday. Anyone who was there, both clients and workers. Speaking of names, how did you learn the victim's name?"

"Why ... uh, there was an identification card."

"An identification card?"

"Someone found it in the toilet."

"Someone?"

"Why … yes," stammered Willie. "It was a cleaning woman who found the identification card."

"A cleaning woman found the identification card?"

"Yes." Willie looked miserable.

"Maybe you will talk to this cleaning woman some more."

"Of course."

"There must have been some man or possibly some woman who supervised things in the brothel, maybe the owner. Someone keeping track of who was working, what rooms were available, and so forth."

Willie's face registered puzzlement. "I don't think we found anyone like that there yesterday."

"Doesn't that seem odd to you?"

"Odd?"

"It seems odd to me."

"I will check it out."

"That will be fine." Marbach frowned. "Now, tell me, what do you think happened at the Hotel Capricorno last night?"

Willie looked perplexed.

"Tell me, and be completely candid. Don't be afraid to sound foolish. What do you think happened at the Hotel Capricorno?"

"I'm not sure … well, it might have been a stagging party. These days a lot of stagging parties involve Gentile girls pretending to be like Jews."

"I agree. All right, we're going to do some careful work on this case. If we don't, there is going to be a big mess. I want you to go back to the Hotel Capricorno and see what more you can learn."

Willie looked confused. He stammered, "I'm not ... I'm not sure I know what I'm supposed to do."

"Detective Rolf Hiller will go with you. He will be in charge. All you have to do is what he tells you to do. But be careful. If the Gestapo shows up, back way off. Don't wait to be told. Get out of their way. Let the Gestapo handle things any way they want."

Gestapo. That menacing word had an intimidating effect on Willie. Gestapo was part of the SS, but the word Gestapo had enough menace to intimidate not only Willie but most of those in the SS who weren't Gestapo.

Marbach stared at Willie for a moment, then stabbed his finger onto the interoffice exchange button next to his telephone, picked up the telephone receiver, and asked to be connected with Detective Rolf Hiller.

Marbach and Rolf Hiller worked together as a team. They were "colleague detectives." There was no closer bond in Vienna Kripo than that between colleague detectives. It was highly unusual for a police inspector and a police detective to call themselves colleague detectives, but that was the way Marbach wanted it.

Using the telephone, Marbach provided Hiller with a quick summary of relevant facts about the situation at the Hotel Capricorno. When finished, he said, "I don't care what else you are working on now. Drop it or get someone else to handle it. Go to the front door as quick as you can get free and join up with Willie Holder ... Yes, Willie. Yes, Police Assistant Willie Holder."

Marbach took a breath and continued. "Willie will be down there in a few minutes. The important thing is to get started on what needs to be done. We've got three army officers and a terrible killing. Judge Thimig's daughter was killed. You know about me and the judge. That isn't important. Find out what happened. Hopefully you will be able to learn something that will keep this situation from becoming worse than it has to be. Any questions?"

After a short pause, Marbach rang off. He took a moment for himself and then gestured for Willie to leave.

Willie got to the door but halted abruptly as a thought suddenly occurred to him. "Shouldn't we take an automobile? We could get there faster."

"No, you will not use an automobile." Raising his voice to an angry level, Marbach said, "Go find Detective Hiller. He doesn't wear fancy suits, but he knows his job. See if Detective Hiller can teach you a little bit about how to do police work. Now get moving."

The door closed behind the young police assistant.

Marbach felt immediate regret. He knew he should have told Willie that using a police automobile would draw unwanted attention in the neighborhood surrounding the Hotel Capricorno. Just because he didn't much like Willie wasn't a good excuse for not explaining things.

But there was something more important than having behaved badly with Willie. Marbach stood up. Terrible news, the worst news in the world, had to be delivered to Judge Thimig—and that had to be done as soon as possible.

CHAPTER SEVEN

When Marbach met with Judge Thimig, he delivered the cruel news bluntly. He had long believed that was the best way to deliver such news, as long as the person on the receiving end could handle it. He felt that when cruel news was told less than bluntly, with pauses, the effect on the person receiving the news could be much worse.

During the meeting with the judge, Marbach concisely stated that Julie was dead, that it looked like she was the victim of a stagging, that she had been dressed like a Jewish prostitute. But very deliberately he avoided saying anything to the judge about the presence of the army officers. Saying anything about them would have resulted in questions. The judge would have demanded names, and when that information couldn't be provided, it was a certainty the judge would use his own sources to get the names, and when that happened, the judge would perish from Nazi wrath.

After Marbach left the judge, he returned to his office and sat in his chair, clenching and unclenching his fists. At best, he had bought the judge a little time. The judge was safe for the time being, but only for as long as he didn't learn about the army officers. But how long would that last? A few days at most.

Still, Marbach concluded, the situation wasn't hopeless. It appeared likely that Lieutenant Neumayer wasn't the killer. Even if one of the other two officers turned out to be the killer, if it could be shown that Lieutenant Neumayer wasn't the killer, the situation might be controllable. Right now the only thing to do was wait and see what Rolf Hiller was going to be able to find out.

Marbach planted himself in his chair and concentrated his attention on an enormous body of paperwork that had accumulated on his desk. Barely an hour later, after staring for a few moments at an unimportant piece of paper, he felt filled with restless energy. Knowing it was too soon to expect Rolf to be back, he pushed aside the papers on his desk. Then, after debating for a moment, he got up from his chair, left his office, walked out of the building, headed up the Schottenring to the Währingerstrasse, and made his way to a favorite place of refuge, the Alpen Café.

He pulled open the front door, went inside, walked down a long, dark corridor, then opened another door, and stood for a moment behind a fencelike iron railing. Eight steps below him was the eating and dining area of the Alpen Café. People were sitting at the marble-topped tables. On the walls were mirrors. There were twenty-four tables in the Alpen Café, but when reflected by the mirrors, it seemed like there were hundreds of tables.

He looked upward. Hanging from the ceiling, multiplied by reflections in the mirrors, were glittering chandeliers. He lowered his gaze. Strategically placed, stoutly rounded support columns separated the floor from the ceiling. Each support column was wrapped in mirrors. With all the mirrors, the effect of multiple reflections was dramatic.

Continuing to stand behind the fencelike iron railing, Marbach looked down at the tables below. The regular clientele were sitting at their usual places. The regular clientele could count on having their tables reserved for them alone, available for them any time of the day or night that the Alpen Café was open for business. Like any really good coffeehouse, the Alpen Café served a variety of functions. It was a place to eat and share good company, sometimes company of a discrete nature. But for many patrons, it was also a place to conduct business. Some patrons routinely had their business mail addressed to the Alpen Café. On all of the tables, there were telephones. Most of the telephones connected only to other telephones within the café, but some of the telephones—for business or for other purposes—connected to callers anywhere in Vienna, and to places far remote from Vienna.

Marbach was still standing behind the iron railing when he heard a voice from down below, a hearty female voice. "Well, look what we have here. The police inspector has arrived. He is almost too late for midmorning breakfast, but we can still scrape up something for him."

The voice belonged to Lena, the irrepressible wife of Franz Krofta, owner of the Alpen Café. Lena was standing with a distinctive feminine presence, hands on her hips, at the bottom of the twelve stairs. Beside her was a familiar figure, the cashier, a gallant man with an empty sleeve. The one-armed cashier was a former mountain soldier.

Lena shouted up at Marbach, "Will you be bringing Constanze here tonight? If not, if that marvelous woman has finally gotten tired of you, I might possibly be willing to temporarily take you into my own bed."

At nearby tables, patrons laughed appreciatively at Lena's bawdy humor. Lena had jet-black hair, high cheekbones, an erect carriage, and powerful physical beauty. She could be earthy and ladylike at the same time. With her strong intelligence, Lena was able to hold her own against anyone, high or low. Her Viennese speech was flowered by Spanish roots.

Before there was time to reply to Lena, a deep male voice shouted from the back of the café, "What about me? Who is going to take me to bed?" With a huge smile on his face, Franz Krofta, Lena's husband, strode out of the kitchen. Fifteen years ago, Franz had been a promising prize fighter. Now, his partly flattened nose was made to order for a face both rugged and handsome. As Franz continued his forward movement, patrons expressed humor at what he had said.

"Oh, such naughty talk," said a young woman, laughing, sitting with some friends.

"I am shocked, totally shocked," said a jovial, heavyset, middle-aged man sitting at another table.

Lena dismissed everything with a wave of her hand. She stared first at her husband and then up to where Marbach was standing at the top of the twelve stairs. "Men are only good for one thing. If it wasn't for that one thing, no man would be worth five minutes of my time."

"One thing?" Marbach laughed as he descended the twelve stairs. At the bottom of the stairs, he acknowledged a humorous wink from the one-armed cashier.

Meanwhile, Franz moved up beside his wife and said to Marbach, "Does Constanze talk as naughty as Lena?"

"All the time," Marbach replied.

Franz laughed, but only for a moment. There was a table far in the rear of the coffeehouse that needed attention, and he moved quickly to attend to whatever needed to be done.

"No midmorning breakfast for me today," Marbach said to Lena. "I couldn't eat a bite. Constanze fixed one of her breakfasts for me this morning. She did something new and awful with eggs."

"Oh … that must have been a Beethoven omelet. She has been learning how to make Beethoven omelets."

Marbach shook his head. "Maybe Constanze should restrict herself to something simple like fried eggs."

"Constanze is not a simple woman. You can't expect a high-class woman like Constanze to make eggs that are merely fried."

"Have you ever actually eaten a meal cooked by Constanze?"

"I am sure anything prepared by my friend Constanze would taste good."

"I wish you'd had breakfast with us this morning."

"Oh, you … *man!*"

"Please … no remonstration."

"Remonstration?" Lena furrowed her brow.

"A word I learned from Constanze."

"Such a word."

"May I have a cup of gold?" he said, meaning rich, black coffee with cream.

"Just a cup of gold?"

"Yes. I can't eat anything. Those omelets are a heavy weight in my stomach."

"Oh, you … *man!*"

While Lena went to get the cup of gold, Marbach made his way deep into the coffeehouse, pausing a few times to exchange a friendly *Gruss Gott* (Greet God) greeting with friends at some of the tables. Finally, at the table permanently reserved for him, his personal table, he slipped into a chair, his personal chair.

Franz, after finishing his chore, joined Marbach at the table and began conversation with a complaint about how bad things were in Vienna since the Anschluss.

Marbach listened for a few moments before saying, "Oh, hell, it was worse after the World War. Back in 1918, there was sickness, starvation, riots, killing. It was much worse in those days than it is now."

"This evil will keep getting more and more powerful until it is destroyed by Communism."

"These bad times will pass; you will see," Marbach said.

"No," Franz said. "Until there is a world revolution, the bad times will keep getting worse."

Marbach studied his friend. Franz had been an early supporter of Austrian Clerical Fascism. Then, five years ago, he met, fell in love with, and married Lena. She was from a Spanish Marxist tradition and had been a dedicated Communist since early in her life. Naturally enough—anyway, it seemed natural—Franz stopped being an Austrian fascist and joined the Communist Party.

For the past several months, Franz and Lena had often talked politics with Constanze, a Democratic Socialist. Constanze's politics were aggressively at odds with the Communists, but the three Reds—two Communists and a Socialist—agreed on one thing: the Habsburg orientation of Police Inspector Marbach was worse than their political differences.

For Marbach, there was one vivid truth: he, a Habsburger, his two Communist friends, and his Socialist lover were bonded together by trust and friendship that was total and absolute.

Franz said, "It is worse today than ever before. Worse than 1918. Worse than 1934. A lot worse than 1934. More and more people every day are finding it easy to give reign to awful meanness, terrible cruelty. This stuff against the Jews. Where is it going to end?"

Marbach grumbled his reply. "It is bad now, but things will get better. You will see."

"Only if there is a worker's revolution."

"You and your Marxist propaganda. Why do you bother me with such nonsense?"

"I only bother you because I like bothering those who are SS," Franz said, staring with exaggerated effect at the button on Marbach's collar, the button with the runic double S of the SS.

Marbach regarded that as a fair blow for the former boxer to deliver. But before there was time for him to figure a way to deliver a counter punch, Lena arrived with a tray containing three cups of gold.

Lena placed the tray on the table and sat down. There was now a ritual to be observed. With eyes shut tight, Lena's black eyebrows demanded silence. And got it. Beautiful Lena had hands that were permanently damaged from a childhood spent doing the rough work of a Spanish peasant. Lena lifted her red-calloused right hand and touched her beautiful patrician forehead, made a quick descent, then touched each feminine shoulder.

Both men followed her lead. Using short, jerking movements, they blessed themselves.

Lena was a woman who gave tenacious loyalty to Communism and a separate, fervent loyalty to the Catholic Church. She was a creature of contradictions: Communist and Catholic. Constanze, a devoted friend of Lena and a creature with her own contradictions, often said that Lena's great strength of character derived from contradictions. Most certainly, Lena possessed powerful strength of character. She was the only person in the world who could get Marbach to pray in a café.

After the saying of grace was completed, Marbach returned his attention to his cup of gold while his two Communist friends discussed profits, losses, supplies, and prices. All of it, as far as he was concerned, was just boring business talk. The business talk continued until Lena used the word "margin."

Marbach decided to do some teasing. He said to Lena, "That word margin. Such a word. Isn't that a word used by the capitalist exploiters of the masses?"

"Oh, shut up," Lena snapped.

"Forget margins," Franz said. "I have to find new sources of good meat and vegetables."

"You better very quickly find cheap sources or we'll soon be bankrupt," Lena said.

Franz answered in a grumpy voice, "It isn't just meat and vegetables. I have to find a new source for the wine and liquor." It was a point of pride for Franz that the Alpen Café was able to offer a broad range of food and drink choices during this time of serious shortages in Vienna. He was always trying to find new sources of food supplies, new sources that weren't formidably expensive.

Marbach didn't pursue more teasing. He sipped his cup of gold and listened while his two Communist friends concentrated on business talk.

Several minutes later, with the business talk between Franz and Lena showing no sign of abating, Marbach found himself thinking about his colleague detective. It was still too early to expect Rolf to be back, but he stood up, paid verbal tribute to Lena, clapped a hand on Franz's shoulder, and made his way past table after table within the coffeehouse. He stopped for a few minutes at one of the tables occupied by friends who were police officers in order to pick up on news and rumors, then walked up the eight steps and out the door.

Outside the Alpen Café, on his way back to police headquarters, he stopped at a kiosk, a small wooden newsstand across the street from police headquarters. Surrounding the kiosk were several metal racks containing newspapers. Checking what was available to be seen in the racks without actually removing a newspaper, he found himself thinking about the judge. He was still thinking about the judge when he became aware of the presence of Kathia, the proprietress of the kiosk.

"Herr Police Inspector," Kathia said, "why is it that you are heading toward police headquarters when you should be enjoying this glorious day in the company of the marvelous Constanze?"

Marbach smiled. The old woman was just one of the countless persons caught up in the broad web of friendships Constanze maintained in various locations across Vienna. He stared for a moment at the metallic swastika pinned prominently on Kathia's smock. Metallic swastikas were being sold at all Vienna kiosks for the price of ten groschen. He had never talked with Kathia about politics, but he knew her to be a good woman. It seemed to him that everywhere he went these days there were good people, old friends, people he'd known for years, who had recently become dedicated National Socialists.

He heaved a sigh, bade farewell to Kathia, and returned to his office. Soon Rolf would be back, hopefully with something that might help keep Judge Thimig safe.

CHAPTER EIGHT

It was late in the afternoon when Marbach's attention to police paperwork was interrupted by familiar voices in the hallway. A moment later, there was a knock on the door.

"Come in," Marbach called out.

Police Detective Rolf Hiller and Police Assistant Willie Holder entered the office. Rolf was from peasant origin. He was highly intelligent, well read, and articulate. But although fascist rhetoric celebrated the peasantry, a Viennese tradition stronger than fascist ideology dictated that a born peasant, regardless of intelligence and competence, would never be promoted above the rank of police detective. Willie, on the other hand, in his early twenties, from a family of prestigious social rank, was almost certain to rise to the rank of police inspector in a few years.

Rolf furrowed his brow and dropped heavily into an available chair. Rugged looking, in his early forties, he had a large gap between his very square, prominent front teeth.

Willie, still on his feet, fussed with his tie in front of the wall mirror.

Marbach kept irritation from his voice as he said to Willie, "Why don't you sit down?"

Willie continued fussing with his tie. He smiled ingratiatingly and continued to fuss with the tie.

Marbach expressed irritation. "Sit down!"

With a startled look on his face, Willie moved stiffly and awkwardly to a chair and sat down.

Rolf smiled a gap-tooth grin.

"What do we know?" Marbach asked, directing the question to Rolf.

When Rolf answered, he spoke in the familiar "Du" Deutsch, leavened by his distinctive peasant dialect. "Boss, I don't know how to say this except to just tell you. We really got a situation here." Using the word "boss" was one of Rolf's many idiosyncrasies. Marbach had long ago given up trying to get his colleague detective to stop using that word.

Rolf pulled a tin container from his coat pocket and withdrew a hand-rolled cigarette. He also retrieved a wooden match and used the nail of his thumb to ignite the match. The lit match produced a bright, sputtering flame. Holding the lit match in his hand, Rolf used the tip of his tongue to assure that the paper on his hand-rolled cigarette was secure before lighting up. After taking a puff, he made a sputtering noise, carefully spit bits of tobacco from the tip of his tongue, and then spoke in a deliberative voice. "What happened at the Hotel Capricorno began earlier in the day at the Café Europa. Julie Thimig was in the Café Europa with the son of the colonel count and two other officers."

"The Café Europa?" Marbach didn't try to conceal his strong reaction to that revelation. The bar at the Café Europa was currently an elite social center for National Socialists, and it had a long history as a notorious gossip center. It was a certainty that in no more than a day or two, everything about Julie and the three officers would be common knowledge all over Vienna. Even if Vienna newspapers bottled up the story, there was no way it was going to be able to be contained.

Marbach heaved a heavy sigh.

Rolf nodded. "Yes, the very public Nazi bar at the Café Europa."

Willie looked offended. A dedicated National Socialist, he found use of the slang word "Nazi" to be offensive. He knew that some National Socialists made free use of the word, but he pointedly offered a correction. "You mean the National Socialist bar."

Rolf cast a dismissive look at Willie, stared down at his open notebook, and said to Marbach, "I got more."

"Go on."

"Lieutenants Paul Neumayer, Erich Ossietsky, and Wolfgang Litzman are all well-known at the Café Europa, although Lieutenant Litzman has been a familiar figure only for the past month. The Café Europa waiters don't think Lieutenant Neumayer really likes Lieutenant Litzman. Actually, nobody seems to like Lieutenant Litzman very much."

Marbach knew Rolf was building up to something.

Taking his time, Rolf slowly pulled an erasure-tipped pencil from his shirt pocket and began writing in his notebook.

While Rolf wrote, Marbach became aware of Willie making an effort to catch his eye. It was obvious that Willie was still disturbed about the use of the slang word "Nazi." Exasperated, Marbach shifted in his chair and pointedly placed his back to Willie.

Rolf closed his notebook and said in a solemn voice, "Julie Thimig was one of two fräuleins with Lieutenants Neumayer, Litzman, and Ossietsky at the Café Europe yesterday. The second fräulein's name is Karen Mann."

Rolf tapped the underside of his chin with the erasure-tipped pencil before continuing. "I will come to the important business of the second fräulein in a moment. First, I will offer my evaluation of each of the three young officers."

Marbach nodded agreement.

Rolf spoke slowly, thoughtfully. "I begin with the least important of them: Lieutenant Ossietsky. He sometimes tries to act arrogant, but mostly he is just an ignorant buffoon. He never went inside the Hotel Capricorno. He stayed outside in an automobile. But buffoon or not, he knows more. Whatever happened inside the hotel, he had no part in, but he definitely knows much that would be helpful for us to know."

Rolf deliberated for a moment, tapped the erasure-tipped pencil against his nose, and then continued. "Let me see. Ah, yes. There is Lieutenant Neumayer. He thinks he did the killing, but he didn't."

"Are you sure of that?" Marbach asked.

"Yes, boss," Rolf said. "Lieutenant Neumayer likes to get drunk and succeeds quite regularly. His lapses of memory about what happens while he is drunk are the stuff of legend. The waiters at the Café Europe say he is a much nicer person when drinking than when sober, but if he doesn't get control of himself, they think he is going to turn into a totally hopeless drunk."

Willie made a slight sucking sound with his tongue, an unsubtle dismissal of the suggestion that Lieutenant Neumayer might have confessed to a crime he didn't commit.

Marbach ignored Willie. If Rolf was going to say Lieutenant Litzman was the killer, which appeared to be what he was leading up to, it wouldn't be just idle speculation.

Rolf put his pencil back into his shirt pocket. "Young Neumayer gets drunk regularly and tends to forget things. And there is the matter of his knuckles. I did some mingling with all three young officers, did some handshaking, especially with Lieutenant Neumayer. A vigorous handshake didn't bother him at all."

Marbach thought about the similar way he had handled handshaking activity at the estate of Colonel Count Neumayer.

Rolf stared defensively at Marbach. "Oh, don't worry. I didn't let on I was checking anyone's hands."

Marbach shrugged.

Rolf continued. "There is something else. I talked with the police chemist about the possibility of poison."

Willie interrupted. "I have seen the chemist report. It is official. There was no poisoning. The Marsh test was negative."

Marbach winced at Willie's reference to the Marsh test, a conventional test for poison, but the only poison it detected was arsenic. If any poison figured in this case, it wasn't arsenic. Julie Thimig's placid approach to death was not at all like the usually frenzied activity of a victim of arsenic poisoning.

Rolf glanced critically at Willie before saying to Marbach, "The chemist is still testing. He knows this has priority. He says it will take maybe another hour to complete the test for hyoscine."

Willie looked confused. "What is …?"

"Shut up, Willie!" Marbach ordered.

Without concealing amusement, Rolf looked at Willie, then at Marbach, and said, "Now about hyoscine … well, it was just luck. I found out from one of my sources that Lieutenant Litzman has a long history with hyoscine, dating back to when he was a boy. Apparently, as a boy he sometimes used it to kill dogs and other animals."

Marbach leaned forward. Rolf had been lucky—an important part of detective work was being lucky. But a crucial thing in detective work was knowing how to make use of the luck, and Rolf was one of the best at making use of any luck that came his way.

Rolf reached into his shirt pocket, withdrew the pencil, fiddled with it.

"What more is there?" Marbach asked, quite certain that there was more.

Rolf put the pencil back into his shirt pocket. "The victim, Fräulein Julie Thimig, was a virgin."

"A virgin?" Marbach made no effort to conceal his surprise.

Rolf nodded. "I have the laboratory reports. Fräulein Julie Thimig didn't have sex at the Hotel Capricorno. She never had sex. Never once in her very short life."

"A virgin in a whore house!" Willie exclaimed.

Marbach and Rolf cast irritated looks at Willie. After a moment, Marbach turned, faced Rolf, and asked, "What are we dealing with here?"

"We are dealing with the murder of a virginal young woman," Rolf answered.

"Go on," Marbach said.

Rolf said, "I went to the officer quarters where Lieutenant Litzman lives. Those officer quarters are a very private place, but there is a sergeant there who owes me a very big favor, and, as long as he is kept out of this thing, he agreed to let me go inside Lieutenant Litzman's room. He even stood guard for me. Inside, I found a very clean trunk with a lock that was easy to pick. There were a lot of newspapers inside the trunk. And there were pictures."

Rolf was silent for a moment and then continued. "The important thing inside that trunk was a diary. From what I read in the diary, the nice, clean-cut Lieutenant Litzman is a *lustmörder* ... a *haarman* ... a thrill killer. Whatever you want to call it, he's one of those who kills for the fun of it. He has killed at least six fräuleins in the past year. There are six names that he put in the diary along with a lot of detail. Enough detail so we'll be able to nail him. He killed four fräuleins in Salzburg and two here in Vienna."

Rolf paused for a few moments before continuing. "Maybe Lieutenant Litzman thought his diary would be safe inside the officer quarters. Or maybe he just wanted it to be where he could look at it whenever he wanted. Anyway, in his diary, Lieutenant Litzman wrote some things down again and again, repeating himself endless times. In that devil's diary, he tells about capturing young fräuleins, making them naked, punching them around, and keeping them alive day after day, helpless in their nakedness. That's real important to him: keeping his victims alive and naked while he takes his time tormenting them. He wrote it all down in the diary …"

Marbach gestured for Rolf to continue.

Rolf took a deep breath. "In the diary, Lieutenant Litzman didn't write anything about actual sex. Just about the nakedness of his victims, and their fright, and the fun there was for him punching them, hitting them, hurting them. Over and over again, he wrote descriptions of their naked bodies. Their breasts … arms, legs. And he recited in detail the frightful pleas they made. In the diary, he says again and again that he never touched their nakedness. He provides the damnedest details about moles, scars, bruises, birthmarks. He writes about how offensive those things are. But the weirdest thing is that he wrote over and over again that he never touched their nakedness. He wrote about putting his hands on their bodies to hurt them, but he also wrote that he never touched their nakedness. Make sense of it if you can. He must have done touching, but he denies it in these private writings intended only for himself to see."

Marbach waited until it was clear that Rolf was finished with what he wanted to say. Only then did he ask about the diary. Of course, Rolf had taken the diary.

Rolf said, "I gave the diary to the genius. He is giving it his full attention."

The genius was Police Inspector Thomas Mastny. He was exceptionally intelligent. So intelligent that everyone in Kripo recognized who was being identified when the words "the genius" were used. He could remember names, dates, incredibly specific details from cases going back over more than twenty years, link what he remembered with current crimes and suspects, and provide helpful suggestions for Kripo personnel to follow.

"Did you find anything else in the trunk?" Marbach asked.

"I had to get out of there. The sergeant allowed me fifteen minutes by the clock. When my time was up, I took the diary. Nothing else. You might want to have someone enter those officer quarters and legally pick up the trunk and anything important I didn't have enough time to see."

"The minute we are done here, you have my authority to give the order for that."

Rolf heaved a heavy sigh. "I saved the worst for last. I said at the beginning of this that there was another fräulein with the three officers yesterday at the Café Europe. That fräulein is missing. No one knows where Fräulein Karen Mann is."

"My God!" exclaimed Marbach.

Rolf took a moment and then said, "I paid a quick visit to the family of Fräulein Karen Mann. Her parents think she is staying in the student quarters at the university. I didn't tell them anything, but I knew their daughter hasn't been seen in the student quarters since yesterday afternoon. I tried to make it seem like I was interested in something unimportant when I talked with the parents, but you know how parents are. They got pretty excited. After my visit, they are certain to check on their daughter's whereabouts, and, any time now, they're going to be coming here in a panic."

Mercifully, Willie kept quiet.

Rolf withdrew a small photograph from his pocket. "I talked the parents into letting me borrow a photograph of their daughter. I have to give it back when we don't need it anymore."

Marbach reached across the desk and accepted the small photograph. It was a family photograph of a young fräulein standing between a man and woman who obviously were her parents. In the background was the main building of the University of Vienna.

"Well, boss, that's what I got," Rolf said. "The important thing is Fräulein Karen Mann. My guess is the lustmörder still has her alive. He'll want to amuse himself with her before she dies. Anyway, I am going 100 percent on that assumption until it is proved false."

Marbach nodded his agreement with Rolf on that point.

Willie didn't agree. He moved around awkwardly in his chair. "If Lieutenant Litzman killed Julie Thimig, he wouldn't take the chance of keeping the other student alive any longer than necessary. She has to be dead."

"We are dealing with a lustmörder," Marbach said. "You never know about those guys."

"I think she's alive," Rolf said.

"We will proceed on that assumption," Marbach said.

There was no more to be said. With a wave of his hand, Marbach brought the meeting to a close.

Rolf rose from his chair, put his hand on Willie's shoulder, and gestured toward the door. "That's a very fine suit you are wearing,"

Rolf said to Willie as they walked toward the door. "Do you suppose your tailor could make me a suit like that?"

"He's a private tailor," Willie said with a perplexed look on his face.

When Rolf opened the door, Marbach looked up suddenly, and said to his colleague detective, "Damn good work. Now I will do what I can do to get started with whatever it is going to take to find Karen Mann."

After the door closed, Marbach sat in deep silence. Because of what Rolf had learned, it looked like it might be possible to keep the judge safe for a while, but a young woman named Karen Mann was wherever the lustmörder had hidden her. Rolf was right. They had to assume she was still alive.

Marbach stood up, left his office, went quickly down the stairs, and walked toward the office of Commander Kaas. Only the commander could do what needed to be done if there was going to be any chance saving Fräulein Karen Mann.

CHAPTER NINE

Marbach approached the desk of the young man who was the head secretary for Vienna Kripo Chief Stephan Kaas. The self-important head secretary sat stiffly behind his desk. A month ago, he would have stood up for a Vienna police inspector. Now, remaining seated, he stared with aloofness. When he spoke, his Viennese-German was conveyed with the affected nasal tone utilized by certain status-conscious Viennese to express their importance.

"Commander Kaas has been called to an important meeting in SS Leader Kaltenbrunner's office in the National Socialist Office Building."

The head secretary for the chief of Vienna Kripo hadn't spoken in a nasal-sounding voice prior to the Anschluss—at least not to a police inspector.

"Chief Kaltenbrunner's office?" Marbach shook his head.

"SS Leader Kaltenbrunner." The correct title was delivered with crisp formality. The self-important head secretary stared imperiously.

Realizing it was futile to say anything more, Marbach turned away and stared down the hallway. He told himself that if he was going to see Commander Kaas as soon as possible, the best thing for him to do was get one of the eager-to-please police assistants to watch the front door and pass on word when Commander Kaas returned. While wondering where he might find a police assistant,

Marbach's attention was drawn to a noise at the far end of the hallway.

The front door was opening.

Marbach stared hopefully and then muttered, "Thank God."

It was the Kripo chief.

Commander Kaas came through the door and advanced down the hallway.

Marbach waited until Commander Kaas was only a few steps away.

"Herr Commander."

"Police Inspector Marbach ... It is good you are here. We should talk about that business involving Colonel Count Neumayer's son. Come into my office."

The head secretary stood up. He formally addressed the Kripo chief and then, after completing required verbal protocol, stood rigidly at attention and said without any nasal sound in his voice, "I have placed some papers for you to sign on your desk. And you have that meeting—"

Commander Kaas interrupted. "Cancel the meeting. Cancel it, and don't pass any calls through to me for a while. Only priority calls. You know which calls are *priority*."

"But—"

"Cancel the meeting," Commander Kaas ordered. "And only *priority* calls." He pushed open the door to his office, turned toward Marbach, and gestured with his hand.

Marbach entered the office and walked to the middle of the room.

Commander Kaas entered the office behind Marbach and pointed to a chair adjacent to a large desk.

Marbach sat down, and Commander Kaas began pacing from one end of the large office to the other.

Marbach leaned forward in the chair.

Commander Kaas walked over to a large office window, stood rigidly straight for a moment, turned around, and fixed his eyes on Marbach. "There will be no charges against Lieutenant Neumayer. There is going to be a cover-up."

Commander Kaas hadn't minced words. He had used the word "cover-up."

Marbach decided to be equally candid. He said, "There is no need for a cover-up. Lieutenant Neumayer isn't the killer. Lieutenant Litzman did the killing."

Commander Kaas pondered for a moment and then said, "It makes no difference who did the killing. There is going to be a cover-up."

Marbach allowed a negative reaction to show on his face.

The commander walked over to the large desk and sat down. "You and I don't know each other very well, but I would like to have plain talk."

Marbach said to the commander, "You can speak frankly with me. Whatever you say to me is private. Just between you and me. You have my word on that."

"I accept your word. Now let's get this out in the open. At the meeting I just came from, SS Leader Kaltenbrunner stated that the entire matter at the Hotel Capricorno has to be covered up. He said that if the Jews are blamed, no questions will be asked."

"Blame it on Jews?"

"Yes."

"I think there is a better way to handle this."

Commander Kaas said, "We obey orders. We obey orders whether we like them or not. We obey orders or we are no damn good."

Marbach got out of his chair and walked over to one of the walls in the office. A picture on the wall had captured his attention the first time he had been in this office, shortly after Commander Kaas arrived from Berlin. He stood in front of the picture and studied it. The picture showed a file of troops and contained words from a training lecture given by General von Eichhorn on January 1, 1915 to the Eighteenth Army Corps at Frankfort-am-Main.

> One day when a staff officer was duly
> carrying out an order he had received, a
> high-ranking general rebuked him, saying,
> "Sir, the Kaiser made you a staff officer
> so that you should learn when not to obey."

Marbach turned away from the picture. "You say we obey orders or we are no good. I don't accept that. Neither did General von Eichhorn. He said that sometimes we don't obey orders. Sometimes we disobey."

Sitting in his chair, Commander Kaas looked beyond Marbach to the place on his wall where the picture from the 1915 training lecture was hanging.

Marbach said, "You are the one in charge. Do we obey our orders?"

"Those words from General von Eichhorn. Oh, my God! I haven't thought about those words in ages. Wherever I go, I like having that picture on my wall. But it's been a long time since I read the words under the picture."

"They are good words."

"Yes …"

"It is time for us to disobey."

"Damn you. Oh, damn you." Commandeer Kaas shut his eyes for a moment. "Don't mind my curses. We are having plain talk. I encourage plain talk. Do you have any more plain words to speak?"

Marbach returned to his chair, sat down, and said, "I came to your office to report what was learned with our Kripo investigation."

"If your report has anything to do with what we are talking about, let me hear it."

"Lieutenant Neumayer and Lieutenant Litzman were with Julie Thimig in the Café Europa early on the day of the killing. There was also another officer—Lieutenant Ossietsky. And there was another fräulein—Karen Mann, a friend of Julie Thimig."

"Those officers were at the Café Europa? With Julie Thimig? Who saw them there?"

"Patrons, waiters … café staff. They made themselves very much noticed."

"The Café Europa! The Café Europa! If Julie Thimig was seen with Lieutenant Neumayer and the others in the Café Europa, there'll be no way to cover this up. It is going to blow up." The commander got out of his chair and strode to the other side of the office. He stood very still, his back to Marbach, and asked, "Anything more?"

"A Kripo investigation has revealed that Lieutenant Litzman did the killing. He is a lustmörder."

"Oh, my God!"

"Surely it is clear that there can't be a cover-up. It won't work."

"That is clear to you and me, but SS Leader Kaltenbrunner won't see what he doesn't want to see. He will insist on going ahead with the cover-up. Right now, the only thing he cares about is keeping the colonel count out of any spotlight until Berlin announces a big economic move, something very big. The big economic move might be announced a couple of days from now—maybe a week. If things can be covered up until that decision is announced, some very important people will become rich, very rich. I'm not ... I'm not saying any of the money will go into the chief's pockets, but I am saying he is determined to protect those whose pockets will be filled. He said he expects he will lose his job if this thing gets messed up. He also said that if that happens to him, before he meets his own fate, he will hand me my head."

Marbach kept silent. He was impressed by the candor of Commander Kaas.

Standing rigidly still, Commander Kaas expressively lifted and dropped his hands.

Settling himself in his chair, Marbach said, "There was another university student. Fräulein Karen Mann was last seen leaving the café with Fräulein Julie Thimig and the young officers. It looks like Lieutenant Litzman has hidden her somewhere. We don't know where."

Commander Kaas went to his chair and sat down. "My God! Is there any way to find the fräulein?"

"We're at a dead end. The only hope we have of finding Fräulein Karen Mann is to get the lustmörder to tell us where he has hidden her."

"Well ... she is probably already dead."

"Fräulein Karen Mann is alive."

"Yes … I understand. I agree. It is our duty to assume she's alive until we know for certain she is dead."

Marbach stared closely at Commander Kaas while saying, "We have Litzman's diary. That's how we know he's a lustmörder. This particular lustmörder likes to keep his victims alive as long as he can. That's something that gives him a lot of pleasure, keeping his victims alive, inflicting horror on them until he chooses to end their lives."

Commander Kaas got out of his chair and began pacing back and forth, from one end of the office to the other. Finally, shaking his fist above his head, he said, "Damn Kaltenbrunner. God damn him!"

Edging around in his chair, Marbach let out a tense breath. "What do we do?"

"I won't have innocent blood on my hands. This is a mess … but it is my mess. No reason for you to be involved. You better get out of here."

Marbach remained where he was sitting. He remembered a time during the war of twenty years ago when he and a fellow mountain soldier had been in a bad place, but instead of staying safe, they had joined together and entered the fight. Before entering the fight, they had shared a moment of laughter that had bound them together.

Marbach began laughing.

Commandeer Kaas didn't understand why Marbach was laughing. "What's so funny?" he asked.

"If I leave now," Marbach said, continuing to laugh, "the next time I am in confession, I will have to tell the priest I committed a sin. I will have to say I left a Berliner alone when he was like a man trying to make love to a woman without taking off his pants. I didn't do anything to help. I just let him fuss helplessly."

"What the ... what do you mean? Make love with my pants on ...?"

Marbach continued to laugh.

After spending a long moment staring at Marbach's laughing face, Commander Kaas joined the laughter. Repressed tension was released in peals of laughter.

While laughing hard, Marbach said, "I have changed my mind. Go ahead. Handle this thing all by yourself."

Continuing to laugh, Commander Kaas said, "You have brass balls, my friend, talking this way to your superior. I have half a mind to put you under arrest."

Pausing in his laughter, Marbach said, "Among Comrade Soldiers, there is no superior and no subordinate."

Commander Kaas's face lit up. "*Comrade Soldiers!* Yes, we are Comrade Soldiers. Those battlefield words apply to us! It can happen this fast. From this moment on, we two are Comrade Soldiers. No superior and no subordinate. We are Comrade Soldiers."

"I would even trust you alone with my wife."

"I don't care about your wife," Kaas said with a laugh. "Would you trust me alone with Fräulein Constanze Tandler?"

"With Constanze?"

"Yes. I have read the records on you, and I have looked at pictures of Volkstheater actress Constanze Tandler. I am sure I could find her to be good company if you would trust me alone with her."

Marbach shook his head and chuckled. "Not for one single minute would I trust you alone with Constanze."

The two men laughed louder than before. They came close to choking in their merriment. They were not commander and subordinate. They were equals. They were Comrade Soldiers.

"We laugh at the devil," said Kaas amidst his laughter.

"We laugh at the devil," echoed Marbach.

Kaas, still laughing, said, "I think we better quit this foolishness. Unless you have a suggestion, I am going to try to do the only thing I can think to do. I can't just do nothing."

Marbach stopped laughing. "If you are thinking of trying to beat on Lieutenant Litzman to try to learn where the victim is hidden, put the thought out of your mind."

Kaas lifted his arms in the air. "What makes you think I am going to … oh, hell. Well, you are right. That's exactly what I was thinking about doing."

"Beating on that man won't work. He knows he is lost, and he will want to have one final victory. He'll have that victory if he sends us off on a series of phony goose chases. Does SS Leader Kaltenbrunner have any V-men working on this case?"

Heaving a heavy sigh, Kaas turned away, shuffled over to his chair behind the large desk, and sat down. "Yes, SS Leader Kaltenbrunner is using V-men. The police leader likes using V-men." Kaas performed an exaggerated spitting activity and then said, "V-men: private cheats and informers. Trusted by no one. For hire by anyone."

"There will be risk for you unless you back away from this," said Marbach.

"If one never takes risk, one is nothing at all."

"We are going to have to lie, cheat, scheme, falsify evidence—"

Kaas interrupted. "We must not call ourselves liars or cheats."

"I disagree. The big trap is to think that because we are honest the dirt doesn't rub off on us when we do things that are dirty."

"I think, Comrade Soldier, we have found something we can disagree about."

"I look forward to many future disagreements with you, Comrade Soldier, but right now, there is dirty business to be done."

"Do you think there is a way to save the missing student?"

Marbach said, "Her name is Karen Mann. The student's name is Karen Mann."

"Yes! Fräulein Karen Mann. Do you have a plan? Is there something we might do to save her?"

"I am going to try to get Lieutenant Litzman to tell me where to find Fräulein Karen Mann."

"Do you think you can get him to tell you that?'

"I think it can be done."

"But you aren't sure?"

"I am sure it can be done. The question is, can I get it done?"

"You are going to try?"

"Yes."

Kaas stamped his foot on the floor. "All right!" He stamped his foot again and said, "I am with you. Just tell me what to do. You know best how to proceed. It is for you to give the orders, Comrade Soldier."

"We will start by getting full background information on all three officers, especially Lieutenant Litzman. We need to learn about financial things, military service, love lives … everything. There isn't much time, but we have Vienna police resources. That means we have the best police resources in the world."

Kaas put his hands on his hips. "Win or lose, I am with you. If SS Leader Kaltenbrunner hands me my head for this bit of mischief, so be it."

"Our biggest enemy is time," Marbach said. "We have to question the three soldiers, all three of them, as quickly as possible."

"I will telephone the colonel count and tell him to have his son and the two others promptly get themselves to police headquarters. It ought to be possible to get the son right away. It may take a while to get the other two."

"Get on with it," Marbach said.

Kaas snapped open a file box on his desk, found the number he was looking for, fixed the telephone in front of himself, put the earpiece to his head, and dialed. After the connection was made, no time was wasted. He said into the telephone mouthpiece, "Hello. Yes … *Gruss Gott* to you, too. Now put the colonel count on the line. Tell him it is Commander Stephan Kaas."

While waiting for the colonel count to get on the line, Marbach caught the attention of Kaas and said, "Be sure to tell the colonel count to bring his son here dressed in civilian clothes. If he isn't in his army uniform, if he is in mufti, he may be less sure of himself. We need every advantage we can get."

Kaas nodded and then came fully alert as he spoke forcefully into the mouthpiece. "Herr Colonel Count, Commander Stephan Kaas here … Yes, I will tell you what I want. I want to prevent a disaster. There has been a killing." There was a pause. "All right, you know about the killing. Now, if we are going to keep this from spinning out of control, I need to have you and your son at police headquarters immediately. And get someone loyal to you to round up the other two officers. I need them here also."

After a short pause, Kaas said, "The other two are with you now? Good. That is excellent. If you do exactly what I say, a disaster may be prevented, but you must do exactly what I say. It is important that you don't let your servants or anyone else know where you and the young men are going. You have to bring the young men here immediately. Do you understand?"

There was a long pause, then Kaas barked aggressively into the telephone mouthpiece: "Good, you understand. No excuses and no delays. No one is to know anything about this. One more thing. I want all the young men dressed in civilian clothes. And keep in mind we have absolutely no time to spare."

When the conversation was done, Kaas slammed down the telephone and brought his hands together in a lusty clap. "All three of those young men were at the Neumayer estate when I called. I may be in the brig before this day is done, and you, my good friend, may lose your fine job, but neither of us will go down without a fight."

"You ballsy bastard," Marbach said with a grin.

Kaas returned the grin. Then, after a brief moment, he became serious. "When this thing gets going, are you going to do the interrogations by yourself, or will you need help?"

"Rolf Hiller and I will do the interrogations."

"I know why I am doing this. I have to ask … what are you doing this for? Are you just a big, sloppy hero?"

"Ask yourself the same question. All you had to do was be a hired dog, fall in line for SS Leader Kaltenbrunner."

"Hired dog, eh? Not me. I am SS. I believe in the Führer, and I have absolute loyalty to the SS. If I thought it would be good for the Third Reich, I would stand back, bury the horror of this within myself, and let the innocent fräulein be sacrificed. But if the police leader goes ahead with this dumb cover-up, it can only end in disaster for the Reich."

Marbach tried not to think about the words spoken by Kaas. He told himself that the important thing was that a good man was taking considerable risk to save the life of a young woman he didn't know.

Kaas said, "We better get started."

Marbach asked, "May I use your telephone?"

"Help yourself."

I took only a few minutes for Marbach to get Police Inspector Thomas Mastny on the line. With an economy of words, he filled the genius in on the case, providing names and critical details.

When finished with the telephone, Marbach turned and faced Kaas.

"You can still back off," Kaas said.

"So can you," Marbach said.

Kaas kept his hand on Marbach's shoulder as they left the office. They went outside the building to wait for the colonel count and the three young officers.

CHAPTER TEN

Marbach and Kaas had been standing outside the police headquarters building for what seemed to them a long time when, finally, the colonel count's limousine arrived. The three young lieutenants, dressed in civilian clothes, conveyed arrogance while getting out of the car. The colonel count, looking subdued, was the last one to get out.

On the alert for anything that might come in handy when questioning would begin, Marbach took note of the arrogance on the faces of the three young officers. Deprived of that arrogance, he thought, each of the three young officers was vulnerable.

The colonel count approached Kaas and delivered unexpected news. "I have to return to my estate immediately."

"Herr Colonel Count," Kaas said, "I wish you would reconsider. Your presence here is important."

"Impossible."

"But ... I really wish you would—"

"No, Commander Kaas. I shall leave things in your very capable hands."

"If you must leave, well ... please let me once again say that it is important for you to not let anyone know about this visit to police headquarters."

"As you wish," the colonel count said over his shoulder as he got back inside the limousine.

Kaas and Marbach stood together and watched the car pull away. It disappeared quickly up the boulevard.

Things were beginning badly.

"Go on inside," Kaas said to the three young officers. "Stop at the main desk inside."

Without speaking a word, the three young officers obeyed.

"This isn't good," Kaas murmured to Marbach as they walked toward the door that had already closed behind the three young officers.

"We have work to do," said Marbach.

Kaas put out a restraining hand. "You are too much the optimist. Hell, this isn't working out. When the colonel count gets back to his estate, he'll start peeing in his pants, and as soon as he feels the wetness running down his leg, he'll call SS Leader Kaltenbrunner."

Marbach didn't reply.

Kaas said, "I excuse you from any further participation. I can't get out of this. Not now. But it will be all right with me if you withdraw."

"If you are going to stick your neck out, you can't expect me to act like a hired dog."

They were only a few steps from the closed front door of the building.

Kaas put his hand on Marbach's shoulder. "Comrade Soldier, eh?"

"Comrade Soldier," replied Marbach.

"Are you really sure you know what you are getting into?"

"I know that I intend to get a confession from Lieutenant Litzman that he alone did the killing. And I know that I intend to do whatever it takes to satisfy anyone that Lieutenant Neumayer had nothing to do with the killing of Julie Thimig. And one way or other, I intend to learn where Lieutenant Litzman has hidden Karen Mann. If doing all that takes luck, I intend to have a lot of luck today."

Kaas shook his head while Marbach reached out and opened the door to police headquarters.

"This is going to end badly," said Kaas.

"You are what you do," said Marbach.

Kaas didn't understand that reply. "You are what you do?"

Marbach held open the heavy wooden front door with his left hand while he moved his half-open right hand in an indifferent, semicircular counterclockwise movement, the characteristic Viennese gesture signifying that there was nothing to worry about. Then he did something he had often done many years ago in the mountains before a battle. He made very deliberate eye contact with the man beside him and put a sappy look on his face.

Kaas recognized what Marbach was doing. He put the same sappy look on his face, a look he had sometimes delivered to Comrade Soldiers before going into battle during the war.

The door closed behind them.

CHAPTER ELEVEN

After getting inside the main lobby of the police headquarters building, Kaas and Marbach separated. Kaas went directly to where the three young officers were waiting while Marbach headed for the basement door. He opened the door and walked down the basement stairs. At the bottom of the long stairway was a telephone switchboard. Next to the switchboard was a small kitchen. All jail prisoners got a cup of potato soup three times a day, nothing more if they only got jail food. Most prisoners had food brought to them by friends or family members. The prisoners who had no friends or family to bring them food, and who couldn't get fellow prisoners to share with them, had to get by on potato soup three times a day.

Marbach walked past the kitchen. He headed toward the small rooms in the back where interrogations were conducted.

As he expected, in one of those rooms he found his colleague detective. Rolf was sitting at a table quietly, pouring tobacco onto paper, and rolling the paper tight. Rolf was spreading the tobacco very precisely before using his thumbs and fingers to expertly roll the paper.

"So here you are," Marbach said.

"Where else should I be?"

"The three young officers are upstairs. Commander Kaas will sign them in, then they'll be split up, be brought down here, and, one at a time, they'll be interrogated."

Rolf gazed thoughtfully at a carefully rolled cigarette.

Marbach sat down on the other side of the table. "Leaves from the floor of the Vienna Woods," he said, referring to the tobacco Rolf used to make the cigarettes. "Whatever happened to that Macedonian tobacco you used to smoke?"

"Vienna Woods is a lot cheaper than the Macedonian," Rolf said. His tie was loosened, his suit jacket badly wrinkled. He picked up a small tin container and shook it. From the sound, the small tin was almost filled with rolled cigarettes. He delivered a gap-tooth grin. "On my salary, I can't afford better tobacco than Vienna Woods, but if you offer me a good cigarette, I won't turn it down."

Marbach hesitated for a moment and then provided one of the Laurens Green cigarettes.

"Wherever did you get Laurens Green?" said Rolf while accepting the expensive cigarette.

"I have my sources."

Rolf put the Laurens Green cigarette in his shirt pocket and grinned. "I'll save this for later. I won't waste such a fine cigarette on the poor company you provide."

For a long time, Marbach had been resigned to Rolf's teasing ways.

Continuing with the cigarette rolling activity, Rolf inquired, "Are you going to tell me the script for how we are going to handle this?"

Good police interrogation required a plan. The worst mistake was to not have a plan whenever it was possible to have one. Because of his affinity for things theatrical, Marbach called his plans scripts. His scripts had a beginning, a middle, and an end, along with as much detail as he deemed appropriate. He prepared scripts when he worked alone, and he prepared scripts when others worked with him. When others worked with him, the scripts specified respective roles to be played, along with cues, sometimes pieces of dialogue, occasionally words to be spoken or to be reacted to in the appropriate way at the appropriate time. The scripts were always kept flexible, subject to change when circumstances changed. The most important thing in any script was the ending: everything was flexible except the ending. The ending was the purpose, the focus, the objective.

Marbach said to Rolf, "There could be trouble with this. Are you sure you want to deal yourself in?" That was the way Kaas had put things to him, and that was the way he now put things to Rolf.

"Just tell me the script, boss."

"All right. First off will be Lieutenant Ossietsky. Information from him will be helpful for the questioning of Lieutenant Neumayer, who will be number two. We can be a little aggressive with Ossietsky—not tough but a little aggressive. But when we get to Lieutenant Neumayer, the questioning will have to be very polite. I emphasize: *very polite*. The son of Colonel Count Neumayer is a very special case. Finally, there is number three, Lieutenant Litzman. He is the important one. He will be interviewed only after we've learned as much as we can from the other two. We need to know as much as we can from the first two if we're going to have any chance of getting Lieutenant Litzman to tell us something that will enable us to find out where he has hidden Fräulein Karen Mann."

With those words, Marbach had provided the verbal outline of a script that was still in tentative form. He seldom wrote anything down for a script unless Rolf or whoever else might be involved needed to have some or all of the script in writing.

Rolf nodded to convey to Marbach that he understood the script. Then he said, "I am the best one to get this started. Mastny has provided a report. I read the genius's report. The information dealing with Lieutenant Ossietsky is very interesting."

Marbach wasn't sure about Rolf going first, but they were colleague detectives, and Rolf had the right to say how he wanted to handle his end of things. Marbach scratched his head. "We have a report from Mastny?"

"Yes. And you haven't read it. Guess who has."

"I repeat myself. There could be trouble for you if you get deeply involved in this."

Rolf made a snorting sound.

"Kaltenbrunner has a big interest in this case," said Marbach, using just the last name. When they were alone, Marbach and Rolf always referred to the SS leader as Kaltenbrunner, with no title. "If Kaltenbrunner ends up displeased, he will provide a lot of grief for those in Kripo he holds responsible for causing him displeasure."

"Kaltenbrunner is often very nasty."

Marbach sighed. "He is determined to continue with the cover-up. He intends to blame everything on the Jews. He thinks he can get away with that."

"It won't work." Rolf lit one of the hand-rolled cigarettes. "How long does he think that trickery will hold up?"

"He will be satisfied if it lasts long enough for a lucrative contract to be finalized between one of the colonel count's companies and Berlin. The announcement of the contract could come quickly, or it might take a few days. Any bad publicity for the colonel count before the announcement is made will almost certainly cause Berlin to find some other company to contract with."

"Now I know what is going on."

Marbach took a deep breath. "Let's get down to work. Kaltenbrunner is going to come charging in here in an hour or two, but a confession from Lieutenant Ossietsky ought to bring him to a halt if it identifies Lieutenant Litzman as a thrill killer who murdered Julie Thimig." Marbach paused. "I'd like a confession from Lieutenant Litzman saying Lieutenant Neumayer wasn't even present."

Rolf smiled agreeably and puffed on his cigarette. "I thought you were the one who never wanted any small dishonesty in police work."

"This time there is going to be lying, cheating, and scheming."

Rolf chuckled.

Marbach said, "Let's get down to business."

Rolf took another puff on his cigarette. "Like I said, I am the one to question Ossietsky. I think I have him figured out. I've read Mastny's report. The genius did a good job. I can make good use of what I learned in that report."

"All right. You get Lieutenant Ossietsky. Do the questioning fast, just don't get too rough."

Rolf crushed out his cigarette but saved the tobacco in a small bag. "Are you telling me how to do my job?"

"Maybe somebody ought to tell you how to do your job."

"If you order me to be soft, most certainly I shall be soft."

"If I order you?" Marbach shook his head at Rolf's tease. He might tell his colleague detective what he wanted done, but that wasn't the same thing as giving an order.

Rolf chuckled.

"What's in Mastny's report on Ossietsky?" asked Marbach.

"The genius provided a very detailed report. If you want to, I can take as long as you want discussing with you what it says about Ossietsky."

Marbach sighed. "I give up. Go and see what you can learn from Ossietsky."

"Don't rush me. I need time to get myself ready."

Marbach was impatient for Rolf to get started, but he understood the ways of his colleague detective. He was obligated to leave it up to his colleague detective to decide how much time to take with temporary mischief before beginning the interrogation of Ossietsky. The mischief was helping Rolf get himself ready for the interrogation.

Marbach said to Rolf, "I may have some use for those photographs you keep in your office."

"Photographs of my family?"

"The ones of your daughter Hannah."

Rolf didn't ask for an explanation. "After I get through talking to Ossietsky, I'll get some of Hannah's pictures for you."

"The ones that show her at various ages."

"Yes."

"Let me say one more time it might be better for you to back off, let me do all the questioning. There is risk here."

Rolf smiled. "You are the one taking a risk, not me. You could end up in prison—or worse. As for me, if this thing messes up, the worst thing that will happen to me is that I will have to line up someone else in Kripo to work with me."

"That would be a sad fate for you, having to get someone else to work with you. Who else would have my patience with you?"

Rolf chuckled and then said, "I've sized up Ossietsky. With any luck, it won't take me long to get a handwritten confession from him, one that points the finger at Litzman and has enough falsehood to exonerate young Neumayer, put him someplace other than the Hotel Capricorno. That ought to stop gorilla Kaltenbrunner and give us a chance to learn what we have to find out in order to save Karen Mann."

Marbach eyed Rolf. "You got this all figured out, eh?"

"Just because I am not wearing a club, don't assume I'm going to go easy on Ossietsky. After all, there isn't a whole lot of time to spare."

"I can see how concerned you are about time."

Rolf grinned. "I think I can get this interrogation done real fast."

Marbach knew it was futile to try to push Rolf to promptly get started, so, at a loss for what else to say, he brought up a totally different subject. "For the first time in my life, I feel what is called alienation. Aside from you and a few other Kripo friends, wherever I go these days, everyone seems to be joining up against Jews while proclaiming total, uninhibited loyalty to Hitler. I feel separate from others. I feel alienation."

Rolf nodded. "There is all kinds of anti-Jewish stuff you never used to see or hear before. Oh, there was always some anti-Jewish stuff, but it was mild compared to what goes on now."

Marbach said, "For me, it is not just those I know in Kripo. Friends of long standing are expressing awful anti-Semitism. They celebrate Hitler, and they say awful things that they never used to say."

"We peasants don't have a problem with this thing called alienation."

"Forget about alienation. There is something I want to know. What do you think about the commander?"

"I don't think about him."

"You don't like him?"

"I give him some credit. He did a good thing for that priest."

The priest in question was Father Merkl, one of the young priests at St. Ruprecht's Church. The worst that had ever been said about Father Merkl was that he wasn't very intelligent. After the Anschluss, the simple, uncomplicated priest took it on himself to protect Jews. He saved more than a dozen Jews before getting caught by the Gestapo. The judgment of Father Merkl's parishioners was that he was too stupid to be a good priest.

Rolf said, "The commander did a good thing when he got Father Merkl away from the Gestapo and had him sent to Munich where the Church will keep him safe."

"So maybe the commander is a good man."

"I don't call him a good man, but as a Kripo chief, he's better than I expected."

"But you don't call him a good man."

"No, I do not call him a good man."

"Sometimes I think you are too critical of people."

"Sometimes I think you are full of excrement."

"Sometimes I am."

Laughing softly, Rolf closed his eyes. When he opened them, he said, "The genius has some good stuff in his report on Ossietsky. It says the young officer's military superiors have concerns about him. The report says he is the nervous type, unsure of himself. Apparently he is afraid of anything that might result in him getting physically pushed around. He stays completely out of sports activities. No soccer, nothing where he might get hurt. I intend to exploit this young officer's nervousness. After I get started, I am going to take him fast. These things are never predictable, but I think I can take him real fast. Hopefully, I can get this done in maybe half an hour."

Marbach kept silent. He was concerned about what Rolf's "real fast" way might involve. He knew that it would likely include some punching around.

Rolf said, "Boss, you are a sorry figure of an SS man. And Regular SS, at that. By the way, they posted your name on the board for not paying your dues."

"*Quatsch*! I haven't had a pay raise in three years, and now I have to pay Regular SS dues."

"Poor police inspector."

"Be grateful that police detectives only have to pay Auxiliary SS dues."

"It is most certainly a blessing that I don't have to pay Regular SS dues."

Marbach frowned. He didn't like it that Rolf had set himself a time limit for finishing his interrogation of Ossietsky and now was taking so much time getting started. He said, "I know you have to work fast—once you get started—and I am not trying to tell you how to do your job, but I'd really appreciate it if you didn't get too tough with Lieutenant Ossietsky."

Rolf stamped out his cigarette and placed the butt in his shirt pocket. "I'll do it tough enough to get the job done. Whenever I can get what I need without being tough, that's fine. But when I can't get the job done by being gentle, I get the job done by being tough, just as tough as it takes."

Marbach knew that what Rolf was saying was what any good police detective might say, whether that detective was working in Vienna, Paris, London, or New York City. His own way was different. He did things his own way because he was convinced it was a better way, a surer way, but he never denied that his way could often be slow compared to the fast way of Rolf and others who did police interrogations.

Rolf, studying Marbach, said, "If I get the picture right, the colonel count didn't realize he would be bringing his son and the others in for interrogation. He thought it would just be to help them get their stories straight with the police before the Thimig family learns what happened."

"What's on your mind?"

"I imagine all three of these characters have been instructed to ask to be turned over to the army if they don't like what is going on here."

"I suppose so."

"These three army officers might lose their gusto if they think they're going to fall into Gestapo hands."

Marbach nodded. The Gestapo were the grand inquisitors of the Reich. They operated under authority provided by a February 10, 1936 text known as "The Fundamental Law" that granted authority to inquire, with whatever brutality was required, into any and all activities hostile to National Socialism.

Rolf said, "If Lieutenant Ossietsky is reluctant to answer my questions, I am going to tell him that we intend to turn him over to the Gestapo. He might get real talkative if he thinks he is going to leave Kripo but isn't going to get transferred into the comforting arms of the army."

Marbach didn't reply. Time was passing, and he wanted to see Rolf get started with the interrogation, He told himself that the best way to prod his colleague detective was to bring up a subject he wouldn't want to talk about.

"When are you going to have dinner with Constanze and me?"

"You ought to stay away from that woman," Rolf said with expected forcefulness.

"Because she is bad?" Marbach teased.

"No. Like everyone, I admire Volkstheater actress Constanze Tandler. She is very extraordinary, and your wife is very ordinary, but your wife is your wife."

"Life would be so much simpler for me if I had your religious faith."

"The Church is always there for you if you sincerely want it back."

"I said life might be simpler for me if I had your faith," Marbach said with a laugh. "I didn't say it would be as enjoyable a life."

Rolf joined in the laughter. They were colleague detectives who had stood beside each other in bad places at bad times, but both were reluctant to explore deeply the things that made them, in important ways, two very different types of men.

Rolf stood up and secured his loosened tie. "I suppose it is time for me to get to work. I hope I can just remember which room they took Ossietsky to."

"Sometimes I wonder if there is anything dumber than a dumb police detective," Marbach said.

Rolf laughed loudly. "Of course there is something dumber. A smart police inspector is dumber." He was still laughing as he left the room.

CHAPTER TWELVE

When Rolf entered the room where Lieutenant Ossietsky was waiting, a friendly exchange was going on between the young officer and a uniformed guard. Rolf didn't like the friendliness, but he knew it would make trouble for him if he expressed criticism about the guard being friendly with the army lieutenant. A low-ranked guard could make trouble for a peasant, even one who was a police detective. That was the way things were and the way things had always been.

The guard waved cheerfully to Lieutenant Ossietsky, cast an aloof stare at Rolf, and departed, pulling hard on the heavy door, causing the room to fill with the noise of a loud metallic slam. The fierce slamming sound usually had a startling effect on anyone about to be questioned, but Ossietsky seemed to be fully prepared. Probably he had been warned to expect the noise.

Rolf moved toward Ossietsky and extended his hand. "I am Police Detective Rolf Hiller." He was interested in seeing the reaction of Lieutenant Ossietsky to the offer of a handshake from a peasant. He had no doubt that the young officer knew he was a peasant.

Ossietsky, sitting on a chair in front of a small table, smoothed a fold in his expensively tailored civilian suit, folded his hands on the small table, stared with disdain at the extended hand, and pointedly withheld his own.

Rolf drew his hand back, looked around, found a chair, pushed it over to a place close to Ossietsky, and sat down.

Ossietsky postured himself in an aloof manner, took a moment, and presented himself in the manner of someone addressing a lowly subordinate. "I am Lieutenant Erich Ossietsky, Fourth Squadron of the Eleventh Cavalry Regiment of the Wehrmacht."

Settling himself in his chair, Rolf didn't return the greeting. He heaved a loud sigh. He was ready to go, and there wasn't time to waste, but he knew it was best to not pump prematurely into high gear.

Ossietsky sat silently, eyebrows arched, as though a social error was being committed in his presence.

Rolf stared at the conventionally good-looking face, took note of the neatly tailored civilian clothes, then, taking his time, removed the small tin container from his suit pocket, extracted a rolled cigarette, and placed it in his mouth. With the unlit cigarette dangling from his lips, he asked his first question. "Herr Lieutenant, what can you tell me about the incident at Hotel Capricorno?"

The reply was provided in the manner of a superior addressing an inferior. "I have no intention of discussing that subject with you. If you continue talking about that, I shall insist on leaving."

Rolf searched in his suit pockets, found a wooden match, pulled it out, held it in his fingers, and examined it closely, aware that Ossietsky's attention was drawn to the unlit match.

Ossietsky said with a small hint of hesitancy, "I think that whatever happened at the Hotel Capricorno yesterday should be put in the past. It is totally of no importance. Colonel Count Neumayer wants it put in the past."

Rolf was almost certain he could ignite the match with one quick, assertive flick of his thumbnail, but he knew this wasn't the time to allow even the smallest failure to be viewed by the young officer. So he scrapped the match on the underside of his chair.

When the match burst into flame, he lit his cigarette, took a puff, and then spoke in a strong, husky voice. "Herr Lieutenant, I want to know what happened at the Hotel Capricorno."

Ossietsky patted his pockets, obviously searching for a cigarette. After a few moments, he gave up the search and said in a voice that seemed to be losing strength, "Hiller, I have no intention of discussing the Hotel Capricorno."

Rolf's last name had been used. No title; not Detective Hiller; just "Hiller."

Lieutenant Ossietsky continued talking, but, as Rolf quickly noted, it was in a voice betraying increasing nervousness. "I ... I suspect it was a mistake to come here. As an army officer, I have the right to demand to be turned over to the army. Am I ... am I free to go?"

Rolf inhaled deeply, took his time, released a long stream of smoke in the direction of the young officer. Blowing smoke in someone's face was a cheap trick, but cheap tricks can sometimes be used to good effect.

Ossietsky, facing the cloud of oncoming smoke, seemed to be determined to show he wasn't intimidated, but it was a long stream of smoke. Finally, he waved his hands, attempted to clear the smoke away. Continuing to wave his hands, he said, "I believe it is conventional for army officers to have the right to be turned over to the army when they are involved in any matter involving the police. I intend to exercise that right. I ... I want to be turned over to the army."

Rolf smiled menacingly. "We have a case here involving the murder of one Gentile fräulein." He continued to smile menacingly as he added, "And the disappearance of a second Gentile fräulein."

Apprehension registered on Ossietsky's face. It lingered for a moment or two and then was replaced by the look of arrogance.

Rolf made his voice a low, growling sound. "To clear up a point, Herr Lieutenant, if you refuse to answer questions, we won't be turning you over to the army. We'll be calling in the Gestapo. If you demand to leave, you'll be turned over to the Gestapo."

"*Gestapo!*" Ossietsky jumped to his feet, almost knocking his chair over. For a moment, he teetered precariously, then he sat back down in the chair. When he spoke, his voice was a gasping sound. "I came here at the request of Colonel Count Neumayer. He assured me that if there was any difficulty, I could ask to be turned over to the army."

Rolf shrugged.

Ossietsky stared anxiously. "I don't see any reason for you to call the Gestapo, Herr Detective Hiller. I hope you will not do that."

Now it wasn't just "Hiller." Not even "Detective Hiller." It was "*Herr Detective Hiller.*"

On a table beside Ossietsky was a telephone. Rolf exercised muscular authority as he leaned over, grabbed the telephone, and dialed a number.

Holding the phone close to his ear, Rolf provided the conventional greeting. "Heil Hitler!" Then he continued as though he was talking to someone on the telephone. He was faking the call. "This is Detective Hiller. I need an automobile to take someone over to Gestapo headquarters." There was a long pause, and then Rolf said, "That is correct. Yes, right away. I want—"

Ossietsky interrupted. "Detective Hiller, I don't think that will be necessary. There is no need for that. Of course, well … uh, of course, I am prepared to discuss this matter with you."

"Hold on for one minute." Rolf clasped his hand over the telephone mouthpiece and said, "One minute is exactly how long you have to convince me that I am not wasting my time." Rolf put an implacable look on his tough peasant face. "It is me or the Gestapo. Take your choice. We know that one victim was named Julie Thimig. She was the one dressed like a Jewish prostitute, the one who was killed. Who was the second fräulein?" Rolf knew the second fräulein's name was Karen Mann, but he had long ago learned that when doing interrogation, sometimes it was useful to ask questions he already knew the answers to.

Ossietsky's voice became high pitched. "All I heard were the first names. The other fräulein said her name was Karen."

Rolf moved his hand back and forth over the telephone mouthpiece, as though undecided what to do next. He waited a moment, then faced Ossietsky and said, "Her name is Karen Mann." His voice was calculated to sound all-knowing. Using his voice that way during interrogation was something he had learned from Colleague Detective Marbach.

Ossietsky looked frightened.

Rolf put a menacing look on his face as he said, "Tell me where Karen Mann is."

"I ... I don't know. I ... I swear."

"Tell me where she is."

"I don't know. Wolfgang ... uh, Lieutenant Wolfgang Litzman was with her when the rest of us went back to the Neumayer estate."

"What happened at the brothel?"

"It is a hotel." Ossietsky's eyes opened wide. "All right, yes it is a brothel, but I don't know what happened."

"Your one minute is almost up."

The miserable young officer leaned forward, dropped his head into his hands, and began sobbing. Amidst choking sobs, he said, "The colonel count told me nothing would happen to me if I came here, and that if you asked any questions I would be safe if I just asked to be turned over to the army. Please. Oh, please … I want to be turned over to the army."

Sitting stiffly in his chair, Rolf peered closely at Ossietsky for a few moments and then hung up the telephone.

Ossietsky stopped sobbing and raised his head.

Rolf put menace into his voice. "Tell me who killed Julie Thimig and tell me where Karen Mann is."

"I want to be turned over to the army."

"Who killed Julie Thimig? Where is Karen Mann?"

Ossietsky began looking less frightened. "When Colonel Count Neumayer learns you are treating me this way, you'll be in a lot of trouble."

Rolf rose from his chair, stood aggressively above Ossietsky, and put added menace into his voice. "I am not afraid of that. You will answer my questions or you will be begging for the Gestapo to keep me away from you. I am the one you should be afraid of, not the Gestapo. Was it Lieutenant Litzman who killed Julie Thimig?"

"I don't have to answer any questions."

Rolf decided it was time to start getting physical. There wasn't a whole lot of time to waste. It was time to start getting physically tough with this young man who was an officer, who couldn't be pushed around too much, but who wasn't the son of the colonel count, and therefore could be pushed around a little.

Rolf grabbed Ossietsky by the hair, roughly dragged the young officer to his feet, and delivered a blow, a hard slap to the face.

Ossietsky reacted with a loud shriek. "Aaaah! My God! Oh, my God!"

With practiced expertise, Rolf continued slapping. Nothing too hard, just open-handed slapping. A couple of times he halted the slapping, but only long enough to select a better avenue of attack. He was careful to not unduly stun the target of his blows.

Finally, Ossietsky collapsed onto the floor. He covered his head and face with his arms and filled the room with loud wailing noises that quickly became whimpering sounds.

Rolf stared speculatively for a few moments. He waited until Ossietsky lifted his head to see what was happening, then walked over to a cabinet and withdrew a sinister-looking truncheon.

Gripping the truncheon firmly, Rolf calculated the stakes: the fate of someone named Karen Mann; dire consequences for some Jews; and Colleague Detective Marbach might lose his job over this. He had to balance all of what was at stake against the immediate distress of this young lieutenant.

Pretending to be going out of control, Rolf waved both of his arms as he shouted, "Look, you rotten vermin, you have no other way to go. You can forget about the Gestapo. I tried to transfer to the Gestapo, but they wouldn't accept me. They said I am too much of a brute. The Gestapo thinks I like hurting people too much. They are right. I do enjoy it. I am going to start hitting you with this truncheon. I will smash your good-looking face so hard you will never look the same again, and I will hammer your genitals to mush. I am going to keep on hitting you until I get every bit of information I need. Do you hear me?"

"Please. Oh my God! Please don't ..." Ossietsky collapsed onto the floor, used his hands to cover his head.

The first blow with the heavy truncheon was delivered across an exposed leg and brought forth an agonized cry. After that, two more blows were delivered, both of them to Ossietsky's legs, neither of them too forcefully, but each of them calculated to cause stinging pain.

Before the fourth blow could be struck, crying sounds became words.

"Stop! I'll do anything you say … anything. Anything you say. Stop. Oh … please, stop."

Rolf dragged Ossietsky by the scruff of his neck to the table and directed the young man's attention to a blank sheet of paper. "Write it out. Write the name of the one who killed Julie Thimig."

"Write …?"

"Write the name of the one who killed Julie Thimig."

"Paul says he did it."

"Do you believe that?" shouted Rolf.

"No."

"Who do you think did it?" Rolf shouted.

"It was Wolfgang."

"How do you know?" Rolf demanded.

Ossietsky made a whining sound while he explained how he knew Wolfgang Litzman had killed Julie Thimig. It was a convincing explanation containing a statement that Lieutenant Ossietsky and Lieutenant Neumayer were not just brother officers: they sometimes had sex together. Rolf took the disclosure about homosexuality in stride. Whether a person was a homosexual was generally his own business as far as he was concerned. He was a peasant, and peasants understood such things.

Rolf said, "Write out your statement. The way you just said it. But leave out that part about you and Lieutenant Neumayer having sex together." Rolf had a reason for saying that. He knew that information about Ossietsky and Neumayer engaging in homosexual behavior wouldn't slow down Kaltenbrunner if he saw it. In fact, it would likely have the opposite effect. Kaltenbrunner would probably see it as something scandalous that needed to be promptly covered up and charge forward to do so.

Rolf looked on while the statement was written. He suggested a few details of his own invention to make the written confession more useful.

When completed, the statement was two pages long. The highly detailed statement made the case that Lieutenant Neumayer wasn't the killer, that Lieutenant Litzman was the killer. There were details that identified the lustmörder proclivities of Lieutenant Litzman.

"Sign it," Rolf ordered.

"Yes."

"Today's date."

"Yes."

Rolf examined the signed and dated statement, and then one final time he asked the most important question. "What can you tell me about the missing Fräulein Karen Mann?"

"I don't know where she is. I swear it. I don't have any idea where she is." The young officer sobbed piteously.

Rolf believed Ossietsky. He picked up the telephone and delivered a quick message. "I need a guard. There is someone here who needs to be taken to one of the other rooms."

A few minutes later, a guard arrived and took Lieutenant Ossietsky away.

Holding the two-page statement in his hand, Rolf made his way to the small basement room where he had left Marbach less than half an hour ago.

Marbach was sitting at his desk, making notes on a piece of paper. He looked up as Rolf came into the room.

Rolf slipped into a chair. "You said we were in a hurry, so I didn't waste any time." He tossed the two pages onto the desk. "This ought to slow down Kaltenbrunner."

"Where is Lieutenant Ossietsky?" Marbach asked.

"He is all right."

Marbach read the two pages carefully, at one point letting out a long, soft whistle. When he was finished reading, he cast a questioning look.

Rolf put a cigarette in his mouth but didn't light it. "There is some stuff I kept out of the statement. Lieutenant Neumayer and Lieutenant Ossietsky are lovers. They are being blackmailed by Lieutenant Litzman. He even has some love letters they exchanged."

"It is good that none of that is in these pages. It might just complicate things with Kaltenbrunner, incline him to bust in here and do whatever it takes to be sure that doesn't get publicized."

Rolf nodded.

Marbach focused on a matter of vital importance. "Did you learn anything that might help us find Karen Mann?"

"Lieutenant Ossietsky doesn't know anything. Maybe Lieutenant Neumayer knows something, but I doubt it. My guess is we'll only learn where she is from Lieutenant Litzman."

"Your guesses are usually right," said Marbach.

Rolf lowered his head for a moment, then looked up and stared directly into the eyes of his colleague detective. "Boss, I didn't use your way of getting this job done, but I got it done quick."

"You sound defensive."

"Go to hell."

"Where is the young man now?"

"I didn't hurt him."

"I'll give you credit for one thing: you are always quick to stop when your brutality has gotten you what you wanted."

"We've talked about this before. Don't call my way *brutal*. There was a job to be done, and I did it. I don't like hearing you say I am brutal because I don't handle things your way."

Marbach closed his eyes, opened them, and said, "Tell me how you would sum up this case right now."

Rolf moved the unlit cigarette from one side of his mouth to the other. "Lieutenant Neumayer confessed to the killing, but he was too drunk to know what happened. Lieutenant Litzman did the killing. Lieutenant Litzman is a lustmörder. The important thing is to find Fräulein Karen Mann, but it is also important to stop this lustmörder from doing more killing."

"Go on."

Rolf yielded a small sigh, then pulled the cigarette from his mouth. "Neumayer wanted to try to have sex with a fräulein. He wanted to prove he could be a man who has sex with a woman, instead of being a man who only has sex with other men."

"Go on."

"Litzman is a lustmörder. He will keep on killing until he is stopped. His next victim will be Karen Mann. He's got her hidden away somewhere, but she's alive. I am certain in my gut that she's alive."

"We will proceed on that assumption," Marbach said.

"We've got to find her."

"Is there anything I ought to think about before I talk with Lieutenant Neumayer?"

"When I threatened to turn Ossietsky over to the Gestapo, that had an effect, even if it didn't last."

"Anything else?"

"According to Ossietsky, Neumayer thinks Jewish females are sexier than Gentile females because they are dirtier. Anyway, Neumayer thought a Gentile fräulein would be sexier if she dressed up like a Jewish prostitute."

Marbach kept silent.

Rolf frowned. "Ossietsky says none of them knew that the fräulein named Julie was from the Thimig family. That's believable. Anyway, I believe it. Ossietsky says the two fräuleins gave fictitious last names."

Marbach continued to keep silent.

Rolf cleared his throat, stared intently, and said, "Ossietsky is believable when he says that none of them, not even Litzman, knew they had picked up someone with the Thimig name."

Marbach asked, "Anything more?"

Rolf recognized what Marbach was doing. They had done this many times in the past. His colleague detective wanted him to talk just to see where the talk would take him, maybe surface something he wouldn't realize was important until the words came out of his mouth.

Rolf's rugged voice became soft. "Ossietsky says Julie Thimig quickly got bit of a crush on young Neumayer. I didn't have to beat that out of him. He offered it. He no longer regards Neumayer as his lover. He was comfortable about Neumayer carrying on with Julie Thimig. Ossietsky said that Neumayer seemed to genuinely like Julie Thimig. He said the two of them spent a lot of time talking together in the café and later in the automobile going to the Hotel Capricorno. She was anxious to please ... so anxious she agreed to dress up like a Jewish prostitute."

Marbach nodded.

"Julie Thimig was barely eighteen," Rolf said. "Karen Mann is the same age. They were both impressed with these young men of the world and couldn't imagine that they would deliberately harm them or allow harm to be done to them ... Well, I need to say this, even nice fräuleins can sometimes behave badly."

Rolf's voice became clipped as he continued. "It is all in the statement you have there in your hands. These young men talked Julie Thimig into dressing like a Jewish prostitute. They said a party was going on where people were dressing up funny—like Jews. It was a stagging party. Some of the fräuleins, the deer, would be dressing up like Jewish prostitutes. There have been lots of stagging parties around the university, so it didn't sound too unusual. On the way to the Hotel Capricorno, Julie Thimig did a lot of cuddling with Neumayer. Ossietsky says he heard her agree to go to bed with him. He says she told Neumayer it would be her first time, and she wanted it to be with him. She wanted to please him. She was willing to do anything to please him. Anyway, that's what Ossietsky said."

Marbach closed his eyes.

Rolf said, "Ossietsky says that in the early morning meeting, Litzman convinced Kaltenbrunner that he killed the other student,

Fräulein Karen Mann, to protect Neumayer. He told Kaltenbrunner it was an accident, but he killed her."

Marbach looked at Ossietsky's signed statement and said, "Well, with what you have here, with this in hand, we ought to be able to stop Kaltenbrunner when he shows up. But the important thing is for me to go and get started with Lieutenant Neumayer." He handed the written statement back to Rolf and said, "You might as well take this to the commander."

Rolf rubbed his hand over his face. He knew why he was being asked to report to Commander Kaas. His colleague detective wanted him to get the full credit while this success would have its greatest impact on the commander.

Marbach said, "I could use those photographs of your daughter Hannah before I see Neumayer."

"Hannah's photographs? Yes, I will get them now."

Rolf left to get the photographs. When he returned a few minutes later, he was wondering what Marbach planned to do with the photographs, but he asked no questions. He knew that soon enough he would learn to what use they were going to be put.

Rolf watched Marbach leave on his way to the interrogation room where Neumayer was waiting. He stood still for a moment, then went to deliver Lieutenant Ossietsky's written statement to Commander Kaas.

CHAPTER THIRTEEN

Marbach made a detour before going to the room where Lieutenant Neumayer was waiting. His detour took him to the office of Police Inspector Thomas Mastny.

For more than a dozen years, the genius had been unable to walk, unable to use his legs. He navigated around police headquarters in a high-backed wooden wheelchair. It wasn't a police injury that had put Mastny in a wheelchair. He was crippled by arthritis. There was always a blanket covering his legs. Although restricted to work performed from a wheelchair, the genius was not at any risk of losing his job as a police inspector. He wasn't just a genius solving cases. When cases were ready for prosecution, he delivered lucidly written case summaries. Prosecutors and judges were highly appreciative of case summaries prepared by Police Inspector Thomas Mastny.

No one in Vienna Kripo, including Police Inspector Hans Rinner, Mastny's colleague detective, knew anything important about Mastny's family, except that he had one. And nothing was known about Mastny's personal interests, if he had any. The crippled police inspector kept his personal life totally private.

Marbach peered through an open doorway into Mastny's very messy office. The genius was on the telephone. He stared at Marbach, rolled his eyes upward, and jerked his wheelchair around.

Marbach backed away. There was no mistaking the unspoken message: *don't interrupt!*

Across the hallway was Police Inspector Hans Rinner's office, and the door was open. Marbach looked inside and received a welcoming gesture.

"Hello, Hans." Marbach always addressed Police Inspector Hans Rinner by the first name, and he always addressed Police Inspector Thomas Mastny by the last name. It was conventional in Vienna to address friends by their first names and others by their last names. Hans was a close friend.

"Here you are, Karl," Hans said, thrusting three new reports at Marbach. "We gave some preliminary reports to Rolf, but these three are much more complete. There is one for each of the three young officers." Hans paused a moment before expressing concern. Using his colleague detective's first name, he said, "Don't go bothering, Thomas. He's been having a lot of trouble with telephone connections to Paris."

Marbach shook his head. "Telephone? ... Paris?"

Hans explained. "The genius is cultivating a Paris lead that may help us with this case we are working on for you. Now take those reports and go. There will be more in another hour or so. Now please leave me alone. I have work to do."

"If you get anything you think—"

Hans interrupted. "Of course. Now get out of here. We assume Karen Mann is alive. Go find her. Do it fast. Don't set off anything that'll get her killed, but do something fast. Find her while she's still alive."

"I'll try."

After delivering a farewell gesture, Marbach walked down the hall while checking through first one report, then another. By the time he entered an empty interrogation room in the basement, he had done a preliminary assessment of all three reports.

The only furniture in the interrogation room was a small, wooden table and two straight-backed, wooden chairs. One of the chairs was very special. It was low to the floor, with an uncomfortable, upward-pitched seat. The special chair had been constructed several years ago. It was a chair deliberately intended to be uncomfortable to sit in, not too uncomfortable, not in too exaggerated a way, but definitely uncomfortable. Marbach shoved the special chair up to the table, moved to the other side of the table where there was a comfortable chair, sat down, and reread each of the reports, one page after the other.

Several minutes later, Marbach folded up the report on Lieutenant Neumayer, the report that had occupied most of his attention, placed all three reports in the table drawer, put his hand into his suit pocket, and confirmed that he had the photographs of Rolf's daughter. The half-dozen photographs included one showing her when she was a tiny child and one taken a few months ago on her fourteenth birthday.

Standing up, Marbach mentally reviewed the script he would use for the interrogation of Lieutenant Neumayer. He would be doing the questioning under a very considerable handicap: the young officer was the son of Colonel Count Neumayer, and this was National Socialist Vienna. It might be possible to be uncivil with Lieutenant Ossietsky and with Lieutenant Litzman, but no one connected with Vienna Kripo could treat Lieutenant Neumayer with anything but courtesy and deference. Hopefully, even though operating under that considerable handicap, it was going to be possible to learn something that would help find Karen Mann.

Marbach affirmed to himself: "Fräulein Karen Mann is alive. *She has to be alive!*"

CHAPTER FOURTEEN

While waiting for Lieutenant Neumayer to be brought into the interrogation room, Marbach was thinking about how he did police questioning. It was different from the way Rolf and others in Kripo interrogated. He might get rough, but he never got physically tough. He was rough when an interrogation called for roughness, but being rough never included physical toughness. He didn't slap or punch and usually didn't do any serious shoving. For him, the important thing was to be as prepared as possible, ask the right questions, listen to the answers, and always be ready to shift course quickly when the situation called for it. He frequently utilized, with whatever modifications were needed, a three-pronged strategy: instill confusion; appear to know everything; and, at the right moment, be the strong protector.

Sitting in his reasonably comfortable chair, he became aware of a hissing sound. Behind him, coffee was brewing on the Primus stove, a bloated, brass-bellied apparatus within which flames—blue and orange—were never allowed to be extinguished. All day and every day, those flames glowed. And all night, every night.

He got up, went to the stove, filled a cup with a calculated amount of cream, and then carefully added coffee. Standing by the stove, he mentally reviewed his script for how he was going to do this interrogation. He was still reviewing the script when the door opened and Lieutenant Neumayer was brought in. The attending guard, properly instructed, quickly left, making the usual loud noise as he slammed the door shut. The noise caused Neumayer to jump nervously. Marbach liked seeing the nervousness. Getting someone nervous was a good way to start getting them confused, a good way to begin the three-pronged strategy.

Marbach walked over and extended his hand. "We met last night. My name is Police Inspector Marbach. Sit down, son."

"I am not your son," Lieutenant Neumayer said in a crisply arrogant voice. Remaining on his feet, the young officer ignored the extended hand. "I am properly addressed as Lieutenant Paul Neumayer, Fourth Squadron of the Eleventh Cavalry Regiment of the Wehrmacht."

Marbach made a point of eyeing Neumayer's civilian clothes as he said, "I don't formally address you as lieutenant when you are here in mufti." After saying that, he returned to his chair, sat down, took a few swallows from his cup of gold, and stared directly into the eyes of the young man. He had learned from the report provided by Hans Rinner that Lieutenant Neumayer seemed to be easily intimidated when people stared hard into his eyes.

Neumayer lowered his eyes.

"Now, Paul, you can remain standing if you want," Marbach said, deliberately using the young officer's first name, a tactic calculated to be provocative. "However, I would very much like to know—it is up to you, of course, but I would very much like to know whatever you might be able to tell me about your friend Wolfgang Litzman and the events at the Hotel Capricorno yesterday."

Neumayer didn't reply. He stood very erect, probed the vest pocket of his civilian suit, brought out a cigarette case, flicked it open, and withdrew a cigarette. Then, after more probing, he brought out a jeweled lighter and, making an effort to look self-confident, tried to light the cigarette.

Marbach observed that the young officer's hand was trembling. He made a point of staring at the trembling hand, kept staring at it as though puzzled. When the staring caught the attention of Neumayer, the trembling increased. The attempt to light the cigarette ended in total failure.

Standing awkwardly, Neumayer threw away his unlit cigarette and shoved the jeweled lighter into his pocket. "None of us will answer any questions about the Hotel Capricorno. We came here … we came here because my father wanted it. He said you would be able to help avoid unwelcome publicity. My father said we wouldn't have to answer any foolish questions. He said that if any foolish questions were asked, we could always ask … we could *demand* to be turned over to the army."

Marbach made use of his eyebrows to convey puzzlement. "How can I help you if I don't know what happened at the Hotel Capricorno?"

"Police Inspector," Neumayer said, fussing nervously with his hands. "You are wasting your time and mine. I have nothing to tell you about the Hotel Capricorno. I think it is time for you to turn me over to the army."

"Paul—"

"I am Lieutenant Paul …" Neumayer's voice trailed off.

Marbach stared at his cup, reviewed in his mind what he had read in the report provided by Hans Rinner about Lieutenant Neumayer's coffee preference, and said, "Would you care for a cup of gold? We have a good brand of coffee here."

"I didn't come to this place to drink your coffee. My father asked me and my brother officers to come here. My father wants the business that took place at the Hotel Capricorno to be cleared up. It is important that my name … my name and the names of my brother officers not be connected to anything that happened. Are you going to do what my father wants done?"

"How can I help clear up the Hotel Capricorno business if you won't tell me what happened? Last night I made clear my loyalty to the colonel count. I brought him all the evidence I had. That was last night. Unfortunately, things have turned up about that incident at the Hotel Capricorno that could cause trouble."

Still on his feet, Neumayer looked confused. "I ... I don't understand. In any event, I will not answer any questions about the Hotel Capricorno. I want to leave this place right now. I demand to be turned over to the army. Am I ... am I free to go?"

Marbach drank what remained of the coffee in his cup. "You can leave any time you want. You came here voluntarily, and I certainly won't interfere if you want to leave, but I don't think your father will like it if you don't help me keep public gossip from turning this into a mess. Tell me something, if you will. Last night when I saw you with your father, were you just recovering from a bout of drinking?"

"What does that matter? You have ... no evidence for the killing. You gave all those things ... everything ... last night to my father."

"Of course I did," Marbach said blandly. "Every last scrap of evidence." He shook his head with an expression of puzzlement, then laughed as though at an enormously funny joke. Still laughing, holding his coffee cup in his hand, he got up and walked over to the stove. "Whatever are you worried about? We both know I will bring disaster on my head if I am personally responsible for causing even the smallest embarrassment for the colonel count."

That was an unpleasant truth, even if told with laughter. Marbach found an extra cup near the stove, looked at Neumayer, poured some cream into the cup, added coffee, then performed the same ritual with his own cup, walked back, and placed the extra cup on the table. "Sit down and drink this cup of gold. It will make you feel better."

"A cup of gold might be good," Neumayer conceded as he stared at the cup of gold on the table. He sat down on the specially constructed chair.

Marbach sat down on the comfortable chair on the other side of the table and sipped his own cup of gold.

Sitting in the uncomfortable chair, Neumayer predictably made no mention of any discomfort. He concentrated his attention on the cup of gold on the table in front of him. Finally, he reached out, took hold of the cup, drank several swallows, and said, "I do not intend to answer any questions about the Hotel Capricorno."

When Neumayer placed his cup on the table, it made a loud clattering sound. Nervously, he drew his hand back. "Am I a prisoner or am I free to go?"

Marbach held his cup in both hands, examined it, took a small sip, and said, "I already told you that you are not a prisoner." He took another sip of the coffee and said, "The colonel count brought you here. By the way, before he left, your father said to tell you that when you are finished here, you should return to the estate by taxicab."

Neumayer sputtered with confusion. "Where is Lieutenant Wolfgang Litzman? ... I don't ... I just don't ... where is Lieutenant Eric Ossietsky?"

"They are both fine," Marbach replied. "Lieutenant Litzman seems to be an interesting young man. What can you tell me about him?"

"About Wolfgang?" Neumayer's eyes opened wide. He tried to settle more comfortably in his chair and twisted awkwardly but made no complaint about how uncomfortable the chair was.

Marbach watched the young officer closely, allowing silence to drag out.

Neumayer nervously cleared his throat. "Father destroyed all the evidence you brought to him."

Marbach furrowed his brow, leaned forward, and said, "Of course he did. The purpose of my visit was so the colonel count could personally see that the evidence was destroyed. Surely you know there is no trickery here. Not when you are the son of the colonel count. Vienna police will never involve the family of the colonel count in what happened at the Hotel Capricorno. Certainly a smart, young man like you can have no doubt about that."

Neumayer opened his mouth and then let it weakly close.

Marbach stared thoughtfully at his cup of gold. "The one who was the killer played you for a fool. Do you want to let the killer get away with a despicable murder? It is entirely up to you. If that is the case, then there is nothing more for us to talk about."

"I ... I killed Julie. I was drunk. I was drunk."

"No, you didn't kill her. I have no doubt, no doubt at all. I am absolutely certain you didn't kill Julie."

"But I did."

"You were drunk. You don't know what happened." Marbach paused for dramatic effect. "I know what happened."

"You are trying to trick me."

"What kind of trick can there be? You are the son of Colonel Count Neumayer."

"You give me your word of honor ...?"

Marbach didn't quickly reply. It didn't matter that what he was going to say was true. It hurt Marbach to profess his honor in connection with this dirty business, but he kept his voice level as he said, "Lieutenant Neumayer, on my honor, I will bring no evidence against you. But more important, on my honor, I know that you did not kill Fräulein Julie Thimig."

Neumayer tried to relax but found it impossible to do that in the uncomfortable chair.

Marbach said, "Don't you think we ought to punish the killer of Fräulein Julie Thimig?"

"Julie …?"

"Yes."

"Julie Thimig?"

"Yes."

"The Thimig family?"

"Yes." Marbach stared at the young officer and added, "She gave you a false last name. Julie was the daughter of Judge Thimig."

Neumayer sat twisting in his chair. *"Julie,"* he said, an aching sound in his voice, his face registering misery. "I was drunk. I get drunk … I have trouble remembering things when I get drunk."

Marbach pushed his coffee cup to one side, leaned across the table, and fixed the young man with an intense look. It was time to make use of what Rolf had learned from Ossietsky. Marbach said in his all-knowing voice, "Let me tell you about yesterday. You and Lieutenant Litzman met these two teenagers on the Ringstrasse near the university. They were very young. They tried to be coquettish and didn't give their real family names. They were thrilled to be taken to the National Socialist bar in the Café Europe. With your influence, it was easy to get them served liquor. They both drank the excellent vodka that was provided to them. Julie Thimig tried to show you that she could be a good sport in the fast life she imagined you live. She developed a crush on you. She tried very hard to do things that might please you. Do you remember how hard she tried to please you? She gave you her trust, all of her innocent, young trust."

Neumayer listened with astonishment on his face, hearing details he recognized as totally accurate.

Marbach kept up the momentum, supplied more details. "Julie agreed to do anything you wanted her to do. When you told her there was a party going on where some of the young women would be dressed in odd costumes, she agreed to dress like a Jewish prostitute. It was easy for you to get her to dress up like that at the Café Europe. There was a room in the café that had clothes available for the taking. Unlike Julie, Karen didn't change clothes. She got drunk. She tried to keep pace with what your friend Lieutenant Ossietsky seemed to be drinking. It didn't take much vodka or much time for Karen to get drunk. Finally, the bunch of you left the café and drove to the Hotel Capricorno. Karen stayed in the car, sleeping off her inebriated condition. Lieutenant Ossietsky also stayed in the car. Lieutenant Litzman made himself very inconspicuous inside the Hotel Capricorno. There was an argument between you and Julie. You trundled off to bury your sorrows in a bottle. You don't know what else happened until you came to your senses back at the estate. You believed Lieutenant Litzman when he told you that you got angry and hit Julie—hit her hard enough and often enough to kill her. What he didn't tell you is that Julie didn't die from a beating. She got beaten all right, but not by you. And the beating isn't what killed her. Julie Thimig was poisoned."

Lieutenant Neumayer shook his head. "I don't understand. *Poisoned?*"

In a sudden move, Marbach reached out, took hold of both of Lieutenant Neumayer's wrists, and pulled them across the table. He held tight to the young man's wrists as he said, "Look at your knuckles. Look at them! They aren't red and sore. Not a bit. Have you seen Lieutenant Litzman's knuckles? Let me tell you. His knuckles are very red and very sore. He beat Julie; then he poisoned her. He enjoys hurting fräuleins. He enjoys inflicting cruelty."

Marbach released his hold on Neumayer's wrists, shoved them away, retrieved a piece of paper from the desk drawer, and pushed it across the table.

Neumayer stared at the piece of paper but didn't pick it up.

Marbach said, "That's the official police chemist report on the death of Fräulein Julie Thimig."

Neumayer shut his eyes.

"Read it," Marbach said in a commanding voice.

Neumayer picked up the official police report. He began reading.

Marbach allowed time for the young man to read and reread the report, waited until the moment was right before he said, "It is all in that report. You can see it all for yourself: name, age, gender … cause of death. There is also information that she was a virgin at the time of her death."

Neumayer groaned as he read confirmation of Julie Thimig's virginity.

Marbach pressed on. "That report documents the cause of death. Julie Thimig was killed by poison. Start using your brain. If you didn't kill her with poison, you didn't kill her."

Neumayer nodded while handing back the official police medical report. Everything made sense to him now.

Marbach said, "You know your own drinking behavior, and you know Lieutenant Litzman's peculiar habits and cruel ways with women. Is it so terribly difficult for you to figure out what happened at the Hotel Capricorno?"

"I didn't kill Julie," Neumayer murmured. "She was poisoned ... a virgin ... she was poisoned."

"That's correct," Marbach said. "You didn't kill Julie. She was beaten around the head and face. Beaten hard. But you weren't the one who gave her the beating. And that doesn't matter. It doesn't matter because she didn't die from being punched around; she was poisoned."

Neumayer looked at his knuckles and then stared gratefully at the man sitting across from him. "Thank you, Herr Police Inspector. I ... I always knew Wolfgang was strange, but I never guessed how vile he might be."

Marbach wished he could look at his wristwatch. How much time had already passed? But he didn't look at his watch. Keeping his eyes on Neumayer, he said, "There is another piece of business. I know Lieutenant Litzman was blackmailing you about Lieutenant Ossietsky. I believe I can help you on that matter if you cooperate with me."

"You know about ...?" Neumayer had confusion and fright in his eyes.

"Yes," Marbach said, speaking in his all-knowing voice. "I know about you having sex with Lieutenant Ossietsky."

"You know ...?" Lieutenant Neumayer lowered his head. "*I am a man. I am a man.*"

"Of course, you are," Marbach said. "But there are *the letters.*" He placed calculated emphasis on the last two words.

"Oh, my God! You know about the letters between me and ..."

"Yes, I know about the letters. I know everything about you and Lieutenant Ossietsky. I also know that you have a fiancée. And I know that Lieutenant Litzman threatened to disclose the letters to her if you don't do his bidding. With your help, I think I can get those letters back. It would be good to get those letters away from Lieutenant Litzman, wouldn't it? Just to protect your fiancée from undeserved pain? What do you think?"

Neumayer had a look of agony on his face.

Marbach waited, kept silent.

Neumayer rubbed his face with shaking hands.

Careful not to break the mood that had been created, Marbach spoke softly, almost gently. "Tell me everything. Right from the beginning."

"They seemed to be ordinary fräuleins," Neumayer began. "Julie and Karen were like any other university students. In SS Leader Kaltenbrunner's office this morning, we called them Reds. I'm ashamed of that. Julie … Julie was not a Red. She was totally faithful to National Socialism. It was wrong of me to let her be called a Red."

Neumayer continued talking, but he was adding nothing of importance. Nevertheless, Marbach encouraged him to keep talking. He listened to the young officer while thinking about Julie Thimig. Her innocence, her sexual innocence up to the moment of her death.

Finally, Marbach decided it was time to do guide the conversation. He made a simple observation. "You walked with these two fräuleins on the Ringstrasse."

"Yes … yes, on the Ringstrasse," Neumayer said, nodding vigorously. "That's where we met them. We walked with them on the Ringstrasse and offered to take them to the Café Europe. Wolfgang Litzman was with Karen, and I was with Julie. Lieutenant Erich Ossietsky just came along, like he always does. That's his way. There weren't any plans for anything. It was just the three of us and the two fräuleins. Inside the Café Europe, Karen got drunk real fast. Julie didn't drink much. She seemed to really like me. Sometimes when I get started drinking … Julie wasn't like anyone I ever knew before. She was so eager to please me. She … she even agreed to wear those clothes. That's why we went to the Hotel Capricorno. We needed a place where Julie could dress herself like a Jewish prostitute. It was exciting because Julie was so Aryan, but also sexy like …" Neumayer's voice trailed off. Finally, he said, "I don't remember much about what happened at the Hotel Capricorno."

Marbach kept silent.

After a few moments of silence, Neumayer's face lit up. "The important thing is that I didn't kill Julie. You said it, Herr Police Inspector. I didn't kill her. I am innocent. I did not commit a murder."

Marbach listened while Neumayer rambled aimlessly. "At the hotel, I … I went off to another room. I remember getting a bottle … When I woke up, we were back at the estate. My father's aides sobered me up. They gave me coffee. Then they gave me something to drink that made me sick. God, it was awful … I got terribly sick."

Neumayer stopped talking, but Marbach intruded his implacable face, and the young officer was unable to keep silent. He began spouting additional details. "Wolfgang said I got angry and hit Julie … that I beat her up. But now I know I didn't kill Julie."

Neumayer continued talking, but he was adding nothing helpful. Finally, Marbach quietly inquired, "Do you think the other fräulein, the one named Karen, is dead?"

Neumayer said, "Oh, I don't know. What difference does that make? The important thing is that I didn't kill Julie. I know that now. Wolfgang is the killer. He killed Julie."

Marbach concealed his reaction to Neumayer's indifference to the fate of Karen Mann. He told himself it was time to do some provoking, but he knew he had to be careful. This was the son of the colonel count. He leaned forward. "Tell me how you feel about Julie Thimig being murdered at the Hotel Capricorno."

The directness of the question shocked Neumayer. "I feel terrible," he said. "Julie was loose with her morals, I suppose, but, still, she was a virgin. I … I don't think she was really a bad sort. How can you ask such a question?"

Marbach delivered his reply with calculated forcefulness. "I want to know how you feel about Fräulein Julie Thimig as a person, as a young woman just beginning her life. As someone who seemed to be falling in love with you. Did you dislike her? Was there something about Julie that made you dislike her?"

Neumayer waved his hand in a gesture of dismissal. "I must say, this chair is most uncomfortable. I don't feel …"

Marbach reached inside his suit jacket, withdrew the packet of photographs Rolf had provided, selected several, and tossed them across the tabletop: a half-dozen photographs of Hannah, Rolf's daughter, at various ages. Hannah's face, hair coloring, everything about her was a match for what Julie Thimig probably looked like at the same ages. The point was that Neumayer was going to believe the photographs were of Julie Thimig.

"Look at these pictures. Do you know who this was?"

Neumayer's face filled with agony and horror, but he couldn't help staring at the photographs. Impulsively, he picked up one of the photographs, the one shoved closest to him. It was the photograph of a happy child grinning impishly into the camera. Neumayer put that photograph down and picked up another taken perhaps a year or two later. The same child standing with other children in a schoolyard. Then he looked at a photograph showing the young child in her early teens.

Neumayer shook his head. "Julie ... oh, I didn't expect anything bad to happen." He pushed the photographs away, collapsed in his chair, swayed for a moment, then pitched forward on the tabletop, his arms stretched outward. Between wracking sobs, he mumbled, "How did this happen? This is a *nightmare*. I was drinking a lot ... but it was poison that killed Julie. You said it was poison ..."

Following his script, Marbach raised the stakes in a dramatic way.

"Tell me about your fiancée."

"Klára?"

Marbach followed up by identifying Klára fully. After that, he said to Neumayer, "Fräulein Klára Zeymer is in love with you."

Neumayer immediately became defensive. "Klára has nothing to do with this dirty business."

"If you and I don't find a way to keep this mess quiet, there'll be no way to keep Klára from learning about those letters between you and Erich Ossietsky."

Neumayer, looking more like a troubled little boy than a young army officer, had his eyes fixed on the photographs he had pushed away, the photographs he was assuming were of Julie Thimig at various ages.

Marbach said, "Tell me about Klára. What kind of young woman is she? Is she religious?"

In point of fact, Klára was very religious. Marbach knew that for a certainty. The report provided by Hans Rinner was specific about Klára's commitment to her religious faith.

Neumayer cast a pleading look. "Yes," he said. "Klára goes to daily Mass."

"Tell me more about her."

Neumayer began speaking. He spoke of his love for Klára. He was a complicated person of weak character, but he was also a young man in love with a religious young woman named Klára.

While Neumayer talked about his love for Klára, Marbach collected the photographs of Rolf's daughter into a small pile, took his time, examined the pictures, then shoved them back again across the table.

Neumayer stopped talking, once again picked up the photographs, stared at them, one after the other, and began weeping. The pitiful weeping sounds continued for a minute or two. Then Neumayer began talking again about his love for Klára. Again and again, he proclaimed Klára's purity, saying she would despise him if she found out about him and Ossietsky.

Marbach listened to repeated assertions about the purity of Klára. While Neumayer talked, Marbach watched and listened and … waited.

Finally, Neumayer seemed to get terribly tired. He let his head drop into a cradle formed by his arms on the table and quickly dropped off to sleep. He looked almost like a little boy falling asleep at a school desk.

Marbach knew that everything up to this moment would be wasted if he made any mistakes. Shallow waters had been plumbed, and deep water lay ahead. He let a few minutes pass. He thought about the script and readied himself to go down into deep water with Neumayer..

A soft snoring noise being made by Neumayer was the only sound in the room. Marbach stared at Neumayer like a predator eyeing its prey. Everything now was calculation.

Marbach roughly shoved the young man's arm.

Neumayer came awake, and his face filled with a sheepish smile that quickly became a look of gratitude.

Marbach said, "You and I have shared some very private things. Sometimes there is nothing to do but find somebody you can trust. Do you trust me?"

"Yes." Neumayer's eyes filled with a pleading look.

Marbach reached across the table and grasped the young man by his shoulders.

"Do you *trust* me?"

"Yes ... yes."

Marbach dragged Neumayer up out of his chair, pulled him upward and forward, across the table.

Neumayer gasped as he hung awkwardly across the table.

Marbach held tight to the young officer while staring into his eyes. "Unless I find a way to stop him, Wolfgang is going to make use of those letters. Klára will learn everything. It will be a horror for her. Are you going to let that happen?"

Neumayer shut his eyes. His pale skin was white and pasty. He hung limply in Marbach's arms while whimpering, "I don't know anything. I don't know ... don't know anything."

"Of course, you do."

"Oh, my God!"

Marbach gripped hard with his strong hands. "Tell me what will help me to deal with Wolfgang."

"I don't understand ..."

"We have to protect Klára. Only if Wolfgang is dealt with will Klára be kept safe from learning about you and Lieutenant Ossietsky. There isn't time to spare."

"Klára …"

"If you want to keep Klára's pure love, you must help me deal with Wolfgang."

"I don't know what you want to hear."

"Tell me something that will help me deal with Wolfgang."

"But I don't know anything."

"Of course you do. You just have to think."

"What?"

"Let your mind relax. Let your thoughts flow. When you are ready, just start talking. Say anything about anything."

Neumayer stared with wide-open eyes.

Marbach kept a firm hold on the young man dangling helplessly across the table. The next few moments would reveal whether the interrogation of this young man had worked or hadn't worked. The script was clear that at this point, under prodding, Neumayer might reveal something trivial, or he might reveal something vital, but he would tell something just to have peace of mind.

Neumayer began talking, and slowly Marbach allowed his hold to loosen. At first, Neumayer wasn't coherent, but then he became like someone having a revelation. He spoke three words: "The Federmann Syndikat."

The Federmann Syndikat!

Marbach let loose of Neumayer, who continued talking. Details came tumbling out. Marbach didn't take notes, didn't do anything that might interfere with the flow of words.

Neumayer talked on and on. Interspersed with details about the Federmann Syndikat were choked pleas to keep Klára from learning about sex between two men.

Marbach organized in his mind what he was hearing about the Federmann Syndikat. Since 1912, an organization called the Federmann Syndikat had been a subcontracting company for Danubian iron and steel enterprises. Although it had prospered after 1918, recently it had fallen on hard times. The stock for the Federmann Syndikat was now selling at a small fraction of the value it had just two years ago, but that would immediately change as soon as word got out that this unimportant company was in line to become the holding company for the transfer of the assets of Danubian iron and steel companies to the Hermann Göring Works. The unimportant Federmann Syndikat was about to become a gold mine! Lieutenant Neumayer's father, Colonel Count Neumayer, was among those buying up old Federmann stock, hoping to profit from the substantial rise in value when the contract with Berlin would be finalized.

Marbach did nothing to interrupt what Neumayer was telling.

Finally, after several minutes, the word flow stopped, and Neumayer said, "I have told you everything."

Marbach kept silent.

Neumayer expressed a concern of importance: "Is there a toilet around here?"

"I will show you where the toilet is. When you are finished, come back to this room. Wait for me here. I will be going upstairs for a few minutes."

After showing Neumayer where to find the toilet, Marbach went upstairs to look for Police Inspector Thomas Mastny. The genius was in his office, pushing his wheelchair from one end of the room to the other. He stopped and furrowed his brow when Marbach stomped his feet in the doorway.

"What do you want?" The genius had an impatient look on his face.

"I want you to get me whatever you can on a business enterprise called the Federmann Syndikat." Marbach provided the spelling for the enterprise and then said, "Look, Federmann is a secret activity involving a lot of important people. You have to be careful. Handle this like a cloaked inquiry."

"*Cloaked inquiry?*" The genius let loose a deep groan, then sat up straight in his wheelchair. "All right, I will be real careful." He gripped the wheels of his chair. "Are you going to save Fräulein Karen Mann? She is alive. I know with every fiber of my being that she is alive."

"I am doing my best."

The genius maneuvered his wheelchair aggressively forward, stopping only in the last instant, just before he would have rammed into Marbach.

"Kiss my arse, Herr Police Inspector."

"You address me as Herr Police Inspector? I am unworthy of such respect from you."

"If you want respect from me, you will save Fräulein Karen Mann." Mastny took a breath. His eyes filled with priestlike authority. "Save the fräulein or be damned for all eternity."

CHAPTER FIFTEEN

A few minutes after leaving Mastny's office, Marbach made his way to the office of the chief of Vienna Kripo and was quickly admitted. Rolf, sitting across the desk from Kaas, flashed his gap-tooth grin while Kaas shouted, "We've won! Detective Rolf Hiller did it! The chief was ready to come charging in here until I read him over the telephone what Detective Rolf Hiller got from Ossietsky. I told the chief we might be able to get a legitimate confession from the lustmörder but that we'll come up with a fake one if necessary."

"Maybe I can get a legitimate confession," Marbach said. "But the important thing right now is for us to find Fräulein Karen Mann."

Kaas pounded his fist down onto the desk. "By all means. Pull out all stops. Do whatever it takes. The fräulein must be saved! That is absolutely the most important thing."

"Yes," agreed Marbach.

"Whatever it takes," Kaas said to Marbach, "I will back you up."

"On the matter of the confession by this killer," Marbach said, "one critical weapon I would like to use is information I have about a highly secret activity called the Federmann Syndikat."

"Federmann?" Kaas had a troubled look on his face. "Look, maybe you ought to stay away from that. Everything about Federmann is highly secret."

"If I can use Federmann, there is a good chance to break down Litzman, a good chance to find out where Karen Mann is."

"What are you asking me to stick my neck into?"

"I'm asking you to let me use a powerful weapon."

At that moment, there was an interruption. A call was coming in from high-level SS in Berlin, a call that had to be conducted privately.

"Gentlemen, if you'll excuse me," Kaas said.

Marbach and Rolf headed for the door.

Just before they got to the door, Kaas put his hand over the telephone mouthpiece and said to Marbach in an angry voice, "Goddamn it! Are you going to find the fräulein?"

Marbach answered in a defiant voice. "Can I use Federmann?"

Kaas made a threatening motion with the hand not covering the telephone mouthpiece and then shook his head. "You rogue. All right, go ahead and use Federmann. If this whole thing comes down around my ears, so be it. Do whatever it takes to save Fräulein Karen Mann."

After saying that, Kaas returned his attention to the telephone call.

Marbach exchanged a glance with Rolf, and they left the office.

While walking down the hallway, Marbach put a hand on Rolf's shoulder. "Does this change your mind about the commander?"

"No."

"He doesn't know Karen Mann, doesn't know her family, probably never saw more than a photo of her, yet he is taking a risk on her behalf."

"What are you saying?"

"I am asking if you are willing to say Commander Kaas might be a good man."

"He's got courage, intelligence, and I'll even grant that he's got a good sense of humor, but that doesn't mean I am going to call him a good man."

"You have a lot of hard armor on you, my friend. What would it take for you to call the commander a good man?"

"I don't think that will ever happen."

"Why?"

"He is SS."

"You are SS, and so am I."

"My heart doesn't belong to the SS. Neither does yours. But his does."

"Commander Kaas is sticking his neck out on this thing with Karen Mann. He doesn't have to, but he is."

"I already told you that isn't enough for me to call him a good man."

"Are you morally pure compared to the commander?"

Rolf put a contrived saintly look on his face. "I went to confession yesterday, and then I went to Mass and received Holy Communion. Today I am in a state of grace."

"That is only because I have taken upon myself your more grievous sins."

Rolf laughed. "You are no one to take on another's sins. You mess with people's minds, yet you keep being critical of me for using—with professional restraint—my fists and my truncheon. Sometimes punched bodies cure faster than wounded minds."

The walk down the hallway continued.

"You better be nice to me. I know your secrets," Rolf said.

"What are you talking about?"

"About you getting Rabbi Leichter to Switzerland."

Marbach wasn't caught off guard. He replied with a laugh, "Why don't you do your duty and turn me in?"

"This isn't for joking. You should have included me in that adventure. At the very least, you should have told me what you were up to."

"Right now we have to concentrate on saving Karen Mann."

"We agree on that. So let me make the observation that while you are finishing up with Neumayer I might get us started on the lustmörder, Lieutenant Litzman."

"I don't know."

"I can get him confused. It could go better for you when you get to him if he's a little confused before you start."

"All right, go get him a little confused but avoid any tough stuff."

"This time I'll avoid the tough stuff."

"It will be good if you get Litzman a little confused. That'll help with a trick I want to try. It is going to involve a newspaper—today's newspaper."

"Just give me an update on the script."

Marbach provided the update. When that was done, Rolf clapped a hand onto Marbach's shoulder and then went on his way to make Lieutenant Litzman a little confused.

Left behind, Marbach remembered something. He grasped the packet of photographs of Rolf's daughter in his pockets, but it was too late to call Rolf back.

CHAPTER SIXTEEN

Marbach returned to the room where he had left Lieutenant Neumayer, who quickly made it clear he wanted to get any remaining business done so he could go home. "I don't want to remain here any longer than absolutely necessary. How long is this going to take?"

Marbach sat down at the small wooden table and said, "This won't take long."

It took about fifteen minutes for a detailed written statement to be completed, a statement containing truth laced with fiction.

The truth was that Neumayer and Ossietsky, accompanied by Litzman, met the two university students on the Ringstrasse, took them to the Café Europe, and then, after a short time in the Café Europe, the group went to the Hotel Capricorno. The fiction was that Neumayer and Ossietsky quickly left while Litzman and the two fräuleins remained at the Hotel Capricorno. According to the fiction, Neumayer and Ossietsky were anxious to go to a party at the Neumayer estate. There had, indeed, been a party at the Neumayer estate, and once the word was given to them, no one who had been at the party was going to say anything that might jeopardize the fiction about Lieutenant Neumayer and Lieutenant Ossietsky being present from the beginning of the party to the end.

Marbach handed the statement to Neumayer and told him to sign it.

When the signing of the statement was completed, Marbach pulled out a separate piece of paper and asked the young officer to write down everything he knew about the Federmann Syndikat. After several minutes of feverish writing, Neumayer handed Marbach what he had written.

Marbach studied the piece of paper for a few moments before saying, "I don't want you to talk to anyone about what we have done here, not even your father. No one at all; nothing at all. Most especially, nothing about Federmann. Do you agree?"

"Yes."

"If your father—or anyone—insists on knowing what you and I talked about, have a story ready that makes no mention of Federmann. I require your word that any story you tell will make no mention of Federmann."

"I give my word."

A few minutes later, Lieutenant Neumayer left police headquarters with a Vienna police release form in his pocket stipulating that the young officer was cleared of any involvement in the killing that took place at the Hotel Capricorno.

Alone in his office, Marbach thought about Karen Mann. She was in some miserable place, hopeless, waiting in terror for the lustmörder to return. Even if the killer didn't return, she couldn't last more than a few days alone in whatever awful place the lustmörder had hidden her.

She had to be found.

Marbach grabbed a piece of blank paper and carefully began writing. When satisfied with what he had written, he gathered up Neumayer's statement and the separate piece of paper, got up from his chair, and went to the office of the chief of Vienna Kripo.

The officious young secretary cast a troubled look but waved him speedily inside.

Kaas stood up behind his desk.

"I have Neumayer's statement," Marbach said. "And on a separate piece of paper, just for you, I had him write up what he knows about the Federmann Syndikat. It is all here."

"Let's see what you have."

Marbach placed Neumayer's statement on the desk while holding back the piece of paper.

Kaas waved Marbach into a chair on the opposite side of his desk, then sat down and began reading Neumayer's statement. "This looks good," he said after a few moments.

"I have a script—how I plan to do the interrogation of Litzman," Marbach said. "There is a role for you to play in the script, if you want."

"What do you mean, a script?"

"I like to plot out interrogations. I use what I call scripts."

Kaas smiled. "All right, Comrade Soldier. Just tell me what role you have for me to play in your so-called script."

Marbach provided the piece of paper. "On this I have written some cues for you to be aware of, things for you to listen for, and some lines for you to speak."

"You can count on me," Kaas said after quickly reading what was written on one side of the piece of paper.

"There is something written on the other side," Marbach said. "It is what I want placed in a phony copy of the *Völkische Beobachter* dated today."

"The *Völkische Beobachter*? The Führer's favorite newspaper?"

Marbach offered a correction. "A phony copy of the newspaper."

Kaas read what was on the reverse side of the piece of paper and frowned. Finally, he said, "Sticking this article about the highly secret Federmann business in a copy of the *Völkische Beobachter* puts my neck in a noose, even if it is a phony copy."

"No one who might be a problem will ever read the phony newspaper."

Kaas hesitated. "I don't know."

"I can use this trick to powerful advantage."

"Who will be printing this phony newspaper?"

"Gunther Menghin."

"Is this a man who works for us?"

"He's a printer with a shop four or five blocks from here. Not a really bad guy, but that didn't keep him from getting into trouble. A few weeks ago—just before the Anschluss—we arrested him for putting misleading information on some of his customers' receipt slips. It amounts to a criminal charge. The important thing for us right now is that Herr Menghin is quite good with a printing press. He can produce copies of any daily newspaper—with today's date— and place what I have written on that piece of paper. Herr Menghin has a very sick wife, and he doesn't want to go to prison. You will be able to size him up for yourself. If you provide him assurance that we will drop the charges we have against him, I guarantee he will keep our little secret. That's my personal guarantee to you, but the decision is yours."

"All right," Kaas said, shaking his head wearily. "I will size this man up, but I am pretty sure what I will decide. I said at the start that we would do this your way."

"If Herr Menghin passes your muster, tell him I want it done within the hour. I know him from past experience. He can do it that fast."

"All right. The important thing is that we are Comrade Soldiers and pledged to save the fräulein."

Marbach walked to the door, paused with his hand on the door handle, turned, faced Kaas, and said, "Yes, we are Comrade Soldiers." After saying that, he opened the door and left the office. He was on his way to Mastny's office.

CHAPTER SEVENTEEN

Marbach peered through an open door into Mastny's office. The wheelchair-bound police detective lifted an arm and waved him inside.

Marbach didn't move. He remained in the doorway, staring at the messiness inside the office. After taking a moment, he inquired, "Does the cleaning lady *ever* come in here?"

The genius didn't reply.

Marbach studied the littered floor for a few more moments, then stepped inside. He maneuvered around a large, upturned box, paused, then proceeded carefully, placing his feet where he wouldn't be stepping on folders, books, or other debris. He navigated his way to a sturdy, wooden chair across the desk from Mastny and, knowing there would be no invitation, sat down unbidden.

Propped upright in his wheelchair, the genius stared at Marbach the way he often did, like a priest dealing with an obtuse altar boy.

"Do you have anything for me? Marbach asked.

Mastny made a snarling sound. Marbach regarded the snarling as a good sign. From long experience, he knew that the genius was at his best when in a disagreeable mood.

Mastny placed a bundle on top of his desk. "I have prepared for you a Suspect Background Report."

On selected occasions when Mastny prepared a report that he regarded as especially significant, he called it a Suspect Background Report.

Marbach opened a bundle that looked like something put together by a child in grade school, the hasty product of what might have accomplished with scissors and dabs of white paste. Scattered throughout the messy pages, pasted onto the paper, were photographs and scraps of paper containing typewritten paragraphs. There were also handwritten notes. On the first page was a note in Mastny's barely legible handwriting:

> Lieutenant Litzman is in many respects
> a perfectly normal man, except that he
> has taken to acting out the dreams and
> fantasies that normal men only fantasize
> about—the torture and murder of young women.

Marbach shook his head but told himself this was no time for him to say anything about Mastny's view of human nature. He continued reading the scribbled handwriting:

> Like the lustmörder executed in Munich
> last year, this lustmörder is terrified
> of losing his mind. That is an obsessive
> fear for him.

Marbach looked at Mastny and said, "He's terrified of losing his mind, eh? That's important for me to know."

There was no reply.

Marbach returned his attention to the Suspect Background Report. After turning a messy page, he murmured, "It says here that Litzman doesn't drink any liquor and that he drinks very little wine. Why is that important?"

"Liquor puts him in terror that he is losing control. He has a need for total self-control."

Marbach flicked away aberrant crumbs of white paste, turned the page, and read one of Mastny's handwritten notes scribbled in the margin:

> *Litzman has attracted notice from his superiors*
> *for his high intelligence and considerable courage.*

Turning that page, Marbach found another handwritten note:

> *Litzman has a strong appetite for hot poppy seed rolls.*
> *He likes them served with Lekvar.*

After that page was turned, another handwritten note caught Marbach's attention.

> *Litzman lies a lot. This has come to the attention*
> *of some of his senior officers. One of them says that*
> *despite his high intelligence, he has a childlike faith*
> *in the efficacy of lies.*

Below that was a note:

> *An army doctor has expressed concern about*
> *Litzman's frequent visits to the hospital to*
> *observe people dying.*

The next page dealt with business records and army records. Turning that page, Marbach found a page with a large, hand-printed note on it.

> *If this lustmörder is able to confuse a*
> *silly police inspector, it will provide*
> *him enormous satisfaction.*

Marbach reread the note he had just read, smiled, and said, "Silly police inspector?"

"Yes!" declared Mastny.

Marbach returned his attention to the report and found buried in the middle of the next smeared, wrinkled page another scribbled note:

> Litzman's army leave record over the
> past year matches a pattern of unexplained
> deaths of six women.

Marbach put a thoughtful look on his face. "Your check of Litzman's leave record matches what Rolf found in Litzman's diary. That was a fast match you did."

Mastny's voice thundered with priestlike authority. "Get on with the reading!"

Marbach returned his attention to the report. He turned page after page, finally stopping when he came upon another of Mastny's scribbled notes:

> Those who like to confuse are often
> vulnerable to confusion themselves. In
> a suitability report, one superior officer
> wrote that Litzman seems to be more
> afraid of confusion than he is of any
> physical danger. He has nightmares.
> More than once in the barracks, he has
> awakened from nightmares shouting he
> isn't crazy.

At the bottom of that page was another scribbled note:

> Lieutenant Litzman is attracted to women
> he describes as stupid. He likes to talk
> about how stupid they are when he is
> with his brother officers. Many of them
> agree with him that the best sex is
> with stupid women.

There wasn't time to waste, but Marbach decided a brief moment might be allowed for some humor. "Why are you so preoccupied with sex?"

"If I know a man's sex life, I know the man," Mastny replied with intimidating self-assurance.

"Why didn't you ever loan your services to Dr. Sigmund Freud? I'm sure he could have benefited from your experience and advice."

"I don't bother myself with amateurs."

"Dr. Sigmund Freud an amateur?" Marbach found that to be an amusing thought but quickly turned his attention back to the report and found another scribbled note:

> *This man has always been vocal and outspoken*
> *about his hatreds: Jews, Reds, homosexuals,*
> *and anyone who possesses human weakness or*
> *vulnerability in any exploitable form.*

Marbach looked up just long enough to spot Mastny staring with concern at a photograph lying among the pile of papers on his desk: the photograph of Fräulein Karen Mann. Quickly, Marbach returned his attention to the report. There was one final scribbled note:

> *Litzman regards his father as awful.*
> *He hates his father for being*
> *a swindler, a mountebank, a crook.*

Marbach laid down the bundle of pages that was the Suspect Background Report, stared at pieces of paste on his fingers, pulled out his handkerchief, and wiped his fingers clean.

Mastny made a snorting sound. "How in hell did anyone as slow and fussy as you ever get up a mountain and save those soldiers during the war?"

"I got to the top of the Ortigara because I don't prematurely rush things," Marbach said. After a moment, he added, "What have you learned about the Federmann Syndikat?"

"*Federmann?* I have learned nothing about that. Not yet. I was busy getting the Suspect Background Report done. I won't be able to get started on Federmann until you get out of here and leave me alone."

"This report is good. It will help me when I have my session with Litzman."

Mastny scowled. "What payment is there for first-class work done on short notice?"

Marbach smiled ruefully as he withdrew a packet of Juno cigarettes, a conventional German brand.

Mastny asked, "What happened to those French cigarettes I hear you have?"

"What's the matter with Juno?"

"I prefer French cigarettes to Juno."

Marbach heaved a sigh and brought the packet of Laurens Green out of his suit pocket. He withdrew one cigarette from the packet and handed it to Mastny. The cigarette was promptly placed in a safe place inside the office desk. Then Mastny patted around in his jacket pockets until he found what he was seeking: a half-smoked butt, which he promptly lit.

Marbach said, "I'll give you your due; you have given me some useful stuff to use when I go after the lustmörder."

Mastny's face became soft. "Please tell Fräulein Constanze Tandler that a friend of Commander Friedrich Tandler, the man of the deed, pays her tribute."

Marbach was surprised. "I didn't know you used to know Constanze. Why didn't you ever say anything? I am sure Constanze would like to hear about her martyred father from you in person."

In a tentative voice, Mastny said, "Many years ago, I knew her father. She was just a small child then. I haven't seen her since those old days—except on the stage."

"You should have told me. I never had a clue you knew Constanze's father. She would be delighted to meet with you. Let me arrange things."

"That was many years ago. She wouldn't remember me."

"If you would come to the Alpen Café some—"

Mastny abruptly interrupted. "There is work to be done."

"Of course. It is just …"

There was no more to be said. Mastny's priestly face was implacable.

"I better get started," Marbach said. "There isn't time to waste."

Mastny stared intently. "If anything significant shows up about Federmann, I will let you know immediately. Are you going to save the fräulein?"

"I will do my best. If there is success, most of the credit will belong to you and Hans."

The genius waved his hand dismissively.

Marbach left the office.

CHAPTER EIGHTEEN

When Marbach entered the room where he knew he would find Rolf and Lieutenant Litzman, he immediately saw that there was trouble. The young lieutenant was sitting in a chair, nursing his face. There was a noticeable reddening along the side of his jaw and a small, red bruise vivid under his left eye.

Marbach looked at Rolf.

Litzman jumped to his feet and glared angrily.

Marbach said to Rolf, "I'll see you outside."

"I demand to see SS Leader Ernst Kaltenbrunner!" exclaimed Litzman, his posture rigid.

Marbach stared hard at Rolf, who lowered his eyes.

Waving his arms, Litzman shouted imperiously, "I insist upon seeing SS Leader Kaltenbrunner to protest this assault on my person."

Marbach turned away from Litzman and walked back through the still open door.

"Wait a minute," Rolf said as he followed Marbach out of the room.

The door slammed shut behind Rolf, who quickly caught up with Marbach. They moved together down the hallway, went through one door, then a second.

After the second door slammed shut, Marbach came to a halt, turned, faced Rolf, and demanded, "All right, tell me what happened."

"I'm sorry. I know I made a mess of things. I had that creep real frustrated. Then he turned things around on me. I should have known better. I'm sorry. I know I screwed up. I know I've let you down."

"Fräulein Karen Mann may be the one you have let down."

"I know that," groaned Rolf.

"Lieutenant Litzman is filled with rage and righteousness. That makes it harder, maybe impossible to get any useful information out of him."

Rolf lowered his head.

Marbach knew Rolf had messed up and had to be held accountable, but he also knew his colleague detective was a good man. He examined the situation and said to Rolf, "You still haven't told me what happened."

Rolf lifted his head and drew a tight breath. "I was doing everything according to the script. I had him frustrated and confused. I thought I was figuring him out, but all the time he was figuring me out. He got onto me for being a peasant. He called me a spinach watcher."

Marbach shoved his hands into his pockets. "You punched him because he called you a spinach watcher?"

"Before he called me a spinach watcher, he let loose with all sorts of nasty things about peasants. What can I say? I blew up. I hit him. I've got no excuse. I behaved like a dumb ox."

Marbach tried to figure out the best way to fix this mess. He said to Rolf, "I assume we have a written transcript of what happened between you and Litzman."

"Of course." Rolf made an upward pointing gesture with his thumb. He was pointing to the recording line between the interrogation room and a room on the second floor.

While watching Marbach, Rolf said, "That recording will rot his mind when he hears it. I wasn't just having fun with him. I followed your script—most of it, anyway. I brought up all the subjects in your script. He wouldn't answer any questions about his father. Absolutely refused. Your script worked real good until I acted like a damned idiot."

"It is going to take a lot of time to break down Litzman."

"Hours and hours for a frightened fräulein to wait."

"We could always do this your way."

"No. My way doesn't work as good as your way. I've known that for years. Even when I'm not punch happy, your way works better than my way."

"We all make a mess of things every so often. I shall put what you did to Litzman behind us."

"Any changes to the script?"

"Litzman must tell us what we need to know before I question Lieutenant Neumayer."

"Years of working with you makes me suspect you plan to work in something related to how Litzman made me look like a damned idiot."

"Correct. Let me write out the part for you to play, maybe some cue words."

"Go ahead."

"The purpose, the focus, remains the same."

"The purpose is to save Fräulein Karen Mann."

"Yes."

Marbach scribbled on a piece of paper what Rolf's role would be when the interrogation of Litzman got restarted. When he was finished, he handed Rolf the script with changes in it.

CHAPTER NINETEEN

After leaving Rolf, Marbach returned to his office to check a few things. He was sitting at his desk when the telephone made a clanging noise. He picked up the telephone and identified himself.

Kaas was on the line. "Karl, SS Leader Kaltenbrunner changed his mind. He is on his way here."

"Is there any way to slow him down?"

"I already tried. It is hopeless. The SS leader is real pleased with us, but someone put it into his head that he ought to take over now.

"What about Fräulein Karen Mann?"

"I tried to bring that up, but the SS leader told me to shut my mouth."

Marbach was filled with appreciation for the plain, clear way his Comrade Soldier was talking.

"It is all a matter of time," said Kaas.

"How much time do we have?" Marbach asked.

"SS Leader Kaltenbrunner will be here any minute now."

"How did Herr Menghin do with that phony newspaper?"

"He brought it to me ten minutes ago, but what good is that now? We've run out of time."

"I don't intend to give up. I am going to keep trying until I know for certain that Karen Mann is lost."

"You are a good man, Karl."

With those words, the telephone conversation ended.

Marbach hung up his telephone, sat in his chair for a few moments, then got up and walked out into the hallway. He kept walking until he found himself confronted by Police Inspector Mastny in the wheelchair.

The genius with the face of a cleric stared fiercely. "You've run out of time. I have my sources. I know Chief Kaltenbrunner is coming, and I know that Detective Hiller bounced Lieutenant Litzman all around, got him into a boiling rage."

"We all goof up sometimes. Detective Hiller is a good man."

"Forget that. The only thing that counts is time. It is a matter of time, a matter of making use of the time that is left."

"You are wasting the little time that is left. With however much time is left, I am going to go and question Lieutenant Litzman."

"Do you think he knows where Karen Mann is?"

"He might know."

"Is there a genuine chance that he might be able to tell how to find her?"

"There is always a chance."

"Don't let the fräulein die."

"With only minutes left, it looks pretty hopeless."

"I propose to you something that might work, even with the little time that is left."

"What are you proposing?"

"Thorn apple."

Marbach shook his head dismissively. "Thorn apple? That drug? You are as crazy as the crazy jerks who use that devil's weed to intoxicate their minds."

"It is the only way to save the fräulein, the only way to give Karen Mann a chance with the incredibly little time that is left. If you don't try it, if you keep plodding ahead, she is doomed."

"All right, she is doomed. I can face facts. Karen Mann is doomed."

Mastny lifted his arms for a moment and then dropped them. "She is most certainly doomed if you don't use thorn apple."

"*Thorn apple!*" Marbach spat the words out.

"Yes, thorn apple," Mastny said with anger in his voice. "Thorn apple. More potent than henbane or mandrake, as hallucinogenic as the best belladonna."

"What awful thing are you asking me to do?"

"I am asking you to give Karen Mann a chance to live," Mastny said, his voice low but fierce.

"Look, I'm sorry, but—"

"Pay attention to me. It was in my Suspect Background Report that Lieutenant Litzman has a terrible fear of going crazy. If done carefully, with very precise doses, the effect of thorn apple can make him think he is going crazy. When you thought you had plenty of time, you were going to use tricks and play on his fatigue. Using thorn apple isn't any different. It is just faster."

"Faster?"

"Karen Mann will have a chance, perhaps only a small chance, but a real chance if you are as skilled in interrogation as some say you are. But she will only have that chance if you use thorn apple.

You had a plan for breaking Litzman down, one of your damned scripts. But your scripts require a lot of time, and there are only a few minutes left. Thorn apple does funny things with time."

"Thorn apple is unpredictable," said Marbach.

"Thorn apple is the only chance to save Karen Mann. It isn't much of a chance, but it is absolutely her only chance. Are you going to let her perish because you are too personally virtuous to do the only thing that might possibly save her?"

Marbach closed his eyes. When he opened them, he spoke slowly. "A friend of mine sometimes uses thorn apple. I've tried it a couple of times myself. Thorn apple makes for some strange feelings—your sense of time goes screwy, things around you change their shape and size. It is … I guess it is like going crazy."

"Use the thorn apple," Mastny pleaded.

Marbach closed his mouth, kept it shut.

"Please," implored the man with the face of a priest.

Marbach spat out words. "Goddamn you!"

"Yes, I am damned," Mastny said quietly. "That doesn't matter. What does matter is that using thorn apple can give Karen Mann a small chance to not perish."

"I don't know … I just don't know."

"Litzman likes poppy seed rolls."

"I guess that's in one or two of the reports we've gotten."

"I figured we might get to this point," said Mastny. "I have taken some thorn apple from the evidence room. I had the cook sprinkle precise amounts of the thorn apple onto some poppy seed rolls. Just enough thorn apple to unsettle Litzman, hopefully not enough to do more than that."

Marbach cursed, shut his eyes, and then opened them and said, "All right."

"God bless you, Karl."

"God help me." Marbach went off to do whatever could be done that might possibly save Karen Mann.

CHAPTER TWENTY

Lieutenant Wolfgang Litzman was sitting in a chair in a small room in the police headquarters building using the tips of his fingers to carefully explore his wounded face. He stopped probing with his fingers when he came to a painful bleeding cut. He quickly pulled his fingers away, hesitated a moment, then touched the fingers to his mouth. Blood from the cut tasted strange, but he savored the strange taste. He felt triumphant. He was a prisoner now, but when he got out of this place, he would be the victor.

As he moved around in his chair, he became aware of pain in his knuckles, especially the knuckles on his right hand. The pain was a reminder of what had happened last night at the Hotel Capricorno. After Paul Neumayer and Eric Ossietsky wandered off, it had been easy to get Julie to take just one more drink. She had been sad because Paul didn't seem to like her. So she accepted a drink, a carefully prepared drink into which had been poured the precisely correct amount of hyoscine. Very quickly, she had dropped off to sleep, and she didn't wake up until fists began pounding against her face. It had been grand hearing her cry, hearing her hopeless cries and desperate pleas.

Litzman's only regret about Julie was that too soon he had run out of time. He wished he'd had more time to torment her, but that hadn't been possible. So he gave her an extra dose of hyoscine, one calculated to send her into a final spiral of unconsciousness, and then, when she was dead, he had rebuttoned her clothes. Such a frustrating thing it was to get her rebuttoned.

Litzman stopped thinking about his frustration with Julie's clothes. He directed his attention to the fact that right now he was wearing no underclothes. When the colonel count had said they were going to police headquarters, he had excused himself, quickly went to the bathroom, and got rid of his undergarments. When he was a young boy, he had learned to enjoy going to exciting places wearing clothes but no undergarments. That still pleasured him. He enjoyed going around fully dressed but wearing no undergarments.

He recollected with delight details about Julie: her beaten face and the fright and the terror she had expressed while drifting in and out of consciousness.

He sat uneasily in his chair. There was a problem. His private member had become dangerously stiff. Pleasurable stiffness had come with recollections of Julie, her terror, and her nakedness. But what if someone noticed the bulge under his trousers? And what if his private member started erupting? The disaster might leak through and show on the front of his plain-colored trousers. The sooner he got out of this place, the better. He checked his watch and wondered how many minutes—how many hours?—before he would be out of this place.

He told himself that the thing to do was get out of this place, get out of this place and be with Karen. The experience with the one named Julie had been good but too hurried. And—in the end—incomplete. With Karen he would be able to take his time, not feel rushed while delivering his full and complete attention to the agonies of a terrified, naked female.

At this moment, to his distress, he found his mind invaded by dreadful memories of what had taken place when he was a small boy. Many times he had been grabbed up by the family laundry woman, ending up trapped between her powerful, naked legs, with his face pushed up toward the middle of her body. She had inflicted herself upon him countless times, and he hadn't been able to tell anyone. If he had told on her, she would have told on him, told everyone about exciting things he had secretly taken from the houses of neighbors.

He tried to stop thinking about having been trapped many times between the laundry woman's legs, the victim of the laundry woman's cruelty. He told himself that was all in the past. The awful woman had enjoyed having him in her power. It was terrible. But now and forever more, he was a powerful one. Not one of those who suffered, but someone who inflicted suffering.

Desperate for relief, he concentrated his thoughts on Karen. He was determined that she was going to be better than Julie could ever have been. He hadn't yet seen Karen naked, but Julie had imperfections he didn't think Karen would have. Julie's large appendix scar and other blemishes were distractions. Even if Karen had distractions, the important thing was that there would be plenty of time. He would beat Karen a little just to get started, then, again and again, he would hit her and listen to her terrified cries, her pleading words. And never would he touch her naked flesh with his fingers, not with his fingers. That was important: not touching her nakedness with his fingers while punching, hitting, and slapping her nakedness. Even if he dug his fingernails into her helpless flesh, it wasn't the same as touching her flesh with his fingers. And her helpless cries would stir him to his very essence.

But right now there was a problem. He realized that the continued stiffness of his private member was getting out of control, risking shame. He knew he had to stop thinking about things that were sexually arousing, so he began thinking about recent interactions with fools. There had been the meeting this morning when SS Leader Kaltenbrunner had wanted assurance that nothing was going to jeopardize the contract between Berlin and the Federmann Syndikat. Federmann—a name so secret the idiotic SS leader barely dared to utter it.

He laughed as he thought about what had happened at the early morning meeting. Right at the very beginning, SS Leader Kaltenbrunner had asked about Karen Mann. The SS leader had been worried that she might cause problems and was relieved when told the lie that in order to keep Karen from causing trouble, it had been necessary to restrain her, and, unfortunately, she had made such a fuss that somehow or other she had ended up dead.

Litzman recalled with pleasure how the SS leader had sympathized with him when he had said that he felt awful about being responsible for the death of the one named Karen Mann. Hard, tough SS Leader Kaltenbrunner, the giant of a man called the gorilla, had been almost fatherly when he said that the killing of the Red slut named Karen Mann had been a service to National Socialism. The SS leader had said that a man must be a man—that the worst thing was to be afraid of being brutal, afraid of being cruel. The gorilla was a talkative man who had talked and talked and talked.

Litzman told himself that those who are fools—those who can be fooled—deserve no respect. Even when they have high status—like SS Leader Kaltenbrunner. But he did concede that approval from those who are highly placed, even the ones who are fools, made him feel good.

Litzman once again touched his fingers to the wounds on his face, but this time immediately drew the hand back. There was awful pain. Hoping to escape the pain, he tried to think of something sublime. The embarrassing stiffness under his trousers was almost gone, making it safe for him to think carefully about Karen. She was waiting for him, waiting to be an ecstasy for him. She was outside him, but he would bring her within him. Not her body—not her naked body—but the pure spirit that radiated out of her. She would fall asleep. He would let her fall asleep, and, when it pleased him, he would wake her up. And when she was awake, fully aware of him in control, he would punch her, careful not to hit too hard. She needed to be conscious of what was happening. He would punch her face and punch her body, but never would he touch her nudity with his fingers. Her nudity would hopefully be clear, pure, and unflawed. But even if Karen did have distractions on her body, she would provide ecstasy.

Litzman took consolation from an upsurge of icy rage. For many years, the icy rage had been his protection. Sometimes hot rage protected him, but he had long known that his best protection was icy rage. The icy rage banished fear, eliminated doubt, invigorated his mind, and cleansed every part of his body.

He thought about the gap-toothed police officer, the peasant who had been too stupid to realize he was being tricked. At the beginning, he had found the peasant's questions to be surprisingly intelligent, but because of his greater intelligence, he had fooled the peasant, turned things upside-down. Still, one thing was troubling: the peasant had expressed a surprising interest in the whereabouts of the senior Litzman, that stupid old man who liked to hear himself addressed as "Herr Direktor Heinrich Litzman." Why did the police want to know where his father was? What did that have to do with anything? His father was in Berlin. Or somewhere. Wherever he was had nothing to do with anything important … that was a certainty, wasn't it?

He had long believed that sometimes life doesn't make sense. Right now, for him, there was nothing to do but suffer the pain from his throbbing wounds. When the peasant policeman had beaten him, he had had taken the blows to his face with courage—no crying, no shouting.

He told himself that those who are superior should feel nothing but contempt for those who are inferior, even when the inferior ones have temporary control over the one who is the superior person. He affirmed that the day would come when no one would be able to have control over him. Made strong by hate, he would become too powerful to be under anyone's control.

Litzman's thoughts were interrupted by noise outside in the hallway. The door opened, and the police inspector entered, followed by the peasant policeman. He wondered where they had gone and why they were coming back now. He studied the police inspector while drawing upon reserves of hot rage, not icy rage. The hot rage was invigorating. At the precisely correct moment, he put some of the hot rage to good use. He shouted, "Herr Police Inspector, I came here voluntarily. I came at the personal request of Colonel Count Neumayer. He said that there would be no trouble or inconvenience for me. I have been subjected to an unspeakable physical assault upon my person. I intend to report what has happened to SS Leader Kaltenbrunner. I demand to be released immediately."

The police inspector said, "I don't see any reason to keep you here much longer."

"What possible excuse is there for *any* delay?"

"The only thing holding up your release are orders we have received from Berlin."

"Why am I being kept here? Where are Lieutenants Neumayer and Ossietsky?"

"They went home about an hour ago. Lieutenant Neumayer is at his father's estate. Lieutenant Ossietsky is back in the army barracks."

"I don't understand why my brother officers have been set free while I am being held here."

"Your brother officers have no connection with our reason for continuing to hold you. As Detective Hiller explained, we have orders from Berlin. Information is needed to help locate your father.

It might be helpful if you corroborated the information we have about the incident at the Hotel Capricorno, but that is not important."

"My father? I don't understand this interest in my father, but I wish you luck in trying to locate him. I don't keep track of his comings and goings. I explained that to Detective Hiller, but he couldn't get it through his thick peasant skull that I have no idea where my father is."

"If you are willing to be helpful, please tell me about the unfortunate business at the Hotel Capricorno."

"I will not discuss that. The peasant policeman asked me about the Hotel Capricorno, and I quite properly told him that I would not discuss that matter in police headquarters. I will only discuss what happened at the Hotel Capricorno with proper authority—with an officer in the Greater German Army. Or perhaps … well, of course, I will discuss it with SS Leader Kaltenbrunner. I think you should promptly put through a telephone call to SS Leader Kaltenbrunner."

"We are investigating the incident at the Hotel Capricorno. We need to clear our records on that case, but the only reason we are holding you is because we have orders from Berlin in connection with a far more important matter."

"A more important matter? What is more important than what happened at the Hotel Capricorno?"

"Nothing important happened at the Hotel Capricorno. From what Lieutenant Neumayer told us, it appears that Fräulein Julie Thimig made offensive statements about the Führer and about National Socialism. Lieutenant Neumayer did what any good German man would do. He hit her. He hit her, and she died. He didn't mean for her to die, but she did. The young woman may have been a monsignor's sister, but we have a full file on her. She was a Red and a slut. As young as she was, she had an extensive record of Red activities. Julie Thimig was active in Red groups around the university. I don't think Judge Thimig will want any public examination into why a good party member like Lieutenant Neumayer did what any good National Socialist would have done. Lieutenant Neumayer would have been a despicable cur if he hadn't dealt with her forcefully."

The police inspector's voice suddenly became like a low hush. The hushed voice said, "I trust that you agree. You do agree, don't you? Lieutenant Neumayer is sorry for what happened, but if he hadn't dealt with the Red slut forcefully, he would not have done his duty. Of course, if you want to say something in defense of the Red slut, your statement will be taken down and officially recorded. Is that what you want to do?"

"No."

"I am going to have a cup of coffee. Do you want a cup of coffee?"

Before there was time to reply, the police inspector reached for the telephone and dialed a number. There was a pause while the connection was made, and then the police inspector said, "Let's have some coffee in here, and something to eat. I want this done immediately."

The police inspector continued to stay on the telephone. He made a connection to another office in police headquarters and began transacting routine police business, something about a small burglary.

An attempt was made to get the police inspector's attention. "Herr Police Inspector ..."

But the police inspector waved an arm for silence and continued talking to someone on the telephone about a small burglary.

"Herr Police Inspector ..."

"In a moment. I have some important business to get done," the police inspector said, and returned his attention to the telephone call dealing with a small burglary.

Suddenly, there was a knock on the door.

"Come in," said the police inspector.

A bored-looking guard brought in a tray with three cups of strong, rich Turkish coffee, along with a pitcher of cream. Also on the tray was a plate of hot poppy seed rolls and a container of Lekvar, the prune butter. Without being told to, the guard placed an extra pot of coffee on the Primus stove hissing in the rear of the room.

Everything seemed to be happening fast, but hot poppy seed rolls had always been a favorite treat. Especially with Lekvar. At the morning breakfast with SS Leader Kaltenbrunner, junior officers had been given nothing to eat. Only high-level officers had been given anything to eat.

A bite was taken from one of the poppy seed rolls. It tasted good even if it did have an unusual yeasty taste. Some Lekvar was pasted on and more bites taken. There came an extraordinary onrush of energy.

The police inspector hung up the phone and said, "I know that the other two officers agreed to keep quiet about that Hotel Capricorno business on your way over here, but Lieutenant Neumayer—once he thought about it a bit—decided, rather wisely I believe, to put himself in our hands. Now we will be in a position to help him when he goes before his military superiors. I don't expect any serious difficulty for him when he goes before his superiors. He is, after all, a good National Socialist. He is a good man who won't tolerate any slurs against the Führer—not by a Red slut or by anyone else."

"You don't expect trouble for him?"

"No. Why should there be any trouble? From what Lieutenant Neumayer told us, he accidentally hit the Red slut too hard. He is a fine young man from a good family. He didn't mean any real harm, but he couldn't let her slurs go unanswered, could he?"

It was impossible to think of anything to say in reply.

The police inspector pushed his coffee cup to one side and said, "The Red slut may have been the daughter of an important jurist and the sister of a monsignor, but our records show she was a vile degenerate and a despicable Red."

"Vile degenerate?"

"Don't let her young age fool you. It is all in our records. She may have acted like a sweet, innocent virgin, but that was just a ruse. Some women are like that. Fortunately, their number is now one fewer."

The police inspector sighed and then continued. "Of course, sooner or later you will either have to corroborate what Lieutenant Neumayer has told us or you will have to challenge it. I had hoped that while we were waiting for the Berlin call you would behave like a good National Socialist and corroborate what Lieutenant Neumayer said."

The sound of the words coming out of the police inspector's mouth was mesmerizing, so enthralling a sound that it was impossible to understand what the words were saying. There was the sound of a drum tapping. The drum-tapping sound was coming out of the mouth of Police Inspector Marbach. The drum taps were words. The drum-tapping voice said, "This is one of those cases that is best handled privately. That will be better for the family of the colonel count. Certainly, a bright young man like you can understand that."

It was impossible to not nod agreement.

The drum-tapping voice continued. But what was the police inspector saying? It was something about that idiot of a father.

In that same moment, something grotesque began happening. The police inspector's mouth started to expand. The police inspector's mouth doubled in size, then tripled in size, and out of the enormous mouth came drumbeat words.

Was this the beginning of insanity?

A folder was shoved across the table. It was difficult to open the folder with fingers that seemed to have become incredibly short and thick, but finally there was success. Within the folder was official documentation—some of it marked SS, most of it marked Gestapo. Page after page described Julie Thimig as an enemy of the Greater Reich, a teenaged Red slut, a Jew lover, an enemy of the Reich.

The police inspector shoved a separate piece of paper across the table. Just a simple sheet of paper, but it made a loud, screeching sound before coming to rest.

The drumbeat voice said, "Write out your statement, and sign it."

The drumbeat voice gave specific instructions: "Write that you and you alone killed the Jew-loving slut, Julie Thimig, that Lieutenant Neumayer wasn't even present."

After delivering those instructions, there was nothing but eerie silence.

The police inspector got slowly to his feet. In that moment, the police inspector's entire body began expanding. It bloated upward and sideways, kept expanding until the police inspector was three or four times the size of any mortal person. The giant police inspector made a dismissive motion with his enormous arm.

The arm movement made by the police inspector was like being rejected by God Almighty! The drumbeat voice began speaking again, but it was impossible to understand what was being said. Part of the problem was that there was a terrible interrupting echo. Words and echoes. Some of the words and echoes were coming from near and from far away at the same time. A cloud of blackness filled the room. The blackness was overwhelming.

Suddenly, the blackness faded away, and there was light. The police inspector's bloated body was beginning another enormous expansion. The police inspector's body kept expanding until it seemed like it was going to fill the entire room.

This was insanity! All that could be hoped for was oblivion. He was rolling over and over on the floor. The rolling couldn't be stopped. Somewhere a child was screaming. It was him. He was that screaming child.

CHAPTER TWENTY-ONE

Police Inspector Marbach stared at the howling, tormented creature rolling on the floor. Less than five minutes had elapsed since Lieutenant Litzman bit into the first poppy seed roll. How many more minutes before SS Leader Kaltenbrunner would show up and bring everything to a halt? Marbach watched and listened until the screams became a series of gasping sounds. Then he moved in close, knelt down, and listened as the gasping sounds became words: "Help me … help me … help me."

Remaining on his knees, Marbach used one hand to loosen Litzman's tie, the other to grasp a shoulder firmly. But suddenly Litzman jerked wildly, pulled free, and did more rolling.

Marbach let Litzman roll. When Litzman stopped rolling, he lay still for a moment, then slowly got to his feet. His head was lowered. Looking limp, he faced the floor.

Rolf moved up beside Marbach, who got to his feet slowly, trying to figure this out. For some reason, Kaltenbrunner hadn't shown up yet. But how much longer did they have?

Litzman fell to the floor and began crying. His crying sounds were like those of a young boy.

Rolf set his jaw. "This is cruel, but it is worth it if it helps us save Karen Mann."

Marbach looked at Rolf. "Most definitely it is cruel. The cruelty befouls me."

Rolf lowered his head for a moment, then lifted it and stared at Litzman who continued crying like a child while crawling toward a corner of the room where he made whimpering sounds while struggling to his feet. He seemed to be trying to cover his lower body with his hands. After a few moments, he collapsed back onto the floor and cried, "Where are my clothes? What's happening to me?"

"My God!" whispered Rolf. "He thinks he's naked."

Marbach walked over to a telephone, picked it up, but kept his finger on the off switch.

One full minute passed while Litzman lay weeping on the floor.

Studying Litzman, Marbach barked loudly into the telephone mouthpiece while keeping his finger on the off switch. "Heil Hitler!" There was a pause, and then Marbach said, "Tell the Gestapo we are finished here. Tell them we will be bringing Lieutenant Litzman over to them."

Jumping to his feet, Litzman cried out almost incoherently: "*Gestapo!* ... Oh, my God! Oh, merciful Jesus! ... I don't know what's happening. Why is it so dark in here? Where ... what happened to my clothes? Gestapo? I don't see any reason ... I don't understand ... I don't know what is happening. My clothes ... where are my clothes?"

Rolf stared at Marbach. The fully clothed Litzman thought he was naked. He was acting like a crazy man. Rolf recalled that the revised script called for being free with suggestions that Litzman was acting like a crazy man. He shouted at Litzman, "You are crazy. Only a crazy man has fits like you are having."

"I am not crazy ... I am not crazy."

Marbach played his part in the script. "Do you have *insane* fits like this often?"

Litzman pushed the palms of his hands tight against his ears. "I don't know what is happening to me. Why is it so dark in here? Where are my clothes?"

"He is a *crazy* man," Rolf said in a loud voice while staring with exaggerated scorn at the fully clothed Litzman.

A moaning sound was yielded by Litzman.

Marbach stepped forward, wrapped an arm around Litzman, and said to him in a comforting voice, "Are you feeling better now? I am sorry, but we can't waste much more time. You must be taken to Gestapo Headquarters."

Litzman stared down at his body and quickly behaved like someone trying to cover nakedness.

Marbach picked up an empty coal bag and passed it to Litzman, who quickly clutched the bag defensively around his body.

"Gestapo?" whimpered Litzman. "I don't understand. Please, oh please … please let me talk to SS Leader Kaltenbrunner."

"There is the telephone," said Marbach. "I don't have any objection to you calling SS Leader Kaltenbrunner."

Litzman stumbled forward. Using one hand to hold the coal bag around the middle of his body, he used the other to pick up the telephone. "Yes … Yes, Operator? I say … can you? … I want to speak to SS Leader Ernst Kaltenbrunner."

Marbach exchanged a glance with Rolf. The revised script covered this. The telephone connection to the office of the SS leader was not genuine. Things had been arranged so that, regardless of what number was dialed from the telephone in this room, the call would go to a telephone two floors up in the building. The police detective answering Litzman's call had been carefully instructed on how to handle the call.

Marbach, feigning disinterest with Litzman, directed his attention to a package lying on the table. He picked it up and handled it as though calculating the weight.

Rolf said to Marbach in a voice intended to be more than loud enough for Litzman to hear, "I think the Spitzer case is in good shape."

There was, of course, no Spitzer case, but Marbach replied in an equally loud voice, "It will be good to have the Spitzer case behind us."

Litzman rapidly blinked while saying into the telephone, "Yes, Operator, I know the chief doesn't have his office in police headquarters. But can you connect me with him? ... Of course, I will wait."

A few moments later, Litzman's voice became loud and excited. He pressed the telephone close to his head. "Hello? Hello? SS Leader Kaltenbrunner's office? Good. Excellent. Let me talk with SS Leader Ernst Kaltenbrunner. This is Lieutenant Wolfgang Litzman calling on a matter of highest importance."

Litzman listened to what was said to him over the telephone. When he spoke, it was with a weak, frightened voice: "You say SS Leader Kaltenbrunner went on an emergency flight to Berlin? No, that can't be true. I need to speak with him. This is awful. I ... I must ..." Litzman's eyes rolled back in his head, and his body swayed and then pitched forward as he fell helplessly to the floor.

Marbach and Rolf watched and waited.

After a minute or two, Litzman staggered to his feet, dangling the coal bag in front of him.

Marbach said to Rolf in a voice he intended Litzman to hear, "It is time to send this young man to Gestapo Headquarters."

Litzman made a loud gasping sound. "Why … why do you want my father?"

Marbach said, "The Gestapo is responsible for investigating treason against the Greater Reich."

"*Treason?*"

"Corruption is treason. The Gestapo fights corruption by treating it as treason."

"Herr Police Inspector," Rolf said. "This *crazy* man is a disgrace to the Reich."

Litzman shouted, "I'm *not* crazy! I'm *not* crazy! What … what is happening to me?" He stared with dismay at the coal bag, let the coal bag loose, and, with a look of dismay, touched his fingers to his trousers, his jacket, and finally his shirt and tie. In an instant, his dismay became anger. He shook his head, kept shaking it, and with the shaking seemed to shake himself free from any affliction. In the matter of a few moments, he seemed to go through a transformation that ended with him looking fully in control of himself.

The man said to be afraid of insanity wasn't behaving as expected. He was showing remarkable strength.

Marbach wasn't ready to give up. Following what had been put in the revised script, he said, "Detective Hiller, I think we ought to get to the bottom of something before Lieutenant Litzman goes to the Gestapo Headquarters. I don't want to have any problems later. Why did you punch him around?"

Rolf followed the revised script. "Herr Police Inspector, the reason I punched this bastard was because he wouldn't provide information that would help us get in touch with his father in connection with a fraud investigation."

"That's a lie!" Litzman shouted. He spoke in a voice thick with anger while pointing at Rolf. "You hit me because I made a fool out of you."

Marbach turned toward Rolf. "Detective Hiller, tell me what happened."

Hearing his cue, Rolf repeated words Marbach had put in the revised script. "Herr Police Inspector, during my questioning of Lieutenant Litzman, I attempted to secure information that might help locate his father in connection with the fraud case being directed against his father. I explained how important it was, but he just started talking nonsense, silly lies in an attempt to get me all confused. When I realized what was going on and grabbed onto him, he insulted me for being a peasant. That bothered me, but the worst thing is that this young officer refused to answer my questions about the fraud case, and he wouldn't profess loyalty to National Socialism. I asked him if he was loyal to National Socialism, and he refused to answer that question. This rat is not a loyal National Socialist."

"You liar!" Litzman shouted at Rolf, his eyes clear and sharp. He stared defiantly at the two men standing in front of him. His anger was giving him strength.

Marbach followed the revised script as he said to Rolf, "Detective Hiller, I need to be absolutely clear on this point. Did Lieutenant Litzman refuse to declare his loyalty to National Socialism? I don't understand why a young man—one who has done a solid service for National Socialism by killing Fräulein Karen Mann—would refuse to acknowledge his loyalty to our cause."

Litzman pumped his head up and down in agreement.

Rolf followed the revised script as he said, "Herr Police Inspector, all this rat did was dispose of a fräulein who was a witness to what Lieutenant Neumayer did to that other Red slut. Kripo has no problem with him killing that fräulein, but he hasn't told us where to find her body. How do we know he really killed her? What if she shows up alive? If that happens, there'll be hell to pay."

"Yes, I know," Marbach said with a loud sigh.

Rolf shook his head as he continued with the revised script. "This young officer is not a good National Socialist. Not once during the time I questioned him did he proclaim his loyalty to the Führer."

Litzman gasped, filled his lungs, and bellowed his rage: "Liar! Liar! When I was questioned, I several times proclaimed my loyalty to the Führer and to National Socialism." He faced Marbach and gestured at Rolf. "This befoulment is telling lies. He is telling wicked lies."

The telephone began ringing, and, immediately, Litzman stopped shouting.

Marbach picked up the telephone. After listening for a few moments, he said into the telephone mouthpiece, "I'm almost finished here. I'll see you later." After saying that, he hung up.

Marbach exchanged a glance with Rolf. The glance was all that was needed to confirm to Rolf that the telephone call was from Commander Kaas and that the commander was ready to play his part.

The commander only knew the original script, but that didn't matter. His instructions had stated he should be on guard for changes in the script and follow any lead taken by Marbach.

Following the revised script, Rolf said to Marbach, "Lieutenant Litzman was one of those latecomers to National Socialism. He didn't become a National Socialist until just before the Anschluss. He still uses the disrespectful slang term 'Nazi' to refer to National Socialists."

Litzman, showing remarkable strength and vigor, shook with livid fury. When he spoke, he confirmed one of the items in genius Detective Mastny's report, the item that recorded an officer as having said that this intelligent young man had *an almost childlike faith in the efficacy of lies.*

"You are a lying pig. I never use the term Nazi. That word is absolutely not in my vocabulary."

Turning in his chair, Litzman pointed at finger at Rolf. "This pig asked a lot of stupid questions, all of them about the Hotel Capricorno. Again and again, I proclaimed my faith in the Führer. I never one time used the word Nazi to respond to your pig friend. I have never used that awful word. Never. Absolutely never. I only use the glorious words 'National Socialism.' And I never disparaged him for being a peasant. When I refused to answer his questions, the pig hit me. He knows that I have influence with SS Leader Kaltenbrunner, and he is frightened, so he makes up lies to defend his despicable conduct. I will trust the good judgment of SS Leader Kaltenbrunner to resolve this dispute."

Marbach turned toward Rolf and said, "Detective Hiller, do we have an automobile ready to take Lieutenant Litzman to Gestapo headquarters?"

"Yes, Herr Police Inspector. I will take him there myself. I've written up my report, with a carbon copy for the Gestapo. I included with my report a copy of the transcript of the interrogation. It was sent down here by messenger just a few minutes before you got here." Rolf paused, then said with calculated menace, "The transcript documents everything said during my interrogation of Lieutenant Litzman. We also have the voice recording. I will provide our copy of the voice recording to the Gestapo."

Litzman made a choking sound. *"Voice recording? Transcript?"*

"Yes," Marbach said tersely. "We make it a matter of routine to keep an open line between interrogation rooms and our rooms upstairs so we can have a transcript of what is spoken."

"Voice recording? Transcript?" Litzman was having trouble balancing himself in his chair.

Marbach took his time before saying to Rolf, "Let me see the transcript of your interrogation of this man."

Rolf handed Marbach several pieces of paper secured into a bound document.

Marbach slowly read what was written in the bound document, deliberately letting suspense build up before he said to Litzman, "You have lied. Why do you lie?" Marbach sighed with calculated dramatic effect before continuing. "I have tried to help you, but all you do is lie. This is the official transcript as recorded by our clerks upstairs from the voice recording. I don't see any expressions of loyalty to the Führer. Not even one. I find that hard to understand. And it is clear, contrary to what you've said, that you use the despicable word Nazi shamelessly. And you disparaged Detective Hiller for being a peasant. It is all in the transcript, and the transcript has been precisely copied from the voice recording."

With a dismissive gesture, Marbach tossed the transcript onto the table beside Litzman who seized it with eyes like those of a trapped animal. His face expressed horror as he read the record of everything he had said, and everything said to him. There was no mistaking the accuracy of what he was reading. There had to be a recording to produce anything as word-for-word accurate as what he was reading.

When Litzman finally stopped reading, he began wailing. "It isn't fair. It isn't fair. It isn't …"

"Do you recognize an accurate transcript of what you said?" Marbach's voice was loud and firm.

For a few moments, Litzman's eyes became like empty pebbles. He was like a man sinking beneath the water of a treacherous swamp. Then, suddenly, for no apparent reason at all, he began laughing.

Litzman, continuing to laugh, was tapping hidden reserves of resiliency. "Herr Police Inspector, I see no reason for you to be in a rush to get me out of here. I am perfectly willing to cooperate with a fraud investigation. If you want to find my idiot of a father, I can give you telephone numbers and addresses in Berlin. With my help, you will have no trouble finding my father."

Litzman stopped laughing and began smirking. "I had private V-men get information about my father. I will provide you that information. My father has a new mistress. So far, he has kept her a secret. She is a vile woman. No older than me. She used to work in a nightclub. That's where my decadent father found her six months ago. And now this nightclub woman lives like a grand lady—better than my mother. I hate my father, and I loathe his filthy Berlin whore."

Litzman kept looking stronger and stronger. Leaning forward in his chair, he said in an angry voice, "Herr Police Inspector, if you are going to find my father, you will need my assistance. I thought I was here only because of that stupid business at the Hotel Capricorno. Your associate, Detective Hiller, was very obnoxious. He was so obnoxious that I sought to antagonize him by forcing him to recognize how stupid he is. I made a mistake when I called him a peasant. I am a good National Socialist. Good National Socialists pay tribute to the peasantry. My loyalty to National Socialism is absolute and total. As proof of that loyalty, I am prepared to give you information that will enable the authorities in Berlin to quickly and securely put their hands on my father. If there hadn't been so much foolishness in the way Detective Hiller handled things, my father might already be in proper custody, but we will put that aside. The best thing for you to do is take me to my home where I can find the addresses and telephone numbers that will enable the people in Berlin to find my father. Shall we get started? Certainly you must agree that the only important thing now is to move quickly before my father's misdeeds get exposed in a way that will be bad for National Socialism."

Litzman was fully in control of himself. He even made a point of fussing with the knot of his tie.

Suddenly, a heavy fist began banging on the door. Marbach managed to look startled, as though he hadn't been wondering why Kaas was taking so long to show up. Hopefully, with Kaas flexibly picking things up from where they were at this moment, it would be possible to break down Litzman's remarkable resiliency. If not, all was lost.

The door swung open, and in strode Kaas holding several newspapers in his hand. It didn't matter that he didn't know what had happened with the interrogation of Litzman since he had been handed his copy of the script. He was ready to go. Making a point of sounding indignant, he said, "Police Inspector Marbach, this story is in all the newspapers. Direktor Litzman has fled to Paris with his mistress. He has taken with him funds swindled from Reichsmarschall Hermann Göring."

Kaas threw the newspapers onto the table and continued ranting. While the ranting continued, Litzman furtively edged a copy of the top newspaper to a position on the table where he could read the front-page article of the prestigious newspaper, the *Völkische Beobachter*.

Litzman yielded a loud, strangling sound. Horror registered on his face. There was a front-page article in the newspaper describing a scandal involving Director Heinrich Litzman. A couple of lines down from the heading was the word Federmann.

Federmann … Federmann

Kaas pointed dramatically at Litzman and recited dialogue from the original script like the words were his own. "I won't stand for any more stalling. I want this piece of tripe sent over to Gestapo Headquarters right now. The story is even worse in the French and English newspapers. The entire world is saying this is SS corruption. It is being called the Federmann scandal."

Litzman's eyes rolled back in his head as he slipped off his chair and collapsed onto the floor with a loud crash. As soon as he hit the floor, his body began to rebel. Stomach contents poured forth. Then there was choking and coughing and more pouring forth of stomach contents.

Marbach took a few steps, knelt down, took hold of the young man, grasped him firmly, and used a cloth to start a cleaning-up process, beginning with Litzman's face. After a few moments, he raised his hand toward Kaas, who, recognizing he was being cued, began shouting, "I want this traitor sent over to Gestapo headquarters right now. No more delays."

Marbach dropped the cloth and pulled Litzman to a standing position.

Kaas shouted at Litzman, "You were involved in your father's fraud. There is no hope for you now. If the Gestapo wants you, they are welcome to you. They have my encouragement to use your body as a target for their whips and their steel-cased truncheons."

"I don't know about any fraud," said Litzman with terror in his voice. His fright transformed him back to the way he had been when he was under the full effect of the thorn apple. His voice was like a whimpering child's. "The drumbeat. That beating drum. Can't someone stop it?"

Marbach clasped Litzman by the shoulders. "Do you want me to stop the drum?"

Kaas and Rolf exchanged a silent look: what drum?

"Oh, please ... please," cried Litzman.

Marbach didn't know anything about any drum, but he trusted his instincts as he said to the young man, "See, the drum is already a little quieter, isn't it?"

"Yes ...? Oh, yes ... yes, it is."

Marbach wiped places on Litzman's shirt where there was still evidence of the disaster with the poppy seed rolls. He spoke in a firm, confident voice. "The drum will keep getting quieter. Soon it will be silent."

Litzman's wildly dancing eyes conveyed gratitude.

Improvising from what was in the original script, Kaas bellowed, "We're just wasting time. This traitor belongs to the Gestapo now."

Litzman yielded a tormented cry. "Herr Police Inspector, please save me."

"I am in charge here," Kaas said to Litzman. "It is important to silence the Karen Mann girl, but I can't afford to have trouble with the Gestapo. They have too many ways of causing trouble. The Gestapo can have you."

Marbach spoke tentatively, as though he was slowly figuring something out. What he was doing had been set forth in the original script. He said, "If the Vienna police held Lieutenant Litzman on a capital crime charge—the murder of Fräulein Thimig—the way things operate, we would have an obligation to withhold him from the Gestapo. That's the law. If there is a capital murder charge, the Gestapo stays separate from what's going on. It is up to Vienna Kripo, exercising SS authority, to get the prisoner into the hands of the criminal courts. The Gestapo stays out of it. That is the way the Gestapo wants things. They don't want it said they are dominating criminal law."

Kaas opened his mouth, almost started to speak, but kept silent.

With his hands covering his face, Litzman stared through the spaces he spread between his fingers. "A murder charge? I ... I don't understand."

Kaas said to Marbach and Rolf, "If this young man showed willingness to help us, I suppose we might hold him on a murder charge."

Litzman's arms dropped to his sides. His entire body was shaking. "A murder charge?"

Marbach paused for a moment, shaking his head as though in resignation. When he spoke to Litzman, his voice was implacable. "The Gestapo will spare nothing. At the very least, they will beat the hell out of you, smash you up in the cruelest way imaginable. The only way Kripo can hold you is if you are under a murder charge. If you confess to a murder charge, we can keep you in our jurisdiction. We don't have to surrender persons charged with murder to the Gestapo until there is a hearing. It will take a day or two before there can be a hearing."

"But if I confess to killing the fräulein, they could hang me for murder."

Marbach shook his head. "By tomorrow, SS Leader Kaltenbrunner will be able to protect you from any ridiculous murder charge. You did nothing wrong, just delivered justice to a Red slut, but tonight, without a confession, all we can do is turn you over to the Gestapo. We have to follow procedure."

Litzman gasped. "I just don't know … I just … just don't know."

"You have to confess," Marbach said. "And you have to cooperate. That's the only way to keep you from the Gestapo."

"Cooperate …?"

"I don't like this," Kaas said in a voice loud enough for Litzman to hear.

Marbach grasped Litzman by the shoulders. "You are an army officer. Certainly, someone as intelligent as you knows that any officer facing a murder charge won't go into a court that isn't an army court. SS Leader Kaltenbrunner probably wouldn't want you to go into an army court, but even if he did, that would mean a military hearing, and, with absolute certainty, you would be exonerated. But right now—for tonight—no one can protect you from a horrible beating if you end up in the hands of the Gestapo, and I'm afraid Commander Kaas, who is in charge here, has already affirmed he will insist on turning you over to the Gestapo."

Kaas spoke with a resolute voice, repeating words from the original script. "My position from the beginning has been that unless this officer gives us what we must have, he goes to the Gestapo immediately."

Litzman gasped, choked on his words, desperately reached out with both hands to grasp the police inspector. "I don't want to be delivered to the Gestapo."

Marbach kept silent.

Kaas stepped forward a few steps but also kept silent.

Litzman's body made involuntary jerking movements.

Marbach spoke to Litzman in a voice that was low and hushed. "I don't want to see you turned over to the Gestapo and get what will certainly be a horrible beating, but what has been started can't be easily stopped."

Kaas stared intently.

Litzman whimpered as he allowed Marbach to lead him back to the table. He sat down in a chair, a helpless look on his face.

Marbach walked to the other end of the room.

Rolf moved up beside Kaas. Side by side, they walked to where Litzman was sitting helplessly in the chair.

Marbach had his back to Litzman and the others in the room. He looked over his shoulder as he said to Litzman in his all-knowing voice, "I want you to tell me where Karen Mann is. I know she is still alive. She must be killed. She can cause trouble. We can't take any chances. And we can't waste time. Maybe the Gestapo …"

"Karen? …"

"I don't understand why you won't tell us where she is. As long as she remains alive, she can cause great harm to the Reich."

"I don't …"

"Just tell me."

Litzman twisted in his chair, looked at Kaas and at Rolf, then focused his eyes on the figure with his back to him—Police Inspector Marbach.

Litzman's voice was a whimpering sound: "Police Inspector …"

Marbach turned around and stared at Litzman.

With a hopeless look and a choked voice, Litzman told where Fräulein Karen Mann could be found. He said she was in a shed in the basement of an enamelware storehouse within the Inner City, barely five minutes from police headquarters. He provided the address.

As soon as the address was spoken, Rolf headed for the door. He wanted to shout with joy. Who else but his colleague detective could have found a way to pull this thing off? He halted at the door when he heard Marbach address Litzman. "I want the letters, too."

"Letters?" Litzman looked confused.

Marbach was persistent. "You must give us the letters exchanged between Lieutenants Neumayer and Ossietsky."

"Why?" Litzman's agonized eyes scanned the walls and ceiling of the interrogation room.

"We have to protect the family of the colonel count. I told you that."

"But the letters ..."

The letters are a small thing, but I must have them." Marbach walked across the room, leaned over, and put his hands on Litzman's shoulders. He pushed hard with his fingers and whispered something into Litzman's ear.

A low moan escaped from Litzman's mouth. When he spoke, his voice sounded almost like a young boy's voice, high-pitched and vulnerable. "The letters are in a wall safe in the basement of the enamelware storehouse." Litzman stared hopefully at Marbach.

Rolf had heard enough. He left the room. The fräulein was alive. She was alive, and she could now be taken from a place of horror to a place where people would care for her. That had to be done as quickly as possible.

CHAPTER TWENTY-TWO

Two hours after Rolf went off to find Karen Mann, Commander Kaas was working in his office when his telephone rang. Leaning forward in his chair, he picked up the telephone and held the earpiece to his head.

Detective Rolf Hiller was on the line. After identifying himself, he used the formal form of address to Kaas and said, "We found Fräulein Karen Mann. We found her alive."

"Thank God!" said Kaas.

"She's alive and safe."

"What is her condition?"

"She wasn't raped." Rolf felt it was important to say that.

"Where is she?"

"I took her to the General Hospital. Her father and mother have been notified."

"Good."

"The fräulein can't stop crying, but she is alive and safe."

Kaas leaned forward and spoke earnestly into the telephone mouthpiece. "Do whatever you can for … for Fräulein Karen Mann and her family."

"Yes, Herr Commander. If I may ask, how close did we come? How long was it before SS Leader Kaltenbrunner showed up?"

"We had some luck. SS Leader Kaltenbrunner apparently went off on some other business. He didn't show up here until an hour ago. When he did finally show up, all he did was pick up Lieutenant Litzman and leave. He didn't ask me for a report, just picked up Lieutenant Litzman and left."

That was all there was to say. After concluding the telephone call, Kaas was filled with a need to share what he had learned from Rolf with the Comrade Soldier who had made the rescue of Fräulein Karen Mann possible. He left his office, walked up to the second floor in the building, went to Marbach's office, and knocked on the door. He heard the familiar voice tell whoever was outside to enter.

He stepped inside.

Sitting at his desk, the Tyrolean hat planted on his head, Marbach was fussing with a file folder.

"So you are still here," Kaas said.

"I was just getting ready to go to the enamelware storehouse," Marbach said while continuing to fuss with the file folder.

"I just got a telephone call from Detective Hiller. Fräulein Karen Mann is safe. She wasn't raped."

Marbach released a deep sigh and clicked off the small lamp over his desk. He stood up. Then he leaned down to lock his desk, reached down to the floor, and picked up a heavy metal crowbar.

Kaas understood about the crowbar. In the enamelware storehouse were the letters between Lieutenants Neumayer and Ossietsky. Those letters had to be retrieved out of a wall safe. The crowbar would be used to open the safe.

With no words spoken between them, Kaas and Marbach left the office together and walked down the stairs. Kaas shared the feelings of his Comrade Soldier.

At the bottom of the stairs, Marbach waved a weary arm and headed toward the front door.

Kaas stood still. He said, "That was excellent police work you performed. I am proud of the role I played in your script."

Marbach was at the front door. He paused for a moment.

"What a ruthless character you are," Kaas said. Then, having delivered what he regarded as a high compliment, he added, "I am proud to be your brother in the SS. You are what a good SS man should be: *ruthless but humane.*" Those words, vital to the SS, were spoken with deep feeling.

Marbach didn't reply. He pulled the door open and walked outside into the evening darkness.

Through the glass window on the door, Kaas watched the tall figure with the crowbar stand still for a moment and then disappear into the darkness.

Kaas was certain he had already delivered the highest possible compliment to his Comrade Soldier, but he felt the need to do something physically expressive. Standing alone in the hallway, he lifted his hand to the place just above his eye and delivered a soldier's hand salute. He held the salute for a few moments before letting his hand drop down to his side. Then, almost without thinking, he proceeded to the door, pulled it open, and looked outside. But his Comrade Soldier was not to be seen.

Kaas looked around, then edged farther outside the door. It was dark, and the air was fresh. He decided to have a smoke. He opened his cigarette case and cursed. All he had was Reemtsma. He lit one of the foul-tasting cigarettes and took a few quick puffs. While smoking, he rubbed his hand over his belt buckle with the powerful SS inscription on it: *My Honor is Loyalty.* He liked those words. He was thinking about how much those words meant to him when a woman appeared. At first, he paid little attention to the woman. She was far back from where he was standing. From behind her, a heavy wind was blowing against the wide brim of her floppy hat.

"Hello," the woman called out. She was an indistinct image in the street shadows.

"Hello," Kaas answered. "May I be of service?"

"I am looking for Police Inspector Karl Marbach. Is he inside?"

Kaas came to an erect posture and clicked his heels. "At your service, Fräulein. I am Commander Stephan Kaas. The police inspector has left to go on a job. He won't be back here tonight."

The woman stepped forward, moved out of the shadows, and came closer to the building, making it possible for Kaas to see her clearly. It was obvious to Kaas that the woman was no street walker. Vienna had beautiful prostitutes walking the streets, even more beautiful than those in Berlin. This woman had a bulky figure, black-rimmed eyeglasses, and a wide-brimmed, floppy hat. No streetwalker would look like her.

Kaas wondered what interest Karl Marbach might have in this woman. Was she one of his information sources? The woman moved closer before stopping. She was only a few steps away.

"Was it a busy day?" The woman spoke with a fetching lilt to her voice, a voice Kaas recognized as mostly Viennese, but with the heavy suggestion of another dialect, possibly Italian.

"It was definitely a busy day," Kaas said, aware of something distinctly interesting about the dowdy-looking woman with the black-rimmed eyeglasses. He was conscious of a need to share some of what had happened to him this day, even if the sharing would be with a stranger. He said, "The police inspector certainly did a good job today. If he hadn't done what he did, as well as he did it, I could have ended up a beautiful corpse."

Kaas paused. He wondered why he was talking so candidly to a stranger. But, after a brief moment, he continued with the candor. "Fräulein, why don't you come inside and leave a message. I think I know where the police inspector went. He had a chore to do. After he does his chore, maybe he will be going over to the General Hospital to see a young fräulein whose life he saved. She's in the hospital now. She is safe. The police inspector saved that young fräulein's life."

The woman with the floppy hat looked up the Ringstrasse. The wind blowing from behind her brought a marvelous flowery scent, like a bouquet of violets. As the flowery scent passed, a musky fragrance remained.

While Kaas breathed appreciatively, the woman delivered him a studied gaze from behind the black-rimmed eyeglasses.

Kaas stared at the odd, lumpy figure, the face, what there was to see of it behind the black-rimmed eyeglasses, and was surprised to realize he was finding the woman fetching. There was, of course, the fragrance. He wondered if perhaps the fragrance explained why this woman was making such a strong impression on him.

Kaas said, "If you would grant me the honor, Fräulein, it would be my pleasure to buy you a drink. I am new to Vienna, and I could use some female company. Maybe we could go to the Alpen Café. Maybe …"

Kaas felt his words freeze in his throat as the woman lifted a delicate hand to her distressed face. "Oh, Commander Kaas, whatever must you think of me? … And just because I dared to say hello to you." There was a loud gasping sound, then a choked cry. "Do you really believe a sweet little lass like myself would go to a coffeehouse with a married man?"

Kaas flushed red. This woman, whoever she was, knew he was married.

"I didn't mean to suggest anything improper, Fräulein ..."

The woman covered her face with both hands, and her body began making a series of jerking movements. She appeared to be crying.

Kaas blurted an apology, but the woman had already backed up several paces. In the next instant, she spun around and began fleeing up the Ringstrasse with her hands clasped onto her wide-brimmed, floppy hat. *"I'm a sweet little lass!"* she cried. *"I'm a sweet little lass!"*

"Oh my God!" Kaas shook his head in bafflement as the woman continued running up the Ringstrasse. *What was that all about?* he asked himself. She wasn't a good-looking woman, even if somehow or other she did convey an explicit femininity.

"Oh, hell," Kaas murmured. He lifted the Reemtsma cigarette for one final puff but rejected the idea and threw the foul thing away.

He took a deep breath and detected a trace of the musky fragrance left by the woman. He peered up the Ringstrasse, but the woman had disappeared. No point thinking about her. For him, one thing was certain: he was going to be a long time in Vienna, and that meant he needed to find a woman in this city. There was no way to bring his wife down from Berlin for more than a few days at a time, and he needed more female company than that would provide. He decided to enlist Karl Marbach to help him find a woman, telling himself that, after all, Comrade Soldiers look out for each other. It wouldn't be unreasonable for him to ask Karl to help him find a sexually desirable woman to keep company with in Vienna.

Kaas took another deep breath. It pleasured him to think that Karl and he were Comrade Soldiers. He affirmed that in Adolf Hitler's Greater Reich nothing would ever break their Comrade Soldier bond.

CHAPTER TWENTY-THREE

It was late at night when Marbach finally returned to police headquarters. He placed the letters written by Lieutenants Neumayer and Ossietsky in a safe place inside a storage room. Then he left the building and headed toward the Ringstrasse.

There was an ache in his stomach. In war and sometimes in police work, there had been many times when he'd had to do bad things in order to keep worse things from happening, and afterward, there was always this ache. When he was a young mountain soldier, older soldiers had explained to him that the ache was "soldier's guilt" and that the worst thing was to not feel soldier's guilt after doing things that sometimes you had to do when there was battlefield fighting. He had been told by the older soldiers to accept his soldier's guilt.

Marbach believed that even though Litzman was evil, and what had been done had made it possible to save Karen Mann, the worst thing now would be to feel no guilt, have no ache. He had done a lot of lying, and the business with the thorn apple had been cruel. He didn't regret what he had done, would do it all again if circumstances warranted it, but he felt it was only natural for him to feel soldier's guilt.

At a fast walking pace, he soon got to the Ringstrasse, and a few minutes later, he arrived at the Alpen Café. Stepping through the front door, he made his way past several men talking to one another in the narrow corridor. He slowed his pace just enough to pass conventional greetings. At the end of the corridor, he pushed open a door, edged forward a few steps, and stood behind the fencelike iron railing from where he was able to look down at the tables and the people below. Far in the rear, despite the effect of the mirrors, he could see Constanze sitting at their table, the table always reserved for them. Her hands were clasped around a champagne glass.

Although eager to be with Constanze, Marbach walked slowly down the eight steps and stopped in front of the one-armed cashier. As always, the initial greeting between them began with formality. The ritualistic formality was a matter of private humor between them.

"Hail, Herr Police Inspector."

"Hail, Herr Cashier."

"You are late tonight, Herr Police Inspector."

"Yes, Herr Cashier. I am late. I see that Constanze is already here."

"She has been here for more than an hour." The cashier's empty sleeve was neatly tucked into the side pocket of his jacket. The arm had been lost in 1916, in a battle so unimportant it had no name.

Marbach turned slightly and looked around. Nothing captured his interest. He faced the one-armed cashier, switched to informal Viennese speech, remarked about the weather, and then asked about the cashier's wife. "Is Frau Fellgiebel doing well?"

"My wife is in an unhappy mood, so she makes my life miserable," replied the cashier.

Marbach said with teasing banter, "Tell Johanna that I am at her service."

The cashier answered with pretended indignation, "You are at my wife's service?"

"Better me than a stranger."

"If you were a rich man, that might make sense, but a police inspector's salary is less than my own." The cashier laughed at his own humor.

Marbach shook his head. "You bring up the subject of money. You sound like a pimp."

"So now you call me a pimp."

"I have always suspected you had that proclivity."

"Proclivity?" The cashier frowned. "What does that strange word mean?"

"I'm not sure. I learned it from Constanze."

The cashier grinned. "She was probably using it to call you a pervert."

"You pimp."

"You pervert."

Both men laughed.

While continuing to laugh, Marbach asked an important question. "What sort of mood is Constanze in?"

"She is like the Constanze of the time before those Nazi bastards made their home in Vienna." Always careful to not be overheard, Marbach and the cashier frequently expressed to each other disparagement of National Socialism and everything connected with National Socialism.

Marbach inquired about the owner of the Alpen Café. "Where is Franz?"

"In the kitchen."

Marbach inquired about Franz's wife. "And Lena?"

The one-armed man gestured with the only arm he had.

Both men stared toward the middle of the coffeehouse where Lena was moving from table to table. Countless times the two men had stood side by side admiring the wife of their friend, Franz. Lena was a woman to look at with appreciation. Her face and figure belonged on a painting. Franz wasn't with them, so they had to be silent in their appreciation. Only when Franz was present did they ever verbalize appreciation while staring at the wonderment that was Lena.

After a few moments, Marbach cast one final appreciative look at Lena, bade farewell to the cashier, and headed for the table where Constanze was waiting. He was conscious of the ache in his stomach as he edged past crowded tables. At one table after another, he exchanged greetings with friends, but he didn't allow himself to be unduly slowed. His eyes were on Constanze, and he was pleased to see she was staring back at him, smiling engagingly. There was no trace of the melancholy. That was important. Also important was that she was wearing the dress of emerald green, a beautiful dress that was one of his favorites partly because of the way it showed off her bare shoulders. It was going to be a grand thing, the two of them sitting together. To make things perfect, she wasn't wearing her elbow-length white gloves. Her marvelous arms were bare.

He imagined how odd Constanze must have looked when she first arrived at the café tonight, with her bulky coat, the wide-brimmed, floppy hat, and those ridiculous black-rimmed eyeglasses. She never allowed him to walk with her after a performance on stage unless they were going to go to a theater party, or a meeting with an old friend, or a collection of old friends. After being on stage, whether a matinee or an evening performance, she usually wanted to have a certain amount of time alone for herself. She very much liked walking by herself to the Alpen Café after being on stage.

He wished he had been here early enough to have seen her entrance. He always enjoyed seeing her arrivals at the Alpen Café after she finished a performance at the Volkstheater. In the place above the stairs, she would pull off her eyeglasses. There were many different ways she had of taking off those spectacles. Then, before going down the eight stairs, she would remove her floppy hat and take off her ill-fitting coat. Never did she take off her coat with any sort of flourish, but always with calculated poise. Most women made an uninteresting activity out of taking off a coat, but not Constanze. And when she got to the bottom of the stairs, she would pass her hat and coat to the one-armed cashier and walk toward the table where he was waiting. She never walked with female exaggeration, but always with feminine assurance. To get to the table might take her only a few moments, or it might require an exceedingly long time, depending on how many cheeks she kissed, how long verbal exchanges with friends lasted.

Marbach recalled an incident he had not witnessed, but which had become one of the favorite stories their friends liked to talk about. As the story was told, with greater or lesser detail depending on which friend was doing the telling, one night about three months ago, a stranger, a boorish character, had reached out and grabbed at Constanze when she walked past his table, and, in the instant that the man put hands on her, she spun around, pushed her elbow into his face, and knocked him backward off his chair onto the floor. Then, as all of the storytellers delighted to tell, Constanze had purred, "Oh, I am so very sorry. My silly, little elbow must have accidentally bumped into your strong, manly face."

There was more to the story. When the man jumped to his feet and cursed her, she cursed him back expressively in Italian and aggressively thrust forward a clenched fist. That had caused onlookers throughout the café to applaud until, with a look of perplexity, the boorish character realized there was nothing for him to do but pay his bill and leave.

Marbach was glad he hadn't been present when the incident took place. He might have spoiled things, ruined a perfectly marvelous story by barging in where he wasn't needed.

Right now, there were a few more steps for him to take before he would be at the table where Constanze was waiting. On the table was a bucket with a bottle of champagne buried in ice. In her hand was a half-emptied glass.

He took the final steps to the table. Then, as he usually did when Constanze was in her chair waiting for him, he stood erect for a moment, bowed at the waist, moved around the table, placed himself behind her, put his hand on the back of her neck, drew her head upward, and kissed her on the forehead.

Remaining behind Constanze, he stared down at her uplifted face and said, "I am sorry for being late. I had some work to do." He stared at the marvelous neat bun of hair wrapped on top of her head.

"Anything important?" There was mischief in the upward lifted eyes.

"Just some work I had to do." Marbach stood over Constanze and watched while she moved her hand up to touch the place on her neck where his hand had just been. The consciously feminine gesture had its calculated effect on him. He let out a breath, then walked around the table, and sat down. He was aware of the amber eyes staring intently as he withdrew the bottle of champagne from the ice-filled bucket, topped off her glass, and filled his own.

Constanze put the glass to her mouth, swallowed, and stared at Marbach. "You never tell me about your work except when you help my friends. Just this one time, tell me what you did today."

Marbach felt a tug in his gut but managed to keep from showing discomfort. "I did nothing today worth talking about." For him, the truth was that he had dirtied himself today by the things he had done to save Karen Mann. He had dirtied himself by using thorn apple. He would do it all again, if it came to that, but this wasn't anything he wanted to talk about with Constanze. Not now, not ever.

Marbach reached for Constanze's hand and was disappointed when she pulled it away. He pretended the withdrawal of her hand wasn't important. Fussing with the buttons on his suit, he said, "Maybe I did something cruel today. Aren't you one of those who is always critical of the cruel things we policemen sometimes do?"

"I have absolutely no tolerance for cruelty. It is a vice. The worst of all the vices. I hate cruelty cruelly."

Puzzled by what Constanze had said, Marbach leaned forward. "Do you really think cruelty is the worst vice?"

"Absolutely!"

"Hate cruelty cruelly? Is that something from philosophy? Which philosopher? Which one?"

"Michel de Montaigne, the great French philosopher."

"I've read some of Montaigne. His work—parts of it anyway—can be found in coffeehouses and lots of places."

Constanze made a huffing sound. "You might try going to a library."

"I have read books. I have read Boethius, but mostly I have been educated by what I have read in cafés and coffeehouses."

"I've said it before. I say it again. Pity the poor police inspector who never got to go to college."

"Who is being cruel now?"

Constanze sat up straight in her chair and, after a long moment, took a deep breath.

Marbach decided to try to change the subject. "How was the theater tonight?"

"It was awful. The play is terrible ... but something good happened afterward."

Marbach wondered what Constanze meant by that. He made another unsuccessful attempt to grasp her hand, but she pulled it away and placed both of her hands together in her lap.

Marbach settled himself in his chair. "It may be a bad play, but you never give a bad performance."

"It is a bad play, and tonight I was terrible in it. Now tell me what you did today."

Marbach put a bland look on his face. "There was a bad case, but I think we got it all cleared up."

"Is that all you have to say?" One of Constanze's eyebrows arched upward.

"You know I don't like talking about police work with you."

"I want to hear what you did today. Is that unreasonable? Is it?"

Marbach felt angry, but he held his anger in check. "Do you really want to hear details about what I did today? Do you want to hear about cruelty? About brutality?"

"I want to hear about the good deed you did today."

"You don't know what you are talking about."

"You saved a young fräulein's life today. She is in the hospital. It is awful of you to be unwilling to share that good deed with me."

Marbach wondered how Constanze had found out about what had happened. After deliberating for a moment, he said, "I wish you hadn't found out what happened. You only know the outcome, not the way it was done. I have no regrets about what I did, but it was a dirty piece of business. And I don't intend to discuss it, not a bit. I am not—"

Constanze reached out and locked hands with Marbach. The amber eyes stared. "Tomorrow I shall go to the hospital. I will find this fräulein, and we shall talk together. We shall talk about the good deed done today by you."

Marbach felt worn out. Maybe Constanze didn't know Karen Mann's name, but knowing Constanze, it was a certainty that tomorrow she would find the young woman in the General Hospital, and the two of them would talk. Yes, they would talk, but they would only talk about how things had turned out. They didn't know how it had been done, the cruelty involved.

While Marbach fussed in his chair, Constanze released her grip on his hands and reached into her handbag. With an impish look, she withdrew a small box of chocolate bonbons, took one out, and handed it to him.

He studied the bonbon and said, "I haven't finished the bonbons you left in my pockets this morning."

Constanze made a laughing sound. "Thank goodness the chocolate policeman hasn't run out of bonbons."

Marbach leaned toward Constanze and took pleasure from simply being able to see her face. There was a room upstairs in the coffeehouse where they would finish this evening. He hoped it wouldn't be long before they were in that room.

But Constanze wasn't ready yet. Marbach could tell that by looking at her. He pondered for a moment, then brought up what ought to be a pleasant subject. "I forgot to tell you, I met a friend of yours in Switzerland. His name is Josef Swoboda. I didn't know who he was. He just came up and introduced himself to me. After we talked for a bit, he asked me to pass on his greeting to you. He's a musician of some sort. He said he's coming to Vienna in the next day or two. I told Herr Swoboda—"

Constanze interrupted. "Josef? Oh … I haven't seen Josef Swoboda in ages. He's a marvelous musician. Is Josef really coming to Vienna?"

"I imagine he's already here. He said he'll be getting in contact with you."

Constanze's eyes were wide open, expressive.

Marbach stared appreciatively at the wide-open amber eyes while providing more details of the meeting he'd had with someone named Josef Swoboda.

While he talked, Constanze enthused about the prospect of seeing her friend again. When he paused, she said, "I'm so glad you like Josef. My God! I haven't seen him in ages. He's such a grand fellow. And a marvelous talent."

On the spur of the moment, Marbach introduced another name. "Do you remember someone named Thomas Mastny?"

Constanze shook her head. "No … I don't think I know that name."

"From years ago."

"I'm sorry. I don't remember the name."

"Thomas Mastny is now a police inspector. He is a good man. He has had a troubled life. Now he is in a wheelchair. He knew your father and you years ago. He calls your father the man of the deed."

Constanze leaned forward. "I don't remember anyone named Thomas Mastny. Do you remember Clara Wolff?"

Marbach just barely managed to not wince. Clara Wolff was one of his former lovers. Constanze had identified another of his former lovers. How many times was she going to do this, identify another of his various former lovers? Keeping his eyes lowered, he answered, "Yes, of course I remember Clara."

"She asked me to pass on her best wishes to you. She is now very properly married."

"Any man who has Clara as his wife is truly blessed."

With a smile, Constanze raised her glass. That was a signal. It meant that there would be a playful ritual, one performed by them countless times while sitting at their table in the Alpen Café. In a theatrical voice, Constanze delivered the champagne toast from *Die Fledermaus.*

"His Majesty, King Champagne the First."

Marbach smiled and returned the toast.

"Her Majesty, Queen Champagne the First."

Constanze lowered her head, then lifted it upward as she half-sang and half-whispered words from *Die Fledermaus*, the great comic opera of riotous extravagance and glorious nonsense: "First a kiss, then a du ..." She continued the liquid refrain owed to Johann Strauss, repeating the flood of *"du's,"* the German word used to address close friends, until the *"du's"* became the single word *"Duidu."*

"Duidu."

"Duidu" again and again.

Only after Marbach finally echoed *"Duidu"* was Constanze satisfied. She silently closed her eyes. One more time the playful ritual was completed.

After a moment, Constanze opened her eyes.

Marbach stared into the amber eyes. "You are pixilated. It is an embarrassment for a respected member of the Vienna police to be in the company of an inebriated representative of the Vienna stage."

"Don't trash the Vienna theater, you boob." Constanze clasped her hands around the stem of her champagne glass.

Marbach held tight to his champagne glass.

Constanze studied her wrist watch for a moment, then raised a finger. The lifted finger was a signal.

Such a signal! thought Marbach. In a lover's wager a couple of weeks ago, Constanze had won the right to have three separate times when she could tell him of her love for him while he had to keep silent. From the beginning of their relationship, there had been lover's wagers. Usually the penalty for losing a lover's wager was modest. Whatever the penalty, it was always agreed to beforehand. Usually the penalty called for doing a small chore, some trivial thing. But for this particular lover's wager, Constanze had introduced an unusual penalty. With the raising of her finger, starting at this moment, for five minutes, he was forbidden to say or do anything. He wasn't allowed to speak a word, wasn't allowed to kiss her or touch her for five minutes. He was obligated, on his honor, to try as hard as he could to keep from showing any reaction on his face while, for five minutes, Constanze had total liberty to tell him without interruption why she loved him and how much she loved him. This was the second time she had collected on the lover's wager. There would be one more time before this lover's wager would be fully paid.

Just nonsense, Marbach had thought before the first time Constanze started collecting on this lover's wager. He had thought it was just foolishness, but he had quickly learned that sometimes love can be very uniquely communicated when one lover speaks and the other lover is required to keep silent and simply listen.

Like the first time she had collected on this lover's wager, Constanze spoke tentatively at first, but quickly became fervent as she told him what was solid and enduring about her love. By the conditions set by Constanze, Marbach could never mention at any later time the things told during one of these five-minute sessions.

Finally, Constanze stopped talking. The five minutes were up. There was, however, one additional feature of this lover's wager. Until she gave permission, Marbach wasn't allowed to speak, couldn't hug her, couldn't tell her how much he loved her. He couldn't do anything that might break the mood that had been created between them for another ten minutes, either another ten minutes or until Constanze signaled that everything was back to normal, whichever came first.

Even more than the first time, there was a lot for Marbach to think about. He hoped that sometime, hopefully soon, he would win a lover's wager that would have the same penalty for Constanze that this lover's wager had for him.

Marbach looked up when Constanze indicated she was ready to go upstairs to their private room in the Alpen Café.

Faithful to the lover's wager, Marbach spoke not a word while they both got up from the table, and he followed her up the stairway. Halfway up the stairs, he pulled at the bun in her hair. Without a glance behind, she loosened her butter-yellow cummerbund and expressed pleasure when he pulled it free.

At the top of the stairway, Marbach followed Constanze into a room. This was their room in the Alpen Café, their very private place. She stretched out on the bed without removing more of her clothing. While he stared at her, she smiled the smile that always touched him deeply, a very special smile, the smile of the sweet, little lass. He moved up to the bed, and began undressing her. Undressing women was an act he always performed with confidence.

Lifting her finger, Constanze signaled that this second penalty for losing the lover's wager was completed. Marbach was permitted to speak.

There was brief talk between them followed by intimate lovemaking, then, after that, more talk, more words. Nothing in the conversation was explicitly related to what had been told during the five minutes when words explaining Constanze's love had been spoken.

Marbach had started to drift off to sleep when he was awaked by words murmured in his ear: "You are a very fine man, Herr Police Inspector. That was a good thing you did for the fräulein today. That commander of yours was impressed. Why couldn't you? ... I wish ... oh, I just wish ..."

Marbach made a grunting sound, but before he could become fully coherent, Constanze said, "Go to sleep, if you must, my love. You don't like speaking to me about certain things that you do, but at this moment, we are closer than we have ever been, and I don't want what I am feeling to end for me yet."

Constanze maneuvered her hands firmly and expertly in a manner that brought Marbach to a state of full alertness. He started once again to engage in intimate lovemaking. "You are beautiful, so beautiful," he whispered.

Constanze pushed at him with one of her hands. "Beautiful? You have seen the scars on my back. Are my scars beautiful?"

Marbach didn't care about the scars on Constanze's body. They were shrapnel wounds, a pattern of scars low down on her back. The largest of the shrapnel scars were two red patches, each almost the size of the palm of his hand. Of one thing he was absolutely certain, the scars didn't diminish in the smallest way Constanze's enthralling femininity.

Constanze said, "We have never talked about my ugly scars or how I got them during the 1934 uprising. You have never wanted to talk about my ugly scars. From the beginning of the time we have had together, I knew which side you were on, and you knew which side I was on in 1934. But we never really talked about it, not really. You never wanted to get into it."

"Your scars aren't ugly. Your body is beautiful. And we don't need to talk about the 1934 uprising." Marbach was about to tell Constanze how impossible it was for him to see any ugliness connected with her when she suddenly jerked upright on the bed, twisted around, and positioned herself so that she was sitting on his chest, one leg on either side of his body. Her nude body glowed in the reflected light from a streetlamp. He stared appreciatively at the perspiration on her nude breasts.

Astride him, Constanze's voice dropped to a low whisper. "We should have talked this out a long time ago. I was wrong to follow your lead and not talk about 1934, but I am going to talk about it now, and you will listen."

Marbach didn't see any reason to talk about 1934, but before he could protest, Constanze said, "We both know I was with the Schutzbund and that you fought on the side of the police and the army." Her voice became intense. "Your artillery smashed us. We were pounded into rubble. The government forces, the army units, and the police crushed us. You demolished us with your howitzers and machine guns and grenades. And those little boxes that enthusiastic citizens threw at us. Little boxes that made noise, exploded, and smashed up things made of wood, or metal, or ... flesh."

"Sweetheart," Marbach managed to say. He wanted Constanze to stop talking about 1934. He never wanted to talk about 1934 with her.

Constanze placed a hand firmly on his mouth.

Marbach stared up at Constanze.

For a long moment, Constanze was silent. When she did speak, it was with devastating force. "I was in the Ottakring Arbeiterheim when it fell. I didn't make it to the sewers like most of the others—the ones who escaped. I remember seeing the young boy who threw one of those paper box bombs at me. He was just a youth—a beardless youth. He howled with the joy of a little boy at play when he spotted me. Then he threw that ugly thing like he was throwing a toy on a child's playground. For me, there was noise and pain, and I found myself lying in dirt gasping for breath. I should have been killed. My mind told me I was dead. There was pain and blackness. And helplessness. I began hearing such awful sounds as no one can imagine. And I wondered if my personal horror was going to last for eternity. I wondered if I was experiencing what death was going to be for me for all eternity."

Constanze took a breath and then continued. "I don't know how my friends got me to the worker's hospital. Later, I was told I kept asking for my papa. He was in charge of the defenders of the Goethe Hof. I was still in the general hospital when I learned my papa was wounded at the Goethe Hof and then captured."

For a moment, Marbach thought that it was going to be impossible for Constanze to go on. She slumped down, but he secured her with his hands and pushed her upward. Holding her firmly by her waist, he felt her strength return. He supported her in an upright position astride him.

Constanze spoke in a gasping, choked voice of things from 1934 she had never before spoken to Marbach about. Of course, he had seen the official police records, but for the first time, he was hearing her tell what had happened.

"They hanged my papa. They hanged my papa. Chancellor Dollfuss had my papa—and others—hanged. My papa was carried to the gallows in a stretcher. My mama went to the hanging. She was fearless, my mama. They couldn't keep her out. She bullied her way to the place where they were keeping Papa just before they led him up the steps to the gallows."

Constanze lifted her head and uttered a cry, but quickly the cry became words. "My papa ... before he died, my papa told Mama to go back to Italy. He said that with the Socialist forces destroyed, Austria was doomed, but maybe Mama would be safe in Italy. Safer than Hitler's fascist Austria was Mussolini's fascist Italy."

Constanze caught her breath. "You don't know what I am trying to tell you."

"I do know what you are telling me."

Astride Marbach, Constanze became rigid, but her head dropped to her chest. After a moment, she lifted her head and said, "It was dangerous for Mama, but she came to tend me in the hospital. She took care of me, then ..."

"Sweetheart, don't torment yourself."

Constanze's voice became almost a shriek as she told more of the horror. "Fatherland Front thugs went to Mama's apartment building, and they threw her out the window, onto the street below. They threw Mama out onto the cobblestones. My mama's body was broken on those cobblestones."

Marbach continued to hold Constanze upright on top of him. He had read about the fate of her father and mother in police files, but they had never talked about this before. That was the way he had wanted it to be. Now, listening to her speak, the details penetrated him to his core.

"Mama's body broken on the cobblestones," cried Constanze. She arched her body, twisted around, got free of Marbach's arms, then grabbed for him, cupped his face with her hands and said, "My wonderful man. My wonderful, wonderful man. You are a brave man. A hero. But you don't know how evil this National Socialism is. It is worse than the Austrian fascism that killed my father and my mother. It is totally about cruelty, about making people feel good about being cruel."

Constanze's voice became a gasping sound. "And don't you dare tell me about Plato. It is wrong to hide behind a wall and wait for evil times to pass. I had to shriek against this evil! I had to do something. Even if it wasn't rational, I had to do something to confront this evil. Just for myself I had to do something! I know it wasn't rational. But … oh, my love, my brave man, my hero …"

Exhausted, Constanze collapsed on top of Marbach, her body heaving in gasping sobs. She cried for more than an hour before finally dropping off to sleep.

Marbach didn't sleep at all that night.

CHAPTER TWENTY-FOUR

At breakfast the next morning, Marbach ate the terrible eggs Constanze prepared. He ate everything on his plate.

After finishing breakfast, he got up from the table, went to the doorway of the flat, turned, faced Constanze, and said, "Give me a kiss that will last until dinner tonight."

She moved forward. They hugged tightly and spoke words of love. There was no talk of the world they lived in, only words expressing their love for each other.

When the love talk finally came to a close, Marbach delivered one final kiss, left the flat, and caught a streetcar to police headquarters. When he got inside the building, he became aware that the ache that had seemed to disappear last night had returned. But it wasn't bad, just a little troublesome. He stood for a moment in the hallway, checked the message rack, found nothing of interest to him, and went to the office of Commander Kaas. The head secretary sounded almost friendly when he said the commander had come down with a bad cold and wouldn't be coming into work until tomorrow at the earliest. Marbach noted that the head secretary wasn't speaking in the nasal-sounding voice.

While proceeding up the stairway to his office, Marbach speculated that the young head secretary must be in a happy mood. After settling himself behind his desk, he aggressively addressed himself to a desk load of hard, demanding paperwork.

Late in the morning, Marbach went down to the basement, into one of the interrogation rooms, and questioned a sophisticated criminal about a complicated crime. His interrogation yielded nothing helpful.

When it was time for lunch, Marbach left his office. He walked to the Alpen Café, opened the street door, went into the long, dark corridor, and encountered four men with familiar faces chatting amicably among themselves. He exchanged greetings with each of the men, then moved on. From behind the door at the end of the corridor, he could hear familiar Viennese sounds of music and happy chatter. The music was Schrammel—the very specialized Viennese folk music. Like all good Schrammel music, it was being played with a touch of sadness. Not too much sadness; mostly the music conveyed to listeners that life can be sweet.

Marbach opened the corridor door, stood for a moment behind the fencelike iron railing, and looked down at the tables below. Of course, Constanze was not to be seen. He had nursed hope, but only rarely did Constanze go to the Alpen Café at this time of day.

After a few moments, Marbach made his way down the eight steps, passed a greeting and a few words with the one-armed cashier, and then made eye contact with the leader of the musicians, Reinhard Delbreuck, a tall, thin man.

Delbreuck set down the concertina he was using for the Schrammel music, smiled, and walked over to the unoccupied piano. Marbach watched while Delbreuck made a tentative movement with his fingers across the keyboard, then thrust a finger in his direction and lifted his hand to the other musicians. Three chords were promptly struck off in rapid succession: E, then E sharp, and finally F sharp. The chords were like three champagne corks being popped. The three chords were followed by a flow of bubbling music.

In a playful tease directed at Marbach, the musicians began playing "Hymn to Champagne," the opening to *Die Fledermaus*. While the music continued, feeling good, Marbach made his way to the rear of the coffeehouse, to his private table, and sat down.

Several minutes later, he was eating his lunch when the musicians began playing one of his favorite songs from *Die Fledermaus*. Throughout the coffeehouse, people joined in the singing. He became thoughtful when familiar lines were sung:

> *Happy is the person who forgets,*
> *What can't be changed anyway.*

He ate slowly, thoughtfully, while *Die Fledermaus* continued. He knew his life was good. He resolved to try to forget Nazi things he couldn't change.

CHAPTER TWENTY-FIVE

After spending an hour in the Alpen Café, Marbach returned to police headquarters. As he worked on police paperwork, he found it difficult to concentrate. He kept thinking about Constanze.

He worked until late that night, when, finally, weary with fatigue, aware of an ache that was present but not too bothersome, he left police headquarters and went to the Alpen Café.

He opened the café door and walked to the end of the long, dark corridor before coming to a halt. Behind the corridor door, he could hear Constanze singing. She had finished her performance tonight at the Volkstheater, and, for the first time in weeks, she was singing in the Alpen Café.

Marbach opened the corridor door, moved up to the iron railing, and looked downward. Constanze was standing beside the piano, her soprano voice making mischief out of an old Viennese song. Reinhard Delbreuck was skillfully working the piano keys. A new man had joined the other musicians. The new man was Josef Swoboda, the fine fellow who had been in Switzerland a couple of days ago.

Marbach walked down the eight stairs, exchanged a silent greeting with the one-armed cashier, and walked to his table while listening to Constanze sing.

He was sitting at his table when, after finishing a song, Constanze nodded toward Delbreuck, who promptly addressed himself to the keyboard. At first, it sounded like a trivial waltz tune was being played, but Delbreuck looked up at Constanze, nodded his head, then started playing a series of notes on the piano that quickly evolved into the famous Oscar Straus song celebrating the chocolate soldier.

Constanze began singing:

> To tell the truth, I never knew
> there were heroes such as you.

Josef Swoboda stepped forward. His rich baritone joined with Constanze in a duet. The two singers continued with the song, finally chorusing:

> In battle I am a soldier,
> A chocolate soldier man.

Throughout the Alpen Café, patrons clapped their hands in musical unison. Standing at his post near the eight stairs, the cashier was slapping his one good hand against his thigh in time to the music.

The song came to its end, but the performance wasn't over—not yet. Delbreuck sat planted behind the piano. He did a piano flourish, and fresh applause broke out but quickly stopped. The patrons in the café realized a different song from the same operetta was about to be sung.

While Delbreuck began the piano introduction, Marbach looked up from his table. Franz and Lena were approaching. He stood up and kissed both of Lena's heavily calloused, very precious hands. His two friends edged into seats beside him. Franz was holding a tray upon which there was a bottle of Armagnac—marvelous French brandy—and four glasses. Franz set down the tray and poured Armagnac into the four glasses. The fourth glass was for Constanze when she would be joining them.

Constanze, her feet planted firmly beneath her, was singing in her full, rich soprano. The coffeehouse became very quiet. Everyone sat in hushed appreciation while Constanze lifted her arms and sang out the most loved of the Oscar Straus chocolate soldier songs:

> *Come! Come! I love you only.*
> *My heart is true.*
> *Come! Come! My life is lonely.*
> *I long for you.*

As the song neared its conclusion, Delbreuck went first to slow waltz tempo on the piano and then quickly built toward the aching, ascending climax. This was the difficult part of the song for any singer, but Constanze sang purely:

> *Come! Come! I love you only.*
> *My heart is true.*
>
> *Come! Come! My life is lonely.*
> *I long for you.*

Marbach felt Lena dig her fingers fiercely into his arm while Constanze continued to successfully match the escalating pace set by Delbreuck. Finally, there was the final line:

> *Come! Come! I love you only.*
> *Come … hero … mine.*

The song was over. The people in the café took a collective breath while Constanze stepped forward and bowed. Quickly, men at various tables—and many of the women, too—got to their feet, shouted approval, and called for the song to be sung again.

Constanze looked hopelessly at Delbreuck, received nodding agreement, and again began singing the song from the beginning.

Marbach wondered if any of the National Socialists sitting in the café cared that the composer of that beloved song was the Straus who spelled his name with one final S, not the double S of the more famous Strauss family. The recent ban against music by Jewish artists was being imperfectly enforced in the Alpen Café. As for Oscar Straus, the old composer, the one who in his youth had been instrumental in establishing Vienna as the operetta center of the world, that old man was somewhere among countless other Jewish refugees who had fled Vienna in recent weeks.

There were calls for more Oscar Straus songs to be sung, and Constanze sang them. Only Oscar Straus songs until, finally, Swoboda stepped up beside her. To enthusiastic applause, she took her bow and walked away from the piano while Swoboda picked up his concertina and began a series of conventional Schrammel songs.

Still being applauded, Constanze made her way toward the table where her friends were waiting, but it took a while for her to get to where she was headed. People at one table, then another, and yet another made claims for her attention.

Finally, she arrived at the table where Marbach and Franz and Lena were waiting. Marbach and Franz stood up. Franz took Constanze by the shoulders and kissed her tenderly on the mouth. She wrapped her arms around him and hugged tightly.

While Constanze and Franz enthusiastically kissed and hugged, Marbach glanced at Lena. Her beautiful face was aglow with happiness.

Constanze finished kissing and hugging Franz, leaned across the table, kissed Lena on both cheeks, and then turned and faced Marbach. He pulled her into his arms, kissed her on the mouth, and guided her into her chair.

When everyone was seated, the four friends touched glasses. Then there was conversation about nothing important, just a sharing of good feelings. The sharing lasted almost an hour until, at the front of the café, Reinhard Delbreuck played an odd chord on the piano and Constanze put her hand on Marbach's arm. She was being beckoned.

For the last song of the night, Delbreuck wanted Constanze to sing the Oscar Straus song that, before the Anschluss, had always closed the Alpen Café. Tonight, indeed, was like nights of old.

Constanze left the table and went and stood beside Delbreuck.

Marbach glanced at Franz and Lena. Franz was fondling Lena's precious face.

Slowly, languorously, Delbreuck played the piano while Swoboda stepped back and Constanze sang alone into the silence of the coffeehouse. Her vibrato-laden voice became nostalgic:

> *Just once again give me your hand to press,*
> *Just whisper once again: I love you so.*
> *Let me enfold you in one last caress,*
> *And then forget me, love, forget and go.*

While Constanze sang, from everywhere in the coffeehouse, voices joined with her. Beside him, Marbach was aware of Lena singing softly, her tear-streaked face filled with joy.

After the song was done, it was closing time, and the patrons of the café began leaving. When the last of the patrons had left the café, the four friends shared private time together.

The shared time didn't last long. First, Franz and Lena went to a room they had rented for the night, then Constanze and Marbach made their way up the narrow stairway to their room, the room where they had spent many precious nights together.

After they got into bed, Marbach and Constanze prepared for lovemaking.

Later, when the lovemaking was finished, Constanze positioned her body in the way she knew would comfort but not arouse her lover. With all her heart, she willed that her lover keep himself safe. While he fell into a deep sleep, she sang softly to him:

Come! Come! I love you only.
Come ... hero ... mine.

CHAPTER TWENTY-SIX

The next morning, early in the day, Marbach and Franz were sitting in the rear of the Alpen Café. Closed curtains blocked out the sunlight. Up near the dimly lit front, Constanze was playing the piano while singing. Standing beside her, singing along with her was Lena. They were doing the "Champagne Song" from Johann Strauss's *Die Fledermaus*. The two women sang:

> *Champagne is the one who is to blame,*
> *tra-la-la-la-la-la-la-la!*

After a few minutes, the singing stopped, and Constanze buried her face in the music sheet. Finally, she spotted what she was looking for and began singing. Lena joined her in the song.

Rising up on her feet, Constanze called out to Marbach, "Karl, my love, join us in the singing."

He called back: "Don't be ridiculous. I can't do the high A."

"*Quatsch*," jeered Lena. "Franz, show up the police inspector. Do the high A."

"Like hell," Franz said in a loud voice.

Both men laughed.

Constanze sat down at the piano, began playing, signaled to Lena, and both women sang:

> *Drink, my sweetheart, drink with me,*
> *Wine will make your heart feel free.*
> *When your heart beats strong and true,*
> *All things will seem clear to you.*

Constanze followed through on the piano, and the music became lazy and sensuous.

> *Happy is the person who forgets,*
> *What can't be changed anyway.*

Marbach lifted his head and silently repeated the words. There were things he very much wanted to forget. Mostly, he wanted to forget that he was in service to the evil that called itself National Socialism.

Constanze clutched Lena, kissed her on the cheek, and then returned her attention to the piano. She played, and Lena hummed until notes were played that caused Lena to stop humming. A totally different kind of music was about to be played.

In a soft, moody voice, Constanze started singing the song called "Sauerkraut."

Franz wrinkled his brow.

Marbach smiled. He knew the American origin of the song. Constanze had identified the American name to him: "St. Louis Blues." He had heard that jazz song many times while in the company of Constanze and Bubili. For him, the music was odd, but he had actually begun to enjoy it.

Constanze sang a few bars in English and then started over. Several times, she did the beginning in English, but again and again she stopped. She wanted to do it better. Finally, Lena grasped Constanze's arm, received a confirmative nod, and began singing the English words:

I hate to see the evening sun go down …
I hate to see the evening sun go down.
Because my sweetheart has left this town.

Franz groaned. "Listen to those words no one can understand. And that awful music. I wish those women would stop fooling with that damned American jazz."

"Jazz isn't so bad once you get used to it," Marbach said.

"I prefer real music, not jazz."

"Jazz is real music. You just have to get used to it, give it a chance."

Franz made a snorting sound. "I hate jazz for the same reason I hate Nazi music. It gets inside people and makes them act strange. You used to feel the same way. A few months ago, you were in the worst temper I have ever seen you in because your daughter was playing jazz gramophone records. It got so bad between you and your daughter that she had to go live with your wife's mother for a few days. I remember you sitting right here, all red-faced, pounding your fist on the table and saying that you wouldn't allow jazz to be played in your house."

"That was more than a few months ago," Marbach said. "And I was wrong. If jazz is good enough for Constanze and Bubili—and if the National Socialists hate it as much as they do—it must be all right. I am very much getting to like it." He cast a condescending look at Franz. "You must learn how to listen for the hypnotic rhythmic pulse."

"The what?"

"The hypnotic rhythmic pulse."

"You have taken leave of your senses."

The two good friends began laughing. While they laughed, at the front of the café, Constanze stopped playing the jazz and again began playing *Die Fledermaus*. She and Lena made a melody of words. Finally, they sang the words Marbach was waiting to hear:

> *Happy is the person who forgets,*
> *What can't be changed anyway.*

A few minutes later, conscious that his ache was totally gone, Marbach stood up and moved toward the front of the café. He nodded at Constanze, kissed one of Lena's precious hands, and left the Alpen Café. There was work for him to do at police headquarters.

CHAPTER TWENTY-SEVEN

Late in the afternoon in police headquarters, Kaas knocked on the door to Marbach's office. He had a book in his hand. "Are you busy?" he inquired.

"No. Come on in."

Kaas entered with a smile on his face. "I just found a book I've been looking for. I'm going to send it off in the mail to my son. Manfred is almost nineteen. I carried a copy of this book all through the trench war. A lot of us did. It is quite a book. Written fifteen hundred years ago, but it still holds up." Kaas passed the book to Marbach.

"*The Consolation of Philosophy.*" Marbach read out loud the title while looking at the book cover. He spoke the name of the author: "Boethius." And he nodded his head. "I carried a copy of this in my pack all through the war. It sometimes seemed to me like it was written especially for those of us who were mountain soldiers."

Kaas said, "Those of us in the trenches found it easy to believe it was written just for us."

Marbach spoke from memory familiar words from Boethius:

"And if the muse of Plato speaks the truth,
Man but recalls what once he knew and lost."

Kaas became excited. "That's right. It is grand that you know those words, that you know Boethius. Remembered wisdom. Wisdom we had before we were born, that we must try to remember.

I want Manfred to learn Boethius. I want him to read *The Consolation of Philosophy*."

"It is good for you to give your son a copy of *The Consolation of Philosophy* to read."

"All young men should read it. I like the image of the beautiful woman who helps the man to understand things."

"I hope I can meet Manfred someday."

"I'd like that a lot, Karl. I'd like Manfred to know a man like you." Kaas became silent for a moment and then said, "Boethius is just one more thing you and I have in common. You and I must talk about Boethius. I look forward to many good conversations about Boethius."

Marbach pulled a desk drawer open, reached inside, glanced at Kaas, and brought out a well-worn copy of *The Consolation of Philosophy*. "Take this copy of the book. You are going to send the new copy to Manfred. You can borrow this one from me. Read up on Boethius. Find something for us to talk about."

"I saw a picture once," Kaas said while accepting the book. "It was in a museum. It showed the execution of Boethius. The picture was ghastly. They had a rope around his neck. They were beating him to death with sticks. That was the fate he knew was awaiting him when he wrote *The Consolation of Philosophy*. Imagine a man facing a death like that and writing something like *The Consolation of Philosophy*."

"I hope Manfred doesn't have to go to war to learn what Boethius teaches in *The Consolation*."

Kaas shook his head. "There won't be a war. Our enemies will be put in their places. Everything will turn out all right in the end. The Führer has promised peace."

Marbach kept silent. It was true that Adolf Hitler was promising peace.

With emotional conviction, Kaas said, "Karl, it isn't the fanatics who will make National Socialism victorious, it will be reasonable men like you and me."

Marbach avoided showing his reaction to what Kaas had said about "reasonable men" like them.

Kaas shoved his hands into trouser pockets. There was something else he wanted to talk about. He spoke tentatively. "I have a favor to ask. It is something that could be helpful in terms of Kripo relations with the Gestapo. I more or less promised my friend—Police Leader Bahr—that it might be possible for us to get some theater tickets, and perhaps even meet some of the Viennese theater company in a pleasantly informal way. You have contacts. Maybe …"

Marbach smiled. "As bad as the theatrical season is this year, for a very low price, I can get you all the theater tickets you want. And it will be easy enough to arrange for you and those who accompany you to informally meet some of the performers. I don't just mean the performers at the Volkstheater. At the Burg Theater, there is Paula Wessely. I know Paula quite well, also her husband, Attila Hörbiger. They're both good National Socialists."

"Do you really know the great Paula Wessely?" Kaas asked, visibly impressed.

"Yes. I know her quite well."

"I saw Paula Wessely do a play in Berlin," Kaas said with a touch of awe in his voice. "In Berlin, she is called 'the Wessely.' She is a great talent."

"Paula is called 'the Wessely' in theaters all over Europe."

"Is she really a National Socialist? I mean … from before the Anschluss?"

"You won't have any trouble confirming that," Marbach said with a laugh. "I'm sure Paula would be pleased to meet with you and your friends. I will make the arrangements."

"It will be thrilling to meet the great Paula Wessely."

"You can meet Paula tonight. I know she is going to be available. Police Leader Bahr can be introduced to her tomorrow or some other night. To avoid possible awkwardness tonight, you need to have an escort. Attila is sometimes intemperate with unattached men hovering around his wife. Yes, you definitely need to be in the company of a woman to avoid trouble with Attila. I think Anna Krassny would be good for that purpose."

"Anna Krassny? Who is this Anna Krassny? Is she old or ugly or what?"

Marbach put a thoughtful look on his face. "Anna old? Ugly?"

"Are you trying to play a trick on me?" Kaas said, laughing. "You strike me as the kind who might line me up with a homely woman just for your own amusement. Pay attention! Hear what I say! Do that to me and I'll put your name at the top of the list of those Vienna police officers who will be required to attend additional National Socialist orientation sessions. There is a new schedule of National Socialist orientation lectures, and I am fully prepared to stick your name right at the top of the list of those required to attend."

Marbach laughed.

"I will do it," Kaas said, making no effort to contain his laughter. In a good-humored voice, he said, "You being a Comrade Soldier means nothing on a point like this. If you try to saddle me with an old woman or a homely woman, I am prepared to keep sending you to orientation lectures until you have a long, white beard."

"Do what you want. I get paid by the month. I can do police work or I can attend lectures."

Continuing to laugh, Kaas said, "I promise you, if this is an ancient woman or an incredibly homely woman, I shall deal with you with absolutely no mercy."

"Anna is an actress. Do you want to back out of being Anna's escort?"

"An actress, eh? Probably one of those homely character actresses. One of those who plays the maid or the unattractive older sister."

"Perhaps you ought to have a preview of Anna so you can decide for yourself if you want to spend time in her company tonight."

Kaas stopped laughing. "A preview?"

"Some pictures."

"You have pictures? Where are they?"

"Across the street. Come with me."

"Go with you where?"

"There is a kiosk across the street where I can show you some pictures of Anna."

Without wasting any time, Marbach led Kaas out of the office, then out of the building, across the Schottenring, and down the boulevard to Kathia's kiosk. The old woman was inside the hut fussing with newspapers. She looked up as they approached.

Marbach shook hands with Kathia, introduced Kaas, and said, "Commander Kaas has indicated he might be willing to take Anna Krassny to a party tonight, but he is concerned that she might be too homely for him."

"Anna homely?" With a smile on her face, Kathia reached under the table in her hut, quickly found a small theater magazine of a half-dozen pages, and passed it to Kaas.

Kaas studied the magazine. Inside were three separate pictures of the actress identified as Fräulein Anna Krassny. Kaas didn't pretend to not be impressed as he looked at the first picture. He studied the exquisite face with feline eyes, like those of a friendly but determined tigress. While turning his attention to the second picture of the actress, he placed a handful of coins on the counter of the kiosk, several times the price of the magazine.

Marbach gave the old woman a conspiratorial wink.

A few moments later, while Marbach and Kaas walked away from the kiosk, Kaas continued to scrutinize the magazine with the three pictures of the actress Fräulein Anna Krassny.

Marbach and Kaas were closing the short distance back to police headquarters when they encountered a small disturbance. A half-dozen teenage boys wearing the white socks that proclaimed their loyalty to National Socialism were having fun at the expense of two Jewish girls barely in their teens. The two Jewish girls were wearing headscarves. The boys in white socks were shouting, "Yids, go home!" Again and again: "Yids, go home!"

The boys shouted other bits of nastiness. "Your matzo soup is waiting." The nastiness got worse. "Ugly Jews, get out! Jews are filthy!"

The badly frightened girls began crying, and, in the way of such things, the crying incited the tormentors to greater excess. A large youth ran up to one of the girls and without warning punched her in the face, knocking her down. A second youth ran up behind the other girl, pulled off her headscarf, turned back to face his friends, and held high his victory trophy.

The girl who had lost her scarf reached down and grabbed the hand of the girl who was holding her hands over a bloodied face. Clasping their hands together, the two girls ran away; they fled down the street.

The youth who had captured the headscarf stopped short when he saw Marbach and Kaas, but he stepped forward when he spotted their SS buttons.

Kaas reached out and grasped the youth in a vigorous embrace.

The teenage boys in white socks clustered around Kaas. They yelled and hugged. Kaas shouted, "Heil Hitler!" and the boys returned the cry again and again. The cry became a chant: "Heil Hitler! Heil Hitler! Heil Hitler! Heil Hitler!" On and on: "Heil Hitler! Heil Hitler …"

Marbach knew he didn't dare be passive. He echoed the Heil Hitler cry. With an effort of will, he put out of his mind the bloodied face of the Jewish girl.

Three of the teenage boys separated from Kaas and ran over to Marbach. He allowed them to hug him, even the one who had punched the Jewish girl.

Finally, after a final exchange of Heil Hitler greetings with the teenage boys, Kaas and Marbach walked the remaining few steps to police headquarters. When they got inside the building, Kaas said, "It was great having fun with those fine young boys, but right now there is something you and I need to talk about. Frankly, I am not sure what I am supposed to do tonight."

Marbach provided an explanation. "When the performance is over, just remain in your seat. Don't do anything. I will arrange to have an usher find you and take you to a room where a good man will be waiting. The good man's name is Josef Swoboda. He will make the appropriate introductions to Anna and Constanze."

"Humor me. Come into my office and tell me about this Fräulein Krassny."

"Anna?"

"Yes."

They entered the office. While sitting in a chair across the desk from Kaas, Marbach said, "If you want to break ice with Anna, you might tell her you are a chocolate policeman—like me."

"Chocolate policeman?"

"Constanze has been calling me that. Anna knows about it. She is one of Constanze's dearest friends, and, I might add, she is an old friend of mine."

"What does 'chocolate policeman' mean?"

"It is some of Constanze's teasing. Calling me the chocolate policeman is Constanze's way of playing on the business of the chocolate soldier in the operetta, *Der Tapfere Soldat*."

"That is a wonderful operetta," Kaas said. "A lot of civilians didn't like *Der Tapfere Soldat*, but those of us who saw army service loved it."

Marbach nodded agreement, then got up from the chair and headed for the door. "I have things to do." He opened the door, stopped, and half-talked, half-sang the theme song from *Der Tapfere Soldat*:

> *Oh you silly chocolate soldier man*
> *Just made to please young misses*
>
> *So sweet you'd melt, if you ever felt*
> *A full-grown maiden's kisses ...*

After Marbach closed the door, Kaas was in good spirit until he remembered that the composer of the song was a Jew. He fussed about that for a moment or two but quickly dismissed his concern. After all, *Der Tapfere Soldat* was an operetta that had brought delight into his life during what could have been a lonely period back in 1918.

CHAPTER TWENTY-EIGHT

At work the next day, feeling fit, no ache at all in his stomach, Marbach devoted himself aggressively to police responsibilities. He read and signed numerous reports, attended three meetings, and prepared paperwork for two cases that would soon be going to court. From time to time, he was afflicted by intruding thoughts about two Jewish girls and a bunch of Nazi boys in white socks, but he managed to banish those thoughts. He told himself there was no point thinking about something he couldn't change.

When it was finally time to leave for the day, Marbach went to a window and saw that it was raining outside. He put on his overcoat, grabbed an umbrella, left the building, popped open the umbrella, and headed for the streetcar stop.

At the streetcar stop, he waited patiently until a streetcar came along. He got on board and walked down the aisle until he found an empty seat. He was aware that waiting for him in his house would be his wife and his daughter. He knew he probably should have gone home last night, but it had been important to be with Constanze. He knew that his wife was a good woman, a very good woman, but a long time ago, inside the house, whenever he was too long in her presence, often just a matter of a few minutes, he felt uncomfortable, looked for an excuse to be somewhere else, in another room, down in the basement, outside in the backyard.

He got off when the streetcar arrived at his stop, opened his umbrella, and walked to the street his house was on. The rain had become only a slight drizzle. His house was a long way up the street. Like all the houses on the street, his house had a painted iron gate.

When he got to his house, he grasped the gate handle and pushed. Despite wetness, there was a squeak as the iron gate swung open. That squeak was a reminder of a household responsibility he neglected. Soon, perhaps this weekend, he would fix that squeak. It was his responsibility to take care of such things.

Upon entering his house, Marbach briskly shook the umbrella, found a place for it on the hallway floor, stamped both his feet, and took off his overcoat.

After that, a familiar ritual began. He stood in the hallway for a few moments sorting the mail that had been left for his inspection in a large dish on a plain wooden table. A considerable amount of unopened mail had accumulated during his absence because of the trip to Switzerland.

While opening sealed envelopes, Marbach avoided looking at his wife when she walked, not timidly but not assertively, to a place in the living room where she could stand and silently watch him.

When the chore with the mail was done, he turned and nodded, and his wife approached. She had an elegance he would never deny.

"Frau Marbach," he said. A lot of Viennese men used the word "Frau" when talking to or about their wives, but he used the word with formal remoteness.

"Karl," Marbach's wife said while kissing him lightly on his mouth. He reciprocated by kissing her impersonally on her cheek.

After the required kissing ritual was completed, with a turn of her elegant head, Marbach's wife addressed him in practiced monotone. She covered important topics of domestic concern. Her mother who hadn't been feeling well recently was now feeling better. Their sixteen-year-old daughter was in the house. Their housekeeper, Fräulein Mitzi, was out visiting some friends.

"Is everything all right with Camy?" Marbach had recently acquiesced to his teenage daughter's wish to be called Camy, not Camilla. He preferred Camilla, but she had made a fuss, and he had acquiesced.

"Camy is upstairs working on a school assignment," Marbach's wife answered. "The assignment requires a paper on the inspiration she derives from the Führer."

Marbach looked at his wife, and she stared back at him. He knew she hated fascism. Any fascism, whether Austrian and sloppy, or German and disciplined. She hated all the fascisms. Usually, he tried to avoid talking politics with her. Like Constanze, his wife was emotional about fascism.

Marbach spoke gruffly. "I thought Camy's paper last week was on that subject." He wondered why he was so often gruff when he was in his house. Gruff for no reason at all. There was no denying it: he was very unlike himself in his own house.

Marbach's wife had a trace of entreaty in her voice, almost a pleading sound, as she replied to what he had said. "The paper last week was on Camy's enjoyment of National Socialist music. This week the paper has to focus on the inspiration she derives from listening to the voice of Adolf Hitler."

Marbach avoided his wife's eyes. He didn't like this any more than she did, but what was there for him to do? The important thing was to keep Camy safe. Teenagers were safe in Vienna only if it was clear that they had total sympathy with National Socialism. What did his wife expect him to do? He could never say or do anything that might put Camy in jeopardy.

Marbach's thoughts were interrupted by a distinctive clatter of shoes tapping an excited dance down the stairs from the second floor.

"Papa!" Camy shouted as she pushed past her mother and thrust herself into Marbach's arms.

Marbach allowed himself to be hugged while Camy described various wonderful things she had experienced during the past few days. Camy's eyes were brown, and her nose was upturned. A delightful pattern of freckles decorated her face. Inexplicably, she hated the wonderful freckles.

Marbach found it grand to share Camy's joy, but finally he pushed himself free. "My feet are wet. The damned rain."

"Karl, are you well?" His wife's face was filled with concern.

Marbach didn't like hearing his wife express concern for him. "Yes, I am well, Frau Marbach."

In an uncertain voice, Marbach's wife said, "You should wear goulashes when it rains like this."

"I don't like goulashes," Marbach said gruffly.

"You look fatigued," Marbach's wife said. "You must be exhausted from your trip. You need to take better care of yourself. You work too hard."

Camy made what amounted to a declaration. "Mama … please! Papa has an important job for the Greater Reich. He can't shirk his duty. He has to work especially hard in times like these."

Marbach stared at his wife and at his daughter and couldn't think of anything to say.

Camy jumped up and down in a burst of enthusiasm. "Oh, Papa, I saw the most exciting thing this afternoon. Some policemen captured a bunch of Yids near the school. It was exciting. I told the police I was your daughter. You can be sure they were very impressed when they heard that."

Camy kept jumping up and down as she continued with excited details of what had been done to the Jewish people captured near her school, Jewish people she referred to as Yids. Her voice was high pitched. "This Yid woman kept crying and hugging her children. Finally, she turned her face to us who were watching, and she cried and cried. Such a lot of crying."

Marbach listened, trying to hear only the sound of Camy's lilting voice, only her precious voice, not the words she was speaking.

Marbach was relieved when his wife interrupted the ugly words.

"Camy, I know how idealistic you are, but is it necessary to use that word 'Yid' all the time?"

"Mama, that's what they are." Camy made her words a challenge.

Marbach stiffened as his wife and his daughter both turned toward him.

He delivered an order: "Camy, you will obey your mother." He hadn't declared his own position, simply taken refuge behind his wife, but at least there would now be peace in the house. Having prevented what might have turned into unpleasantness, he said, "I am going to take a hot bath before dinner."

"A pail of hot water is on the stove," Marbach's wife said. "There is water in the tub."

Marbach left his wife and daughter and went upstairs to the bathroom. His moodiness dissipated when he noted with relief that the pail of hot water on the small Primus stove was boiling. He was glad that he had a small Primus stove in his home. The full-sized bathtub was already partly filled with cold water. All that was needed was to add the hot water. He poured the pail of hot water into the tub and then wasted no time getting undressed.

Marbach didn't want to think. And he didn't want to think about why he didn't want to think. He got into the tub. The warm bathwater felt good. He settled into a comfortable position and soon fell asleep.

When Marbach woke up—unsure how long he had been asleep in the tub—the recollection of Camy's words about Jews hit him with fierce intensity. The bathwater had become cool. He sat in the cool bathwater and told himself that Camy was good. She had the goodness of the innocent. She was still a child. The worst thing—the very worst thing—was to think of doing or saying anything that might put her in jeopardy. She wouldn't be safe in National Socialist Vienna if she didn't say hateful things about Jews. Her awful words were keeping her safe. The important thing was to keep Camy safe. That was the only thing that mattered.

The bathwater was no longer warm, but it was still tolerable. Marbach's thoughts became lazy. He thought about Constanze, recollected the scent of musk, and allowed himself a few more minutes of refuge in the bathtub.

CHAPTER TWENTY-NINE

The next day at breakfast, Fräulein Mitzi, the Marbach family housekeeper, worked hard to keep things in a happy mood. She had a way of drawing unto herself all of the positive feelings that the others in the house could muster. Short and considerably overweight, for more than a dozen years Fräulein Mitzi had loyally provided her services to the Marbach family. She had her own private room on the second floor of the Marbach house. The relationship between Fräulein Mitzi and Frau Marbach was like that of sisters.

Fräulein Mitzi hovered over the table while the members of the household ate what was placed in front of them. On most days, Marbach rarely ate anything at breakfast in his own house. On this morning, he ate everything placed on his plate.

After finishing her breakfast, Camy stood up and pushed Fräulein Mitzi into the chair.

A ritual was being performed that Marbach had enjoyed seeing when Camy first started doing it at about the age of five. It had developed into a family ritual that had lasted until a year ago when Camy stated she had outgrown childish things. But now, without any explanation, the ritual was being repeated. Fräulein Mitzi sat in Camy's chair and was served breakfast by Camy. It began with a cup of rich, black coffee. Marbach could think of nothing except how incredibly adorable Camy looked fussing over Fräulein Mitzi.

When Marbach finished his breakfast, he got up from the table and prepared to leave for work. He walked around the table, pushed his hands down firmly on Fräulein Mitzi's chubby shoulders, then went to where Camy was sitting, and kissed her on the forehead. He tried to ignore the expressive tears running down the young face.

Finally, before leaving, he approached his wife, sitting silently in her chair. He looked at her upturned face, into eyes that were blue and warm. He surprised himself by speaking her name: "Alma." Captured in the moment, he kissed her warmly on the lips. As he walked out the door, the taste of his wife's kiss was sweet on his mouth.

CHAPTER THIRTY

Marbach left his house and walked toward the streetcar stop. He thought about the kiss he had shared with his wife. It was a wonderful kiss. When the streetcar arrived, he got on board. He was still conscious of the effect the kiss had on him when the streetcar brought him to the stop near the police headquarters building. Getting off the streetcar, he wondered if he was being faithful to Constanze, taking pleasure from a kiss from his wife. After thinking about things for a moment, he asked himself what sort of comic opera character he was, feeling guilty because of a kiss shared with his wife.

He entered the police headquarters building, remained standing for a moment in the hallway, then went and checked the report board, the record of recent police activities in Vienna.

There was nothing of interest to him.

He walked up the stairs to the second floor, paused for a moment, and then looked upward toward the third floor where the file room was. At this early morning hour, it ought to be possible to get into those files and please Constanze by making Marianne Frish a little safer.

On the third floor, Marbach stopped in front of a door upon which hung a clipboard with a log sheet for the signatures of those admitting themselves to the file room. Separate from the log sheet was a key hanging at the end of a piece of string. Before entering the file room, one was supposed to sign the log sheet and make use of the key. The key was covered with red powder. If the key was used to unlock the door to the file room, it would no longer be covered with red powder. A police clerk used the red powder to keep a check on things.

Marbach had no intention of leaving a record that he had entered the file room today. That meant he wouldn't be signing the log book or making use of the file room key. He had a key of his own, a remarkable skeleton key that could open countless locked doors in all kinds of buildings.

After using his key to get inside the file room, Marbach glanced at a written notice declaring dire consequences for anyone who entered the file room without signing the log, who did not accurately record in the log their name and title along with the date and the exact hour and minute of arrival and departure. But he wasn't too worried. It wasn't likely he would get spotted this early in the morning. If that happened, well, he would probably be able to handle it.

Getting on with the job at hand, Marbach edged silently up and down narrow pathways between towering file cabinets until something unexpected caught his eye. He stopped. On a large table was a special set of files—a collection of cards with the number 175 on them. The 175 cards identified homosexuals. The SS had dictated that arrests of people with 175 cards would soon get underway, but the SS had also made it clear to all Vienna police that the arrests would be done with a minimum of embarrassment for loyal servants of the Greater Reich.

Always there are special privileges for special people.

The important thing about the 175 cards on the large table was that they presented Marbach with an unexpected opportunity to get two separate chores done, even if it meant taking a few extra minutes.

Some of Constanze's friends might be identified on those 175 cards. Several times in recent weeks she had expressed concern for her 175 friends.

Even though the 175 cards were stacked alphabetically, it was more difficult than Marbach originally expected, but finally he managed to find 175 cards for two friends of Constanze. He liked thinking how grand it was going to be presenting the cards to her. There was one problem: the search had taken almost ten minutes.

Aware he was spending too much time in the file room, Marbach put the two 175 cards in his pocket and explored around until he found the collection of cabinets that had files for everyone in Vienna, files that, since the Anschluss, had been used to document legitimacy. To move in or out of the city, to get a job, to obtain a driver's license, for countless routine matters, what was in these files documented legitimacy or brought people to grief.

Marianne Frisch hadn't found it necessary in recent weeks to do anything that would require her legitimacy to be documented, but sooner or later that was sure to happen, and if the file showed that she was a Jew, the consequences would, at the least, be stressful for her.

It didn't take Marbach long to find Marianne Frisch's file. It surprised him how young she was, barely sixteen. His mind flashed onto the faces of the two teenage Jewish girls who had been bullied by aspiring young Nazis. How old were they? But he resolved to not waste time thinking about that. He studied Marianne's file. The letter J was recorded on the cover of the file. J for Jew. He removed the J. After that, probing inside the file, he made several erasures and removed one entire sheet. When he was finished, there was nothing left in the file to identify Marianne Frisch as a Jew. Her safety was substantially increased.

Noise out in the hallway was a reminder of the risk Marbach was taking by remaining too long in the file room. He cautiously left, went down to his office, and addressed the considerable amount of paperwork needing his attention.

Two hours later, a sizeable amount of his office paperwork disposed of, Marbach decided to take a short break. He went downstairs to the main hallway and stood in front of the report board, curious about what might have happened since he had checked the board earlier this morning.

He stiffened.

Words on the report board had a devastating finality:

> Early this day, Bubili Mirga—Gypsy—was shot and killed by Vienna Police Corporal Maximilian Duper. A group of citizens had confronted the gypsy and one of them tore off the gypsy's scarf. The gypsy was missing an ear. He had obviously been caught years ago in a gypsy hunt.
>
> In wild frenzy, the gypsy fought the righteous citizens. Police Corporal Maximilian Duper appeared on the scene. With courage and decisiveness, Police Corporal Maximilian Duper shot and killed the gypsy.

Marbach felt overwhelmed, first by a sense of loss, then by rage. Bubili was dead. Shot and killed. Murdered because he was a Romani.

Moving mechanically, Marbach left the building, hailed a taxicab, got inside, and sat staring out the window, not seeing anything at all as the taxicab moved slowly around the Ringstrasse. All he could think was that he had to tell Constanze about Bubili, that it was going to be terrible telling her what had happened to her new but deeply loved friend. He hoped she would be strong.

The taxicab picked up speed.

Marbach told himself that Constanze was going to grieve terribly. She was a creature of her emotions. Her pain was going to be a terrible thing, and there was no way to spare her. She had to be told the awful news before she read about it in a newspaper or learned about it from some other source.

When the taxicab arrived in front of the familiar building, Marbach paid the fare and got out. His feet were like heavy lead weights as he walked up the stairway to Constanze's flat. He fumbled clumsily at the door until a surprised Marianne let him in.

Marianne put her finger up to her mouth. "Please be quiet. Constanze is asleep. She is so happy. The play has been cancelled. There will be no theater performance tonight. The awful play is closed, but we must be quiet. She is sleeping." Marianne's eyes opened wide. "Oh, did you hear what happened last night at the theater party?"

"No?"

"I wasn't there, but they told me about it when Constanze's friends came over here to have a party. Everybody was so excited. They treated me so good. Such important people, and they treated me so good. They knew I am a Jew, and it didn't matter. Of course, Constanze did a little bossing around, but I must say all of her friends were very nice to me."

"What happened at the theater party?"

Marianne lifted her hands in the air. "Oh, I wish I had been there. It must have been glorious. Everyone said it was glorious. An SS man called Constanze a Jew, and she threw a glass of wine in his face. That was why her friends came over here." Marianne's eyes were shining. "They came to celebrate Constanze throwing that glass of wine. Such wonderful people they all are."

Marbach took Marianne by her shoulders. "Are you sure there is no trouble?"

"There is no trouble. Absolutely no trouble. Oh, you should have been here. We had a marvelous party. While we partied, everybody kept talking about how wonderful Constanze was."

"Do you know who the SS man was?"

"I forget his name. A lieutenant, I think."

"An SS lieutenant? Are you certain there will be no trouble?"

"I was worried about that … at first. But everyone said there is nothing to worry about. Everyone at the party treated it like an enormous joke."

Marbach let his arms hang at his sides. He could think of nothing to say to Marianne. The marvelous eyes staring at him widened. He made a lame attempt to nod agreeably.

After a moment, they both turned around and looked toward the room where Constanze was sleeping.

"Let me be alone with her," Marbach said.

"Has something bad happened?" asked Marianne.

"Someone has been killed." Marbach didn't speak Bubili's name.

"Oh my God!" gasped Marianne.

Marbach said, "Leave us alone. Please … I must talk with Constanze."

Marianne clutched Marbach tightly for a few moments, until, with gentleness, he managed to push her away. She looked lost as she slipped out the door of the flat.

Slowly, Marbach entered the bedroom. He picked up a chair in front of the dressing table and dragged it behind him as he approached the bed.

Constanze was lying face up, the way she always slept. He sat in the chair and waited for her to wake up. After several minutes, he finally made a soft stamping sound with his feet and then coughed several times.

Constanze began stirring. Marbach watched her roll over onto her side and slowly open her eyes. He took her hand.

"Sweetheart, how marvelous," Constanze slurred sleepily. With friendly lust, she tried to pull Marbach into bed beside her. "I don't have to do that damned play anymore. I am free of it."

Marbach drew back. "Sweetheart, I have something terrible to tell you. I wish there was some way to protect you from this. I have to tell you something terrible, and you have to be brave. Can you be brave?"

Constanze jerked upward in the bed. "Where is Marianne?"

"It isn't Marianne. She is safe." Marbach's mouth was dry. He spoke awful words in as direct a manner as he could muster. "Bubili has been killed."

"Bubili?"

"Bubili is dead. Killed. Murdered on the streets." Marbach continued talking. He spoke with mechanical flatness, but the odd thing was that he couldn't stop talking. With men, when comrades were killed, he had always kept his words to a minimum. But now, with Constanze, he couldn't stop talking.

The details Marbach provided became jumbled and incoherent, but he kept on talking.

Constanze pulled Marbach into the bed beside her. Lying in her arms, he kept talking until his words became a moaning sound. He was still moaning when he surrendered to oblivion in Constanze's comforting arms.

CHAPTER THIRTY-ONE

Constanze lay as still as possible on the bed, concerned that any slight movement or sound she might make would wake her lover. She was staring at his face when a sudden contraction of the muscles of his body pitched him upward, out of her arms, straight up in bed.

Karl turned slightly and looked down at her. His face registered confusion for a moment, and then he sat rigidly on the bed with his head fixed straight ahead.

She knew this was a delicate moment. Even when he was sick with influenza last fall, he hadn't tolerated being "babied" by her. Many of the toughest men she had known in her life were eager to be babied at certain times, but not him. Never him. He always hid vulnerability. He was a good man. He was her hero … but she hated it that he always hid vulnerability. He was strong, stronger than anyone she had ever known, but it was wrong of him to hide all trace of vulnerability.

Apprehensively, Constanze watched while Karl remained upright in the bed. Moving carefully, she pulled him back into her arms and, hoping it might soothe him, began humming an Italian song from her girlhood.

He lay silently beside her, his body rigid.

She continued humming the Italian song until she heard a mumbling sound. She moved her head in order to better hear the words being spoken to her and was immediately stabbed with pain.

"I shamed myself. I don't—"

Constanze placed one of her hands firmly on Karl's mouth to quiet him. She didn't say anything. She knew this wasn't the time for her to talk. Now, the thing for her to do was use her arms and her body. She fondled Karl for several minutes, and, finally, they had a sort of lovemaking. A quick, sudden release. Not at all like their usual lovemaking. As soon as the lovemaking was finished, he fell asleep.

Constanze remained awake while Karl slept.

A half hour later, Karl suddenly woke up. Without saying anything, he rolled over in bed and got to his feet. Constanze didn't speak. She watched while Karl made his way into the bathroom. She followed him there.

Inside the bathroom, Karl broke the silence. "Marianne has gone off on some sort of business."

Constanze didn't say anything in reply to that. Of course, Marianne was gone. Anyone could see that.

Karl was standing in front of the mirror. Constanze approached him from behind, took hold of him, turned him around, drew his arms around her, moved her hands up to his face, and held his face in her hands.

But all Karl did was yield a fatigued smile, let Constanze loose, and begin fussing with the bathtub. The round-shaped bathtub had high metal sides. It was barely three feet in diameter. He turned on the tap water and then sat fully clothed on the toilet seat, looking fatigued. The bathtub began filling with the water from the tap. It was unheated water. Some boiling water was needed, and there was no hot water heater in her flat. Boiling water had to be hauled to the flat from the basement where large heaters operated round the clock.

Constanze decided to do something she had never before done. Sometimes Karl hauled hot water, but most times she got someone, usually the maintenance man, to bring the heavy pails of boiling water to her flat. Now, without speaking a word, she walked out of the bathroom, put on a robe, went down to the basement, and, a few minutes later, brought back a large pail of boiling water. Her arms ached terribly as she clumsily poured boiling water into the bathtub already half filled with cold tap water.

Constanze rubbed her arms while Karl got up from the toilet seat. Lost in his thoughts, he undressed, checked the temperature of the bathwater with his fingers, then got into the bathtub, rubbed shaving soap on his face, and began shaving with a freshly sharpened straight razor.

Constanze continued to rub her arms, trying to make the pain go away. Finally, she sat down in a chair in front of the cabinet mirror and pretended to fuss with herself. With quick, furtive glances in the mirror, she watched Karl sitting in the tub shaving. She was glad that he was beginning to look like his old self.

After a few moments, Constanze became aware Karl was staring at her. The cabinet mirror made it possible for him to stare into her face while she had her back to him. She looked into the mirror and returned the stare.

Karl paused with the shaving and said, "I never realized you could be so useful. No man could ask for more—a woman who will haul his hot water for him."

Constanze purred an obscene Italian curse.

Karl yielded a short laugh and resumed shaving.

Constanze fussed with her hair and said, "The next time, we go back to the old way. You haul the hot water for both of us."

Karl made a slight laughing sound.

Constanze adjusted the cabinet mirror, the better to watch Karl.

Before continuing with the shaving, Karl stared at the razor in his hand, then studied Constanze through the reflection in the cabinet mirror, and said, "In some cultures, women do all of the hauling of the water. It is a sign of respect toward their men."

Constanze chuckled at the small joke while wiping the cabinet mirror in order to see Karl more clearly. After a moment, she shifted slightly and stared at her reflection in the mirror. "I wish I had higher cheekbones," she mused.

"You have marvelous cheekbones."

"My hair looks terrible."

"Do you want me to fix it for you?"

Constanze shook her head and then glanced at Karl. It had long fascinated her the way he shaved in the bathtub without using a mirror. His explanation was that whenever he tried to use a mirror while shaving in the bathtub, it just steamed up and became useless. She found it difficult to imagine that there might be other men who shaved without using a mirror.

Constanze said, "I think I may alter my perfume. Perhaps something with a floral scent."

"Why would you do that?"

"For the sake of change."

"I don't like change."

"You are too much the Habsburger." Constanze frowned. "I am thinking of trying a floral bouquet, something new and interesting."

"Your perfume is interesting enough now."

"It should be mysterious," Constanze said as though deep in contemplation. "A woman's perfume should be mysterious."

Karl wiped some of the soap from his face and said, "When are you going to tell me what happened between you and an SS man that caused you to throw a glass of wine in his face?"

Constanze faced herself in the cabinet mirror. Using her hairbrush, she attempted to bring order to her hair while providing a pithy one-sentence summary of what had happened the previous night: "Lieutenant Eichmann did something I didn't like, so I threw a glass of wine in his face."

"*Lieutenant Adolf Eichmann?*"

"Yes."

"Lieutenant Eichmann doesn't have high rank, but he does have strong connections. There could be trouble from this."

"I doubt it." Constanze studied her hair, then the hairbrush, and then used the reflection in the cabinet mirror to stare at Karl. She was aware he was using the same mirror to stare back at her.

"Tell me all of it. There could be trouble. I ought to know everything that happened."

"There won't be trouble."

"Will you please tell me what happened?"

"It isn't necessary."

"Do you need an audience before you will tell what happened?"

Constanze laid down the hairbrush, rolled her hair into a bun on the back of her head, and pinned it down firmly, conscious of being closely watched. She fussed some more with the bun and sat resolutely in her chair. Using the cabinet mirror, she saw that Karl was staring at the bun in her hair. During her melancholy period, he had often tied and untied the bun, expertly arranging and rearranging her hair. She would always be grateful to the woman, whoever she was, who had taught him how to expertly fix a woman's hair.

Constanze said with directness, "You almost never tell me about your triumphs. Why should I tell you about all of mine?" She regarded that as a fair thing to say. There were so very many of his "good deeds" that he didn't share.

Constanze made a slight adjustment to the cabinet mirror so she could stare at Karl as directly as possible. He had finished shaving. His feet were planted firmly against the end of the bathtub. He looked comical keeping himself upright by pushing his feet up against the end of the tub. The water was almost above his shoulders. If he wasn't careful, he might slip. She examined that possibility. It would be comical. He wouldn't hurt himself, not considering the construction of the bathtub. Definitely, he wouldn't hit his head. He would just slip down in the bathtub, get covered by water.

Karl said, "I tell you my good deeds. I told you about Rabbi Leichter, didn't I? I told you about Rabbi Leichter, and now you hold back from telling me about tossing wine in Lieutenant Eichmann's face."

Constanze sat stiffly in her chair. Karl was the one who didn't share, not her. Using the cabinet mirror, she stared at him relentlessly for a moment, then leaned forward in her chair and playfully began speaking in rapid Italian that she was sure he wouldn't be able to understand. It pleased her that what she was saying was certain to sound earthy and obscene to him. It was, in point of fact, very earthy and totally obscene.

Karl edged around in the round-shaped bathtub. "Maybe I should be jealous of Lieutenant Eichmann. Maybe he was just having a lover's spat with you last night. He is the sort I might expect you to be attracted to. He gets chauffeured around Vienna in a Rothschild limousine. He meets with all of the important officials.

And in the evenings, he dines in great splendor. Yes, it is possible to imagine you greatly enjoying Lieutenant Eichmann's attention."

Constanze ignored what she regarded as silly talk, uttered an especially obscene Italian curse, and focused her attention on her reflection in the mirror. Karl laughed, and she wondered if he had been able to accurately translate that obscurely phrased, very obscene Italian curse.

Karl toyed with the bathwater, laughed louder, and said, "Poor Lieutenant Eichmann. One defenseless SS officer standing alone against a Tormenta, one of those terrible Italian mountain storms. The poor man never had a chance facing a Tormenta launched by Constanze Tandler."

As Constanze helplessly joined in the laughter, her mind dwelt on the times in recent weeks when she had lost control of her terrible temper and cursed Karl for cooperating with the Nazis. He was a very good man, a wonderfully good man, but he did cooperate with the Nazis. Somehow a way had to be found for them to talk about that ... yes, but not now. This was a time for merriment.

Constanze lifted a hand to her hair, glanced over her shoulder, and made eye contact with Karl while he said, "I appreciate the vulnerability poor Eichmann must have felt as he faced the overwhelming power of a Tormenta."

Constanze faced the mirror and contemplated the mischief that could happen if Karl got careless with his feet.

He said, "Being cursed by you is a terrible thing, as I can well attest. And this time, you cursed the man in public. At least I have had my scoldings in private. Poor Adolf Eichmann had his scolding in public. Everybody must be laughing at him today."

Constanze laughed. She yielded to the enormous depth of joyful passion she felt, but after a moment, she abruptly stopped laughing.

She was afflicted by concern for Marianne. The important thing right now was to get Marianne back to the safety of this flat.

Still, she told herself, there was a little time, a few moments right now, enough time for her to tell about last night's encounter with the SS creep named Lieutenant Adolf Eichmann. She wouldn't tell an elevated version, like it might be told in front of their friends. Right now, this man she loved would hear the story raw, the way she would tell it to especially close women friends.

Sitting in her chair, Constanze looked into the mirror and molded her face into a caricature of mock fury. She had her lover's full attention. Whatever anyone might say about her, she was an actress who knew how to capture her audience, whether many, or few ... or only one, this time the one who was the most important audience of all possible audiences.

Constanze transformed her face from fury into a serene mask. A dramatic performance involves calculation, especially when the performance has to be conveyed through a bathroom mirror. When she spoke, it was with disciplined control of her voice.

"Sometimes oafs approach you on boulevards. Other times at parties. Like the oaf he is, Lieutenant Eichmann came up and with an awful grin on his face pushed the lower part of his body up against me. Men who do that are creepy men."

Constanze smiled when her large lover, sitting in the small bathtub, brought himself to an upright position.

Eagerly anticipating what could happen if Karl wasn't careful in the bathtub, Constanze became more provocative. "The oaf who is Lieutenant Eichmann likes to practice cruelty to people by calling them *Jew*. He pushed the stiffness in his crotch up against me and asked which part of me was Italian and which part was Jew. He said it would be interesting to do an inspection and find out for himself."

Constanze got out of her chair and headed for the bathroom door. She took delight in the thought that her very large and now extremely angry lover was perched precariously in the small, circular metal bathtub.

With theatrical calculation, Constanze spoke provocatively over her shoulder. "Just before I threw the wine in Eichmann's face and before I did my little march out of that place, I told that Nazi turd that if he pushed his stiff, little dick against me one more time, the Italian part of me would bite it off and the Jewish part would stuff it down his throat."

Having delivered her exit line, Constanze walked out of the bathroom, slammed the door behind her, then stood in front of the closed door, and listened to a loud splashing sound. There was a bubbling sound and a coughing noise. A lot of water was being splashed on the floor of the bathroom.

Karl's voice called out while he was still choking from the water: "Wait … where are you going?"

Constanze shouted through the closed bathroom door: "I have chores to do." She heard loud splashing noises. Standing firm, she resolutely faced the closed bathroom door and waited for it to open.

Karl emerged with a small bath towel around his middle. Constanze couldn't help thinking that even in a moment like this, he had his foolish modesty.

Constanze signaled with a wave of her arm that she had no time to waste. "I have to get going."

Karl said, "I fixed Marianne's police file. I took out everything identifying her as a Jew. There is something else. I picked up two 175 cards identifying friends of yours as homosexuals."

"Where are the cards?"

"I put them on the table."

Constanze went to the table, picked up the two 175 cards, studied them for a few moments, and then shoved them into her purse. She turned away, pulled on her oversized coat, placed her floppy, wide-brimmed hat on her head, put on her black-rimmed eyeglasses, and grabbed a large bundle from a table near the door. The bundle contained some of Karl's clothes that needed to be taken to the cleaners.

Karl said, "Where are you going, sweetheart? I want to …"

Constanze said, "I thank you for what you did for Marianne and my friends. You are my chocolate policeman. No doubt about it. Indeed, you are my chocolate policeman."

Karl moved the small bath towel to more completely cover the middle of his body.

Constanze posed in front of the large mirror in her living room, put down the bundle of clothes for a moment, picked up a perfume bottle, and added a dab to the nape of her neck and on each wrist. Then she picked up the bundle, held tight to her purse, took a few steps, and pulled open the door. "There is this cleaning to be taken out, and I have to find Marianne. It isn't good for her to be out on the streets alone. She has probably gone over to the hotel where Anna is staying. Don't worry about the 175 cards. I won't be careless with them."

"Let me go with you."

Constanze held onto the opened door, stared speculatively, and said, "I am a respectable member of the Vienna stage. I would lose my respectability if I was seen on the streets with an undressed man."

After that, laughing in E-flat, Constanze closed the door and went on her way.

CHAPTER THIRTY-TWO

Karl Marbach stood with the small bath towel in front of him. He could hear Constanze's footsteps going down the stairway. He breathed the scent of her musky fragrance, but only for a moment. Recalling what had happened when he brought her the awful news about Bubili, he gripped his fingers into clenched fists and shut his eyes. He was ashamed.

Finally, resolved to put the feeling of shame in the past, he stood in front of the gramophone collection. He wanted to listen to some music. He fussed around, finally selected one of his favorite albums, withdrew one record platter from the album, and placed it on the gramophone. Then he laid out the other platters from the album. It was going to take a half-dozen platters to play all of Beethoven's *Pastoral*.

While listening to the beginning of the symphony, he went into the bedroom. In Constanze's modest-size flat, it was possible to be in the bedroom and listen to music playing in the living room. He went to a dresser drawer, his private dresser drawer in Constanze's flat, and took what he needed. After putting on trousers and a shirt, he went to a closet filled mostly with Constanze's things and found his extra suit jacket, the one he always kept there. Then he examined the three ties he always kept in the closet and selected the one that seemed the most suitable.

When he felt properly dressed, he went to the bed, lay down, took care not to wrinkle his clothes, and listened to more of the *Pastoral*, getting up only when it was necessary to replace a platter.

He didn't mind that some of the platters were being played out of order. It was all the *Pastoral*.

Time passed.

He had just replaced a platter and was standing in the living room when the gramophone began with what he recognized as the second movement of the symphony. He stood very still, listened closely, waited until the musical notes became like the patter of raindrops, and then waited a while longer until the music became dark and moody.

While listening to the second movement of the *Pastoral*, he stood in front of a mirror and put a proper knot in his tie. Continuing to fuss with his tie, he walked around within the flat, stopping only when it was necessary to tend to the requirements of the gramophone in order to continue hearing the music of horrible torment and infinite rapture.

Almost an hour later, he was still turning record platters over, listening and relistening to his favorite parts of the *Pastoral*, when he heard sounds in the hallway.

He cocked his head, listened, went to the door, and pulled it open.

Directly in front of him was Marianne. Constanze and Anna Krassny were huddled behind her, talking about something. Marbach wasn't surprised to see Anna. Constanze and Anna were close friends.

Marianne's large, brown eyes brightened as she listened to the music playing on the gramophone. Her head began weaving in delighted response to a familiar, carefree tune in the *Pastoral*. Marbach grasped the teenager's hand, pressed it to his mouth, and drew her forward. She smiled shyly. He smiled back in a reassuring manner and then shifted his attention to Constanze and Anna.

Anna stared at him, took one step backward as though to gain momentum, and then rushed forward.

No hand kiss would suffice for Anna. She demanded a hug and got it. Then she demanded a kiss on the mouth and got it. A few years ago, he had loved Anna in the romantic way. Now there was no romantic feeling, but sometimes it was fun for them to pretend in front of Constanze.

Anna drew her head back to peer over her shoulder at Constanze. The two women exchanged mischievous grins.

While Anna returned her attention to Marbach, Constanze remained standing in the doorway, the wide-brimmed hat pushed back on her head, the black-rimmed eyeglasses resting precariously close to the end of her nose.

Anna laughed a throaty laugh, pulled Marbach close, and said over her shoulder, "Constanze, if you were not my best friend, my very best friend, my best friend in all the world, I would take this one back from you."

With Anna in his arms, Marbach became aware of a familiar fragrance. He recognized Anna's perfume. She lifted her head upward and stared at him. He was filled with appreciation for her wonderful face, her marvelous blue eyes. She settled comfortably in his arms, slowly moved her head back and forth. Her hair danced lightly on her shoulders. There was one problem: the music had stopped. Anna lifted an arm and waved at Marianne, who immediately understood what was needed and went to change the platter on the gramophone.

When the next platter began playing, Anna made a distinct movement with her body. It was her way of signaling she wanted Marbach to dance with her to Beethoven's music. Even with a piano, a sofa, and several chairs, the living room was large enough to accommodate two people dancing.

Marbach and Anna walked together to the center of the living room and began dancing, turning around and around, dancing like lovers, moving in short, gliding movements to the beginning of the third movement of the *Pastoral*.

Marbach treasured the taste of Anna's kisses on his mouth. Never would either of them betray Constanze, but Anna's kisses were always sweet. These days, the sweet kisses she bestowed were not erotic. It was friendship kissing, but even so, only permissible because Constanze was watching them. Whenever Constanze wasn't present, they never shared more than one quick friendship kiss, but Constanze was present, so several friendship kisses were exchanged.

The dance continued. Marbach held Anna in his arms and guided her across the floor. Despite his size and modest skill, Anna was able to make their dancing look graceful. Finally, they glided to a halt in the center of the living room, where, for a moment, Anna became rigid in Marbach's arms. Her arms tightened around his neck, and he heard her whisper in a low voice that only he could hear: "I am so terribly sorry about our wonderful Bubili." After saying that, she hugged fiercely, pressed her face against his chest. No additional sound escaped her lips, but she was unable to totally keep her emotions in check. A sobbing sound escaped her tightly closed mouth.

When Anna finally got fully in control of herself, Beethoven's music was still playing. She pushed at Marbach until he figured out how to hold her in the way she needed to be held so they could begin dancing again. Their dancing began with a long circling movement that ended with Anna making an expert dipping motion.

While holding Anna in his arms, Marbach stared into her blue eyes and said, "L'Heure Bleue." It was the name of the perfume she was wearing.

The music ended, but Marianne moved quickly and placed another platter on the gramophone.

Anna came erect, stepped back, took measure of what was playing on the gramophone, drew Marbach close, and guided him into another series of dance steps. She smiled, made a difficult maneuver with her feet, and, skilled dancer that she was, helped Marbach join with her in an agile dipping motion.

The music continued. Anna made herself a pleasing weight in Marbach's arms for a few moments and then edged herself free, rolled her shoulders, and let her blue eyes flash mischievously. Speaking loud enough for everyone in the room to hear, she said, "Karl … so you still recognize L'Heure Bleue. Indeed, I haven't worn this perfume for ages, simply ages. It is so terribly difficult to get these days. Constanze got a bottle from a Frenchman who joined the theater company a few days ago, and she made a gift of it to me. It has been a long time since I last wore L'Heure Bleue. Karl, do you still believe it is a perfume made only for blue-eyed women?"

"Of course," answered Marbach. "Every woman has her fragrance. For you, Anna, L'Heure Bleue matches your blue eyes. A man is reminded of the color when the sun has set, but the night has not yet fallen."

Those words drew a hearty laugh from Anna. "So you still speak those words to blue-eyed women." After saying that, she separated from Marbach, turned around, faced Constanze, smiled broadly, and ran toward outward flung arms. The two women hugged tightly.

Finally, Constanze made a beckoning motion for Marianne to join them, and the three women bundled together, laughing and hugging. After a few moments, Anna lifted her head from Constanze's shoulder and said, "Karl, in the old days you were always giving blue-eyed women samples of L'Heure Bleue. But you had different perfumes and other fancy talk for women with eyes of other colors."

All three women laughed.

"What is your perfume?" Marianne asked Constanze while snuggling close. "I love that musk fragrance."

Constanze held tight to both of her friends and said, "My perfume is my mystery. I have it made up for me. But I may change to a different fragrance. Tell me, Karl, do you think something along the lines of Insidia would match my eyes?"

In the spirit of the moment, Marbach made an exaggerated moaning sound. "Insidia is a perfume for women with greenish-blue eyes, not a woman with amber eyes."

Constanze relaxed her hold on her two precious friends and said, "Marianne, sweet one, dear sweet one, please find some drinks to freshen us. Include one for yourself. There is some marvelous Schilcher Rose for those of us who have the taste to appreciate good wine, and for this oafish man, give him a glass of his schnapps—his kümmel."

"One for me?" gasped Marianne.

"Yes. It is good for you to learn proper drinking in the company of older folk who care for you deeply."

Marbach smiled. He knew that Schilcher Rose was the favorite drink of Marianne's young sweetheart, Emile, a couple of years older than Marianne. Two weeks ago, Emile had fled with his parents and two sisters to France, and Marianne desperately missed her sweetheart. Marbach thought it was grand of Constanze, at this time, in this place, to ask Marianne to serve the favorite drink of her sweetheart.

"You will find the wine and liquor in the cabinet over there, Marianne," Anna said, adding with melodious diction a colorful obscenity that more amazed than shocked Marianne. Anna, even more than Constanze, had a way of making outrageous obscenities sound like innocent mischief.

Anna joined Marianne at the cabinet, found four glasses, and set them on the cabinet: three long-stemmed, crystal-clear wine glasses for the women, and a plain, flat-bottomed glass for the man. Anna and Marianne tended to the preparation of the drinks while Marbach remained where he was and stared at Constanze, standing across the room from him. Her head and her shoulders were moving in time to gaiety in Beethoven's music that was spilling forth from the gramophone.

Constanze's amber eyes suddenly locked onto Marbach's eyes. He stood absolutely still, stared back at Constanze, and half-whispered but deliberately made the half-whisper loud enough for all three women to hear: "Musk in a woman's eyes and fragrance in the woman's soul."

Constanze stood resolutely still for a moment and then rushed across the room into Marbach's arms, laughing in musical E-flat. While being held close, she lifted her head. "You made me laugh," she said, her eyes dancing, the words a playful accusation. She secured herself in Marbach's embrace, laughed some more, and then became silent, and they started dancing, following the flow of the music.

While Constanze and Marbach moved their bodies in rhythm to the dance, Anna walked over to the gramophone, stared inquisitively at the spinning gramophone record, edged a few steps away from the gramophone, settled onto the piano stool, and peered at a music sheet.

The gramophone record platter played to the end, and Anna began toying with the piano keys. Her musical doodling suggested a fetching tune. With calculated affectation, Anna looked over her shoulder and said, "Tell me, Constanze, what are these changes on this music sheet?"

Marianne stopped fussing with record platters and walked up behind Anna to ponder the music sheet. In a quick reversal, Anna stood up, slipped behind Marianne, and guided the young woman onto the piano stool.

At that same moment, Constanze separated from Marbach. He held out his arms, but she stepped away, placed her hands together, and said, "Marianne, sweet one, please play what is on the music sheet."

Marbach knew that mischief was about to begin.

Perched in front of the piano, Marianne furrowed her brow as she studied the music sheet.

"Go ahead, Marianne," Anna said, balancing her hands on Marianne's shoulders. "Play the music."

"Yes, Marianne, please play what is on the music sheet," Constanze said, moving back beside Marbach and drawing his arm securely around her.

Marianne, at the keyboard, began playing. Expertly, she worked her way through the first part of the piece until Anna, standing directly behind her, peered at the music sheet for an instant, picked up the melody, turned around, and began singing in her trained soprano. The music was Oscar Straus, but the lyrics had been changed.

> *Oh, you great big chocolate policeman*
> *You are far too sweet and pretty*
> *Oh, you funny chocolate policeman*
> *For you I feel great pity.*

Oh, you silly chocolate policeman
Just made to please young misses
So sweet you'd melt, if you ever felt
A full-grown maiden's kisses …

Anna dissolved into helpless laughter when the song was finished. Beside her, Marianne continued the final refrain on the piano while laughing giddily.

Taking her time, Constanze slid around behind Marbach and began a steering motion toward the sofa. "My chocolate policeman," she said, while maintaining a forceful shoving movement. "Keep moving, my chocolate policeman. I will tell you when to stop."

"Chocolate policeman, indeed," said Marbach, with a sigh of resignation. He allowed himself to be deposited at one end of the sofa and then reached up, grasped Constanze's hand, and pulled her down beside him. She smiled as he drew her close.

Marianne came over to them holding a tray of drinks. Marbach reached out and secured for Constanze a wine glass filled with Schilcher Rose, handed it to her, and then took from the tray the glass containing his kümmel.

Anna walked over, retrieved from the tray a glass filled with Schilcher Rose, and made herself comfortable in a heavily stuffed chair facing the sofa. After setting aside the tray, Marianne took a glass of Schilcher Rose for herself and sat at the far end of the sofa.

Drawing Marbach's arm close around her, Constanze lifted her glass and proclaimed an ancient Greek toast, a very special celebration of hospitality she reserved only for people to whom she felt especially close: "*Guest Friends!*"

Anna held up her glass and echoed the toast: "Guest Friends!"

Marianne looked puzzled but lifted her glass and spoke the toast: "Guest Friends!"

With one arm around Constanze, Marbach used his free hand to raise his glass. He spoke the toast with solemn deliberation: "Guest Friends!"

With the ancient Greek toast completed, Anna was determined to return the conversation to playful mischief. "Well, Marianne, do you agree that Karl is the chocolate policeman?"

"I am not really sure," Marianne said. "Isn't the police inspector too experienced with women to …" Her words trailed off as she surrendered to a torrent of giggling.

Anna waited till Marianne's giggling had almost ended before she said, "Karl is successful with women because he is willing to be a little afraid of them."

"That is true," Marbach said. "Without some fear, there is no awe, and without awe it is impossible for a man to fully appreciate a woman."

Constanze and Anna shared a glance and then began laughing.

Anna's deep, throaty laughter joined with Constanze's musical E-flat laughter. Their laughter blended into a melody. Marianne's playful giggling leavened the melody.

Marbach shook his head and drew his arm more tightly around Constanze. He nodded contentedly when she made an abrupt movement that ended with her head resting on his chest.

Marianne stopped giggling long enough to say to Constanze, "I haven't told you yet, but I got a letter from Emile. He is fine in France. I have told you that Emile and I met at the Musikverein. That was six months ago. You have never told me. I wonder … where did you and the police inspector …?"

Constanze placed her hand on her lover's stomach. "We are Guest Friends. Don't call him police inspector. You may call him

Karl or Guest Friend, but nothing else. Not tonight. Not in this place. Guest friendship is about equality. Now, to answer the question you were starting to ask, Karl and I met in the Café Central last year."

Marbach looked down at Constanze's hand. He hoped she was going to keep it on his stomach. He said to Marianne, "The first time I saw ever Constanze was not one year ago. It was ten years earlier. She was on the stage playing the part of Margarethe in *Faust*. I must say I never saw any other actress play the part of that handmaid of goodness with such expressive femininity."

Constanze lifted her head. She kept her hand on Marbach's stomach as she said to Marianne, "Margarethe was virtuous but not timid. It is a common mistake to play her as the timid handmaid of goodness."

"The night I saw it," Marbach said, "you made her sensuality very obvious." He knew it was safe to say that. He knew Constanze was proud of having played the part that way.

"Oh, what a great play!" Marianne exclaimed to Constanze. "I wish I had seen you in *Faust*. It is my favorite tragedy."

Marbach felt grateful when Constanze's fingertips began tapping on his stomach. Constanze said to Marianne, "Tragedy? Well, if it is a tragedy, the tragedy is not what happens to Faust. The tragedy is what happens to Margarethe! Faust made his bargain and acquired all the material things the world has to offer. But that wasn't enough for him. He wanted more. He never stopped wanting more."

Constanze paused, took a breath, and continued. "But Margarethe was different. That's what I love about her. Absolutely adore. She was a woman who gave her love with generosity and courage, and paid the price for that love with her own life. Then, Margarethe's love and generosity were so powerful that she was able to return from the grave to save her man."

For a few moments, no one spoke.

Finally, Marianne broke the silence with a hushed whisper. *"Oh, my."*

Marbach looked at Constanze and spoke the immortal line from *Faust*, keeping his voice low. "The eternal feminine image that leads men on." He made a pretended gasping sound when Constanze shoved her elbow with playful force against his ribs.

Anna laughed cheerily, decided it was time to switch from Goethe to Oscar Straus, and softly sang,

> *So sweet you'd melt, if you ever felt*
> *a full-grown maiden's kisses …*

"I am assaulted from all sides," Marbach said with exaggerated weariness. Then he abruptly changed the subject. Looking at Anna, he said, "Tell me what Constanze did last night to that poor Lieutenant Eichmann when he asked her which part of her was Jewish."

"Oh, it was grand!" Anna exclaimed. "I wasn't ten paces away. Those were the best lines spoken by a Viennese actress all year. Even the National Socialists in our crowd have been calling me with compliments."

"National Socialist friends?" Marianne looked suddenly apprehensive.

Anna's eyes filled with concern as she looked at Marianne. "Yes, I have National Socialist friends."

Marianne lowered her eyes.

For a moment, there was silence. Then Constanze said, "Of course, Anna has National Socialist friends. So do I. If we didn't have National Socialist friends, we … we would be ejected from the company at the Volkstheater. But both Anna and I hate National Socialism and the evil it is inflicting on the world."

Marbach took advantage of an unexpected opportunity. "I'll bet there are more Nazis working in the Burg Theater than there are in all of Vienna Kripo, and keep in mind that Vienna Kripo is much larger."

Constanze shook her head. "That is nonsense. How do you do the counting? Do you exclude Commander Kaas from being a Nazi?"

Marbach interjected humor. "Just who is and who is not a Nazi is something I decide for myself."

Constanze and Anna groaned in unison.

Marianne stared at Marbach and shook her head with gentle reproach. She couldn't resist showing everyone that she recognized the play on words: "Didn't a former Viennese mayor say something like that? Only didn't he say it about Jews?"

Anna stared fondly at Marianne. "You are precious."

Marbach decided to continue to pursue mischief. "I still haven't heard all the details about what Constanze did last night."

Constanze said, "You certainly did. I told you all about it."

"You told me some of it, but I suspect there is more."

Laughing raucously, Constanze shook her finger at Anna. "Don't you dare tell him about my stage exit. Don't you dare."

Anna laughed and shook a finger back at Constanze. "*Dare?*" She laughed some more. "Dare? I *dare* you to try to stop me. I was part of that stage exit. It was a grand moment. I am going to tell Karl about it, and I am going to tell our wonderful Marianne, who must be thinking what an awful person I am for having National Socialist friends. Well, maybe I am awful, but last night I participated in a grand march. I marched shoulder to shoulder with two marvelous comrades after a perfectly good glass of wine was tossed in the face of an SS creep."

"I am betrayed!" Constanze wailed, enjoying herself totally. She drew Marbach's arm tight around her.

Anna sat up straight in her chair and directed herself to Constanze. "You will have plenty of occasions to tell the story, but it also belongs to me. I was part of that grand march. So was the wonderful Josef Swoboda. It was truly a wonderful moment, the three of us marching side by side, linked arm in arm."

"Swoboda?" Marianne didn't recognize the name.

"A good man," said Anna. "He didn't come to the party to celebrate Constanze's deed because he was able to talk a young woman into letting him take her home. I never saw him before last night. He has some age on him, but he is a man with brass balls."

Marianne's eyes opened wide with shock at Anna's salty talk. Then, after reflecting a moment, she broke into laughter. At the other end of the sofa, familiar with Anna's way of freely expressing herself, Constanze rolled up tight against Marbach and laughed helplessly.

As the laughter died down, Marianne, tears of laughter running down her face, managed to get herself under control long enough to say to Constanze, "But what happened last night was dangerous. Why did you do it? Why didn't you just tell the lieutenant that you don't have any Jewish blood in you?"

"Come, now, Marianne," Anna said, "would you have Constanze do anything to give support to the evil notion that there is something wrong with having Jewish blood?"

Marianne stirred herself to an upright position at the end of the sofa. "I am a Jew." Immediately, she looked unsure of herself.

Constanze didn't miss a beat. "I am a Red."

Anna was quick to chime in. "I am an actress."

Marbach laughed as he said, "I am a Habsburger."

They all laughed. There was nothing else to do but laugh. They laughed joyful laughter that bound together four Guest Friends.

CHAPTER THIRTY-THREE

After the toast was concluded, the three women talked among themselves while Marbach sat and listened. He came fully alert when Marianne began talking about something that had happened to her a couple of days ago.

"I was … stagged," Marianne said in a tentative voice. "They put hands on me. Why do men do such things? One of them was the son of Colonel Count Neumayer. It wasn't as bad as it might have been, but it made me feel terrible. It could have been worse. I wasn't … but still it was awful."

Marbach leaned forward. "The son of Colonel Count Neumayer?"

"Yes, the son of Colonel Count Neumayer," Marianne said. "He had some friends with him. They were all together in a car."

Anna had an angry look on her face. "What happened?"

"Nothing." Marianne shut her eyes, kept her eyes closed as she continued using words that came at a fast clip. "Oh, I wish it had been nothing. It wasn't awful like it might have been, but it was bad. A man got out of the car and said he was Lieutenant Krebs. I'll never forget the name, *Lieutenant Krebs*. He grabbed … he grabbed me and said for me to be a good little deer."

When Marianne indicated with her hand that she had no more to say, Anna delivered an expressive curse and said, "Stags and deer. A game for freakish boys and awful men."

"Damned stagging," Marbach said.

"I managed to get away," Marianne said. "But not before he put his hands all over me, touched private places. I wasn't hurt, but it … it was …"

There was silence.

Anna broke the silence. "Lieutenant Krebs, whoever he is, most definitely is a rotten character."

Marianne stared anxiously and then seemed to gain strength as she echoed the words spoken by Anna. "Lieutenant Krebs is a rotten character."

Constanze looked with concern at Marianne and deliberately changed the subject. "My sweet Marianne, my very sweet Marianne, we are friends, we are Guest Friends. So, as a Guest Friend who will speak nothing but the truth to another Guest Friend, what do you think about me doing Euripides's *Hecuba*? What do you think about me playing the role of Hecuba?"

While Marianne thought about what she might say in reply to Constanze, Anna separated herself from the other two women, got up from the sofa, and headed back to her chair. Once seated, she faced those on the sofa and said, "Sweet Marianne, Guest Friends share truthful emotion and honest talk. That is why I say I don't have a high opinion of that play."

Constanze pointedly stuck her tongue out at Anna.

Anna made a fist, gestured with defiance at Constanze, and then fussed to make herself comfortable on the heavily stuffed chair across from the sofa.

Marianne said to Constanze, "Oh, I don't know … I just don't think that is the correct part for you. That woman is good at the start, but she becomes evil by the end of the play."

Constanze hugged Marianne. "That's why I want to do this play. Someone good becoming evil. If they let me, I want to end the play making the sound of a howling dog. A good person who becomes a howling dog is a warning that the multitudes who are now embracing National Socialism very much need to hear."

Marianne gasped softly, apprehensively.

"It is a good play," Marbach said, offering his considered judgment.

"It is a great play!" declared Constanze.

Waving her arm, Anna signaled there was something else she wanted to talk about. "Enough about that play. Listen, my sweet Karl, you and Stephan Kaas are friends. I know he is married. I know how to handle that sort of thing. What I mean to say is that he is a man who stirs my feelings, and I need good, uncomplicated sex right now. Well?"

Marbach knew he had to be candid. "I made a lame joke with that nonsense about me being the one who decides who is and who is not a Nazi." He paused for a moment. "We are Guest Friends. So I am required to assert the plain and simple truth that I like Stephan Kaas. He has intelligence, courage … but he has placed himself in dedicated service to the great evil of our time. He is a committed National Socialist."

Anna stared at Marbach. "I trust my instincts. Stephan is a good man. I like Stephan. I am ready to share my bed with him."

Marianne's eyes opened wide.

Constanze shook her head. "I don't know. I just don't know."

"What don't you know?" Anna stared angrily at Constanze.

"I *just* don't know," Constanze said defensively.

Marianne stared from one woman to the other.

"I like Stephan," Anna declared, directing herself to Constanze. "Yes, he is SS, but so is Karl. Stephan is like Karl in many ways. They even look a lot alike. They are both strong men, and … I need a strong man right now in my terribly empty bed."

Marianne made a soft gasping sound.

Constanze didn't like having this conversation in front of Marianne. She believed it would be better to have it later, hopefully soon, but not with young Marianne present. Because Marianne was present, Constanze decided to change the subject. Working her fingers into Marianne's hair, expertly teasing it into a more attractive arrangement, Constanze said, "You are so beautiful. What you need is your own perfume. A perfume to match your marvelous brown eyes. You've been wearing Violetta Tatiana. That is not precisely the right perfume for your eyes. It is good enough for most brown eyes, but not yours. On Monday, I am going to take you to a perfume bar. We will find a fragrance for you. Your own fragrance. One that will match your lovely brown eyes."

"But you gave me the bottle of Violetta Tatiana," Marianne said.

Constanze leaned back on the sofa and brought Marianne into a tight embrace. "You need your own perfume, one specially made only for you and your very special brown eyes."

"A perfume made just for me?" Marianne had incredulity in her voice.

"Yes. Have you ever been to a perfume bar?"

Marianne exclaimed, "A perfume bar! I have heard of them, but I've never been inside one."

"You have much to learn, my sweet, and I shall be your teacher. On Monday I shall take you to a perfume bar, and we will arrange to have a perfume made especially for you and your lovely brown eyes."

"I think your brown eyes are marvelous," Marianne said to Constanze. "I wish I had brown eyes like yours."

"Constanze has amber eyes," Marbach said, as though offering a serious correction.

Sitting in her chair, blue-eyed Anna said to Marbach, "You used to say the best eyes are blue eyes. Have you changed your mind?"

Marbach replied, "I'm in an amber phase right now. Actually, it is a permanent phase. Just amber eyes for me from now on."

"It better be a permanent phase," Constanze said.

There was laughter in the room. No one laughed louder than Anna.

After a moment, sitting alone in her heavily stuffed chair, Anna decided to return the conversation to the subject foremost on her mind. "Stephan is a man. I like him. He doesn't talk politics with me. He avoids talking about lots of things, but one thing he did mention is that he is going to take a civilian job."

"A civilian job?" Marbach was surprised to hear that.

Encouraged, Anna sat up straight in her chair. "Yes, Stephan told me about a new job he may be getting. If he gets the new job, he will be leaving Kripo. His new job … I'm not sure I have the name correct. I think it is called the German Earth Works Corporation."

Marbach's voice was dark and forbidding as he provided the correct name: "German Earth and Stone Works Corporation."

None of the women knew why that name should bother Marbach. All three women directed their attention to him while he addressed

Anna with anger in his voice. "What can you tell me about this new job Stephan Kaas wants to take?"

"Stephan says it is a very important position," Anna said with a troubled look on her face. "He says it is a chance for him to start a new career—earn a lot more money." She looked apprehensively at the others in the room. "What's the matter?"

Marbach angrily shook his head.

Anna's face lit up. "There was a man at the party last night, a Gau Inspector, the man who is going to hire Stephan. Oh, Constanze, you were with us. What was his name?"

"Gau Inspector Schachermayr." Constanze knew the name of the Gau Inspector. One of her many gifts was an ability to remember names of people she met only casually.

Anna clapped her hands together. "Yes, that was his name. Gau Inspector Schachermayr said they had a very good position for Stephan, one that will pay a lot more than what he is earning now."

All three women stared at Marbach, who was scowling darkly. Finally, he said, "I heard about the job, but I didn't know Stephan had any interest in it. The German Earth and Stone Works Corporation is going to operate the new Mauthausen concentration camp. It will be a profit-making enterprise for the SS. They will be opening it this summer. Mauthausen will be like it was twenty years ago ... maybe not that awful, but pretty bad."

Anna's face constricted with revulsion. *"The Mauthausen camp! The Mauthausen camp!"* Her voice filled with rage as she continued. "I thought Stephan was talking about some sort of construction business, maybe some sort of security work. But the Mauthausen camp! I heard stories about that place when I was a child. Now they're going to open it again. How could Stephan want to have a job at the new Mauthausen camp? That is loathsome! It is … *absolutely loathsome!"*

Marbach opened his mouth, then shut it tight.

Anna's voice was loud and filled with anger. "My God! Oh, my God! Stephan didn't say it was Mauthausen. He didn't say anything about a concentration camp—about a torture camp. Twenty years ago, the Serbian war prisoners were kept there. I saw pictures in books when I was a little girl. Nightmare pictures! The Serbian war prisoners were worked like slaves in a quarry. They were worked to death. Mauthausen was condemned all over the world."

"How terrible," Marianne said weakly. She allowed herself to be grasped securely by Constanze.

Anna leaped up from her chair, unsteadily holding her drink in her hand. "What kind of a man is Stephan? How could he want to be a part of that sort of evil? I am a hypocrite. I am selfish, and I am shallow. I know that about myself. I have National Socialist friends … I was ready to sleep with Stephan, but even with all my faults, I won't bed down with Nazi rottenness."

Marianne cried out.

Swaying on her feet, Anna gave out a shrieking sound and swung her arms around, spilling part of her drink on Constanze's carpet. Immediately she looked down, and her face filled with distress at the sight of what she had done to the carpet.

Constanze jumped up from the sofa. "Throw the damned glass."

Anna stared at the glass in her hand.

Constanze pointed at the wall and in an authoritative voice said, "Throw it."

Anna stared at the wall as though seeing it for the first time. She examined the pattern of stains, took aim, and threw the glass.

It flew across the room and exploded against the wall. A bright red stain was created at the point of impact. Almost immediately the red stain began taking on a bluish color.

Constanze lunged toward Anna. The two women clung together. The weeping of one became the crying of the other. Making a crying sound, Constanze led a sobbing Anna into the bedroom.

The bedroom door slammed shut behind them.

Marbach knelt down and started cleaning up traces of wine on the carpet. Marianne joined him. She trembled while using a piece of cloth to scrub one stain and then another. From behind the closed bedroom door, they could hear crying. First, Anna crying, then Constanze crying; finally, both of the women crying together.

On his hands and knees, Marbach looked at Marianne. Her entire body was shaking. Tears were dropping from her face onto the carpet. There were so many tears she couldn't possibly see what she was cleaning. She crawled forward, went beyond the place on the carpet where there were wine stains, but kept scrubbing vigorously.

Marbach moved over beside Marianne and put a hand protectively on one of her shoulders. She turned her tear-stained face toward him and smiled. Then, blinded by her tears, she resumed scrubbing.

CHAPTER THIRTY-FOUR

A few minutes later, Marbach and Marianne were still on their hands and knees when Constanze and Anna came out of the bedroom holding hands.

Anna, nestling her head on Constanze's shoulder, reached out toward Marianne and made an unspoken plea for her to join them.

Marianne jumped to her feet, rushed across the room, and secured Anna in a tight hug. After a few moments, Constanze moved around, got between her two Guest Friends, and held them both in her arms.

Finally, Anna separated from Constanze and Marianne. She took a few steps and reached out toward Marbach. He stepped forward and hugged her. They clung together until Anna stopped hugging long enough to say, "Karl, I shouldn't have compared you and Stephan. You two aren't alike. He is not like you at all."

"We are alike," Marbach said.

"No, you are not alike," Anna said.

Marbach took his time, spoke slowly, thoughtfully. "It is clear to me at this moment, in the company of Guest Friends, that I have no choice but to acknowledge how much alike Stephan Kaas and I are. The two of us think alike, and we work the same way. The only difference between us is that I have immunity to the appeal of National Socialism. Having Constanze in my life probably gave me the immunity."

Constanze shut her eyes. There was a lot for her and the man she loved to talk about, but there would be time for that later. She opened her eyes, stared at Anna, and said, "I think your most recent contribution very considerably improves the art work on these walls."

Anna returned the stare of her Guest Friend Constanze, and then she looked at all four walls and filled her face with clownish pride. "The art work on these walls is very expressionist. I now have three of my contributions on these walls. But this new one is my very best. It is next to the splash left by that Italian singer a couple of years ago who sang an aria from *Tosca* before throwing his glass."

Marianne's eyes grew large as she looked from one wall to the other. "Which one is yours?" she asked Marbach.

"I have thrown just one glass. I'm not sure which stain is mine."

"Oh, surely you must know which one it is," Marianne persisted.

Marbach pointed to a large stain. He knew he would be corrected. He eagerly looked forward to being corrected as he said, "Maybe that one. How can I be sure?"

"You know very well that one belongs to Constanze!" Anna shouted.

Constanze let loose a loud burst of laughter while she pointed dramatically toward a place near the floor. "That small stain is Karl's. It is from the only glass he ever threw against these walls."

"Oh, my God," Marbach murmured. He was enjoying himself with this mischief.

Constanze continued pointing at the modestly small stain. "That is where Karl threw his glass on an afternoon when there was a spider on the wall—a great big spider—and I was headed for it with a rolled-up newspaper."

Marbach said, "I couldn't let cruelty be done to a kindred soul. If I have done no other honorable deed within this flat, let it at least be recorded that I created a diversion. I threw a glass of wine that enabled Herr Spider to escape."

Anna laughed. "Oh, Constanze, I will always remember it. You were still mad at Karl when you got to the theater."

"It is such a small stain," Marianne said, her giggle erupting into laughter.

Marbach grinned. "The important thing is that Herr Spider got away."

"Outrageous," Constanze said with laughter.

"Herr Spider escaped the wrath of Constanze," Marbach said. "I saved a kindred soul."

"Rotter!" Constanze said.

The four Guest Friends joined together in laughter.

Finally, still laughing, Constanze said, "Well, my Guest Friends, I don't know about the rest of you, but I could do with another glass of Schilcher Rose." She put an arm around Anna, and they walked together to get fresh drinks.

Marbach led Marianne back to the sofa.

"Constanze and Anna are so wonderful," Marianne whispered to Marbach after she sat down in the middle of the sofa.

"Yes, they are," Marbach said, settling himself at the far end of the sofa.

When Constanze and Anna returned with a tray of fresh drinks, Marbach accepted from the tray a fresh glass of kummel. Constanze took two glasses from the tray and sat down at the other end of the sofa from where Marbach was sitting, She beckoned Marianne, and the two of them huddled together, tightly grasping their glasses of wine. Marbach sat alone at his end of the sofa.

Anna, holding a glass in her hands, sat again in the heavily stuffed chair facing the sofa.

Constanze pursed her lips while studying Marianne's hair. "You have beautiful hair, but we must get it fixed properly."

Marianne lifted her head and stared with adoration at Constanze. Determined to end the look of adoration, Constanze ran her fingertips over Marianne's stomach. The giggling that erupted from Marianne ended the look of adoration. Constanze and Marianne joined together in helpless laughter.

Marbach winked at Anna sitting in the nearby chair.

"Let the children play," Anna said.

Marbach looked around as though he was in a strange place. "Where is the telephone? I know now that I have to separate from Kripo, but I am not yet separated, so I better check in."

"Karl, are you going to report Constanze to the police?" Marianne chirped, eager to show she could do teasing.

Marbach contemplated his glass of kummel and said, "I have changed my mind. I will call my office later. There is no rush. I am too delighted to do anything to spoil this moment. My day is made. Marianne has addressed me by my first name."

Marianne shyly clasped her hand over her mouth. Constanze reached over and pulled the hand away. "Guest Friendship!" she declared. "In Guest Friendship, we are all equals."

Anna rose from her chair and propelled herself onto the sofa. She squeezed between Constanze and Marianne, and grasped them with her arms. The three women rolled together and laughed like children at play.

Four people occupied the sofa: three women laughing merrily, and one man separate from the women but joining with them in laughter.

After a few minutes, Constanze brought up an important subject. "Marianne, you aren't safe in Vienna. You have to get out of Vienna."

Marbach agreed. He said to Marianne, "You must leave Vienna. No Jew is safe in Vienna."

Constanze stood up, stared at Marbach, and then went to the telephone. She dialed with quick, vigorous thrusts. When the connection was made, she spoke instructions in French into the receiver and then said she would wait for Paris to return her call.

She remained standing by the telephone for a few minutes. The others in the room kept silent. Finally, a high triple note rang through the flat, the sound made when an out-of-country telephone call was coming in.

Constanze held the telephone to her ear and spoke in rapid French.

The three people sitting on the sofa focused their attention on Constanze, transfixed by French words that were mostly unintelligible to them.

A few minutes later, after the telephone call to Paris was completed, Constanze stood in front of the sofa and said, "Marianne, there is a job waiting for you in Paris. Also one for Emile, if he wants it. Everything is all settled."

"I can't speak French," said Marianne.

"Your new employers know that," replied Constanze, facing her young Guest Friend. Finally, with a deft movement, she took a graceful hop and placed herself on the lap of the overwhelmed Marianne. In the same moment, she stretched out her legs and grinned when Marbach captured both of her feet in his hands. Caught in the middle, Anna gave out a loud, joyful gasp.

It was a good moment—but too brief.

At the very moment when everything seemed so good, a different sort of ringing sound filled the large flat. There was no high triple ring, just one ring after the other. It was a local call. Constanze quickly got off Marianne's lap, ran over to the other side of the room, and picked up the telephone. A smile was on her face as she turned around to face her friends while exchanging greetings with the telephone caller.

Constanze's smile became a frown. "Oh, police work," she said, waving her hand at Marbach. He got up from the sofa, walked over, and took the telephone from her.

A moment later, still holding the telephone in his hand, he faced the women and announced he was going to have to leave. "I am sorry," he said. "I have to go. I'll be resigning as quick as I can, but right now there is a case demanding my attention."

"My love," Constanze said, "right now, for just a few moments, I require your presence. Just you and me alone."

Quickly, Anna secured Marianne's hand, and they fled into the bedroom.

Marbach and Constanze were alone.

"Whatever happens, my love," Constanze said, "my love for you is everlasting. I know you are about to make a big change in your life."

"I am going to stop being a Nazi policeman."

"You have an obligation to your wife and your daughter. I know how important that obligation is for you. Don't worry about me being a problem. Just do what is right."

There was no more talk between the two lovers, only kissing. They kissed silently, fervently, until, with reluctance, Marbach separated from Constanze, left the flat, and went to police headquarters.

CHAPTER THIRTY-FIVE

It was late at night when Marbach finished doing the work that had required him to return to police headquarters. With a troubled mind, he decided to not return to Constanze's flat. Soon his life would be changing in a profound way. The thing for him to do now was go home, see his wife, talk to her about … things.

He took the streetcar home and soon was sitting with his wife and Fräulein Mitzi at the kitchen table. A large pot of hot coffee had been brewed. Camy was upstairs in her bedroom.

Marbach sat and sipped coffee while his wife and Fräulein Mitzi talked to each other about matters of no interest to him.

Suddenly, the telephone began ringing in the living room.

Marbach said, "I'll answer it." He rose from his chair, pushed his way through the swinging door that separated the kitchen from the living room, and walked directly to where the telephone was. When he put the telephone to his ear, he heard the familiar static sound that meant someone was calling from a public telephone booth. He identified himself. "Police Inspector Marbach."

There was a mechanical clicking noise that meant a connection to a public telephone booth was being made.

After a moment, a voice spoke. "This is Police Corporal Bruning."

Marbach recognized the name. Police Corporal Bruning was someone he would recognize on sight but didn't know personally. What he did know was that the police corporal had a good reputation.

"Go ahead, Police Corporal Bruning."

"Herr Police Inspector, I'm terribly sorry …"

"About what?"

"There has been a stagging. One of those god-awful staggings. I'm sorry, sir."

"Yes?"

Police Corporal Bruning delivered the news bluntly and directly. "One of those killed by this stagging is known to you. I'm sorry, sir, but Volkstheater actress Constanze Tandler is dead."

Marbach grasped the telephone tight, and spoke one word: "Dead?"

"Yes. I have been at the scene. There is no mistake."

Marbach struggled to keep control of himself. Constanze was dead … Constanze was killed … Constanze was dead.

His stomach felt heavy inside of him, but Marbach kept his voice devoid of emotion as he spoke into the telephone mouthpiece. "Police Corporal Bruning, tell me what you know."

"Volkstheater actress Constanze Tandler and a woman named Marianne Frisch—a Jew—were killed by a half-dozen soldiers on a stag hunt. The soldiers were after the one named Marianne Frisch. One of the officers was Lieutenant Paul Neumayer, the son of Colonel County Neumayer. Lieutenant Neumayer was pretty drunk. By the looks of him, he may not have had much to do with the killings, but he was there."

"Do you know anything more?" Constanze was killed, and Marbach was behaving like he would if this telephone call involved a victim unknown to him.

Police Corporal Bruning told more. "I heard Section Leader Brandl say that the official police story is going to be that this was no stag hunt. The section leader says the official story is going to be that Marianne Frisch, who they are going to call a fugitive Jewess, murdered Volkstheater actress Constanze Tandler. There will be no mention of any stag hunt ... I feel shame about this awful thing. I feel shame. How is it possible that things could change this fast? We are Kripo. We in Kripo are supposed to do our work with honesty."

"Yes."

"I am at your service, sir. I am now off duty. You don't know me except to pass a greeting, but I swear to you that you can trust me."

"I trust you. And I have a request. I need a car."

"I am in the police garage. There are plenty of cars here."

"I will need a driver for the car. I want three people taken to Czechoslovakia. My wife, my daughter, and another woman. They are here now."

"I will be the driver."

"Thank you. I appreciate—"

Police Corporal Bruning interrupted. "I will be at your house in no more than fifteen or twenty minutes. I have your address ... I am most terribly sorry for the awful news I have delivered."

The telephone call ended. Marbach hung up the telephone and stood still for a moment. With difficulty, he managed to take a breath. A febrile blackness engulfed him. He deliberately made a connection with hate and, in that moment, found it possible to take a full breath. One thought was fixed in his head: *kill ... kill ... kill.*

At that moment, the swinging door between the kitchen and the living room was suddenly pushed open.

His wife entered the living room, stood still for a moment, then rushed toward him. "Karl, you look so … something awful has happened."

Marbach let his wife hold him for a moment, then separated from her and came to an erect posture.

The door opened again, and Fräulein Mitzi stood in the doorway.

Marbach said, "Come in here. I have something to say to both of you." His wife grasped Fräulein Mitzi's hand, and the two women went to the sofa and sat down. He knew there was no time to waste. He had to get his wife, his daughter, and Fräulein Mitzi out of Vienna. He had to get them on their way to safety in Czechoslovakia before he could start killing. He was going to kill the son of Colonel Count Neumayer. And there would be others he would kill. He was going to do a lot of killing before … before the end of things.

Planted heavily on his feet, Marbach looked at the two women sitting on the sofa and said, "You both have to leave Vienna immediately. And Camy must go with you."

Marbach's wife got to her feet and delivered a look of helpless entreaty.

Marbach stared at his wife. The plea was made with his eyes; not a word was spoken.

Silently, Marbach's wife sat down.

Marbach addressed both women. "That telephone call … the caller will be here very soon in an automobile. You must take your passports and whatever light hand luggage you can manage. You will be taken across the border to Czechoslovakia."

Marbach had told the women what he wanted them to do. Now he knew he had to do some explaining. He stared anxiously at the good woman who was his wife. It pained him to look at her, but he didn't lower his eyes.

"Nazis have murdered two people of importance to me. I intend to have revenge. I intend to kill the Nazis responsible for murdering two good people."

Turning his back on his wife and Fräulein Mitzi, Marbach was conscious of rage welling up inside him, rage that drove out anguish. Keeping his back to both women, he said in a voice that was toneless, "Get yourselves ready. Don't waste any time."

Fräulein Mitzi released a deep, strangled gasp. "Can't you come with us?"

Marbach turned around, faced both women, and said, "I am not going with you." He paused for a moment. "I have made my decision."

Marbach was aware of his wife staring at him, as she had so often in the past, striving to give him something, and, as so often in the past, over things large and small, he was giving back nothing in return.

Marbach said to his wife and to Fräulein Mitzi, "The telephone call I just got was from a policeman. He will be here in about fifteen minutes. Nothing about him or anything connected with this business of getting the three of you to safety can ever be disclosed to anyone without putting that policeman in jeopardy."

Marbach felt it was important to say that. A fine man, Police Corporal Bruning, was taking a big risk. It was important to protect him.

Marbach stared at the remarkable woman who was his wife. "Gracious Lady, I have done you much wrong. Right now, my honor is a shabby thing, but it is all I have. On my honor, I am truly sorry.

For so many things over all the years that I have done that hurt you … I am truly sorry."

Fräulein Mitzi put her head in her hands.

Marbach froze when his wife said to him, "I love you."

There was silence in the room.

Finally, Marbach stepped forward, reached out with an awkward gesture, took his wife's hand, and brought it to his mouth. After a moment, he released her hand and stepped back.

While Marbach stood erect in front of her, his wife said, "I won't let you say farewell to me with a hand kiss." She moved up close and drew him into an embrace. Her mouth was sweet. He held her until she pulled away, left to go and fetch the things she and Fräulein Mitzi were going to need.

Standing alone, Marbach felt engulfed by confusion until he got back in touch with his hate.

Marbach was still in touch with his hate several minutes later when he became aware that an automobile had pulled up outside. He walked out of the house.

Uniformed Police Corporal Bruning got out of the automobile. Marbach and Corporal Bruning shook hands and talked together until Frau Marbach, Fräulein Mitzi, and Camy came out of the house holding bags and packages.

After everything was packed into the automobile, Marbach hugged Camy, shook Fräulein Mitzi's hand, and then approached his wife and kissed her on the mouth. He was taken aback when she clung tightly to him for a moment before releasing him. With terrible pain in her eyes, she turned away and got into the automobile. He wished he could tell her he loved her, but he wasn't able to speak the words. Constanze was the love of his life. Even if she was dead, Constanze was the love of his life.

Marbach watched the automobile drive away and then reentered the house. He found his service weapon, his 7.65 mm caliber Walther PP, checked the handgun, and shoved it under his belt. Then he moved his truncheon behind him and secured it under his belt. When he couldn't immediately find his Tyrolean hat, he grabbed a fedora and left his house.

There was killing to be done.

CHAPTER THIRTY-SIX

Marbach walked toward the streetcar stop at the end of the street. He was on his way to the Neumayer estate. He was determined to kill Lieutenant Neumayer. He was determined to also kill the colonel count. In addition, other Nazis were going to be killed. He took a deep breath. He was determined to kill and keep killing until he was dead, until he was delivered to the blessing of nothingness.

Wearing a plain brown suit, walking toward the streetcar stop, he tried to look like he was only out for an early evening walk. He hadn't gone far when he saw two neighborhood women approaching from the opposite direction. Their faces were familiar to him. He touched the brim of his fedora and slowed his pace slightly, but not enough to indicate he was inclined to stop and chat.

He continued past the two neighborhood women. Concealed under his tightly buttoned suit coat, the Walther PP was snug against his stomach. In addition, secure against his back, held tight by his belt, was his truncheon. The only weapon that really counted was the Walther PP, but it felt good having the truncheon. It felt good thinking about cracking a skull or two.

He released the safety lock on the Walther. The manual on/off switch was "on." There was a round in the chamber. It was hazardous carrying a Walther that way, but if there was a sudden interruption by anybody, it would be possible to blast away without wasting any time.

It didn't take him long to get to the streetcar stop. A few minutes later, the streetcar arrived, and he got on board, rode for several stops, and then transferred to another streetcar. After a long ride, he got off the second streetcar and walked the short distance to the Neumayer estate.

Standing in front of the Neumayer estate, Marbach surveyed the scene and saw no sign of the Gestapo, no sign of anything unusual. He studied the main entrance and then walked several steps until he was able to see the rear entrance. He kept walking until he got to where he could see a third entrance, not far from the rear entrance. The third entrance was for servants and merchants doing business with the estate. He quickly decided that was the entrance he would use.

He moved up close to the third entrance but quickly hid behind a tree when a man carrying some boxes suddenly appeared and passed through the gate with no interruption. It looked like there wasn't a guard on duty at the third entrance. After debating a moment, he made his decision and walked through the apparently unguarded gate.

"Halt!" barked a voice.

Marbach halted.

The voice that had stopped him belonged to a very young guard who looked like he had just woken up. The sleepy-looking, young guard was aiming a rifle at him.

Marbach tried to look like his only concern was that he was being temporarily delayed. The weapon being aimed at him was a Mauser Gew 98, a bolt action, single-shot rifle with a five-round magazine, a weapon that couldn't be fired unless the bolt was pulled back. Marbach told himself an experienced guard would have pulled on the bolt as soon as any intruder was spotted, even if the bolt had already been pulled back; on the other hand, an inexperienced guard might have never pulled the bolt back, and this sleepy, young guard looked very inexperienced.

Marbach identified himself. "I am Police Inspector Karl Marbach," he said. He knew that the only thing to do was use his own name. It was a certainty he would be asked to show identification. While waiting for a reaction from the young guard, he used his left hand to draw attention to the SS insignia on his collar. With his right hand, he undid the button on his suit jacket and subtly edged that hand behind him until he was able to grasp the handle of the truncheon.

The boyish face of the guard looked excited and made an odd laughing sound.

Marbach was familiar with that sort of odd laughing sound. Inexperienced soldiers in the mountain war of his youth had sometimes made that sound before excitedly firing a weapon. And in police work, it was common knowledge that an odd laughing sound was sometimes heard just before certain types of characters fired a weapon or made use of any weapon.

Marbach made up his mind. He decided to move fast. He threw the truncheon with a forceful underhand motion.

At the same moment that the club crashed into the face of the young guard, there was a loud exploding sound from the Mauser Gew 98.

Marbach felt a crushing force slam into his body. For a moment, there was only blackness for him.

When the blackness slipped away, Marbach found himself on his feet. The bolt on the Mauser Gew 98 had been pulled back.

Marbach staggered, stumbled back a step, but somehow managed to remain on his feet. Clutching his stomach, he made a labored attempt to suck air into his aching body. His left arm was hanging helplessly at his side. The middle of his body felt like it was on fire. With an effort of will, he steadied himself on his feet and moved forward step by step until he was standing above the young guard who was now lying on the ground.

He reached down and with his still functioning right hand grabbed the dazed youth firmly by the collar. "Tell me your orders."

"I … I shot you!" the disoriented young guard exclaimed.

"Tell me your orders."

There was no answer.

Marbach used his good hand to tighten his grip on the young guard's collar. He managed to cut off desperate attempts to take a breath, waited a moment, and then loosened his grip while still holding firm to the collar. He stared at the boyish young face as it filled with an unspoken plea. He continued to stare while the young guard said in a choking voice, "They told us you wouldn't be here until … until later tonight. Later tonight, if you … if you … if you came. A full guard will be posted around the estate beginning at midnight."

"Are the colonel count and his son in the house?"

With a confused look on his face, the young guard nodded and gestured toward the main residence. Marbach stared in that direction, then let loose his grip on the young guard, and the youth fell backward onto the ground.

Marbach looked around. There was no sign that anyone had heard the shot, but it was impossible to be certain, and there was no time to lose. The truncheon was on the ground. He reached down, picked up the wooden club, and with a swift, powerful motion, swung it hard across the unprotected left side of the boyish face.

There was a cry like a child might make, then silence.

The effort of striking the blow and the crying sound caused Marbach's stomach to burn hot, but he was resolved to not permit any distraction. He headed toward the main residence. As he moved forward, he deliberately renewed his contact with hate. His hate made it possible for him to not think about the young guard's boyish face, but he was having trouble breathing. His injured arm felt like it was being dragged down by a heavy weight; his stomach and his thigh were one large, aching wound.

While moving forward, limping awkwardly, he put his hand to his head. The fedora was gone. Idiotically, he regretted losing the hat. He hated having lost the fedora, even if he couldn't imagine that he was going to have any more use for hats.

He kept going, kept moving forward. The important thing for him was that he was going to do some killing, and then, after that, there would be an end of things. First, some killing … then oblivion.

He noted that there were no whistles going off, no bells being ringing, no shouting voices. He hadn't yet run out of time, but most certainly there was no time to waste.

He got to the main building and found a door beside a series of darkened windows. The door yielded to his quietly forced entry.

Inside the building, he shuffled down one hallway, and then a second, until he arrived at a glass-handled door where he stood still for a moment and listened. From behind the door came the sound of recognizable voices. One of the voices was Lieutenant Neumayer's. A second voice belonged to the colonel count. An unfamiliar third voice could be heard.

A fourth voice spoke up. There was a fourth person in the room. The fourth voice belonged to Stephan Kaas.

Marbach didn't like it that Stephan Kaas was in the room. In the killings to come, it would probably be necessary to kill Stephan Kaas. Marbach didn't like thinking about killing Stephan Kaas. The new job at Mauthausen sounded bad, but Marbach wondered if maybe it was just going to be a detention center this time, not the horror place it had been twenty years ago.

Marbach concentrated on what he had come to the Neumayer estate to do. He formed a picture of the inside of the room in his head. Since the war of his youth, he had believed that when you go into battle or any potentially violent situation, it is important to have a picture in your head of where you are going. Right now, he speculated on the number of men who might be in the room. Hopefully, there wouldn't be more than four. It would be difficult enough to handle four.

Marbach turned around and looked at a gun rack hanging above an ammunition box. They were exactly the way he remembered them from his first time in this place. There was the 12-gauge, double-barreled shotgun, just the way he remembered it. Using the shotgun, the powerful weapon, would add to the pleasure of blasting people into eternity. Only one thing mattered: *Kill! Kill! Do some killing!*

He secured the shotgun from the gun rack, balanced the weapon in his one good hand, popped it open, shoved it under his wounded arm, selected two shells, loaded the shotgun, and nursed the weapon shut, making only a quiet clicking sound.

With the shotgun fairly secure under his useless left arm, he used his one good hand to probe his coat pocket and brought out a small packet wrapped in a scented handkerchief. Inside the handkerchief was one chocolate bonbon. He stared for a moment, then stuffed the handkerchief containing the bonbon back into his jacket pocket.

It was time to get started, but first he knew he had to find out how badly he was wounded, get some sort of estimate of what he was going to be capable of doing. Slowly, tentatively, he checked his wounds. His left arm was almost helpless. The really bad pain was low down in his body. There was a sharp throbbing in his upper left thigh.

He did detailed checking and was surprised at what he found. He wasn't badly wounded. One bullet from the Walther Gew 98 had hit the Walther PP stuffed in his belt, causing it to discharge, releasing a round to tear its way through the upper part of his left thigh. The one round from the Walther PP had ended up in his nearly helpless left arm, but there was no bullet in his stomach. There was a lot of blood on the front of his shirt, but he was going to be able to do what he came here to do.

Kill! Kill! Kill!

With the shotgun tightly secured under his injured arm, he used his free hand to place his damaged Walther PP in the gun rack, picked up what looked like a serviceable Walther PP, loaded it, placed it in his suit pocket, and walked back to the glass-handled door. He listened again, took confidence from the feel of the shotgun under his arm, drew strength from his hate, grasped the doorknob, and quietly opened the door.

CHAPTER THIRTY-SEVEN

Marbach slipped quietly into the cavernous room. He stared up to the front where four men were standing. *Kill … Kill … Kill.* First, kill Colonel Count Neumayer and Lieutenant Neumayer. Cleanse the world of their foulness. There was also an officer in the room. The officer was a major. He would be killed, whoever he was. Stephan Kaas was the fourth man in the room. Yes, Stephan Kaas … Well, if he didn't get too far out of line, maybe he wouldn't have to be killed.

Marbach edged over to one side of the room, got behind a long row of very high bookcases, and moved forward until he was close to where the bookcases ended, very close to the four men. He grasped the shotgun in his right hand, used his thumb to quietly secure the safety switch, stepped out in front of the bookcases, advanced several steps, lifted the weapon in an upward motion, and brought it down hard on the unprotected head of the major. The blow was delivered at a precise angle and with calculated force to risk no damage to the shotgun. The man collapsed onto the floor.

Immediately, the colonel count and his son cried out.

Marbach used his thumb to release the safety catch on the shotgun. Then he stretched his arm forward. Holding the shotgun almost like it was a hand gun, he pointed the weapon at the colonel count.

"Oh my God!" the colonel count called out. Beside him, Lieutenant Neumayer looked totally terrified.

Standing off to the side, Comrade Soldier Stephan Kaas made a small, distracting movement.

Marbach swung the shotgun around. If Stephan Kaas made a threatening move, he would be killed.

Facing the twin barrels of the shotgun, the image shrugged, reached inside a suit jacket, and withdrew a Luger. In this moment the image became Stephan Kaas. He hesitated a moment before tossing the weapon onto the floor. Then he stood in a relaxed manner with both hands at his sides.

Marbach pointed the shotgun off to the side. He didn't let his face show how he felt seeing his Comrade Soldier behaving with characteristic courage.

Marbach's thoughts were abruptly interrupted when the colonel count called out, "I don't want to die. Have mercy. Don't shoot me. Please … don't shoot me." Marbach took note that the father was standing beside his son and pleading only for himself.

Lieutenant Neumayer quickly made the same plea as his father: a plea to not shoot "me."

Conscious of the shotgun in his hand, Marbach swung the weapon around and stared with unconcealed disgust at the father and the son. Each of them pleading only for himself. He felt strengthened by the hate that had momentarily slipped away but once again surged.

Lieutenant Neumayer cried, "I didn't kill anyone. I was drunk. I was drunk. I didn't do any killing. I was drunk. Oh, please … please don't kill me."

Marbach pointed the shotgun directly at Lieutenant Neumayer.

"Please … please," cried Lieutenant Neumayer.

Looking terrified, the colonel count edged one step away from his son, then a second step, and a third.

The father and son couldn't be allowed to get too far apart. Marbach delivered an order: "Halt!"

The colonel count stood rigidly still, his arms high over his head. He uttered a plea. "In the name of God, have mercy! Don't shoot me!" The colonel count made additional pitiful pleas, all of them for himself. "I didn't have anything to do with what happened. I am innocent. I am innocent. Have mercy. Oh please have mercy." Eyes distended, the colonel count stopped speaking words. Instead, he made noises like an animal caught in a trap.

Marbach tightened his grip on the shotgun and let his surging hate speak for him. "I am going to kill you and your son."

"Please ... please," sobbed the colonel count.

Marbach wondered if there could be any feeling in the world as grand as the feeling when befouled creatures are going to be killed and you are the one who is going to do the killing. There were two rounds in the shotgun: one for Lieutenant Neumayer and one for the colonel count. After that, the butt of the shotgun would be used to smash in the skull of the unconscious man on the floor, whoever he was. Stephan Kaas was going to behave himself, but these other three could be killed. The thing to do right now was empty the two rounds, one into the Lieutenant Neumayer and one into the colonel count.

"Please don't kill me," gasped the colonel count. "Please don't kill me. I will do anything you say. Only please don't kill me."

Lieutenant Neumayer, standing helplessly off to one side, turned his face away from his father.

Marbach took pleasure imagining how he was going to end things, but there was one problem: his arm holding the shotgun was aching badly. To ease the ache, he lifted the weapon above his head, held it upright for a moment, and then, with a decisive motion, he rubbed the aching arm across his forehead.

In that instant, he found himself breathing the fragrance of musk. Somehow on his sleeve there was a trace of Constanze's perfume. How did it get there? How long had it been there?

The fragrance of musk.

Constanze's fragrance of musk.

Marbach swayed on his feet. The surging hate was gone. That quickly it was gone.

Lowering his arm, Marbach held the shotgun steady but aimed it in no particular direction. Words and sounds were rushing through his head: Constanze's words and the sound of her voice. He could hear her voice exactly as it had sounded when, in front of her Guest Friends, she had talked about Hecuba, the role she had wanted to play because it was about a good person going bad, a good person becoming a howling dog.

Marbach continued to sway unsteadily on his feet. He realized Constanze's warning applied to him. He had become a howling dog. One doesn't have to make barking sounds to become a howling dog. The hate he had been carrying within had corrupted him. Hate had turned him into a howling dog.

He slowly lowered the heavy shotgun, took a moment, then said to the father and the son, "Get out of my sight."

The son ran for the door. The father kept his hands in the air as he timidly inquired, "Do you mean I can go?"

Marbach delivered a weary wave of the shotgun, and the colonel count ran out the door behind his son.

As the door closed behind the colonel count, Marbach's helpless left arm became a painful weight at his side. He tried to hold onto the shotgun, but it dropped from his hand, clattered onto the floor. He watched helplessly while Kaas stepped forward, reached down to the floor, picked up the shotgun, emptied it, and let the shells spill onto the floor. He continued to watch as Kaas reached down a second time and picked up the Luger.

While trying to stand steady on his feet, Marbach checked his lame arm and the bloody area around his belt.

Standing in front of Marbach, Kaas made a foot shuffling motion. Finally, he said, "You are doing a lot of bleeding."

Marbach dropped both hands to his sides. "What happens now?"

"You need a doctor."

"I'm not as bad off as I probably look."

"It's for sure the colonel count won't waste time sending the SS here. You better get going. If you get picked up, it will be all over for you. Can you make it on your own?"

"I'll be all right ... but if I get away from here, if I can't be found here, won't that make trouble for you?"

"Don't worry. All I have to do is say that you had a weapon, and I had none, that you were determined to leave, and I had no way of stopping you. With your reputation for handling yourself, I won't have any trouble making that sound believable. There will be no discredit directed at me." A pause. "Are you sure you can make it on your own?"

"I'll be all right," said Marbach. He was deeply conscious of the Comrade Soldier bond as he glanced around the large room. In a mirror wrapped around a thick marble column stretching from floor to ceiling, he saw a reflection showing distinctly recognizable images of him and Kaas. He watched as the two images in the mirror blended together into one, then with any slight movement by either of them, in a fluid motion only one of them was reflected in the mirror, then the other. Again … and again, first one of them, then the other.

Kaas walked over to the unconscious major, knelt down, and checked him over. "It looks like you just knocked this character out. I think he will be all right."

"I was more concerned about not damaging the shotgun than I was about busting his skull."

"You're a real tough character."

Marbach turned away and headed toward the door. After taking a few steps, he stopped, turned, faced Kaas, and said, "We only had a short time together, but we became Comrade Soldiers."

Kaas stopped fussing with the unconscious officer and stood up. "We are, indeed, Comrade Soldiers. We saved Fräulein Karen Mann. I should say you saved Fräulein Karen Mann. The part I played in that is one of the things in my life that I will always be proud of, but you are the one who set it up. You set it up, and you kept it going. I just followed along."

"We did it together." Marbach stared at Kaas, this man to whom he was bonded, this man he knew to be brave, intelligent, good humored, generous—everything one looks for in a Comrade Soldier.

Kaas suddenly became very solemn. His voice dropped to a low pitch. "In this final moment together, probably the last time we will ever be together, the best thing we can do is share words that are fine and good." Kaas shifted the luger from his right hand to his left, lifted his right arm, and spoke words like he was reading them from a hymnal. "*One People, One Reich, One Führer.*"

Marbach realized his Comrade Soldier expected him to repeat the words just spoken. What was there to do? What was there to say?

In a troubled voice, Kaas asked, "Why are you so slow to repeat those words? We never talked about this … I guess there wasn't time, but I expect to hear you agree with me that the Führer is the greatest man who ever lived and National Socialism is the grandest force imaginable." Kaas was silent for a moment. Then he said, "The Jews rule Russia and England. They even rule the United States. But the Führer has awakened the German people. We will conquer this corrupt world. We will turn this befouled world into a paradise."

An ominous silence filled the room.

CHAPTER THIRTY-EIGHT

The two men stood facing each other.

Kaas reached out toward Marbach. "Karl, show me you are the good man I know you to be. I am asking you to speak the glorious words: *One People, One Reich, One Führer.*"

Marbach knew that the sensible thing—the rational thing—would be to repeat the words Kaas expected to hear. They were words he had spoken many times in recent weeks. Why cause a fuss? Just repeat the words.

But before he could speak, before he could repeat the words, pain from his wounds erupted, and his thoughts became confused. He found it difficult to remain on his feet.

Kaas stepped forward. "Karl, are you all right?"

Unbidden words came tumbling out of Marbach's mouth. "Murdered … Constanze murdered … Constanze and Marianne."

Kaas stared at Marbach. "Marianne?"

Marbach struggled to clear his mind of confusion. A question had been asked. Stephan Kaas had asked about Marianne. It was a question that had to be answered fully and completely.

"Marianne Frisch was the … the wonderful young woman, the precious young woman who was killed alongside Constanze."

Kaas shook his head. "Wonderful young woman? I read the reports … I am sorry about Constanze Tandler, but, well, I *did* read the reports. The one named Marianne Frisch was a *Jew*. She was a *Jew!*"

Marbach clasped his hands together. "Marianne was wonderful. A precious young woman." Struggling with confusion, it seemed to Marbach that he was repeating words he could hear Constanze speaking.

But in the next instant, Kaas spat out words. "Precious? *A precious Jew*? How can you speak such nonsense?" Kaas paused a moment. When he continued, it was obvious he was trying to be conciliatory, trying to find common ground. "Almost all National Socialists have had Jewish friends in their lives. Some still have Jewish friends today. I used to have Jewish friends. When I was a small boy, I had a friend who was a Jew. But all Jews, willing or not, belong to a malignant force that is determined to rule the world. No Jew has the humanity that Aryans have. Karl, people like you and me must recognize the evil that is in the world. An evil that will bring great horror onto the world unless we make use of what strength we have to scrub the world free of all trace of Jewishness."

Marbach started to reply, but he was afflicted by another surge of pain from his wounds. He hoped he wasn't going to pass out.

Kaas stepped forward. "You are in bad shape. Let me know what I can do to help you. Don't be reluctant to ask for anything I might be able to do to help you. We are Comrade Soldiers."

Marbach felt overwhelmed by the Comrade Soldier bond that connected him with Kaas. He spoke clearly. "Yes, we are Comrade Soldiers. In the struggle to rescue Karen Mann, there was some danger, not much compared to what we both have known in battle, but however much there was, it was enough to make us Comrade Soldiers."

Kaas also affirmed the Comrade Soldier bond. "Yes, saving Karen Mann bound us together. And there was more. We connected with philosophy. We shared appreciation for Boethius."

Marbach let words slip out of his mouth. "Boethius is great, but there is another philosopher from long ago who has recently captured my attention. That other philosopher is Montaigne. It is possible to find some of Montaigne's wisdom on pieces of paper placed in coffeehouses."

Kaas nodded agreement. "Like you, Comrade Soldier, I got the best part of my education in coffeehouses and cafés. Berlin has wonderful gathering places, maybe not as many as Vienna, but more than a few. In one of those Berlin places, I learned about Montaigne. I repeat Montaigne's words: *What do I know?* Those are good words. *What do I know?* Montaigne also said, *All that is certain is that nothing is certain.*" Kaas paused. "I especially like what Montaigne said about friendship. It was from Montaigne that I learned to say I celebrated a friend *because he was he, and I was me.*"

Marbach was moved. Montaigne's words about friendship had long been important to him. He spoke the words. "*Because he was he, and I was me.*" Then he added, "Yes, those are good words. I have long treasured those words. If I should be asked by anyone why I have friendship for you, those are the words I would speak."

Kaas whispered with fervor, "*Because he was he, and I was me.*"

Marbach allowed muddled words to come out of his mouth. "There is much to learn from Montaigne. He instructs us that cruelty is a vice, the worst of all the vices. He instructs us that cruelty is something to hate and despise ... whether we find it in ourselves or in the people around us."

Kaas reacted with shock. "I don't remember Montaigne saying anything like that. In the Berlin coffeehouses, I never read anything like that. If Montaigne said that cruelty is a vice, he was wrong. If he said what you say he said, there is excuse for him, but there is no excuse for you. You were taught by National Socialism to celebrate cruelty."

Marbach realized he had blundered into dangerous territory.

Kaas spoke with a voice filled with fervor. "Those of us who are enlisted in the cause of National Socialism must cultivate cruelty within ourselves. Cruelty sustains us as we make the fight for the beautiful new world promised by the Führer. Before the Führer took charge, everything was hopeless. Ten years ago, there was hopelessness, but now there is hope! The Führer gave us hope. We must be worthy of the Führer, and to be worthy of the Führer, to serve him faithfully, we must nourish cruelty in ourselves. The Führer has told us that we must be as cruel as nature. The Führer says that it is not by the principles of humanity that we must live, but rather by means of brutal struggle. In your SS classes, you were taught that. You were taught that cruelty makes the followers of National Socialism strong! No one is tolerated in National Socialist ranks who has even the smallest reluctance to inflict cruelty on Jews and on any and all enemies of the beautiful new world promised by Adolf Hitler."

Marbach's mind was clearing up. He took a few steps toward a nearby door while exploring one of his coat pockets. Finally, he brought out Constanze's handkerchief, the handkerchief containing one chocolate bonbon. Hoping to reduce some of the tension in the room, he tossed the bonbon to Kaas, who caught it in one hand, the one not holding the Luger.

Kaas delivered an order. "I don't give you permission to leave!"

Marbach stopped. He was only a couple of steps from the door.

Kaas threw the bonbon onto the floor.

Avoiding any movement that might be provocative, Marbach put the handkerchief back in his pocket, reviewed the situation with a mind that was now totally clear, pulled the door open, and, with tightness in his gut, stepped out into the hallway.

After the door closed behind him, Marbach stood stiffly still for a moment. While facing the closed door, he could hear the sound of a mirror being smashed and loud, angry cursing. Amidst the cursing, one word was shouted again and again: *"Traitor! Traitor! Traitor!"*

Marbach headed quickly to the end of the hallway, pulled open the main door of the house, and moved at a fast pace down the path leading toward the front gate of the Neumayer estate. He was only a few steps from the gate when he heard the sound of feet pounding behind him.

Closing up from behind, Kaas shouted, "I repudiate our Comrade Soldier bond. I have never before repudiated the Comrade Soldier bond, but I do that now with you. I thought you were a good man, but I was wrong."

Halting in front of the gate, Marbach thought about the Comrade Soldier bond he had shared with Kaas, and then about the Guest Friend bond that had linked him with Constanze, Anna, and Marianne.

Kaas halted a dozen paces behind Marbach and aimed the Luger.

Suddenly, back at the house, there was the sound of a door slamming.

Both Marbach and Kaas turned around. They stared toward the house. Colonel Count Neumayer was running down the path with a shotgun. Behind the colonel count was Lieutenant Neumayer.

The colonel count moved up close to where Marbach and Kaas were standing, came to a halt, and aimed the shotgun.

"Father, let me shoot him!" shouted Lieutenant Neumayer as he grabbed his father by the shoulders. The colonel count pulled free from his son, and in that moment the shotgun let loose with an explosive charge.

Bam!

Marbach tensed. Instinctively, he grasped his stomach, but in that same instant, he realized he wasn't hit. Close by, he heard an agonized cry. He turned and watched while Kaas stood stiff for a moment, then fell to the ground.

Marbach tried to make sense of things. He hadn't been hit by the shotgun blast. It was Kaas who was hit. He looked around and saw the colonel count's face fill with horror. He continued watching while the colonel count and Lieutenant Neumayer fled back toward the house.

A minute later, the sound of a slamming door was distinct in the night air.

By that time, Marbach had already moved to where Kaas was lying. He remained standing still for a moment, then knelt down and used his one good hand to loosen Kaas's tie. After that, he began checking the wound.

While Marbach checked the wound, Kaas coughed, gasped for breath, and attempted to reach for his Luger that was lying nearby.

Marbach edged around, retrieved the Luger, shoved it under his belt, and said, "Take it easy. I don't think you took the full effect. It looks like most of the blast missed you, but you have a hole in your side."

Kaas ground his teeth and gasped, "To think I thought of you as a Comrade Soldier. If I ever get another chance, I will do my duty. I will kill you! If I ever get another chance, I won't hesitate. I will kill you on sight!"

"Settle down. We are both doing some leaking, but we will both be all right. When all is said and done, the important thing is to have luck."

Kaas rolled on the ground in a spasm of pain.

Marbach grabbed onto Kaas, pressed one of his hands down hard on Kaas's shoulder.

Kaas contorted his face as another wave of pain hit him. He pushed Marbach's hand away and shouted, "You are befoulment!"

Marbach looked up. Noises were coming from the house. Lights were going on. Getting to his feet, he tried to make sense of things. Until a few minutes ago, he and Stephan Kaas had been Comrade Soldiers, and now Stephan Kaas hated him. They were enemies because Stephan Kaas had a total commitment to National Socialism, a movement that celebrated cruelty. Constanze and Marianne were dead because of National Socialist cruelty. Why had he been so slow to recognize the total evil of National Socialism? How many people all over the world were going to perish because of the cruelty that was the driving force of National Socialism?

Marbach recalled the fervor in Constanze's voice the many times she had called him *Nazi policeman*. He had thought it was unfair of her to speak those words, but she had been right, totally and completely right. He had been a *Nazi policeman*. His highly prized rationalism had allowed him to be a passive partner in the cruelty practiced by National Socialism. Why had he been so slow to recognize that Constanze had been correct each and every time she had called him *Nazi policeman*?

Marbach reached into his pocket, found Constanze's handkerchief, lifted it to his face, took a moment to breathe the musk fragrance, and then carefully put the handkerchief back in his pocket.

Kaas made a coughing sound.

Marbach said, "I am sorry for your pain."

Kaas coughed some more, then said, "I swear my eternal hatred for you. I see you now for the totally befouled creature that you are. You have set yourself against what is good and pure and true. Adolf Hitler is leading the way toward goodness, purity, and truth. Everyone says that. Go out on the streets in Vienna, or in Berlin, in any city in the Greater Reich. All of the German people, except those who are hopelessly befouled, agree that National Socialism is good and pure and true. Shame on you for betraying the multitudes of good people who can be seen every day all over Greater Germany celebrating Adolf Hitler and National Socialism."

"I guess I have some sort of immunity to National Socialism."

"Immunity?"

"Yes. If so, I got the immunity from Constanze Tandler. Knowing Constanze Tandler, being around her, being close to her, gave me immunity, enough immunity so I wasn't caught up in the whirlwind of excitement generated by Adolf Hitler and National Socialism. Constanze was such a good woman. I loved hearing her laugh. When her laughter was pitched up high, it was the most feminine sound imaginable."

Holding his stomach, Kaas rolled on the floor in pain. He shouted, "*You aren't normal!* Look around. See the National Socialist Volk. We National Socialists are the normal ones."

"I want no part of Nazi normality."

"Damn you! You pig dog! You befoulment!" After getting those words out, Kaas did a lot of hard coughing.

"Take it easy," said Marbach. "I have to go now. One of the few things I have left is my Habsburg honor. Even though I failed it recently, I believe I now have my Habsburg honor back."

"My Honor is Loyalty!" The SS words were shouted as a retort to what Marbach had said.

Marbach turned away from Kaas and walked to the gate. When he got to the gate, he stopped, took one final check of his wounds, and then buttoned his suit coat all the way up to the collar button. After he got away from this place, it wouldn't be good if his bloody shirt drew unwanted attention.

Feeling stronger by the minute, he thought about what he was going to do. He was going to go to Czechoslovakia and find Alma and Camy. He owed his wife a lot. Maybe she could forgive him. Thinking about his wife and daughter, he stood very still for a moment and then turned around.

Kaas was rolling from side to side. "Goddamn you, Police Inspector Marbach! Goddamn you to hell! Goddamn everyone who doesn't support the Führer and National Socialism. I wish I had a weapon. If I had a weapon, I swear to God I would kill you with a pure and righteous heart."

Marbach stared at the brave, intelligent, generous man who had been his Comrade Soldier, a man to whom he still felt tied. He told himself that the wrong question to ask is what makes an evil person do evil. The important question to ask is what makes good people do evil. Stephan Kaas was a good man who had dedicated his life to Adolf Hitler and National Socialism. Millions of good people, caught up by the noise, music, and words of Adolf Hitler and National Socialism were willing to inflict cruelty on behalf of a movement they believed was beautiful, noble, and true.

Marbach faced the gate. He wondered if there was any force in the world that might be able to stop Hitler and National Socialism.

He told himself that National Socialism wasn't going to just dissolve. It had to be defeated, but was that going to be possible? The answer to that question was discouraging: Russia was looking after itself; England and France were hopelessly weak; and, as for America, that country that had once been powerful was now weak, divided, unsure of itself.

Marbach put out his right hand and shoved hard against the gate.

The heavy gate began moving, but only slowly at first. As he continued shoving, the gate suddenly swung all the way open, and he felt like a powerful force was drawing him forward.

Far off in the distance, he could hear the clanging bell of a streetcar. If he walked fast, he ought to be able to catch that streetcar. He shoved his hand into his pocket, found Constanze's handkerchief, and grasped it tightly. He only had a few scraps of paper money and a couple of coins. He would have nothing when that was gone, nothing but the clothes on his back ... and his Habsburg honor.

Marbach told himself that if he could manage to get into any army fighting Hitler's Germany, he would try as hard as he could to be the best soldier it was possible for him to be. He remembered when he was a young mountain soldier twenty years ago. He remembered that the very best soldiers were those who abhorred cruelty. He wondered why he hadn't recalled that during conversations with Constanze when she had talked to him about the philosopher Montaigne and the need to hate cruelty cruelly. He thought how odd it was—the things one doesn't remember when it might be helpful to remember them, things that are only remembered at some later time.

Marbach spoke words out loud. He thought that maybe speaking the words out loud would help him to atone for the way he had been living his life. *"If I had hated cruelty cruelly, I would never have allowed myself to be a Nazi policeman."* It helped speaking those words out loud.

He continued to move forward. He was determined to fight as hard as he could against the evil of Hitler's Reich. He was determined to be a warrior, but he knew he had to be vigilantly on guard to not be seduced by the lure of cruelty. He found himself remembering a piece of paper with words from Montaigne on it that he had read in a coffeehouse a long time ago. Odd, but it was a long time since he had thought about that piece of paper and Epaminondas, the Theban general of the fourth century BC who, Montaigne said, was famous for keeping his head clear when swords were clashing around him. When he had read what was written on that piece of paper, he had committed to memory the name of the Theban general, but he had never thought about mentioning Epaminondas in any of his conversations with Constanze. It simply hadn't occurred to him.

Marbach resolved to keep his head clear in the fighting to come, to not let cruelty distort his judgment and keep him from seeing things clearly. He would use soldier's guilt to help him reject the lure of cruelty, help him be the best fighter he was capable of being in the fight against the evil of National Socialism.

He put one foot in front of the other. He kept putting one foot in front of the other.

ABOUT THE AUTHOR

Tom Joyce worked in Ohio jails and the Ohio State Penitentiary. During his military service, he took ex-Nazis to Frankfurt, Germany, for de-Nazification proceedings. After military service, he got a PhD from Cornell University. He has taught courses in criminology and sociology to FBI agents, police officers, and college students. For a lot of years, he has been writing and rewriting stories about a Vienna police inspector in the 1930s and 1940s. He has three novels and a dozen short stories gleaned from chapters in the novels. He is now working on novel four.

ABOUT THE BOOK

This story is the first of three completed novels in which fictional Vienna Police Inspector Karl Marbach is a central character. It takes place in mid-April of 1938, one month after the Anschluss, the Nazi annexation of Austria. In the war that began in 1914, Marbach was awarded the highest medal bestowed by the Austro-Hungarian Empire. Now he works for Vienna Criminal Police—Vienna Kripo. Although born into a poor family, he identifies with the deposed Habsburgs. From that identification, he derives his strong sense of honor. In his work and in his life, he prides himself on being guided by reason, not emotion. His lover is Volkstheater actress Constanze Tandler. He is concerned that his actress lover's highly emotional, deeply passionate hatred of Nazism is futile and is putting her in danger. In addition to his lover, he has a wife, who is a very good woman. His teenage daughter, to the distress of him and his wife, is attracted to Nazism. But they both recognize that if their daughter doesn't openly profess devotion to Nazism, she won't be safe in post-Anschluss Vienna.

Marbach's Habsburg honor permits him to have both a lover and a wife, but sometimes he feels guilt. He indulges Constanze's teasing when she starts calling him "the chocolate policeman," making teasing comparisons between him and "the chocolate soldier," a character made famous by George Bernard Shaw and popularized in Viennese operetta by Oskar Straus. She says that, like "the chocolate soldier," he prefers bedroom merriment to doing his duty on a battlefield.

In Marbach's police work, there is a killing. The victim, initially believed to be a Jewish prostitute, turns out to be a university student from a prominent Aryan family. Marbach investigates and quickly establishes that the killer is a lustmörder, a thrill killer. Marbach works with the new chief of Vienna Kripo, Commander Stephan Kaas, and the lustmörder is captured, but there is another missing young woman. The lustmörder has her hidden and won't say where. Marbach refuses the suggestion that he use fists and a truncheon to learn where the young woman is hidden. He has a better way. He uses interrogation skills and trickery to exploit the weaknesses of the lustmörder and learns enough to save the captive young woman.

Even the leader of the SS in Vienna, Ernst Kaltenbrunner, expresses pleasure with the police inspector's handling of the case. Marbach and Kaas call each other "Comrade Soldier," cementing the bond between them with words both of them used for close friends on battlefields twenty years earlier. Everything seems to be going well for Marbach until a group of young Nazis chase after a young Jewish woman who is under Constanze's protection, and both Constanze and her Jewish friend are killed.

In Nazi Vienna, no action will be taken against the killers of Constanze and the young Jewish woman. Marbach sends his wife and daughter to Czechoslovakia and then goes after the Nazis who did the killings. He becomes a fugitive and is pursued by Kaas, who repudiates their Comrade Soldier bond. Kaas puts his sense of duty above that bond and professes loyalty to his Nazi faith.

Marbach manages to escape from Kaas and heads for safety in nearby Czechoslovakia. He has come to recognize that his rational approach to Nazism was incomplete. He was wrong about a lot of things. He treasures the image of his lost lover, Constanze, and then thinks about his wife and daughter. He knows he is unworthy of his wife but hopes she will take him back. Putting one foot in front of the other, he heads for Czechoslovakia.